Early praise for *The Developers*

" ... it doesn't take a super sci-fi buff to see the potential implications of an Internet superpower and the American government operating out of people's homes hand in hand. And that is just the tip of the iceberg. Imagine having a serious love jones while trying to begin a new chapter in the world of technology ... With the recent Internet chatter that has been surfacing about larger, more powerful internet companies, the book's message appears to be eerily relevant. This is a must for anyone who really dug *1984* or *Brave New World* but also likes to surf the Net from time to time, preferably with the idea in the back of your head that Big Brother could be watching."

- Katie Richardson, *Buzz Magazine*, Champaign, Ill.

"*The Developers* is a startlingly original and somewhat curious debut novel. The earnestness of the writer, the diversity of the characters, the originality of the presentation and the clarity and understatement of the prose combine to make it one of the most surprising releases of 2005. Woods' first book gives reason to expect some kind of masterpiece somewhere down the road."

- Paul Kopasz, *Louisville* (Ky.) *Eccentric Observer*

"The Internet concepts are enough by themselves for a novel. But Woods wraps the technical aspects of the story around the company's five 20-something employees, who try to balance work with their love lives, marriages, Richard Simmons fixations, stalker ex-husbands and secret lives in dangerous miniskirt cults."

- Jim Mayse, Owensboro (Ky.) *Messenger-Inquirer*

continued ...

"Thank you for your kind words and sense of humor. You are a gifted man!"
- Richard Simmons, Hollywood, Calif.

" ... a novel about a little bit of everything - in the mode of *Seinfeld*, with a helping of *Dilbert* on the side."
- Rebecca Coudret, Evansville (Ind.) *Courier & Press*

"Ben Woods lucidly and quite pleasantly describes some of the issues surrounding the establishment of a new company in the Internet age. He clearly understands plotting and structure and can put together a story with a good rhythm and pace. I look forward to reading further installments from Malorett or from wherever his imagination sets to work next."
- John Walsh, BookPleasures.com

"*The Developers* is a frank and honest, and truly humorous window into the creative economy. The characters we meet in Woods' novel are the prototypes for the engines of our future. Whether it is the author's imagination or reality, I'm sold. These are people I'd like to know. Or at least people I'd like to have working for me."
- Randy Smith, Destinations Bookstore, New Albany, Ind.

" ... Each character ... adds drama and humor to the events leading to .comU's launch as personal issues intervene in regular daily work ... "
- Mel Robertson, Crawfordsville (Ind.) *Journal Review*

THE DEVELOPERS

By Ben Woods

 KING PRINTING COMPANY, Inc.

To help debug future versions of this book, please send corrections and comments to info@benwoods.com.

The Developers
First Paperback Edition: **May 2005**
ISBN-10: **0-9764322-8-5**
ISBN-13: **978-0-9764322-8-9**
Website: **thedevelopersbook.com**

Publisher:
King Printing
181 Industrial Ave
Lowell, MA 01852
 adibooks.com
kingprinting.com

Designers:
Amanda Stewart
Ben Woods

Author Website:
benwoods.com

To my grandparents, who have given me the opportunity to succeed and enough material to never stop writing.

Special Thanks:
Brad Cathey
John Condray
Miranda Der Ohanian
Linda Elsey
Ross Hayden
Andy Lampton
Bill Rising
Mary Rising
Amanda Stewart
Betty Weber
Elizabeth Woods
Rusty Woods

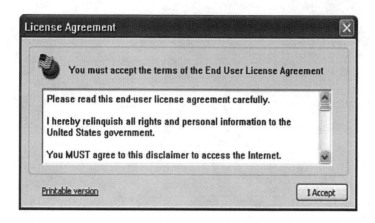

License Agreement

You must accept the terms of the End User License Agreement

Please read this end-user license agreement carefully.

I hereby relinquish all rights and personal information to the United States government.

You MUST agree to this disclaimer to access the Internet.

Printable version

I Accept

ONE

On occasion, Matt wished some technologies, like telephony, had never advanced. He envisioned the days where human operators had to make call connections, plugging wires in a Battleship-like board that covered a wall the size of South Carolina. Not that Matt was old enough to ever witness one in action; the only images he had of a working model were from *Andy Griffith* reruns.

Back then, it was surely easier just to ignore a call, assuming the operator punched the wrong hole. Or better yet, one could always pick up the call and use a disguised voice, claiming to be Edna at the corner grocery store or Ludwig van Beethoven, and the operator would have no choice but to disconnect.

Unfortunately, the 21st century brought about the rise of the cellphone, and even though its dependability was sketchy at best, it was difficult to avoid. Matt reasoned he could ignore one or two calls, and even a message could be discounted and blamed on being out of range, the snowy weather or cosmic forces. But there was no way he could ignore eight calls and four voice mails from the office, especially as the owner. Matt gave in and called Kevin to say he was on his way to the LAB.

But Matt wasn't on his way yet. It was 10 p.m., and 3 inches of snow had fallen in the past four hours. Even in his 4x4 it would take him at least 30 minutes to get to the LAB. After two years of working there, Matt had actually started calling it the LAB. To him, it was just some cheap office space on the south side of Malorett. Is Malorett, Michigan, even big enough to have a south side? This question perplexed Matt often, usually for 12 seconds during breakfast. Of course when he ate breakfast with others, it bothered him for a good 17 seconds.

It just became increasingly difficult to explain to prospective clients that this 2-year-old computer software company was working out of two bedrooms in a pre-1900 house. Even still, could it be called software? Matt had decided long ago it was too cumbersome to explain his company's services: website development, database programming, website hosting, computer technical support, advertising, marketing, writing, pretty much anything a customer wanted. Software had to be the best way to explain it, even if it wasn't always software.

The group couldn't really disguise a setup like that in a historic district-turned commercial area. Instead, Kevin came up with LAB, the Local-Area Bedroom, and the WAB, the Wide-Area Bedroom. These names were spinoffs from local-area network and wide-area network, types of networks an IT professional could discuss for weeks. The workers here, Matt thought, were far too busy to explain technological terms to the public. The group performed most of its programming and development in the WAB, while they left the LAB for the big-time stuff: meetings, table tennis, strip shows, that sort of thing. Once they even managed to find a stripper who could play Ping-Pong while giving table dances. Surely Matt wasn't being called to the LAB just for that.

Either way, Matt Severson never had to explain where he was going again. He could just say LAB or WAB. Most people either thought he was an evil scientist — because he always was carrying around something that resembled a test tube — or always performing a bad Elmer Fudd impersonation. Matt didn't care because the supposed test tube was just a large pen. It was one of those multicolored pens that had blue, black, green and red ink, and if you tried to click all four colors at the same time, it was broken forever. The pen was Matt's favorite, even though the black ink was currently empty. He had signed the first contract for The Developers with it, and many more had followed. But this next contract, well, that was a whole other ball game.

There was never any traffic on a Tuesday night in Malorett. Wait a minute ... there was never any traffic in Malorett at any time. Winter seemed like it should have ended a decade ago, but it was still March. The city had received 4 inches of new snow during the day, and 3-6 inches more were expected that night. Malorett pretty much looked like Hoth, minus Darth Vader and storm-troopers, for five months out of every year. The snowdrifts were particularly impressive this morning as Matt's vehicle sloshed through a sand/salt/snow mixture. Tauntauns would have made the trip more interesting, he decided, but it would have also made it more arduous, at least without a lightsaber and a droid or two.

Matt drove down Main Street past several empty three-story buildings. Matt had made the trip hundreds of times, yet he still couldn't grasp the emptiness of the town. Malorett isn't a ghost town; the ghosts have even left Malorett. What was once a booming town in the 1880s with 100,000 people had dwindled to about 10,000 or so. The city had flourished due to rich mineral deposits in the region, but once those dried up, residents quickly vacated. The Developers kind of stumbled onto the town through Moxee Tech, which is just minutes away. Matt graduated from Tech eight years ago, while Kevin just picked up his degree last year.

Matt finally pulled into a small parking lot next to yet another three-story building. It was almost 11. He hoped he wasn't late. Matt looked up and saw bright lights coming from the left side of the second story, which was supposedly vacant. Matt estimated the last time those lights were on had to have been last month. He momentarily lost track of what he was doing when Katy appeared.

"It's about time!" Katy said. "What the hell are you wearing?"

Matt looked down and realized he still had on shorts. That made sense considering he was ready for bed, expecting to make it back into work at 7:30 Wednesday morning. Once, Matt had worn yellow and green Zubaz pants, and everyone laughed. He just assumed people would hopefully shut up if he wore shorts when it was 20 degrees outside. No one made fun of what Sarina wore — or better yet, what she didn't wear — at these temperatures.

"Why does it matter what I'm wearing?" Matt said. "What the hell is going on down here that's so important?"

"We had some ideas, and we wanted to fill you in. Don't you want to be here for it?"

"Yeah, but can't it wait until the morning?"

Matt assumed Katy had been at the office since he left, around 7 p.m. It had been a pretty busy month so far for the group: not that any other month in the two-year history of The Developers had not been busy. The target date for the big launch, though, was less than a month away, and the group had just two full days to prep for a major site demonstration.

Katy and Matt walked up a small set of stones to the main door of the building. She had left the door wide open because once it was closed, it was tough to get back open. Not only was the door made out of solid wood, but someone had tried to turn it into one of those Dutch doors, with a top and bottom. It didn't work perfectly, but worse, the person put the door back together so miserably that the top half sometimes would not budge unless it was heated. The Developers spent most of the previous winter just traveling through the bottom half and making multiple visits to the doctor for scoliosis testing.

"You are never going to believe some of the things we forgot," Katy said. "We may want to have a few more volunteers look over everything. How could we do this?"

Katy was almost breathless, and she never gets that way, Matt thought. Well, at least she usually didn't outside of the bedroom. If Matt told her that, though, he might get his head shoved through the top half of the door, even if he knew that from personal experience.

The two walked down a small corridor and approached a non-Dutch style door. Even though the door was shut, Katy and Matt could hear full conversations, which appeared to be either shouting arguments or audience members trying to coerce game show contestants to make the right moves.

"Dude, it's not THAT big of a deal!"

"What? I can get into this user profile without even knowing the password! How is that not a big deal?"

"Dude, you programmed it! Do you think other people are going to figure that out?"

"Yes ... and stop calling me dude, slick!"

Drew, as the oldest Developer, usually passed his ideas directly to Matt. But Matt wasn't there, and a major issue had arisen, which left Kevin with the job of getting Drew under control.

It wasn't working tonight. Matt and Katy had finally reached the door.

"You've got to be kidding me!," Matt said. "You need me here at practically midnight because you don't think the site's secure? This couldn't have waited until the morning?"

Nothing was said for 20 seconds as Matt sat down in his industrial-strength swivel chair and booted up his Macintosh computer. He originally thought this was going to be some big deal and was happy to make the trip into the LAB. OK, maybe not happy, but at least intrigued, considering they had been over the demo at least 50 times, and everything checked out.

"Uh, Drew, do you have anything to say?" Matt said.

"Yeah ... why the hell are you wearing shorts?" Drew said.

"I was planning on going swimming once the snow melted ... 43 years from now," Matt said. "What is going on?"

Drew wasn't dissatisfied with the project up until this point. He wasn't discouraged by what he had found. He just didn't understand how they had gotten this far and he had never seen this.

"OK here's the deal," Drew began. "If someone logs in, everything's cool. If someone who doesn't have a login account tries to access the site, they have to sign up. That's cool too. But if someone signs up, then logs out immediately ... they really aren't logged out."

"But that's not true!" Kevin said. "We just need more specific instructions, like to close the browser. Maybe we need a little note saying without closing the browser, a hacker can steal your identity. What would that be worth, a Taco Bell burrito?"

Drew continued to gaze at his screen with a blank stare as Kevin rocked in his easy chair. Kevin looked at Matt and Katy, trying to figure out what was going through their minds. He checked his watch and realized they had only 4 minutes alone, so that wasn't enough time to break their hookup record. That had happened just after they had broken up for the third time, or was it the fourth? Kevin could hardly remember, nor did he really want to keep track of it all. He had called the *Guinness World Book of Records* to check if they had a category called Fastest Breakup Sex, but unfortunately, the event hadn't been verified, and Kevin didn't want to see the evidence.

Even though Matt's computer had chimed on startup, he still held his head down in his lap. With an early morning meeting, this was a complete waste of his time.

"Please do not call me in for this shit," Matt said. "We've got plenty to finish by Friday. I like Kevin's idea. If we need to change it, we can change it. Katy, what do you think?"

Katy had been rather silent during the whole ordeal. Matt assumed she had already made her comments before he got there. Now he wondered if she was thinking about something else, or him.

"Yeah, that's a good plan," Katy said. "Sarina can work on that with the other help features in the morning. Even though we are showing the demo for the second time, it doesn't have to be perfect."

"It would be nice to actually make some money from something we built," Kevin said. "Drew, are you going to live? Do you need a taco?"

"I could always use a taco," Drew said. "Is everyone leaving?"

It was midnight. The group had invested so much time and energy the past few weeks that Matt had implemented a midnight curfew, just so everyone would be at least a little conscious the next day. As they inched closer to the release of .comU 1.0, each person's mood seemed to go back and forth daily. But the four members who were there Tuesday night felt extremely confident, if not a little cocky, that they finally had something that, like MC Hammer, couldn't be touched.

And the biggest hope was that they would finally reap the benefits of this website that would, in turn, benefit the entire city of Malorett.

Matt remembered something that he noticed before he originally entered the office.

"Does anyone know why the second-floor lights are on?" Matt said.

"No way!" Drew said. He jumped out of his chair, raced out the door, through the hallway and stepped under the top half of the front door. Apparently Matt wasn't the only one perplexed about the lights.

"Damn!" Drew shouted.

Matt, Katy and Kevin speedily walked to join Drew out front. The lights were off.

"Sarina said she would give me 20 bucks if I saw the lights on!" Drew said. "Don't you remember her saying that?"

"Where is Sarina tonight?" Katy said. "If she's within 20 miles, I'm sure she could just run on down here."

"True," Kevin said. "Is anyone cold?"

With temperatures barreling toward zero, they figured it was a good idea to go back and grab their coats before they left for the night. Drew continued to stare motionless at the upstairs window, while Katy maneuvered her way between Matt and Kevin back inside.

"Does someone live up there?" Kevin said. "Are they just on business trips or vacation or maybe they can see in the dark?"

"Don't be crazy," Drew said. "I saw a lady up there once. Well, I didn't really see her, but I thought I saw her."

Either Drew was making absolutely no sense, or Matt was shivering too badly to understand what he was saying. There was a slight possibility that his legs might suddenly become warmer if he spoke, Matt thought.

"Come on. Either you saw her or you didn't," Matt said.

"OK, I didn't," Drew said. "I saw a shadow."

"And the shadow looked like a lady?"

"Actually the shadow looked like Grimace, and it appeared to be carrying what resembled a purse. So I just assumed it was a bigger lady."

"All right, let's check with the Butch tomorrow. He'll be able to straighten everything out."

Having said this, Matt realized he could just go start his truck and warm up by turning on the heat. After being giddy for most of the day due to the excelled site development, then being pissed off after making it down to the LAB to see virtually nothing wrong, then being frigid while standing outside at night talking about a ghost, Matt had completely lost his mind. Matt ran down the steps, avoided two snowdrifts that were right between his truck and the office building and pulled up on the door handle. For some odd reason, he locked it, so Matt fumbled through his shorts pockets, found the keys and opened the door. Katy made it outside and handed Drew and Kevin their coats.

"Thanks, Katy," Kevin said. "So can I again interest you in becoming Mrs. Kevin Gentry?"

"Have you interested me in that before?" Katy said.

Drew walked slowly down the steps, still dumbfounded by the second-story lights. He had already forgotten about the earlier problem with .comU.

"If Butch doesn't have an answer, I will find out myself," Drew proclaimed.

"Landlords never have answers!" Matt said.

"That's not true," Kevin said. "Remember that time we were watching *Jeopardy!* and he knew about that Buddhist temple?"

"Why yes, of course ... the one that looked like a spaceship," Matt said. "He does have answers. We shall get to the bottom of this!"

"Matt, you can't say 'shall,' " Drew said. "Programmers don't say antiquated terms like that. Maybe 'shell,' but really."

Katy had been soaking in the dialogue while she tried to finish bundling up in her heavy coat. She was still focused on preparing for the demonstration Friday and had stayed out of what she dubbed "petty conversation."

"Come on, let's get out of here," said Katy, walking just behind Drew while motioning to Kevin to walk down the stairs. Finally, everyone made it to their vehicles and plowed through the snow toward home, already preparing in their minds for the next day of fun.

>:¢ - Katy
@:) - Matt
>:P - Kevin
>8. - Drew
:D - Sarina

TWO

"Will this damn thing ever start?"

Sarina wasn't late. At least not yet. But by the way her Geo Metro had been acting lately, she was looking at late days for the rest of the year. Every day since last Thursday, she had gone through the same thing: She starts the car, it seems to be going, but right when she shifts to reverse, it dies. Her uncle Barry claims it's just the cold weather. It was damn cold this Wednesday morning.

After staring out the windshield for two minutes, Sarina tried it again. It started immediately. She put it into reverse and backed out of her normal parking space at the Evergreen Way apartment complex. Sarina had lived there since she moved to Malorett a year and a half ago, when the group started working on the project. Sometimes Sarina wished they could have picked someplace else, like maybe closer to Indianapolis, her hometown, but overall, she didn't have many complaints. There were plenty of empty streets for running, and that's all she really needed to get away.

The route from Sarina's apartment to the office was probably the easiest of the group. She lived just south of downtown Malorett, and it was a straight shot there. On an early day, she did see a little bit of traffic, but nothing like a larger city, which seemed more regular to her.

This, Sarina thought, was about as far from a regular city as you could get.

Luckily, the snow accumulation after midnight was less than an inch, and the sun was even shining, which made the drive a little more pleasurable. Sarina noticed a few snowmen down a side road, and she knew the sun would eventually bake at least a portion of their bodies away. If only some of their clients who failed to pay melted away once the sun came up, Sarina thought. And if it were still this cold outside, she could leave a few articles of clothing hanging on their mushy remains. Right when she pulled into the small lot at

9:45, she noticed Matt's truck and Drew's car. As she got out of the Metro, another car screeched around the corner and pulled into the space right beside her.

"Hey there, Kevin," Sarina said. "Did you get out of here at a decent time?"

"No way!" Kevin said. "Matt even came in for a little while because Drew found some problem with the security on the site."

Kevin and Sarina chatted as they walked into the building and made their way into the LAB.

"What did you do last night, run to Vegas?" Kevin said.

"I did run, but at home on the treadmill," Sarina said. "It's usually too cold to run at night here. I hate that. In Indianapolis you can run outside sometimes in January."

"Can't you just wear a bunch of clothes?"

Drew was already at his desk scrutinizing over something. He held his head in his lap as he tapped his right foot slowly on the carpet. At least he wasn't talking to himself like usual.

"Are you still working on the same thing, Drew?" Kevin said as he sat at his computer and logged in.

"Yes and no," Drew said. "I think I've found a better way around it, but it might create another problem on some browsers. I can just make the cookie and the session expire and go to another page or something."

Kevin checked his email as he noticed the clock on his computer read 9:55 ... five minutes before they would be moving the discussion to the WAB. The group needed just another short walk through of a few .comU features if they were going to make the demo work properly Friday.

Kevin had 23 new emails, just since last night. Of course, most of it was junk: three for Viagra, two for penis enlargement, one for breast enlargement, three for financial stability and a host of others. There was, however, a message from his sister. Jennifer was in her second year over at Moxee Tech, and she usually had questions for Kevin on her homework. But that was just small talk because she was always near the top of her class in high school, and so far, college was no exception.

Hey, Kevin! I'm stuck on my calculus AGAIN. Will you have a chance to come by and help me out later today? I've got three classes, but I'll be done by 2 or so. Do you wanna do dinner? You need to take a break from the project before Friday!

She couldn't be more right. Kevin Gentry was the last full-time man in on the project, but his contributions had been crucial for .comU. Kevin was placed on the entertainment section of the site ... well, not actually placed. Kevin begged Matt to work on that portion ever since day one. Matt had hoped for a little help from Tech, so he approached one of his former professors a few months into the project. Out of the handful Matt met, Kevin was the one who stood out. Kevin might not have been the smartest or the most creative, but even from the beginning, he always did a superior job. He also had a knack for promotion and making things sound a whole lot better than they actually were. In this way, The Developers were able to grab the attention of many college students for volunteer help through the first couple of drafts of the site.

Luckily for Kevin, he could still escape and go hang out with Jen every once in awhile. She had a lot of cute friends, all of whom Kevin had dated at least once, with the exception of Jane Wilson. Jane was Jen's best friend and, as far as Kevin was concerned, off limits. Plus she seemingly always had a boyfriend, so there was really never much of an opportunity to go out with her anyway. Being the one girl he couldn't have just made Kevin want her even more. He decided he would hurry and reply to Jen before the meeting began.

Yeah Jen, I can make it over for dinner. You wanna go out or eat at your place? Bring Jane if you can. She doesn't have basketball practice, does she? I have a meeting right now, but I'll check back by noon at the latest. I'll try to give you a call later to see what's up.

While Sarina and Drew were still plugging away at their machines, Kevin got up to stretch a bit.

"Has Katy made it in yet?" Kevin said.

"She'll be here," Drew said. "I guess Matt is already over in the WAB."

The WAB was down a longer hallway than from the front door to the LAB, and luckily, there were no Dutch-style doors. It seemed more logical that The Developers could have rented rooms closer to each other, but supposedly, the room right across the hall wasn't available. Sarina saw Butch carrying a couple of boxes in there at some point, but no one else had seen anything go in or out of that room. The guys also thought it was strange Sarina was the only one who ever saw anything unusual in the entire building.

Drew entered the WAB, followed by Sarina and Kevin. Matt was sitting at the far end of the meeting table, jotting down a few points. Katy snuck in at last, and she already had her pen and paper in hand.

"I know we've gone over this at least 564 times, but let's give it another run through," Matt said. "I think it would be a good idea now for everyone to briefly rehash their parts, mentioning the new matters we've corrected or changed in any way since two weeks ago. Sarina, go ahead and start with the overview."

"Hold up a sec, Matt," Katy said after setting her stylus and PDA down. "Isn't this meeting geared more toward potential investors for the project?"

"True ... we do need to make sure to thoroughly explain the importance of the city not only bolstering population but also commerce in general," Matt said. "We did fairly good at that last time, with Kevin's report on site traffic and name recognition of .comU products."

"Thanks slick. Should that be worth maybe another burrito?" Kevin leaned back a bit in his wooden chair. The five members of The Developers sat around a kitchen table in the WAB, which occupied the room most likely numerous years before any of them were even born. Drew, at 31, was the oldest, and Kevin, age 22, was the youngest. Sarina just hit 30 last month, Matt's a year behind her and Katy just turned 26 on Christmas.

"While we are going through this today, if you have anything to add that directly details advertising or revenue-generating parts of the site, say something," Matt said. "OK Sarina, go for it."

Sarina grabbed her water bottle and moved closer to the laptop Matt had set up before the meeting. The Developers despised PowerPoint but found the clients in the area thought PowerPoint was a better invention than fire.

"Like last time, I'm just going to give the outline of .comU: the reasons this system is necessary for Malorett, how we will get people involved, features of the system, potential problems and remedies and/or ways to prevent them, advertising opportunities and a time for questions," Sarina said. "I think I should mention the person's name who will cover the certain topics, that would work nicely. Is that it?"

Drew and Kevin scribbled notes on paper and didn't even seem to realize Sarina was finished. Matt almost looked as if he were asleep, prompting Katy to nudge him.

"Welcome to .comU," Sarina continued. "We are glad you could make it today for this short presentation, devoted to explaining the features and possibilities of .comU. I, Sarina Metcalfe, will discuss the reasoning behind developing this community portal for a town like Malorett. Katy Terrill will discuss the ways the community will be able to get involved and intertwined with the product. Drew Davis will talk about the many site features. Kevin Gentry will go into detail about the advertising and sponsorship capabilities. Lastly, Matt Severson will follow up by answering any questions and also discussing the pricing."

Sarina opened a black folder with a few more notes. Although all of The Developers were fairly thorough in their work, Sarina was the most meticulous of the crew. She had three sheets of notes, mostly typed with notes written in the margin. Every mark was just as clear as the type, and every word was written in bold block lettering. It was frightening to think the audience probably could read her notes a good 20 feet away.

But her current audience — at least the male portion of it — wasn't paying attention to her notes but instead noticing she was wearing a black miniskirt that would have been short on Emmanuel Lewis. Matt, Kevin and Drew thought it was immensely bizarre to wear a miniskirt during such cold conditions, but they were afraid if they confronted Sarina about it, she would stop wearing them. Instead, they played dumb and just enjoyed the view.

"Many of you are wondering why a city like Malorett, Michigan, would need a community website," Sarina said. "With a population hovering close to 10,000, how could this benefit the city? Well, first off, we anticipate that if people use this system to its full potential, it could possibly double the city's population within three years."

Sarina stopped for a moment. Drew and Matt glanced at each other, contemplating the last comment.

"Three years?" Sarina said. "I've thought about this the past couple of days. Do we really believe our system could double the population in that amount of time?"

"We have to," Matt said. "We can believe it, or we can pretend to believe it. If we pretend to believe it long enough, then we will believe it."

"I'm not sure that made any sense, but OK," Sarina said. "I'll continue. With a growing population, there will be a need to keep track of people moving in, keep track of those already living here and keep commerce on technology's edge.

"Getting the word out about .comU should be a piece of cake, considering we hope to have up to 65 percent of local businesses involved at startup and more than 85 percent after one year. This site, in a sense, will be a way to let the economic development of the city govern the influx of people in the area.

"Most cities this size could not handle a situation in which so many people were flocking to the area. That's where Malorett stands apart and is the reason we selected this town to begin development. With so many empty buildings, housing will not be hard to come by. Property value will start out small and will steadily increase due to the constant flow of people, either touring or actually moving here.

"The talk of Malorett will not stop here. There will be people accessing this site all over Michigan, all over the US, all over the world, just seeing this virtual city ... the first of its kind. Sure, they will be able to get a taste of Malorett online. But can you really experience a city without actually showing up there, at least once? That's the kicker, and that's how even tourism will rise."

Sarina had reached her stopping point and hoped she hadn't gone too much into Katy's part. Sarina didn't even need her notes to give her speech. The only reason she needed them was to make sure she stopped. Sometimes her ambition got the best of her.

"Katy Terrill will now continue and give an overview of just how we will get the public involved and sold on .comU," Sarina said.

Sarina walked to the far side of the table and sat down, pulling the bottom of her skirt down as much as possible, which wasn't very far. Katy, on the other side of the table, jotted down a final note before she stood to take her turn. Drew leaned over to say something to Kevin, and Kevin gave a short chuckle. Katy glared at them, but both gave her innocent glances. Katy proceeded to the head of the table and made sure her part was ready on the laptop.

"Will Malorett embrace .comU overnight?" Katy started. "How long will it take before people in the city are using the site as a portal for their own lives? We've used a host of methods to attempt to determine the life span on the site, where people will go, what they will do and how long they will stay entertained. Needless to say, all the results were positive."

Katy clicked the laptop mouse to unveil a screen split in three rows. The first, shaded light blue, was labeled "IN THE SCHOOL." The second was a lime color and said "IN THE WORKFORCE." The last one, a light violet, read "IN THE HOME."

"Our first focus group consisted of children and young adults, ages 12-20," Katy said. "That is an extremely broad group, and possibly the most important group. For a website like this to have longevity, the children must be involved from the beginning. During the early phases of .comU, we interviewed 30 boys and girls, young adults, of different backgrounds, different races, etc., to determine what would pique their interests. We found what we expected: This age group is on the computer a large portion of time; they want to see a lot of games and contests; and they want to keep in touch with their friends and meet new ones.

"The workforce group was quite possibly the trickiest to pinpoint, mainly because the age group stretched the largest. The most common needs of this group had to do with keeping up with local business, networking, knowing what is going on with their children and recreational activities. Most businesspeople use their computers at work, but about 70 percent had home computers as well. The most astonishing statistic we found from these initial interviews was that most people in the workforce considered themselves computer literate, even though they lacked numerous online abilities. This gave us a few more ideas of things to add to the site.

"The final group included some homemakers and elderly folks. It has been rumored for some time now that most people age 60 and over do not know how to use computers and do not want to know. It was interesting to us, then, that over half the people we interviewed age 60 and up had a computer. Most said their son or daughter bought it for them but really never told them how to use it."

Katy had her presentation practically memorized. This gave her time to think about other things, like why the hell Matt was wearing glasses, if Kevin would look cuter in blue or green and whether or not she was wearing her new black underwear. If she were wearing them, they most likely were not showing through her khaki-colored pants, because if they were, Kevin would have already made a comment about it. Wait a minute though, what if that was what they were discussing before I got up here, she thought. As long as he knew that would be the only chance he would have at looking at her underwear, it didn't really matter.

Katy continued with the presentation.

"In the months that followed the focus groups, we incorporated the new findings into what we had already built. Back in January, we brought back many of these same people to have them take test drives through the site. Every single person we brought back — 64 in all — stayed past the time we allocated for them. Now, Drew Davis will delve deeper into the features on .comU."

Matt was again having trouble staying awake. Maybe he should have held the meeting a little later, just to get a breath. Then again, it was already 40 percent or so over, and Sarina and Katy had both performed perfectly. Matt tried to play off the fact he felt as if he hadn't slept since the project originally started, or the fall of the Roman Empire, whichever came first.

"Great, Katy," Matt said. "You might also want to mention that parents wanted to see educational tools on the site."

"Sure Matt, I'll put that on the list," Katy said.

Katy was already writing away. She remembered more things than Matt thought was humanly possible. Maybe that's why he was always wondering how much she remembered about him — and them — but he was too tired to even daydream about it right now.

"Also, we need to explain a little about the test groups, maybe what the breakdown is of different ages, genders, etc.," Matt said "I know we have the statistics booklet, but we need to give them a general base to start."

"Definitely," Sarina said. "We need to prove to the business people that we didn't just make this shit up."

Drew took the stand. He was supposed to discuss every feature on the site, but that would be nearly impossible. He typed into the web browser the address of the .comU that was accessible only as a testing ground. Although the staging server could be viewed from any browser, there wasn't a way to get to it unless you knew the exact URL. This would come in handy in the upcoming weeks, when each of the five Developers would be traveling around town, giving the rest of Malorett its first glimpse of the city's future.

The front page loaded, and even though everyone in the room had seen it thousands of times, it was still breathtaking to all of them. They had built something based on prior sites and prior designs but had woven it so intricately that it would be greater than anything before it.

"Hello. I would like to discuss some of the features that .comU users will see immediately when they visit the site," Drew said. "As you know by now, we expect this will be the city's meeting place and portal to find just about anything in Malorett. To do this, we need to be connected in every way possible. As you notice on the front page, we have simple navigation at the top for entertainment, sports, education, government, connect and store.

"Under entertainment, we'll have restaurant listings, area events, community activities, an events calendar, things of that nature. Users will be able to input their own events and add contact information and pictures with their events. There will be an additional section for restaurant and book reviews, which users will be able to submit as well.

"For sports, results of all local games will be available, as will professional sports, along with fantasy leagues. We even hope to have chat sessions with some of the more prominent coaches and players so the fans can feel like they are part of the game.

"Considering that we are hoping to bring in many new families, the education section might be the most important. There will be information from the public and private schools for parents, as well as a way for teachers to get homework and papers to and from the students. And of course there will be games and activities for children of all ages to browse."

Katy set her pen on the table and stopped Drew.

"Do you think we are rushing through this?" Katy asked. "Some of the people are going to be hearing this for the first time. Are they going to be expected to remember it all?"

"There won't be a quiz afterwards," Kevin said. "Unless you want to make a quiz and place it in the education section. Get on that, Sarina!"

Sarina rolled her eyes, which for some bizarre reason, Kevin used to think meant true love. Unfortunately, he had been given some bad advice by a fortune teller during a trip to Florida. On top of that, Kevin later found out the fortune teller got hit by a bus the next day.

Katy started to chime in with another comment, but there was a shuffle near the door. Everyone froze; at 10:30 a.m., there was never anyone else in the building but The Developers. On top of that, there was no way for anyone else to get in the first floor, unless the door was unlocked. So much for this site, we are going to get diced by an ax murderer, Kevin thought. The door swung open, and there was a bright light shining in the WAB.

The light finally came into focus as a smiley face T-shirt.

"Jesus, Butch, what the hell are you doing?" Katy said.

"I came to collect the rent check," Butch said.

"Didn't I leave that in your mailbox last Friday?" Kevin said.

"Yeah, but I left it in my drawers and ran it through the washing machine," Butch said. "I tried to piece it together, but it was missing the signature."

Butch Hodges was the epitome of a local, whether it be a southern town or upstate Michigan. Butch wore torn jeans (not the kind teenagers tried to bring back in style; the kind that had been torn during a tractor pull or a hoedown of some sort), sometimes a baseball cap (today it was the John Deere version) and, as always, a smiley face shirt. You would think someone would grow out of that phase, not horde 10 assorted colors and rotate them daily. He rarely came around during the day; in fact, this was the first time in at least three weeks most of The Developers had even seen him. Butch lived in the building next to the one that housed the LAB and the WAB. He owned both buildings, and that's about it.

"I'll write you a new check, as soon as I stop payment on the last one," Matt said, making a note in his PDA.

"What, ya don't believe me?"

"I believe you, but we are trying to get some things squared away for Friday. Do you need it today?"

"It is bowling night. I just loooooove bowling alley onion rings."

"OK, after the meeting I'll bring it over."

Butch grunted loud enough to let everyone know he was somewhat dissatisfied with the results of the discussion. Then again, Butch thought, they could just move out and move into one of the other random empty buildings in Malorett.

"Hey Butch, any idea why the lights upstairs were on last night?" Kevin said. Sarina perked up a bit.

"That was me up there," Butch said. "Oh wait, that could have been two days ago. Or three days. I need one of those organizer thingys."

Butch pointed to Matt's PDA, shook his head and walked out the door. Matt turned to Drew and told him to continue.

"OK, following the education section comes the government aspect of the site. We plan to leave this area as a public forum for people to voice their opinions about anything and everything. We will also use it for town meetings and debates during elections times.

"The Profiler, in its simplest terms, is the way community members will contact and interact with new and existing community members so that even in a town this size, everyone will have the chance to know everyone. People will be encouraged by giveaways, contests, etc., to enter profile information and find out more about their neighbors. This method has worked for personal sites and social networking sites for years, and we want to prove it will work for communities to grow together as well.

"Lastly is the store, which will be open to any business in town that wants to sell products and services. It will be similar to the Yellow Pages but much more innovative and useful."

Drew was pretty much finished with his part, except for one last question.

"Should I field questions during my presentation?" Drew said. "Like if someone wants to know if his kid is going to get fat by sitting in front of .comU all day?"

"I think we wait to answer questions at the end," Matt said. "But if they have an urgent question, go for it. Kevin are you ready for your part?"

Of course I'm ready, Kevin thought. He could do this in his sleep, but just to be safe, he determined he should remain awake. Kevin had been known to doze off and occasionally enter a world similar to the one Walter Mitty visited, but it normally involved a very large buffet at an all-you-can-eat joint. This was too important to the rest of the group to screw up.

"Is there a rule about not cussing during the presentation?" Kevin asked. Katy had just taken a small sip of her water, and luckily, she barely managed not to spit it right on Drew. The comment drew a small chuckle from Sarina as well. Matt, still rubbing his eyes, glared at Kevin.

"Just do the presentation. I don't give a shit if you cuss," Matt said.

Kevin began.

"Imagine you are the media — newspaper, radio, TV, whatever — and a prospective advertiser asks 'Will my ads reach my target audience?' Wouldn't it be great if you could respond, 'It will reach your entire target audience, even the target audience you didn't know existed.' Well, I have good news. With .comU, you will be able to give that answer every time.

"As you've learned by now, this site will be the community, meaning this will also be the place to advertise. When people sign up for anything they will have to give information. This information can be processed to determine what areas of the site people visit the most, what stories are the most important, how long they stay on the site, etc. The privacy policy will be clear, in that no names or email addresses will be distributed. To your advertiser, everyone will just be a number. But those numbers are the ones that will be adding up to dollars.

"Our recommendation is to concentrate heavily on sponsorships of site areas, rather than annoying banner and popup ads. Those used to be cool. No wait, those were never cool. The whole idea is name recognition. You have a contest sponsored by a few companies, you print up T-shirts, hats, whatever, with company logos and you have walking billboards. In a sense, .comU becomes another media source.

"As investors of the site, the returns should start immediately with the advertising and sponsorship that can be gained right away. Now, Matt Severson will conclude our presentation by fielding questions and discussing pricing."

Sarina gave Kevin a golf clap, and Kevin bowed, then waved just like the Queen of England. As Kevin took his seat in between Drew and Sarina, Matt stood and walked to the front of the group.

"All right, surely people are going to ask me questions," Matt said. "There's a good chance I will point in any one of your directions to help answer a question. I'll be prepared, but it would be helpful for you to think of some potential questions that might be asked."

Matt yawned and leaned to his right side slightly. His right foot slipped briefly, but he caught himself to not make too much of a scene. The other four glanced mostly in disbelief back at him. Matt was occasionally tired, but never during a meeting he called. On top of that, this was a meeting he had called two weeks before, and Matt rarely holds to meeting times.

"Hey, Matt, are you going to be OK?" Drew said.

"I just had a rough night," Matt said, still rubbing his eyes.

"Well your part is just the Q&A, so there's not much more to go over," Katy said. "Let's just go ahead and get back to working on the site. There are still some features and bugs we need to discuss before Friday."

Matt seemed to liven up a bit.

"Good idea!" he said. "Meeting is adjourned. I need a nap!"

Sarina pulled a small piece of plastic out of her pocket. At first, Kevin thought it was a balloon, but then he realized it resembled a Whoopie Cushion.

"Who carries a Whoopie Cushion with them?" Kevin asked, grabbing his PDA and standing up from his seat.

"It's a blow-up pillow," Sarina said. "For Matt to use."

Sarina handed it to Matt and showed him how to inflate it.

"Did that come with your blow-up Rick Astley doll?" Kevin asked. "You know I'm never going to give you up."

Sarina, and the rest of the gang, ignored Kevin's '80s music comment and exited the WAB.

THREE

Always in the car, always in the car, Kevin thought. Maybe if I weren't always trying to get on every girl back at school, I wouldn't have to always be in the car. But then what fun would it be to live in the middle of nowhere in northern Michigan?

Kevin was headed to his sister Jen's place. She had promised him that Jane would be there. OK, maybe it wasn't a promise per se, but he expected her to be there. He really hadn't gotten very far with Jane in the past, but this was a new day. Kevin figured after dinner, he could try to make his move, which usually consisted of just trying to get her phone number and not spilling his food in the unsuspecting girl's lap. So far, he was 0-for-5 with Jane. Like Jen's other friends, though, he was giving her seven chances. Usually by the seventh, there was another friend to attempt to pick up anyway. Kevin had heard a rumor through some other friends that Jane had broken up with her boyfriend recently after he missed one of her basketball games. Maybe she wasn't off limits anymore after all.

It was about a 20-minute drive from the office to Tech's campus. Jen lived on the west side of campus, in one of the few dorms. She was planning on getting an apartment for her junior year, but her dorm wasn't too bad. And it didn't bother Kevin going to visit ... it was, after all, an all-girls dormitory.

Normally Kevin was fairly focused on seeing how many of Jen's friends he could manage to bump into, but today was different. Friday was the big day, and that was just two days away. Kevin had finished plenty of touching up after the meeting: He talked with Drew about the user authentication problem, he worked with Sarina on a few design things and he talked briefly with Matt about a couple of new advertising ideas that could be used during the presentation.

The group still had all day Thursday to iron out anything, but Katy had a couple meetings with clients for other projects, and if Matt stayed in the same state, he would have to get some rest. Kevin overheard Matt telling Katy he had an additional meeting at 3 and that's why he couldn't leave. Kevin assumed it was with other potential investors of .comU, to remind them of the impending meeting Friday, but no one knew for sure who these people were exactly. In fact, Matt had had two short meetings Wednesday morning and never gave any indication what transpired out of them. Matt wasn't the kind of person to hide things, but he was the type to make sure things were right before divulging information. Drew figured that was the case, but Katy was a little more suspicious. Then again, Katy was suspicious of everyone.

It was almost 5 p.m., and Kevin figured Jen would be in her room, since her email said she would be back from class after 2. He hoped his email didn't lead her to believe he would call her first. Kevin finally made it to the dorm's parking lot and found a spot almost instantly. Jen lived on the third floor of a five-floor dormitory, while Jane lived on the second floor, but at the other end of the hall. Kevin walked into the guest area to call Jen. He had forgotten once again to just call from his cellphone. Surely after six months of having one he would remember the thing. He called, but there was no answer. That was a bad sign.

While he was trying to determine his next move, Kevin noticed a McDonald's bag sitting in the foyer. Kevin was hungry, so even though he was supposed to meet his sister for dinner, he thought a fry or two wouldn't be bad. He wasn't a huge guy, but he wasn't skinny either. It had been at least 18 hours since Kevin had eaten a French fry, which was entirely too long. He thought it might even be a record. Kevin had completely abandoned his search for his sister due to his large appetite for McDonald's. He approached the unattended bag and opened it. JACKPOT! A Super-sized fry and two Big Macs. Even if it might ruin his dinner with Jen and Jane, he was too hungry to pass up a snack.

While Kevin was debating with himself in between bites if he should eat all the lost food, he noticed a girl talking on one of the guest phones was holding a McDonald's drink. Thinking the food must be hers, Kevin attempted to quietly step away from the remaining grub. At least he had somewhat quelled his hunger with a few fries and two bites of a Big Mac, but now he had to make a quick getaway.

Kevin sprinted over to the stairs, but before he made it, he heard a loud "KEVIN!" He spun around, praying it wasn't her. But it was. Crissy Calhoun, perhaps the most annoying and most intelligent slut at Moxee Tech. Drew and Matt had tried to explain this paradox to Kevin. Yes, she was a good student in the computer science department. Yes, she had slept with every professor in the department, which included eight males and two females. Drew and Matt agreed that the strangest person in Moxee was the girl dressed like Captain Ahab; the second-strangest was the guy who always smelled like steamed carrots and cotton candy; and the third was the computer-geek sex-fiend Crissy.

"It is sooooo good to see you, Kevin Cakes!"

Oh my God, Kevin thought. She just said Kevin Cakes.

"Hey, Crissy," Kevin said. "Have you seen my sis?"

"Now why would you need to go looking for her when you can stand here and see this?" Crissy slid her right hand inside her pants, tugging gently and revealing a black thong.

"That's nice Crissy, but I'm already late. Where is she?"

Crissy seemed slightly mad but quickly got over it.

"I saw her walking down the second floor. But she might be over ... "

Kevin left quickly to run to the phone book. Wilson, Wilson, Wilson ... Jane ... 63487. He dialed the number as fast as possible.

"Hello?"

"Jane! What's going on! How have you been?"

"Kevin, is that you?"

Whoa, Kevin thought. He was getting really excited. She knew it was him, and he didn't even say his name!

"Yes, it's me! Have you been waiting for me to call?"

"Kevin! It's me, Jen. Are you crazy?"

"Sorry Jen, it's hard to hear on these dorm phones. Are you and Jane ready for dinner? It's on me!"

"Yeah, we'll be ready in a sec."

Kevin was hyped again. After he took a seat in the lobby, he peered over to the left and noticed Crissy showing another helpless victim her underwear. Finally, Jen and Jane appeared at the main double doors, both looking like they were ready for a night on the town. Kevin hurriedly rose to meet the two at the exit door.

"Glad you could make it," Jen said tapping her brother on the arm.

"I'm glad to see you too!" Kevin said, glancing at Jen then peering at Jane. "That is, 'too' as in 'also,' but also 'two' as in 'greater than one.' " Jane smiled at Kevin's attempt of homonym play. "So girls, where are we going to eat?"

"Well, Jane and I were just talking, and we want Italian. So we thought about the Olive Garden. Is that OK?"

"All the salad and bread you want?" Kevin said. "That sounds great!"

Kevin, still starving even after his earlier Big Mac sample, wondered if this was the first time in history that three 20-somethings agreed on a restaurant without any debate.

***

"So am I going to be able to use the system?"

"Yes and no. It's for Malorett, but anyone anywhere will be able to use it."

"So you will have stuff for school on there, right? Like our basketball schedule?"

"Yes, definitely. And hopefully the school will buy into the system and add other stuff in there too."

"Yeah Jane, maybe you'll be able to meet a new boyfriend on there!"

Kevin and Jane both blushed after Jen's comment in between bites of pasta. Jane had always been aware of Kevin's love for females, especially her. The two first met last year when Jen moved into the dorm her freshman year. Kevin had graduated and just started working on a project for The Developers with the school. Jane lived two doors down from Jen. Kevin knew about Jane from the basketball team — she was a highly regarded recruit from Texas who played every game as the first sub off the bench. She was slightly shorter than Kevin — she stood 5 feet 10 inches, while Kevin was right at 6 feet. Kevin loved tall girls, especially ones as cute as she was.

"Actually Jane, there will be a personals section," Kevin said, almost whispering into Jane's ear while clutching her right arm. "Maybe I will see you on there."

Jen had had enough of this flirting game.

"OK, Kevin that's enough," Jen said. "I'd rather not tell Jane the story about Crissy and the squirrel."

"Huh?" Kevin and Jane said in unison.

"Never mind," Jen said. "So what do you think will be the best feature of the system?"

"Man, there are so many, it's hard to pull out just one." Kevin paused to ask the waiter for more salad. "The idea itself will revolutionize the way community websites are handled in the future. The biggest difference is the community model people are used to seeing. Sites like Geocities, Friendster, whatever, urge people from all over the world to get closer together, like they live down the street or something. But .comU urges people already near each other to just get closer, so you really get to know them. Just think how many people you walk past on a daily basis, in the store, on the street. Think if you knew the person, or knew you had something in common with them, the chances of you approaching this person and having a friendly conversation would be greater."

Jane and Jen looked mostly interested, taking short pauses to nod as they gnawed on breadsticks and nibbled on linguine.

"Some of the research we did was by interviewing people from really, really small towns — places with populations fewer than 1,000," Kevin continued. "We wanted to know why they lived in such small places, what benefits they had, what they knew about others. Those are the kinds of things we want to bring to Malorett. We anticipate almost immediately this should have a great impact in driving people to the town ... at least as tourists, and hopefully as a new home for people."

"Don't you think people will be turned off by the lack of privacy?" Jen said.

"People don't have to put every ounce of information on the site," Kevin said. "They can put as much or as little as they want. The key, though, is public record. Records available to the public will be searchable in a multitude of ways, and should work as fast as Google. Maybe we can get different people to update it, sort of like the Wikipedia. If you wanted to find the property value of a specific piece of land in Malorett right now, you have to go to city hall, to the basement, and flip through a couple of books. With this system, you can do one quick search and whoomp, there it is."

Jane's eyes brightened.

"Wait a minute, couldn't this alienate them even more?" Jane said. "If you didn't have to leave your house to do anything, everyone will just be sitting at home, in front of their computer, instead of being out and about."

Kevin took a drink of his iced tea and nearly finished it in one gulp.

"No, no, no," he said. "That's the whole thing. You will still have to go out to check the land you want to buy. You'll still probably go to the grocery, the mall, etc. But this system gives you options — so if you're sick, or you want to stay in, you don't have to go out. Plus, when you do venture to other parts of town, you won't have to waste time finding things. You've already found it on .comU."

Kevin couldn't tell if Jen and Jane were completely in awe or bored out of their freakin' minds. Jen already had heard his .comU spiel plenty of times, and Jane never seemed very impressed about anything Kevin did. But maybe it was just a front. Maybe she was just playing hard to get. She did manage to find her way to be around more often lately when Kevin visited. And she almost always wore a tight shirt, like the red and black striped one she was wearing today, or some article of clothing that made her stand out like a Girl Scout at a biker bar. But the last time I checked, Kevin thought, Girl Scouts don't wear tight shirts. But it was wild how much bikers enjoyed Girl Scout cookies, especially Thin Mints.

The trio had come to an ease in eating. Kevin appeared to be eating the final breadstick, only because it was there. Jen was debating on whether or not to take the remainder of her linguine dish, which was about three-fourths complete, back to her dorm fridge. Jane appeared to be staring into space or possibly at the two kids standing outside the restaurant, apparently calling a three-legged dog toward them.

"Uh-oh ... I gotta get to study table," said Jane, looking at her watch. The basketball team had an hour each night for mandatory studying. Once a week they would also have an evening practice, but this week, that happened to be on Thursday. "We'd better get going, I have to be there by 7 or else."

"Or else what?" Kevin said.

"Or else I have to run an extra mile tomorrow before practice."

"Can I run with you?"

"I don't think coach would like that."

"Why, would she be jealous?"

As they were leaving, Kevin figured now was the time to pour it on heavy. Starting Friday, when .comU was going to be revealed, there wouldn't be much time for a social life. If he could somehow talk Jane into a date on Saturday, at least he would have an excuse to leave work for a few hours. And if all went well, then maybe it would be for more than a few hours.

Kevin picked up the tab — as promised — and followed Jane and Jen to the front of the restaurant. Jen walked out the entrance first and hurriedly made her way back to Kevin's car. Jane leisurely strolled behind, giving Kevin the opportunity to make his final descent.

"So Jane, is there any way I could interest you in dinner on Saturday?" Kevin said.

"Are you being serious? You just bought me dinner tonight?"

"Well, I was hoping it would be just the two of us," said Kevin, nodded at Jen, who appeared to have trouble finding Kevin's car.

"Let me think about it. I'll check my schedule. No wait, let's do it."

Kevin's eyes perked up as Jane realized what she had said. Before she could knock the vision Kevin had of herself undressing in front of him, he had already affixed his attention elsewhere. Matt and another gentleman stood three car lengths away and appeared to be in deep conversation. While Kevin and Jane were still a row from the car, and Jen stood at the car as if she had been there since just before the Civil War, Kevin made a move over toward his boss. He made it quickly between a parked car and van headed for the road.

"Dude, what are you doing here?" Kevin said.

Immediately, the conversation between Matt and the man came to a halt. The other man, wearing a three-piece suit with a thin red tie, even turned slightly away from Kevin.

"Hey Kevin, what are you doing here?" Matt said.

"I'm just eating with Jen and her friend."

"Are you getting some action?"

"Well ... not yet. So seriously, what are you doing over here?"

The other man still gazed in the opposite direction and had not acknowledged Kevin's existence.

"Oh. I came over here for a late meeting with another potential client," Matt said. "Kevin, this is Doug Morris."

The other man nodded and shook Kevin's hand.

"Client ... for .comU?" Kevin said.

"Possibly," Doug said, with a firm handshake. Doug and Matt gave wry smiles to each other.

That answer didn't relax Kevin, but Doug and Matt sure appeared to be at ease. Kevin heard talking behind him. It was Jen and Jane, practically yelping to each other. This was most definitely a sign for Kevin to get the hell out of there. Oh yeah! He was in the process of asking out Jane.

"All right, I need to get out of here," Kevin said. "I'll catch up with you in the morning, Matt. Nice to meet you, Doug."

Kevin turned around and quickly made it back to his vehicle. Matt had mentioned a meeting with a new client, but The Developers figured it was in the initial stages, like giving the potential client broad background on .comU. But this was no intro ... they were at Olive Garden! Something was just strange. The only time Matt is ever this smug is when he is questioned about his relationship with Katy. This was something completely different.

"Come on, Kevin. I need to get to study table!" Jane said.

Kevin found the right key and opened the passenger door for Jane.

"If I get you to practice on time, then can we have dinner Saturday?"

"Let me think about it one more time."

Jen, standing next to the driver passenger door, threw her arms in the air.

"Jane just say 'yes' or he will never stop!"

"OK then, yes. You can pick me up at 8."

Kevin all of the sudden felt as if his legs were going to jiggle completely off. Here is the future Mrs. Gentry, he thought. Thoughts of Matt and the mysterious Doug dressed for a big business deal quickly dissolved and were replaced with images of Jane wearing, well, nothing.

FOUR

"N-40."

"Boo!!!!!!!!" the crowd yelled. Drew, of course, was perplexed. Why was everyone booing at the last called number?

"Get the hell out of here, ya freak!" yelled some elderly woman from the second table. Wait, elderly isn't the right word for her, Drew decided. She might have been the only person in the hall who had a walker for her lucky troll.

"What do you want from me, Ethel!" Drew was not happy. His day at work was hectic enough. Now he was being ambushed by the most unruly group of citizens in the world: losing bingo players. "I call the numbers, you daub your paper. It's that easy. I have the hard job. I have to pull the Ping-Pong balls out and call the numbers. They make it look easy on the lottery show, but damn, it's not easy at all!"

This caused more ire from the crowd. The next ball was already positioned to be called, yet the audience was hostile and rowdy. Drew was even more confused.

"Drew, we are playing Big X," Ethel said. "There are no 'N' numbers. Just throw that number out for crying out loud. Don't read numbers we can't use!!!"

Of course, the Big X doesn't include "N" numbers, because the free space is the center of the X. The crowd looked relieved, as did Drew. He now had to wait five minutes for Ethel to get situated again. It's kinda funny, Drew thought, as he remembered when Ethel McMahan was a little more civil, back in the good ol' days, when she was under 100. Even the troll gave Drew a dirty look.

Drew had more important things on his mind than bingo. Granted, he still enjoyed calling games two nights a week at St. Pius, where Drew and Jessica, his wife, were members. The definition of a church member these days, it seemed, was that you donated money to its ongoing projects. So considering Drew almost always bought some nachos during his bingo nights, he counted that as contributing. So maybe Jessica didn't count after all, even though they were forced to have their picture taken for the church directory.

"OK, OK ... on with the game," Drew said. "Let's get it on!"

The audience roared in pleasure. Bingomania was on again.

Drew called one final number for the Big X — G-49 — and Jimmy Dickson picked up the victory. By Drew's calculations, Jimmy had bingoed four of the last six weeks, which would put him among the league leaders in victories. But alas, there was no league, and no leaderboard, so Jimmy settled for his $150, $10 of which went to Dale Washington's granddaughter, Becky. She was the Bingo Helper who yelled out Jimmy's winning numbers to Drew to verify the win. This also allowed Jimmy to work his other game a little more, since he flirted with Becky and all the helpers. The main problem was that Jimmy was 71, and Becky was 17. Jimmy swore up and down to Becky and the others that his age was transposed on his driver's license, but they always wondered how come he never mentioned it two years ago.

Another game of straight bingo for the approximately 250 in attendance — Martha Singleton, a.k.a. Big Martha Triplebutt, took the win in six numbers — was followed by a short intermission. Drew had Becky bring him some nachos and a Dr Pepper, and before she made it back, he was furiously writing down notes on a piece of scratch paper. Drew jotted down a few items about The Profiler before he forgot them, but roars from the crowd overwhelmed his concentration.

"Get your lazy ass on with the calling, bee-yatch!" Ethel said.

Ethel gets ugly sometimes, especially in the drought she is in. The lady hadn't won at St. Pius in four years. For one of the top 10 earnings winners in four straight decades, that wasn't acceptable. Some people thought she was getting too old to play. It's hard to justify what is too old to play bingo, though. At 104, she definitely wasn't the youngest in the building.

Becky started to walk away from the caller's table when Drew motioned for her.

"If we do more testing on The Profiler, we could use your help," Drew said. "You could be one of the first people on the system!"

"Awesome!" Becky said.

The comment seemed to brighten Becky's day, more so than Jimmy trying to rub her shoulders. The raunchy men, combined with the thick layer of smoke in the room, made for an unappetizing atmosphere for most of the Helpers. But it was kind of fun, especially when the debate between Bob Barker's best years, black hair or white hair, resonated through the hall. The discussion had grown to a point that two years ago, the room was actually divided into Blacks and Whites, based on Barker's hair color. With the help of Drew, the group finally decided he was good both ways, but the difference was since his hair turned white, he made a stronger effort to control the pet population.

Drew was ready for the second half of this Wednesday night's escapade. But at the same time, he needed to get his shit together for Friday. Drew spent most of his afternoon determining the various fields to be used for The Profiler.

Initially, Kevin was going to work on the project with Drew, but he opted to go visit his sister. From the aura surrounding Kevin the early part of the afternoon, he expected things to go well with one of his sister's friends. After Kevin left, Sarina filled Drew in a bit with Kevin's desire to date one of her friends. Oh to be young again, Drew thought. Not that he was old. At 31, Drew was the oldest Developer. He had lived in Malorett longer than any of the others in the group. After graduating from Georgia Tech, he did some grad school work at Moxee Tech and eventually taught classes for a couple years there. That's how he met Matt, and from there, the two pretty much started The Developers. The group was just an idea on the back burner, until four years ago, when Matt told Drew he had enough clients to do development for a living. Drew joined Matt shortly thereafter, still teaching at the university. Finally, the work was overwhelming enough that Drew cut back to part time, then left completely about two years ago. It was definitely going to be good to see the .comU project come to fruition.

Game 17, dubbed the "Double Floating Postage Stamp," was Drew's favorite. All a contestant has to do is cover two squares of four numbers on the board. There was heated debate once as to whether or not your boxes could overlap, and as of now, the rule was that the boxes could, indeed, overlap.

Strangely enough, this debate paled in comparison to the Bob Barker debate, and thankfully, unlike that one, no one was injured.

As Drew called the game and munched on his nachos, he remembered to call Jessica quickly and let her know he wouldn't be eating dinner at home. Drew and Jessica had been married for eight years. Jessica taught at Moxee Tech in the math department, as she had since they moved there. She was happy with her job, but she wasn't extremely pleased when Drew decided to leave the school for The Developers. Drew worked many long hours the first year or so, and Jessica usually saw him only on weekends. But lately, they had become closer, with Jessica being relegated to just part time during this year, and Drew being home more often. They decided it would be time to start a family when things were basically settled, hopefully in the next year or so.

Chet Marshall took the big prize in coverall. The extra jackpot, which is given out only if a player bingos in fewer than 50 numbers, was up to $650. After 44 numbers, Big Martha was only two away, but Chet had three of the final five numbers to win it outright. Big Martha was crushed, but not nearly as crushed as her seat cushion, when the final number she needed appeared on the monitor just after Chet yelled "bingo." At least Martha won one game, which is better than most, and she would be able to get double cheese on pizzas for at least two weeks.

Drew was tired when he arrived at St. Pius, but by the time Game 20, the final game, rolled around, he was thoroughly exhausted. Between numbers, Drew caught a message on his scrap paper he hadn't noticed. It just said "Need help, call me later, Katy." This was extremely bizarre, Drew thought. When did Katy write this on his paper?

Katy didn't appear to be in the best mood by the end of the work day. She had to answer a couple of voice mails, mainly dealing with Friday's meeting. The news leaked to the press — of course, Kevin was the leak, done with plenty of tact. Kevin would call the newspaper and the local TV and radio stations and give them great insider information all the time. And when they would ask his name, he would just say "Deep Throat." Maybe the media companies would think that their Deep Throat did have some amazing information, but unfortunately, all he had turned up so far was a small apartment fire (which he started), a person streaking down Main Street (Sarina, of course) and any of their big meetings. Kevin sometimes talked about wanting to meet the real Deep Throat, and possibly having him call the places in Malorett, just to prove he did have some connections. He sent Pat Buchanan, who both Kevin and Drew think was the original, an email once, but unfortunately, there was no response.

Katy told all media outlets that the .comU meeting scheduled for Friday was closed to the public, but that a press release would be sent just after the meeting. With every call, and every request for more information and/or interview, Katy obliged to as much as she could. Drew and Sarina overheard some of her conversations, wondering if she was spreading herself too thin. Then they remembered, this is what Katy lives for anyway. She can handle it.

Just before 5 p.m., Matt returned to the office with a man that Drew, Katy and Sarina had never met. Matt and the gentleman seemed to be in somewhat of a rush.

"Katy ... Katy ... are you here?" Matt said, as he and the man looked into the WAB. Katy just happened to be in the corner, looking through files, for a contact from the newspaper. The person from the newspaper had said his name on the phone minutes before, but either he didn't speak clearly, or he was eating a sub sandwich while trying to imitate Charles Bronson.

"Yeah, I'm here, Matt. What's going on?"

"I need those papers, Katy. The ones we were talking about earlier."

"How much earlier?"

"You know. THE papers. The .comU papers."

"Which papers? Contracts? Site specifications? Privacy and legal documents?"

Matt was scrambling around on Katy's desk as she spoke. Katy noticed the paper rustling and spun around.

"Matt! What papers?"

He didn't answer for 20 seconds, then held up five sheets that had been connected by a paper clip.

"Never mind. Here they are. Let's get out of here, Doug. Sorry it took so long."

Doug, the previously unnamed man, shrugged his shoulders and walked out just behind Matt. Katy, Drew and Sarina all just looked at each other, stunned.

"What just happened?" Sarina said.

"Who was that guy?" Katy asked, looking specifically at Drew.

"I've never seen that guy in my life," said Drew.

Just as Drew finished his sentence, Matt poked his head in the doorway once more.

"Let's get this place looking a little better," Matt said. "We are going to have visitors Friday, and we can't have papers all over the place."

Katy was already irritated that Matt flipped through her papers. Now he was telling her to pick them back up?

"What the hell?" Katy said. "We aren't going to dirty the place up for company. We have to get this other stuff finalized. Sarina is reading over and editing policies. Drew is finishing the database modifications. I'm ... "

Matt didn't let her finish.

"You," said Matt, pointing at Katy and then at her desk, "will clean up the mess at your desk. Immediately. There's no need to discuss this further."

Matt left, and Katy turned toward her desk. Drew and Sarina looked at each other, not knowing if they had missed something. Katy and Matt seemed to be on good terms personally earlier, although that never seemed to last long. Business-wise, though, things were always conducted appropriately.

"Are you OK?" Sarina asked Katy.

"Yeah, why wouldn't I be?" Katy began stacking her papers into two piles in an orderly fashion. "That client must be someone important."

"If so then why do we still not know him?" Drew said.

Drew never found an answer to his question. Not that the answer would appear at bingo, but maybe Katy had found it. Maybe that's why she wrote the note on the paper.

Finally a winner, Drew thought. Sid Mench grabbed Game 20 with an eight-number bingo, a simple small diamond. Sid was best friends with Jimmy Dickson, so they were going to celebrate their double win, perhaps with a steak dinner at Ponderosa. Sid gave Becky a tip, and as Drew was packing up his things, she came over to the caller table.

"Guess what, Drew?" Becky said. "Sid and Jimmy want to take all three of us helpers out to eat. Do you want to come with us?"

"Sorry Becky, I gotta run," Drew said. "I need to finish up some stuff from work, plus Jessica is expecting me home soon. Have fun though!"

Becky grimaced, but she waved, spun around and headed back over to where Sid and Jimmy were sitting. Drew normally stayed around and chatted with the bingo patrons, but he needed to get out of there and call Katy. Drew checked his watch — it was almost 10. Surely that's not too late, especially with the type of note in his pocket. He made it to his car and dialed Katy's number on his cellphone. After four rings, her answering machine picked up.

"Hi, this is Katy. I'm not in right now. Leave a message and I'll get back to you soon. Unless, of course you are Michael. If you are Michael, or one of Michael's friends, NEVER, NEVER, NEVER CALL THIS NUMBER AGAIN!!!! BEEP!"

Drew was unsure if he should leave a message or pray that Michael never called her again. He checked the scribbled note, and took the first option.

"Katy! It's Drew. Sorry I'm calling so late ... "

He was interrupted by Katy picking up.

"Drew! It's me! Thank God you called. Things have been crazy both in and out of the office lately. Sorry about the message. I just made it a few hours ago."

"Oh? He's back again?"

"Who the hell knows. There was a message on my answering machine when I got home tonight. He called again an hour later. Doesn't he get it? I put up with his shit long enough when we were dating and when we were married! I don't have to deal with that anymore!"

Drew seriously doubted he had time for another Katy tirade regarding Michael. They had been together about three years, one and a half married, and then they separated for one year. The divorce was final about five months ago, but every month, he called Katy with some ridiculous request. Drew was waiting at a stoplight, but he had approximately five minutes until he made it home. He was beat, so he needed to figure some way out of this mess. Maybe he could tell Katy he had to go to the bathroom, or possibly he was just in a 27-car pileup. No, at 10 p.m. in Malorett, there probably weren't 27 cars even in operation. The bathroom thing was the best he could do in such short notice.

"Katy, I'd love to talk, but I have to go REALLY bad."

"Go? I thought you were driving someplace now?"

"Yeah, I'm almost there. I have to go REALLY bad."

"Aren't you going there now?"

"No go! As in go to the bathroom!"

"Dude, you used that excuse last time I told you a story about Michael."

"Did you just call me dude?"

"Drew, I didn't call you about Michael. I called you to talk to you about what happened at the WAB today."

Relieved, Drew closed his eyes for a second, which is a pretty dumb thing to do on a two-lane highway. A semi narrowly avoided Drew's vehicle as it crossed over the center line for a fraction of a second.

"I thought you were OK with everything, Katy," Drew said. "That Matt was just in a bad mood or trying to get stuff done or something?"

"That was the easiest thing to say at the time. But that's not the case. He's thinking about me again, Drew. I can just tell it. I can tell it every time."

"Well of course he's thinking about you, Katy. He kinda has to. I mean, you are an integral part of .comU."

"No, he's thinking about me in other ways."

There's only one thing worse than hearing Katy talk about Michael, and that's hearing about Matt, Drew thought. Well there are a couple of worse things ... like the time Ethel and Big Martha decided to mud wrestle to raise money for St. Pius. As Drew was rambling to himself in his head, he realized he was discussing something with Katy, although he couldn't remember what it was. So he used a standard question to refresh his memory.

"How do you know?" Drew said.

"I just told you!" Katy said. "I can tell!"

"You can tell what?"

"That he's thinking about me!"

"Who is?"

"Matt! Have you been listening to me?"

Oh yeah, Matt and Katy. Now he remembered.

"Of course I have, Katy. I just wanted to make sure. So he said something today when he was talking about cleaning the place? What was it?"

"Well ... nothing just then. But the whole day, the way he was looking at me, the way he glanced at me, pretending he wasn't. The way he said different things to me, in the meeting and afterward. The way he looked through my papers. He doesn't do that to everyone."

"But remember Katy, he had a client with him! He was in a hurry. I don't think it was anymore than that."

"How would you know, Drew? Have you ever dated him?"

Drew thought for a minute just to make sure he was absolutely positive of the question.

"Um, no Katy, I haven't. But that shouldn't matter. I don't think he's thinking about you like that. He has too much else on his mind."

The garage door opened at Drew's house. He had made it home. Katy was going nowhere with this, plus they all had to be there by somewhat early in the morning.

"I don't think so, Drew," Katy said. "He wanted to know what I was doing for lunch Thursday because he wanted to go somewhere and get a fish sandwich."

Drew hit his head with his right hand. This was more serious than he thought. The fish sandwich was a dead giveaway.

"Katy, I made it home," Drew said. "Let me call you right back after I tell Jessica the situation. We have to be to work early, but we have to take care of this tonight."

FIVE

It seemed as if it were 342 years ago, but actually, it happened for the first time barely more than two years back. Drew managed to find himself right in the middle of something he had no conceivable notion of determining. And of all the things, he had to bring up that brown paper bag, sitting innocently in the refrigerator.

Drew and Matt had just started The Developers. Work and new clients were coming in fast, so fast that Drew had just quit his teaching position at Moxee Tech to devote all his time to bigger and better things, including theorizing about the system that would eventually become .comU. Technically, Matt was his boss, according to the actual business structure, but they always looked at each other as peers. With the increase in work, and the chance that the chores would grow exponentially in the upcoming year, Matt and Drew decided it was time to expand the business further. At first, the two thought bringing on one additional person should do the trick. Instead, they opted to open it up and find the best people for the job, even if that meant hiring more than just one new employee.

Thus began the circus called by some businesses as human resources. Within a week after publishing an ad in the Malorett newspaper, Matt had received 48 resumes. He was initially worried that instead of posting their simple ad:

DEVELOPERS NEEDED:
We are working on new ways to combine computer-based technology with various types of marketing. If you have a strong background in programming, writing, designing or any combination of these things, we need you. Please send resume and references.

The newspaper quite possibly published this ad:

Matt remembered the last time he read that in the paper. The models ended up being elephants! Someone at the newspaper had played a joke by leaving out key elements to the ad. Unfortunately, that same person who played the joke accidentally included his address in the ad.

Needless to say, there were still strange specimens showing up in the resumes. One guy said he had never seen a computer before. Another man mentioned he had invented the calculator. A woman said her daughter was "developing" but wasn't positive that was needed. She even enclosed a fairly large training bra with her resume and references. The problem was, though, that Michigan state law prohibited 11-year-olds from working full time.

After scanning the resumes, Drew and Matt decided they didn't need a boatload of people who had no clue what they were doing. They also determined that four would be the magical number, but probably one of those employees would be part time only. Kevin was mentioned early in the selection process, mainly because he came with the highest recommendation from Professor Jones.

Sarina was the only person qualified from the stack of resumes. She also was mentioned by various Tech professors as an obvious choice. She had just gone back home to Indianapolis for the summer, but she immediately returned for the job opportunity.

The final piece of the puzzle, however, wasn't so clear. In fact, if Drew hadn't gotten out of bingo early that day, he might have been talking to a fast-maturing 11-year-old.

Occasionally Drew called Friday's 2 p.m. summer bingo down at St. Pius. On this particular August day, as the church prepared for its annual picnic, Drew found himself calling only 15 games. This worked out nicely because he needed to get over to the office to finish a couple of things before the weekend. With no intermission, Drew never had time to get his nachos, so once the bingo ended, Becky brought him a brown paper bag that included two fish sandwiches. Thank God for Becky, Drew thought. Thank God for bingo, Ethel McMahan thought all day EVERY day.

Drew got to the office, ate one sandwich and threw the other into the refrigerator. Matt was supposed to be back from a meeting around 4, which would give Drew time to finish a few things and plan for the upcoming week. Sarina was on her way to Malorett and was going to start the following Monday; Kevin had already been familiarized with the system and was to start part time on Wednesday.

Drew had just finished reading an email from a maintenance client when he heard a knock at the door. It hadn't quite registered with Drew that it was, indeed, a knock at the office door. He and Matt had just relocated there two weeks beforehand, as they both just worked at home prior to the planned expansion. Up until that point, only three humans knocked on that door: Drew, the day before he had a key; Matt, the day he forgot his key; and Butch, the landlord, to make sure the door worked. Butch claimed a squirrel occasionally ran into the door as well, bringing the total to four knockers.

Matt couldn't have forgotten his key; the door was locked when Drew arrived. Or perhaps Butch was "testing" again, but he usually didn't appear until later. Drew moved down the hall toward the door and saw the silhouette of a young woman, maybe in college, standing impatiently outside. It was possible she just had to use the restroom, but her uneasy movements made Drew approach the door slightly faster. Even from a distance, he had a hunch she was attractive, and he wasn't disappointed when he opened the top of the Dutch-style door.

"Can I help you, young lady?"

"I'm not really that young, but yes you can help me. I have a resume to give to Matt Severson concerning the job opening in the newspaper. Do you think you can give it to him?"

The girl handed Drew a resume. He glanced over it and noticed she actually had qualifications: some programming experience, some writing and a business degree from Tech.

"So, Katy ... you are Katy Terrill, correct?"

"That's correct."

"Do you currently live in town?"

"I live in Moxee. Well, I did live in Moxee. Or, I still live there, but not in my house. I mean, my husband and I ... "

"Never mind the question, Katy. I didn't mean to pry."

"It's OK. Honestly, what's bothering me more is talking through this half door to you. I feel as if I'm at the back door of Pee Wee's Playhouse."

Partially embarrassed, Drew introduced himself and invited Katy inside. He noticed she was still quivering either from nerves of delivering the resume, or possibly divulging her personal life to a complete stranger.

"Where are you working now?" Drew said.

"I'm a manager at the Lazarus in Moxee," Katy said. "It's OK, but I would like a little more out of life than managing teenagers at their first job and 40-something lifers who are never going to move up anywhere. I've been trying to find something more worthwhile. That's when I saw the ad for The Developers."

"Well, I think we found all that we needed actually. I'm sorry, but ... "

Katy stopped him, much like a school crossing guard stops first-graders immediately after the first bell rings. Drew wasn't moving, so he shrugged and wondered if she really intended to make him stop, or if it was some new "Vogue" move that Madonna had not yet perfected.

"What is that smell?" Katy said. "Is that fish I smell?"

"Well it's possible!" Drew said. He led Katy to the breakroom, opened the refrigerator and pointed to the brown paper bag that contained his fish sandwich. Katy grinned and blushed, while Drew entered into deep thought, trying to explain how anyone could grin and blush after being shown a brown paper bag containing a lone fish sandwich.

"How did he know?" Katy asked.

"Huh? How did who know?"

"How did Matt know I would be coming here?"

"I seriously doubt he did. What makes you think he knew you were coming?"

"The fish sandwich, Drew! The fish sandwich!"

"Did I miss something?"

Katy started to answer him, but there was a rattle down the hallway. Matt had returned from his meeting and shouted a "Hello?" down the hallway. Immediately, Katy shot out of the breakroom and sprinted down toward the door. She greeted Matt with a huge smile, an oversized hug and the biggest surprise in this building since the day Butch forgot to wear a smiley face T-shirt.

"Katy, what are you doing here?" Matt said, barely able to breathe from the Hulk Hogan-style bear hug being applied.

"I've come to work for you," Katy said. "Just like old times! And I see you were expecting me!"

"How could I have been expecting you?" Matt glanced around Katy at Drew, who shrugged.

"Duh, Matt! The fish sandwich in the refrigerator!"

Matt still didn't get it. He hadn't put anything in that refrigerator in three days, yet somehow he was responsible for its contents. Drew must have brought the mysterious sandwich, Matt thought. At this point, Matt decided to just play along.

"Oh yes, I forgot about that," Matt said. "It is really great to see you again, Katy. Um, let's go in here and discuss the job opening."

Drew looked over at Matt, stunned. They still had an opening?

"Uh, Matt, I thought ... "

Matt cut off Drew, took Katy by her arm and started walking toward the LAB.

"Drew, we'll be right back," Matt said.

Still trying to determine what was happening, Drew went back to the WAB and continued working. Matt filled in the blanks for him later that evening: Matt had met Katy while he was a teaching assistant at Moxee Tech. They dated briefly following the class, but it didn't last long. Matt was engulfed in his work, while Katy met a guy named Michael Fletcher, another student at Tech. Katy dropped Matt soon thereafter. At that stage, with Matt theorizing about The Developers' potential, he just didn't have time for her.

While they were dating, which lasted about three months, Matt and Katy discovered they shared an adoration for eating fish. Almost weekly, the two visited various fisheries around Malorett, Moxee and other nearby towns. Katy was a salmon girl, while Matt was more a grouper-type guy. That never brought about a discussion, but everyone knows a salmon girl and a grouper guy will eventually lead to some kind of rift.

About an hour later, Matt and Katy walked into the WAB.

"Drew, meet the fifth Developer, Katy Terrill."

"Actually, we already met, but again, it's good to meet you," said Drew, extending his hand.

"Yes, good to meet you again as well," Katy said.

***

Drew made it inside his house. It was late, but Jessica was still awake. She usually stayed up until he made it home from bingo, mainly to see if Ethel had finally ended her losing streak. Drew explained the Katy situation, and Jessica rolled her eyes, as usual. She always wondered how Matt and Katy could ever possibly work together, or have some sort of platonic relationship, given their past. Drew was at a loss because he, too, had no idea. But what could he do?

***

Kevin and Sarina had no problems adjusting to their new jobs, but it was evident early on that Matt still looked to Katy as his right-hand man. Everyone suspected they were sleeping together, but no one had the urge to ask. It didn't affect their work performance negatively, and on top of that, it may have helped it.

With Drew and Matt, the work was too thick to even comprehend. Matt had worked on his fair share of hosting and development contracts with clients for a few years, and Drew maintained some website development customers plus a few who contracted for IT support. They assumed the first six months would be pretty meager money-wise, considering the .comU project would be taking off shortly. During the initial months, Sarina and Drew took care of the existing clients, while Matt, Katy and Kevin focused on finding new business and outlining .comU. Things progressed far better than anyone had expected: The Developers picked up enough new clients to allow the group to spend time working on the community project. Matt had said in the beginning he expected a launch of 3-5 years. But after six months, that was trimmed to three years maximum.

In fact, Matt and Katy spent many a night theorizing the moment when the project would launch, how it would be presented and what type of slogan they could use to promote it. Of course, most of this time was spent under the sheets.

"Here's the best one yet, Matt," Katy said while tugging at Matt's muscular arms. ".comU — You're not a number ... you're not a name ... you're a username and password."

"Not bad Katy, but what about this one?" Matt said, gently massaging Katy's shoulders. ".comU — There's an 'I' in community, but there's also a 'U.'"

Katy was in the midst of breaking up with Michael, who she had been seeing since Matt could remember. Michael and Katy always got along just fine. In fact, they had many similar interests, including their computer science majors, and agreed on music, movies, sports, that sort of thing. But Katy sensed that Michael had an intolerance toward her working as much as she did. He worked for an IBM sector located in Moxcc, putting in 45-50 hours a week himself. Katy never realized anything like this until they started living together. Michael expected her to take care of many of the household duties, which was difficult, considering the hours she was putting in as a Developer.

Matt wondered if Katy really didn't realize this because once she started working at the LAB, she wanted to be there more and more and more. Finally, Katy moved out for a brief period of time, only going back to grab more clothes and important belongings. Most of the stuff ended up at Matt's, and he didn't mind. They could get even more work accomplished, without even leaving the house!

Even though she was happy with The Developers, and Matt, it became too overwhelming to live at work all the time. She began to miss Michael, and he, in turn, became aware of Katy's work ethic and came to appreciate it. The couple were engaged not too long thereafter, and things seemed better for awhile. Matt and Katy never had trouble working together, but their time spent outside of the office was obsolete. A few months down the road, however, Michael was up to his old tricks, and again, Katy came running to Matt.

But Michael always made amends quickly, and Matt was quickly forgotten, at least, outside of work.

***

I can't even remember the rest of the details of Matt and Katy's relationship, Drew thought. After everything Matt had told me about them, and after he "accidentally" read a few email threads between the two, all he could come up with was a basic outline of how they met, when they got together and when Michael came into the picture. Oh, and there was the time they broadcast themselves from Matt's home webcam. Matt was just testing it for .comU when Katy made a special appearance at his house wearing very little.

Drew called Katy to briefly continue their conversation, even though it was now 11:30 p.m.

"Hello, Drew?"

"Yeah Katy, it's me. How are you feeling?"

"I'm feeling a little better. But I still don't know what to do about Matt."

"What did you tell him when he asked you if you wanted to have a fish sandwich?"

"You mean after I almost fell out of my chair? I told him he was crazy. He is you know. He's CRAZY! Tomorrow, we should probably just act like nothing happened, and we didn't have this conversation. Is that OK?"

"Yep, that sounds good. Good night, Katy."

***

One full day from the launch, Drew thought as he reviewed his new email. One day while there's a snowstorm heading this way, Matt thinks it's mating season and Kevin STILL hasn't asked for the burrito I owe him. Maybe this really does signal the apocalypse.

"Drew, do you have time to work on The Profiler now?" Sarina said, entering the WAB. Drew looked at his watch. It was already 10 a.m. Shit. He had hoped to get there a little earlier, to finish some other things, but it was a long night.

"Yeah, Sarina, let's fix the stuff that needs to be fixed. We should be OK for tomorrow anyway, with the demo, but this needs to be fixed soon."

"What are you going to show them in the demo?"

Drew typed in the URL for the testing area of .comU. He clicked on The Profiler link, which brought up boxes for Drew to type his username and password. It worked, which was a stark difference from yesterday, when everything seemed to bomb every other time. Sarina's idea about the session variable helped with this problem, too.

Drew and Sarina needed to complete the demonstration of the member listings. When users come to The Profiler to do lookups, they will enter as much search criteria they have — most likely a name, or possibly even an address. The search would return a list of potential matches, and users could find out more information or even find a map to their address. And with The Developers' advanced mapping system, users could zoom in so far to not only see who they found in their search, but they could also see their next-door neighbor or anyone around the block, if that information is available.

Sarina rolled her chair back to her computer. She grabbed her water bottle from a bag on the floor, took a sip and typed something on her machine.

"Where is everyone this morning?" Sarina said. "I thought they were supposed to be here?"

"Do we have another meeting?" Drew said. "I think bingo fried my B-5, I mean, my brain last night."

Just as Drew finished, Katy walked in the LAB. She looked as if she hadn't slept more than 14 minutes the night before. Drew turned and nodded, while Sarina just stared.

"Girlfriend, what's wrong with you?" Sarina said.

"I'm OK," Katy said, moving toward her desk. "I just didn't get much sleep. Did anyone call this morning?"

"Nope," Drew said. "It's been pretty calm. Almost ... too calm."

Katy was content with that answer. She booted up her computer and began her daily ritual of checking email and scanning her task list. Then she spun around, as if she just remembered she left her car running.

"Are we supposed to have a meeting this morning?" Katy said.

"I don't think so," Drew answered. "But I couldn't remember either."

"I mean, we practically have meetings EVERY morning," Sarina said. "Maybe the three of us should have a meeting."

"About what?" Drew said.

"About what the hell Matt was thinking last night," Sarina said. "What was that all about, just brushing you off the way he did?"

At first, Drew and Sarina didn't think Katy was going to answer, but finally, she faced them.

"Sarina, he's crazy," Katy said. "But it's OK. Everything will be OK."

"You aren't falling for him again, are you?" Sarina said.

"What the hell?" Katy said. "No, it's not like that. It's ... I just want to move on with this project. That should be more important than any personal issues."

Sarina, not content to let the conversation end, changed subjects slightly.

"So Michael called you again?" Sarina said. "What is he doing, spying on you?"

"AHHHHHHHHHHHHH!!!!!!!" Katy screamed and ran out the door. Evidently, that was the wrong thing to say this morning.

Sarina and Drew walked out of the LAB, down the hall and caught up with Katy in the kitchen. She appeared to be fine, pouring herself a mug of coffee.

"Um, you just ran out like you were possessed by the devil or Grendel or something," Drew said.

"I'm OK, guys," Katy said. "I really am. Thanks for your help though. We just need to focus on .comU, not past boyfriends or stalking ex-husbands."

"So he IS calling you!" Sarina said.

"Yeah, he called twice last night," Katy said. "I think he wants his Hall & Oates CD back or something. First off, I gave that back to him when we separated. Secondly, I had it by accident. Thirdly, why would anyone want that CD?"

"Uh, I have that CD," Drew said. "Maybe he wanted it so next time he called you, he could play 'Maneater' in the background."

Katy had put up with this on a monthly basis ever since they were divorced. Michael would call for some ridiculous reason and try to coerce her into meeting him in some dark part of town. Katy finally decided to get caller ID and stop answering his calls. Then he started calling from pay phones, so Katy decided not to pick up the phone until someone tried to leave a message. When she first instituted this policy, she pissed off a lot of people because she set her phone to pick up on the 26th ring. Luckily, her mother cussed her out when the answering machine finally kicked on.

Katy had more suitors than Matt and Michael, and others didn't even have names that started with 'M.' Katy was always sought after heavily but tried to focus as much as she could in moving up in life without having to sleep her way to the top. She just blamed it on Malorett, the Nothing Going On Here capital of the universe. The Developers decided Malorett just barely beat out the strip joint in the Vatican for that title.

The reason everyone fell for Katy was not just her looks, but her style, or her flair, and her ambition. She had the ability to stand up to even the most confident guys, look them in the eyes and say "You're wrong, dumbass." She had light brown hair, deep brown eyes and a tiny mouth, except when she cracked a smile, which turned her freckled face into a pristine painting.

Katy, Drew and Sarina made their way back down the hallway to the LAB. Kevin and Matt had apparently arrived recently, as they both were still wearing their coats.

"Hey guys," Matt said, removing his gloves. "If it's OK with everyone, I think we should have a dinner meeting this evening. Is everyone in?"

Everyone nodded.

"Then it's settled," Matt said. "Is six o'clock OK? That will give us time to review all that we've done today. I need to make some calls and see if all invited are coming tomorrow. Katy, have you received any cancellations?"

"No Matt, everyone should be here, as far as I know," Katy said. "It probably wouldn't hurt to again check with the chamber. I'm not positive they know the media will not be attending."

"We don't want the media covering the meeting?" Kevin asked.

"We will send a press release out after the meeting is finished," Matt said. "That will protect the integrity of our potential clients. The media will know about it, don't worry about that."

Kevin hit himself in the head a few times to try to wake up. Sarina and

Drew continued to finish their work on The Profiler. Katy sat down at her seat, hoping Matt had not noticed she looked like a wreck. It was useless for her to think he wasn't thinking about her, but he was thinking about her. It made Katy dizzy thinking about her last thought, so she decided to just make more items on her task list and accomplish them.

SIX

Kevin was the first to arrive at Dave's Burger Bonanza. If it had to do with food, Kevin was always the first one there. Well, except one time when he misunderstood directions and ended up being late for the meal. All The Developers were surprised, but not entirely surprised when he showed up with a Big Mac container in his pocket. "I got lost ... I was scared!" Kevin replied after arriving that evening.

But he didn't need directions to his favorite place to eat. Dave's was nestled between a gas station and a law office on the east side of Malorett. Drew initially discovered the place, and ever since that time, The Developers have used it as an off-campus meeting place. As the name suggests, Dave's specializes in burgers, but not just the ordinary hamburger, or even just the cheeseburger. In fact, the Manager's Special consists of a turkey burger, chicken burger and hamburger stacked on a poppy seed bun, topped with lettuce, pickles, onions, black olives and special sauce. As strange as it may sound, it was definitely Kevin's favorite.

While he waited for the others to arrive, Kevin popped open his glove compartment. He found dozens of menus and coupons, just in case he ever got the urge to visit any of the local restaurants. He pulled out Dave's menu and reviewed his choices. I haven't had a Cheezie Wheezie in awhile, Kevin thought. A Cheezie Wheezie had four different types of cheese, melted on a single hamburger patty. The catch was the cheese types changed each week, so he would have to wait until he entered to determine if that was the burger for him.

This sounded grand to Kevin, but then again, just about all food sounded grand to Kevin. The one exception to this rule was pumpkin pie. He couldn't even eat it with a large dab of Cool Whip on top. Kevin would rather STARVE than eat pumpkin pie. Considering he was looking on the stout size these days, coming in at over 200 within his 6-foot frame, it was evident the pumpkin pie firing squad had not been by his house lately.

Finally, 12 minutes after Kevin arrived, Sarina and Katy pulled into the parking lot, followed immediately by Matt and Drew. All four had left directly from work; Kevin had to run home fast beforehand to check on his fish. Everyone assumed he just wanted to make sure Jane hadn't called his home phone to cancel. He was still amazed she was really going on the date Saturday with him. They were planning to have dinner and then go bowling. There was still a lot of time for her to cancel, Kevin thought.

Kevin jumped out of his car, carrying Dave's menu, and the others made it to the front door. The crowd had died down a bit, as it was already 7:30 p.m. Sarina held the door for two departing customers. Both were men in their mid-40s who definitely ate right eight days a week. You know it's a good sign, Sarina thought, to go into a restaurant where large folks eat, especially when they don't even have a buffet.

The group was seated immediately. Drew picked up a couple of crayons at the hostess counter as he walked toward the table. They opted for a six-seat circular table in the center of the main room. The table was adjacent to a mammoth tree that couldn't have been real. The branches were too high to determine anything, and no one dared try to touch the trunk. Photos of customers and paintings of Indians adorned most of the walls, and there were lantern-type side lights above every other booth. The dim lighting made Dave's burgers look even more scrumptious than anyone could fathom.

Matt, Katy and Sarina scrutinized over the menu; Kevin waiting patiently for everyone to decide what they wanted; and Drew colored the placemat slowly and unassertively.

"Hey Drew, if you were going to color something, don't you think you should color something that's not already colored?" Sarina said.

"Well, if they aren't going to bring me a kids placemat/menu, then I'll just have to make do with what they give me," Drew said. "I can't help it if I like to color."

"Does everyone know what they want?" Kevin asked. "I think I'm going for the Cheezie Wheezie. I'll gladly pay you Tuesday for a hamburger today."

For a split second, Katy could have sworn Kevin turned into Popeye's best friend, Wimpy.

"I think I'm ready to order," Matt said confidently. He then turned to Katy. "What are you having? The fish sandwiches here are pretty good too, but not as good as Walt's Wharf up the road."

"Yeah, I've had their fish here before," Katy said. "But I'm going to stick with a regular burger. I haven't had one in awhile."

Katy didn't intend to sit right next to Matt, but the odds were against her from the beginning. Drew and Kevin sat down instantaneously, side-by-side, and Matt grabbed a chair opposite of them. Katy chose the seat next to Kevin so that if he tried to rub Sarina's thighs, like last time, he would have to make a long stretch. Not that it hadn't happened before, but it was slightly more difficult.

After a short wait, the gang ordered food. Everyone, except Kevin, ordered cautiously, not knowing if this would be coming out of their pockets or the company's. Matt usually waited until the end to reveal what would happen. This seemingly helped everyone; no one ate too much, and the company usually got off without paying a ridiculous amount for grub.

Sarina ordered first. She asked for the veggie burger with all the fixings. Wait, aren't the fixings really just the veggie burger itself anyway? Sarina had tinkered with a no-meat diet for a period of time, but she was off that kick for now. Every time she went more than two weeks without eating enough protein, she could never finish her two-mile run. Some people can get through it eating peanut butter, eggs, etc., but Sarina would rather just stick with a juicy steak every once in awhile. This time, ordering a veggie burger signified nerves, but no one else could have recognized that.

Not that there was anything wrong with being nervous about getting ready to launch such a large product as .comU. But Sarina had been on the outside looking in for much of the project. She brought many good ideas to the table, but for the most part, the basic premise had been decided well before she was a Developer.

Even still, she was part of it now, and an important part at that. Sarina had shared responsibility with Katy for marketing and promotions and with Drew for the actual programming. Sarina had a major in computer programming and a minor in business, so she could stretch different ways for the project.

Although Sarina was great with each member of the group, she spent quite some time to herself. There was no bona fide reason why she did this; she was always included in get-togethers with the group. But outside of The Developers, Sarina had few friends around town. While the others had somewhat of a life outside the WAB, Sarina's extracurricular activities included basically staying in shape. She had plenty of opportunities at dates, mostly from the guys gawking at her at the gym. Sometimes she went along with it, but usually, she was satisfied with the job and taking care of her cat, Beppo.

Unlike his owner, Beppo did not run anywhere. At the very least, he occasionally scooted from one side of Sarina's love seat to the other. That, in itself, could have been a mini-series. Beppo had to be the slowest cat alive, and it may have been beaten out by a few dead ones as well. One time Kevin arrived at Sarina's place for a "date" and accidentally sat on what he thought was a nice rug. Ever since that time, Beppo was rude to Kevin on return visits.

Kevin seemed to "date" a lot of girls, Sarina always thought. But she wasn't looking for anything serious, so she didn't mind hanging with him every once in awhile. He knew a lot of places around town to go, plus he seemingly had friends everywhere. And Kevin didn't mind being Sarina's tour guide. The first minute Sarina left for the bathroom during their outings, Kevin made it clear to his friends that yes, she was the girl who ran in the freezing cold, wearing just a sports bra and spandex shorts. But Kevin didn't let them take pictures, because that would just be tacky.

Sarina had on plenty of clothes at Dave's Burger Bonanza, which was a good thing because it had to be below freezing in the place. Maybe the gigantic tree was removing the heat in the room in search of oxygen, because it certainly wasn't retaining much carbon dioxide, being bothered by waitresses all the time. At least the autograph hounds took Thursdays off.

Although she was nervous, Sarina had confidence in the project, and her part of .comU. She had worked with Drew to fix an integral part of The Profiler earlier in the day; on Friday, after the .comU preview to the city, she had planned on testing other sections more thoroughly.

While Sarina committed to memory the important things she needed to check on, Drew was busy coloring. At least he refrained from ordering off the kids menu; He, like Kevin, ordered the Manager's Special with an order of onion rings.

Drew relished these few minutes away from work. He liked to use the minutes to think about absolutely nothing. I mean, unless you count trying to stay inside of the lines on a place mat, then he wasn't thinking. He knew Friday would be the day to think again. Drew's section of the talk was one of the shortest, but it was the most crucial, at least in his mind. He had to touch on every single feature within the .comU structure. It wasn't possible, but he had to do everything in his power to make it possible. Fortunately, Drew's demeanor never fluctuated much, so he was prepared to go along with his speech. Whether or not cows showed up to listen to him, Drew would deliver when it was his time. The only chance he wouldn't be able to do so would be if someone started throwing crayons.

It was Drew's thinking that the only way this project would succeed and come to fruition as planned was if everyone did his or her part. The Developers, up to this point, possessed something that no other work group Drew had known before had possessed: true teamwork. There was plenty of minor complaining, including Kevin always being hungry, Katy always going delirious over Matt and her ex and Sarina always nitpicking at Drew's programming style. But all of this was thrown out the window when it came time to get things done.

But not everything always went as planned. For instance, Drew had not intended to throw his green crayon underneath the table, and for that matter, make it bounce into Sarina's purse. He tried to play it smooth, and quickly snaked his foot into the purse's side pouch. The purse's balance, though, was compromised, which caused the purse to fall. Luckily, Sarina, Matt, Kevin and Katy appeared to be in a heated discussion. He rolled the green crayon with his left foot, back to the side of his chair, gently scooped it up and turned his focus on Katy.

"We went over the entire presentation yesterday," Katy said. "How could we go wrong? The only chance we have at blowing this is if someone doesn't show up. Everyone will be there, correct?"

"I guess what worries me, Katy, is an off-the-wall question," Matt asked. "We've trained for everything we think is possible, but there's always that possibility someone will come up with something we haven't heard."

"What could someone ask or say that would completely screw this up?" Kevin said. The group thought for a second and was interrupted by the waitress bringing their order. The woman served Kevin first, appropriately, and he began chomping on his onion rings immediately. Matt and Katy stared at Kevin, still contemplating the last question. Sarina fumbled for her napkin, while Drew finally put down the crayons.

"See, Kevin, that's the point," Matt said. "If we could think of the question, then we wouldn't have to worry about it. But what if it's something we can't think about?"

Kevin then tried to speak even though his mouth was stuffed with what composed about one-fifth of his meal.

"Matt, this is too philosophical to discuss at Dave's Burger Bonanza."

But Matt wasn't ready to let the talk end.

"Guys, there's something I need to tell you before the presentation tomorrow," Matt said. "I had contemplated holding out, but I think everyone needs to know."

Everyone immediately quit eating and looked at Matt.

"I have been told by two people who are relatively close to the people making decisions that we have already won them over. The final presentation scheduled for tomorrow will just be customary, almost like a show, for everyone involved to get one last good look at the system before it's approved."

"Approved?" Drew asked. "Approved by whom? We don't need approval, we need sponsors."

"I know Drew, maybe that wasn't the best choice of words," Matt said. "I mean, if the city is ready, then we go forward with the project. Apparently, the city is already making a specific fund for this particular project acquiring certain keystone sponsors for the system. It doesn't even look like we'll have to do any hard selling to many more clients."

"Um, Matt, I don't get it," Kevin said, grabbing an onion ring and devouring it without missing a beat. "The businesses I've contacted are interested in sponsorship for various parts of the system. Other companies are planning on running banner ads or even smaller ads on the site. What are we doing about them?"

"Oh sure, Kevin, they will still exist," Matt said. "That's not what I'm saying. We aren't so much changing our plans for the system. Well, we aren't changing them, so much as accelerating them."

"Accelerating them?" Katy inquired. "How can we do anything faster? We don't have any funding yet!"

"That's precisely what I'm saying," Matt said. "There's a good chance that tomorrow, the city will request to PURCHASE the .comU. The system would still remain as property of The Developers, but the city would actually take care of some management, especially how certain areas are sold and which companies fit in which places."

"This gives us virtually no control over how .comU will grow," said Drew, shaking his head. "I don't understand this at all."

"Me neither," Sarina said. "I thought the plan was that we told the city how to use it, not the city telling us what to do with something we built."

"I know that's what it looks like, guys, but I haven't told you the whole story," Matt said. "I've met with some well-to-do people here in town recently, and I have to tell you, the money these people have could drive the people in charge. Everyone sees the potential, and the city wants to be the first to jump on it."

"We can't sell to the city!" Katy said. "This is a complete change of plans. Don't we have any say in the matter?"

"Yes you do, Katy," Matt said. "That's why I'm bringing this up now. The presentation tomorrow will contain members of the city government and local business leaders. But I've come up with a way to avoid problems."

"And that would be?" Drew said.

Matt took a bite of his fish sandwich. "We need to promise a system in a box, ready to go, whenever they are ready for it. This means moving the launch up sooner than expected. If we do this, no one can outbid the other for our services. We will still control the launch, the system and anyone who wants to be a part of it."

Drew, Sarina and Kevin all had bewildered looks on their faces. What Matt was telling them didn't make much sense. In order to keep control of the site, they had to get it done faster? Wasn't it already completed?

Katy, though, wasn't indiscreet about her feelings.

"Matt, this is bullshit. You have been keeping this from us all along? So on one hand, we have companies and possibly the city wanting to buy ownership of the system, but at the same time, we are planning on keeping it? It seems to me we are going to piss a lot of people off."

"I feel like the homecoming queen," Kevin said.

"What the hell is that supposed to mean?" asked Drew, chewing on his burger.

"Well of course everyone wants a piece of the homecoming queen. But she doesn't give it up to anyone, not even the homecoming king. Maybe her biology teacher, but that's about it."

"Well, what about the homecoming king?" Sarina said. "I mean, couldn't it be about him too? Maybe he thinks he's too good for all the girls."

"Sarina's got a good point, Kevin," Drew said.

"WOULD EVERYONE SHUT UP AND STOP TALKING ABOUT THE STUPID PROM?????!?!?!?!?!" Katy said.

Katy wasn't very happy, so Drew declined to remind her they were discussing homecoming, not prom. When everyone was quiet, Katy again tried to make her point.

"So what's the verdict, Matt?" Katy said. "We are going to wait for everyone to jump back on our bandwagon after we turn them all down in this meeting?"

"I think you are blowing this out of proportion," Matt said. "I'm saying that they think they will be able to make us relinquish control. And from what I'm hearing here tonight, no one wants to do that. It's our project, and we will be the drivers behind it. I completely concur. Our deal should work something like this: We have an exclusive deal with the city. We work with the city on determining pricing for companies, schools, whatever to be associated with the system. We come up with a realistic way to split the revenue. But for any of this to work perfectly, we are going to have to get .comU running immediately."

"So when is immediately?" Sarina said.

"If what I'm hearing from my sources is true, they might expect something as early as Monday."

Matt's words were shocking.

"WHAT WHAT WHAT!" said Kevin, scaring the waitress as she refilled everyone's drinks. "I don't mind putting in extra work on the weekends, but I have the date with Jane on Saturday. It might be my only chance with her. You saw her Matt, she is FINE. I can't turn that down for any amount of money. Well, unless, it included some McDonald's coupons and ... "

"If I recall, everyone was telling me Wednesday the system was ready to go, right?" Matt said.

Everyone nodded.

"Well if it's ready to go, what's the big deal?"

"Adequate testing," Drew said. "Not just on the systems, but the quantity of people possibly using it. I'm not sure how much bandwidth we have, we need and we want."

"I understand," Matt said. "I don't think anyone will expect it to function perfectly from the beginning. But if we promise them a soft launch, at least it will be up and running, if people do want to use it. I'd like to schedule our first promotion sometime early next week, maybe for the beginning of next month. If we show we are serious about moving forward rapidly with this, everyone will be happy, and everyone will pay to be apart of it. I don't see how we can go wrong."

"This is starting to make sense now," Katy said. "With the city having an ambassador-type control, we should be able to drive local businesses to take part in the site, so we will benefit directly from them monetarily-wise and also through the city itself, cementing .comU in the eyes of the local population.

"Exactly," Matt said. "That will make .comU the most successful, and in turn, will make The Developers a major success in the process."

Once again, it appeared the quintet was on the same page. While Drew appeared somewhat skeptical the soft launch could work, he still felt they could do it. Although left unspoken, it was apparent everyone would be working during the weekend. This included Kevin, but hopefully not during his date with Jane.

Matt went ahead and picked up the tab. It was 10, but no one had much energy remaining.

"I'm going to get out of here, guys," Kevin said. "Does anyone need a ride back to work?"

"Go ahead, Kevin," Sarina said. "I'm going to run Katy home. Drew, where is your car?"

"Drew's car is up at work, but I have to pick up a few papers anyway," Matt said. "So yeah, Kevin, get out of here. Go home and dream about Jane or something."

"Screw that. I'm living out my dream Saturday!" With that, Kevin exited.

Katy waved at Kevin as Sarina pushed her out the door. Matt just stood beside the exit, waiting for Drew. For the fifth time in a row, Drew had forgotten to return all the crayons to the basket on the hostess counter.

#:o - Jane
>:P + #:o ... ;-)

SEVEN

It wasn't extremely surprising to Katy that Thursday night brought 7 inches of snow to Malorett. The snow was always the heaviest in late January in this part of Michigan, but there was still usually a good shower or two in March. Besides, complications were bound to appear on Friday morning at some point. Why not start late Thursday?

Katy found herself behind a snowplow on her way to work. The meeting was scheduled for 10 a.m., and The Developers were supposed to arrive by 8:30. The snow had subsided enough that traffic was moving at an average pace. Katy checked her clock — 8:15, and she was just a mile away. If you could ever count on any of The Developers to be on time, it was Katy. She was always on time, always prepared, always organized. Sometimes, though, she would overprepare, or overorganize, and become flustered with her condition. Surely, for a big presentation like this one, that time wouldn't occur today.

As Katy pulled into the office parking lot, only one other vehicle was there. Matt's 4x4 was parked in the front spot, and Katy reluctantly parked beside it. She was still somewhat shaken from the confrontation two days ago, and since that time, the two had not been alone together. Without looking suspicious, she couldn't avoid him this time. Katy started up the stone path to the door, and one step away from the front door, she noticed the bottom half was slightly open. Considering it was approximately 25 degrees outside, with wind gusts that prohibited forward movement, now was not a good time to keep the front door open. Katy approached the door and gave it a gentle nudge. As she leaned on the bottom, she also opened the top half and peered inside.

Just then, both halves swung wide open, as Katy almost fell to the ground. She managed to catch herself to see Butch standing over her.

"Damn squirrels!" Butch said, rubbing his hands on his purple smiley face

T-shirt. By the looks of the red and yellow fingerprints on his shirt and jeans, Butch had apparently gotten into a container of cheese puffs.

"There are no squirrels out there, Butch," Katy said, standing up and making sure she had not been sprinkled with cheese puff dust.

"They knocked! I heard them! They are out to get me!"

"Butch, calm down. Are you going to be here all day? We have a big meeting with investors today in the LAB."

"Are you trying to tell me I should leave?" Butch frowned, but it might have been because he was out of cheese puffs. She noticed an empty plastic container in the corner of the foyer.

"If you stay, you'll have to get cleaned up. These are big-time people."

"Will they bring me more cheese puffs?"

Katy shook her head and walked down the hall. She overheard Matt talking on the phone just before she walked in. Katy walked to the far right-hand corner of the room to her desk. Matt sat just inside the office door, and his desk was up against the wall to the left. Katy had already started to go over the checklist of things she needed to do when Matt hung up his phone.

"Big day today, huh?" Matt said.

"Sure Matt. Big day," Katy said. "I think we'll be OK."

Katy peeked out of the corner of her left eye to see Matt reluctantly standing up. She continued what started out as sorting .comU company sheets, alphabetizing a small group of questionnaires already completed by businesses around town. But Katy had a hard time concentrating as Matt slowly walked toward her. She pretended not to notice, with her head buried in the sheets of paper. What seemed like an eternity finally ended as Matt finished his journey to the far right corner of the WAB.

"Katy, are you OK?"

"Sure, I'm fine."

"I mean from the other day? We never had a chance to talk about it."

Matt grabbed Sarina's chair and sat close to Katy, awaiting her answer. Katy thought for a minute.

"Um, yeah, I had totally forgotten about it."

"Come on now Katy, I know you better than that. Surely you didn't forget. Well, I just wanted to apologize. I've been under a lot of stress lately, and I know that is no excuse, but that's the truth."

Katy continued to sort the papers, but looked up for a split second.

"We've all been under a lot of stress," Katy said. "You're right, that's no excuse."

"I know. What I'm trying to say is I wasn't trying to single you out or make an example of you. Plus, with the new client ... just never mind, it's no use trying to explain."

"That's exactly right."

"OK, so I'm sorry, and it won't happen again."

Matt waited for a response from Katy, but it never came. He walked back to his desk and continued his morning business. Katy finished sorting her files and crossed it off her checklist. She was satisfied with Matt's apology, but at this point, it really didn't matter to her. Matt wasn't someone who went on tirades against individuals anyway, unless it was a person who screwed him in a business deal. But Katy still wondered if he was just trying to make up for the sake of The Developers, or for the sake of trying to patch up their relationship. She brushed aside that thought immediately, because there was no time to worry about it.

Matt and Katy barely noticed Sarina, hands full of notebooks, enter the office. Sometimes Sarina took home things to review, but it appeared as if she had reviewed every single note she had ever taken as a Developer.

"Did you go through all of that stuff?" Katy asked.

"Oh, I thought about it, but no," Sarina said. "I was looking for something, but I forgot what it was. I thought a late run last night would remind me, but it didn't. It probably didn't help I got snow all in my pants."

Just as Sarina uttered the last sentence, Kevin and Drew walked into the WAB. And they weren't about to let her get away with saying something like that in their presence.

"What was his name?" Drew said.

"Whose name?" said Sarina, still facing her monitor.

"Joe?" Kevin said. "Joe was in your pants?"

"SNOW, if that's what you are referring to," Sarina said.

"Who is snow?" Drew said. "Do you have a picture?"

"Snow, the substance." Sarina grew tired of this charade quickly.

"I thought you wore shorts to run?" Kevin said. "I mean, if you even actually wear those."

"It was cold and SNOWING, which is why I got snow in my pants."

"Hey Matt, maybe you should let Sarina borrow those Zubaz pants you wore the other night," Kevin said. "I'm sure they'd look better on Sarina than you!"

Sarina opened the PowerPoint presentation on her screen to check it one last time before the meeting. Kevin and Drew removed their jackets and also started preparing for the meeting. It was 8:45, and all five group members knew that the next hour and 15 minutes would possibly be the longest in their lives. At least with a glance out the window, they noticed the snow had completely stopped. Maybe people would show at the meeting after all.

***

"Because this is the first meeting between many of us here, I'd like to take a minute to introduce our team."

Matt scanned the room, just to make sure everyone who was supposed to be there was there. He didn't notice any unfamiliar faces, and by his quick count, the six-member audience was correct. It was a good number, because any more wouldn't have fit in the LAB. Drew and Kevin moved the meeting table up against the south wall and grabbed a couple of extra chairs scattered through the building. They sat in front of the right side of the table, facing the crowd. Katy and Sarina flanked Matt on the left side. Sarina gave the stack of handouts to the people sitting in the front, while Katy opened the presentation and made sure it was positioned correctly on the wall. There's no need for a projection screen when you have a nice-sized white wall.

"I'm Matt Severson, the founder of The Developers, which if you don't know by now, maybe you are in the wrong room. This is Drew Davis, the vice president and head systems engineer. This is Katy Terrill, our projects coordinator and product designer. This is Sarina Metcalfe, programmer and marketing specialist. And lastly, this is Kevin Gentry, our sales director. Sorry, we don't have a secretary treasurer or secretary of homeland security, although I can promise you that for your safety, we have unlocked the fire escape doors down the back hallway."

Matt took another glance around and checked off the audience again: Susan Messer, Malorett Chamber of Commerce representative; Rick Kepling, publisher of the *Malorett Times*; Doug Morris, CEO of Foundation Technologies; Lynn Davis, from the Malorett Public School System; Phil Harris, founder of the Harris Hotel Enterprise; and Steve Tillman, mayor of Malorett.

"Everyone should have a copy of the outline we will attempt to follow this morning," Matt said. "Does anyone have any questions before we start?"

No one moved. Matt wasn't sure if anyone was still alive, but then Mayor Tillman sneezed, so he figured that was a good sign.

"All right, I'm going to turn this over to Sarina Metcalfe."

Matt took Sarina's seat. He wasn't anxious, but the words that Doug had mentioned to him the day before were still haunting him. Matt wasn't sure he, or for that matter, the rest of the group, was ready to get the system going by next week. But if anyone could do it, it would be his group, his team, his people that were about to put Malorett on the map.

One by one, each person delivered each section of the presentation flawlessly. Most people in the crowd seemed interested. The first questions weren't asked until Drew was about halfway finished with his discussion. Lynn Harris asked how the children would be kept interested with .comU. Drew had anticipated this and gave her a list of options.

"I realize this system will be accessible from the Internet," Lynn said. "But some of our elementary schools have only modem hookups right now. How will they be able to use .comU effectively?"

"Every business, whether it's schools, restaurants, whatever, can still log-in to the site using dialup," Drew explained. "We have been told by both the cable company and the telephone company that high-speed Internet access would be available citywide and almost countywide by this summer. We've also been informed that a new wireless Internet connection may be offered by the city in the near future."

"We just started offering high-speed in some of our hotel rooms, and it has been a big hit," said Phil Harris of the Harris Hotel Enterprise. "It's kind of senseless to put it in every room because, well, most of the time, there's no one in those rooms anyway."

Phil came to Malorett with the hopes of building onto his growing chain of hotels in Michigan. He renovated three of the bigger downtown buildings and turned them into state-of-the-art hotels. There was decent traffic in the winter months, mainly due to the skiing areas that surrounded much of northern Michigan. But for much of the fall and spring and during the entire summer, there weren't as many vacationers to venture into town. With some of the promises made by Matt about the potential population burst expected with the system launch, Phil salivated at the opportunity.

And as the success of the system increased, Phil planned to increase his monetary contributions to The Developers. Phil had the financial backing Matt and the group would need. Kevin asked Matt if Phil could also throw in a bunch of those hotel bars of soap, because he preferred those over store-bought soap. Matt decided today wasn't the best time to ask, and surely, Kevin wouldn't take it into his own hands.

"So what will be the slogan for the system?" said *Malorett Times* publisher Rick Kepling.

Drew thought for a split second.

"With the initial launch, the slogan will be downplayed somewhat because the new product should suffice," Drew said. "But we do have a few ideas for slogans."

"Actually, I have our master list of slogans," Katy said. "Would you all like to hear them?"

The crowd seemed interested.

"OK, here we go ... 'We need U,' with 'U' being a letter, not the word. Let's see, 'Unity starts with .com,' 'Thousands of users all waiting for U to be a part of it. Again, the 'U' as the letter. Oh, and 'There's an I in community, but there's also a U,' and lastly, 'You're not a number ... you're not a name ... you're a username and password."

"We are still working on a few more slogans," Matt chimed in while the commotion between some of the representatives continued. "We figured at this point, we could either try to come up with a better slogan or hold off a little while longer to make something better."

"I like the unity aspect to it all," Mayor Tillman said.

"How about 'Usernames bring unity,' " Kevin blurted out.

"Well, we don't have to decide this today," Matt said.

"What if we didn't have plenty of time to think about it," Doug said. "Like what if we moved up the launch date?"

The audience actually began clapping. Somehow, Matt had forgotten after an hour and 10 minutes into the talk that this might happen.

"How soon are we looking at moving up the launch?" Matt said.

"Well, how soon is as soon as possible?" said Doug, acting as if he had asked his dad for the keys to the car that he had just totaled the week before.

"The system is ready to go," Matt said. "There's some testing that needs to be done. I don't see any reason why it couldn't be up and running to the public by Monday."

"But ... " Katy tried to get her wisdom in, but it was too late.

"Ladies, gentlemen ... who would like to see this thing launched Monday?"

This time, it was a resonating applause by the panel.

Matt looked at the other Developers and shrugged.

"We would like for nothing better to get this up and running immediately," Matt said. "But Monday ... that's pretty soon. There's just a lot of testing that still needs to be done."

"A LOT of testing," Drew said, softly in the background, but loud enough that everyone heard him.

"But Matt, you just said a minute ago the system was ready!" Doug said.

"Well, about a minute and a half, but who's counting."

"Come on Matt, you are stalling on us. What's the deal?"

"What if some of the testing was done while the system was running?" Susan Messer said. "Would that be a bad thing?"

"Not really," Matt said. "We've reached the stage where we could launch the site, but some of the features might not be there immediately. That would buy us time to finish important things on the site. What does everyone think about this?"

"Sounds good to me," said Phil Harris. "As long as the things associated with the tourism in Malorett are addressed soon."

"I do worry, friends, that everyone will want their part of the deal first,"

Matt said. "One thing I've discussed individually with each of you, but not as a whole today, is .comU funding. I was going to hold off on this, but because we are now moving up the launch date, there's no better time to discuss it."

Matt walked over to the laptop that was used during the presentation.

"We have calculated total operating costs of the system for the first year," Matt said. "Most of this money will be spent on the hardware, software and employee expenses. As of now, we are keeping our team intact, with the intent of adding as many as three full-time people in six months to a year. During the first year, we may also add part-time people, and we are working on an internship program with Moxee Tech and possibly the local high schools.

"We will run the site from here, but we'll mirror it through an outside hosting provider."

"I guess I'm kind of confused," Lynn said. "So are the schools going to be paying a percentage of the total, or how will it work?"

"Right now our primary financial backing will come from two places: Foundation Technologies and Harris Hotel Enterprise. We'll use some of the funds to develop a marketing budget, to be used for advertising around town as well as in nearby cities. Word of mouth should be the most powerful marketing tool we can use. And hopefully a little good press from the media."

Matt made a subtle head tilt toward Rick Kepling.

"We'll see what we can do over at the paper," Rick said. "People around town are already somewhat aware of the system, so by telling them they can now actually go to the site, well, that's going to be the clincher."

"So it's settled?" Doug said. "We are going to attempt a soft launch on Monday?"

"That's what it sounds like," Matt said. "Let's just hope it survives at least until Tuesday."

Matt, Katy and Drew spent the next 10 minutes conversing with the committee members on their way out. All three were still in shock over the enthusiasm that remained in the LAB. On the other hand, these people had never given them a reason to doubt that .comU would be received well by local officials and the public. It was just amazing to see it actually happening, like a dream that seemed real until the alarm clock blared.

Meanwhile, Kevin and Sarina immediately returned to the WAB. Their first notion was to continue working on the system, but they were a little too frazzled to do that.

"Matt has overestimated us this time," said Kevin, swiveling in his chair. "How is this possible? Even if we worked every hour this weekend, there would still be glitches we would miss. It could be a month before we get everything worked out. I just don't know anymore."

"Chill out, Kevin," Sarina said. "We've got enough to keep Malorett users busy."

"That's only if people are using the system. We are counting heavily on word of mouth for this soft launch. That's a lot of words with not a lot of mouths."

"But all the people in the meeting are investors, to a certain extent. They benefit from a successful run. Why wouldn't they promote it?"

"But why would they promote an unfinished system? Who benefits from that?"

Katy and Drew joined Kevin and Sarina in the LAB. Both sat down and let out a sigh of relief.

"So ... did you guys finish the system while we were sending people on their way?" Drew asked.

Sarina rolled her eyes at her computer screen, and Kevin didn't even acknowledge the question while perusing Slashdot.

"We've got a lot to do this weekend," Katy said, again shuffling through papers. "What is everyone's availability? I would imagine Matt is going to expect everyone to be here every day."

"That suits me fine," Kevin said. "But I am not missing my date tomorrow night. And if things go well, I might not be in until a little later Sunday."

"If things go well?" Drew said. "You mean, like your date gives you a few of her McDonald's french fries?"

"What? I would never take a first date to McDonald's. I've already got it planned, we are going to Shoney's."

"Don't forget to go late enough to get the breakfast buffet," Sarina chimed in. "I can't think of a better turn on than watching a guy devour biscuits and gravy. Yum yum!"

"You guys can discuss the date later," Katy said. "But I want to know when everyone will be here."

"Tell us when you'll be here," Drew said, "and we'll think about our hours too."

"I was thinking of working late tonight, then probably coming in tomorrow at 10, staying until 9 or so, then working Sunday as much as possible," Katy said. "I need to avoid my home and especially Michael. I have a feeling he's going in for the kill this weekend. This is a good excuse."

"I'll be here, too," Sarina said. "I don't have much going on. Hell, it's too snowy to run for too long anyway."

"Actually, someone might need to make a trip over to Tech," Matt said, entering the room after finishing with the committee members. "Doug Morris mentioned that he spoke with Professor Malcolm Jones earlier this week about suppling student testers."

"I'm going to be over there," Kevin said. "But I'm going to try to avoid the school premises, unless Jane wants me to chase her through the library."

"I can be here all day Saturday and Sunday afternoon," Drew said. "But Jessica and I are going to the movies tonight, and I have bingo-calling duties Sunday."

"That sounds good," Matt said. "For the rest of the day, I'm going to work on getting these student volunteers, putting together the marketing packages for prospective clients and doing some random testing. I'll be here tomorrow and Sunday as well. Just let me know if you guys need my help on anything that you are doing."

"I'll look through the site and test whatever," Katy said. "Sarina or Drew, do you guys have a list of what needs to be examined?"

"Yes, and the list is growing," Sarina said. "But it's manageable right now. If we can get the main features of The Profiler set up just as it is specked out, I think that will make the users fairly happy."

"It appears everyone is on the same page as far as getting .comU off the ground," Matt said. "Will we really be able to do this?"

There was silence for a good 10 seconds.

"If we don't," Kevin said, "at least we can say we went down trying. If we do, we can get the newspaper to take a picture of us all holding up a computer, similar to the guys holding up the flag at Iwo Jima."

EIGHT

"I cannot be late for this. I cannot be late for this. I cannot be late for this."

Kevin was late for everything, or at least everything that didn't involve Mexican cuisine. Jane had chosen the steak place near Moxee Tech, and it didn't even serve nachos.

Kevin sped through Moxee, repeatedly looking at his car clock. He was supposed to arrive at 7:30, and it was already 7:36. He still had to drive across the city to campus to pick her up. This wasn't the best way to enter a first date, that's for sure. At the very least, Kevin called Jane at 6 and said he was still at work. She didn't seem too disappointed; in fact, she was trying to rest after her basketball game earlier in the day.

The only thing worse than being late is calling to say you are running behind, then giving a time and being even later.

But Kevin wasn't going to give up just yet. He had waited long enough to finally have a chance at Jane, even if it were mostly a friendly date. He was definitely content to settle for that. And if things went a little further ... Kevin was never one to back down from a beautiful, tall woman.

He made it to the dorm parking lot at 7:42. Immediately upon pulling into the lot, he dialed Jane on his cellphone.

"Jane? It's Kevin. I just made it here. Sorry I'm late."

"That's cool, Kevin. I just finished getting ready. I'll meet you in the front lobby, OK?"

"All right Jane, I'll see you in a minute!"

Kevin was relieved. Not that he had expected Jane to be upset, but he was glad she understood his work situation. He even thought to himself how understanding Jane was about a lot of things. It somewhat scared him to believe he was thinking things about a girl that weren't physical. It had been a long time since that occurred.

Immediately upon entering, Kevin grabbed a seat in the middle of the room. The lobby was bustling with co-eds. Kevin assumed most of them must be getting ready to go to some party. But at 7:45? Maybe there was something else going on, like a basketball game, a streaking contest, a Beer-Pong tournament or anything that would bring so many college students together at once. Kevin theorized as he sat and waited for Jane. He noticed five girls in the center of the lobby, speaking so loudly and so closely to each other that Kevin couldn't comprehend a single word. There probably hadn't been that much excitement at the dorm since Carrot Top was on campus. Or maybe Carrot Top had decided to come back to defend his Beer-Pong title.

As Kevin tried to concentrate on what the girls were saying, he felt two extremely soft hands cover his face. Even on a Saturday night, Crissy was going to harass me, Kevin thought. He reached up to lift the hands away, but he still couldn't help noticing how delicate her hands were, regardless if they seemed almost the same size as his.

"Crissy, get away and stop bothering me!" Kevin stood up, removed the girl's hands and turned to face her.

It was Jane.

"Well, if it's going to be like that, I've got better things to do," Jane said, walking back toward the door.

Kevin was not a runner. He had never run track in school, he had dissed Sarina many times just running through Malorett and the last time he moved faster than walking was to get out of the way of Butch's speeding car. But for an instant, Kevin turned into a world-class sprinter, hurdling over a chair and darting in front of Jane. It happened so fast that even the girls who were most likely not talking about Carrot Top noticed.

"Wait! I'm sorry," Kevin said. "Crissy always harasses me. There are so many people in here, and with all the commotion ... but I've been thinking about this date ever since we left the Olive Garden parking lot, and I'm not going out like that."

Jane stopped and tried not to make eye contact. She smiled and said, "You're going to take me for some floozy, show up late and expect me just to go somewhere with you? If you weren't my best friend's brother, I'd go find a bingo. Let's go."

"You want to go play bingo?" Kevin said.

The pair walked to Kevin's car. Even though the parking lot was dimly lit, Kevin thought Jane beamed radiantly as usual, wearing jeans, a long-sleeved T-shirt under her jacket and a cute winter cap. She didn't wear tall shoes, so their heights were pretty equal, with Jane measuring in just below Kevin. As Kevin opened the passenger door for Jane, he noticed her checking him out for the first time ever. He hoped that "cleaning up" a bit, including wearing new jeans and a new shirt, couldn't hurt his chances.

"How was the game today?" asked Kevin, pulling out of the lot.

"Not bad. We won a close one. We were up by a bunch, and they came back, but we hung on at the end."

"How many points did you have?"

"I think seven. I don't know, sometimes I don't keep track. I played a lot, though, so I was pretty tired today."

"How was your nap? I sure could have used one of those the last few days."

"I didn't sleep too long. I had to finish some calculus homework today. Integrals are not my favorite things."

"Well why didn't you say so? You should have brought your homework along. I love integrals. At least what I can remember of them."

"What? You've been out of school only a year!"

"Time flies when you're stuck in an office and a real job all day."

Jane had envisioned the "date" to be somewhat uncomfortable, considering it was the first time she had ever been alone with Kevin. But all in all, she felt at ease with the situation. Maybe she had expected Kevin to come on stronger, but she was picking up good vibes, like that he really liked her, instead of her just being a boy toy.

Meanwhile, Kevin was trying to focus on the date and get work out of his head. The last 36 hours had been freakin' insane. First they were preparing the presentation. Then the presentation goes well, until they find out the system needs to be ready by Monday. Kevin, along with the rest of The Developers, pretty much worked the rest of Friday and a large portion of Saturday as well.

While Matt and Katy handled the majority of the paper work, to system contributors and media, Sarina, Drew and Kevin thoroughly tested main site features from just about every angle feasible. Kevin's top priority was platform compatibility, so he switched from his PowerBook to the office Dell machine frequently during the day. The problems were minor enough as to not thwart the project, although they would have to find ways around these peculiar oddities at some point. It just wasn't going to happen by Monday.

Kevin and Jane arrived at the Heartland Steakhouse. The driving conditions were fairly good, especially considering the snow fall from the day before. Saturday's temperatures rose almost to 40, which was high for March. But a slushy mess ensued every time someone entered and exited a vehicle, although at the moment, neither Kevin nor Jane seemed to mind. They were both starving.

The two walked in and were seated immediately. The bar was pretty full, but the rest of the restaurant had plenty of open seats. Apparently, at 8:30 on a Saturday, not many people still needed dinner.

"So why were all the people in the lobby at your dorm?" said Kevin, removing his jacket and taking his seat in a booth.

"I think ... there was some concert on campus," Jane said. "I'm not sure what type of music it was. Shows how much I pay attention."

"Well at least you got some homework done."

"Yeah that was a good thing ... so tell me about this launch on Monday. Jen said something about it earlier this morning. I thought you guys weren't going to open this site for another month or so?"

"Well, I guess plans change. The investors and the city officials want it now. There really hasn't been enough testing from the populace, though, so it might turn out that this soft launch is the best thing overall."

"What do you mean by soft launch?"

The waitress stopped by and took their orders.

"A soft launch just means that we aren't going to heavily advertise that the system is up and running. Basically what we are going to do with .comU is not have everything available to the public. We'll still be able to test some of the other things, while people will be on the site."

"That makes sense. But do you have enough people to provide tech support and still test the site?"

"Supposedly, we are working out a deal for a couple of interns through Tech, which will allow us to take care of the higher priorities. One of the professors is a good friend of mine and Matt's, so I think they are even going to potentially count it as classwork or something. If as many people as we expect are on the system, and need help, there's no way we could handle that."

Jane spent most of dinner asking Kevin questions about .comU. Kevin didn't mind answering them, but he wanted to get away from work, not rehash it. He tried to change the subject numerous times, but it just wasn't working. Finally, while Jane was chewing an oversized bite of steak, Kevin found his opportunity to switch gears a bit.

"So Jane," said Kevin, taking a sip of Dr Pepper, "whatever happened to your boyfriend?"

Jane stopped chewing, looked up and just stared at Kevin for a minute. Kevin realized he had said something wrong.

"I guess he's still here somewhere," said Jane, setting her fork down. Her facial expression turned somewhat somber.

"I'm sorry ... I wasn't trying to invade. It's just that Jen never told me."

"Oh, it's not your fault. It's just stupid. And I don't really talk about it, that's probably why she didn't tell you."

"My bad. Let's talk about integrals or something!"

Jane laughed, picked up her fork and started eating again. Kevin almost fouled out again, by opening his big mouth. From here on out, Kevin decided, he would open his big mouth only if he were going to shove steak into it.

Kevin had originally thought about asking Jane to go see a late movie, but he knew he had plenty of work to do. Plus Jane had mentioned she had to get up early to work on a group project for one of her classes.

They decided it was time to take off, so they made it to the front register and out the door. There wasn't much said on the way home, perhaps because Kevin was unsure of ending the date, and Jane was unsure where the hell Kevin was going. Kevin was just thinking over and over that maybe he was wrong to think of Jane anymore than a friend, because surely she didn't think of him any other way.

As they pulled into the dorm parking lot, Jane smacked her head with her hand.

"So THIS is where you were going," said Jane, shaking her head.

"What do you mean? I thought this is where we were going."

"Kevin, why would you think that?"

"You said you had to get up early and ... "

"And what? It's not even 10:30! Whatever."

Jane opened the car door and got out. Kevin sat there for a minute, still not understanding what was going on. He figured at the very least, he should walk Jane to the front of the dorm. He turned the ignition off and got out.

"Jane, wait up."

Kevin caught up with Jane quickly, as she was just a few steps ahead of him.

"Did I screw up?" Kevin said.

Jane stopped.

"I know we didn't have anything planned, but I thought we were going to do something else, go somewhere else, after we ate."

"Yeah, me too, but you have to get up early and ... "

"It's not that early."

"Well, I have to be at work too, and I just thought you were hinting ... and all that about your ex ... I just figured it would be better to bring you back. Did you have a good time?"

Jane rolled her eyes.

"Yes Kevin, I had a good time. I always do when I'm around you."

"So you mean we can do this again?"

"Sure!"

"Hopefully next time I'll be on time. Then we can hang out longer. I mean, I still have to make the drive back to Malorett."

Jane took a step away from Kevin, then turned back toward him. She paused for a moment, noticing Kevin trying to figure out what she was doing. She thought for a split second, then crept closer, leaned across the conversational space between them and kissed him on the cheek.

"What if you didn't have to drive back to Malorett?" Jane said.

"Are you suggesting ... "

"I'm not suggesting anything. But you can stay up here a little longer if you want."

Change of plans, Kevin thought. Work was again out of his mind. He grabbed Jane's hand, and they strolled quite briskly toward Jane's warm, cozy dorm room.

***

Sarina stared at her screen. She had been staring at it so long that she couldn't determine if there was anything on there, or if she was just imagining it.

"Drew, could you check this out? Do you see what I see?"

"Unless you have some way to see what's on your screen without turning it on, Sarina, I do not see what you see."

It was 10 Sunday morning. Sarina had just entered the WAB 10 minutes before, but it seemed as if she had never left. Sarina was the second-to-last to leave the night before, around midnight. Drew had exited around 9, Jessica's orders; Katy got out a little thereafter, to avoid being burnt out; and there was no telling when Matt left. Or he may have never left, because when Drew arrived at 9, Matt was there. The stress definitely wasn't depleting yet, but surely the worst was behind them.

Most of Saturday was devoted to .comU testing, and things went fairly smooth, as Drew and Sarina debugged The Profiler. Sarina had also been trying to finish compiling a list of local cellphone numbers, called CellBook. Matt had spoken with Michigan area cellphone companies about producing an available list of cellphones. At first, the service providers were not willing to jeopardize their customers' privacy. But The Developers came up with the notion of activating .comU accounts, which in turn, could activate a cellphone number listing. When users go to sign up at .comU, they can enter a cell number, and by doing so, automatically become a part of CellBook.

By itself, the cellphone service companies were not convinced. That's where the site's contest promotions became the key. Those users who activated their cellphone number usage would be entered to win something provided by sponsors. On top of that, these same providers could advertise within The Profiler, which could then turn into more cellphone users. That entire package wasn't as difficult to sell as just putting together a phone book of cellphone numbers.

While Drew and Sarina sifted through their items gracefully, Katy was swamped with sponsors and the media. She was amazed at how fast word spread that .comU would be operational by Monday. She was pleasant to those who called, even though she said the same things over and over and over because everyone asked the same annoying questions. Yes, the site would be accessible Monday. No, not every feature would be available. Yes people everywhere could sign up. Yes, she was wearing underwear.

Luckily, Katy had a simple spreadsheet that broke down .comU revenue by company. There were a variety of ways Malorett businesses were involved in the project, but most were signed up with simple ads in various site sections. Katy already had confirmed 15 banner spots. She was also working on sponsorship for various site sections, which could even include promotional items and giveaways. Then, of course, there was the short list of companies who were major contributors to the site.

Katy had a short break between advertisers when she spoke with *Malorett Times* reporter Gene Simons for almost 40 minutes Saturday afternoon. Due to the soft launch, everyone decided it was best to promote the site was available, but to not go too deep about the features, etc. Simons assured Katy that the story would be buried either in the A or the Region section, so she could live with that.

Somehow, Katy managed to keep her business under control. On the other hand, Matt became the state fair information booth. Many corporate sponsors needed assurance that everything was going to work. Matt gave them that, even with his fingers crossed behind his back. He continued to display confidence in the system, and very few people questioned it. Susan Messer of the Malorett Chamber of Commerce was probably the toughest sell to this point. She seemed bewildered how the chamber would benefit, but Matt explained a chamber membership would mean additional site features and would bring a better reputation to those companies.

Late Saturday evening, Matt put together a features list and a timeline in which things would be implemented. Many items on the list would be ready by Monday, but there was still a huge chunk remaining. A lot was dependent on the amount of working time The Developers would have during the next few months. The solution to this problem, Matt decided, was to include interns and possibly part-timers. Professor Jones came through for Matt on Friday, giving him 10 names of excellent students from his classes. Matt wanted to meet these people as soon as possible, so the professor suggested an informational meeting at noon Sunday at Tech. Matt figured that would work out great, seeing as that would give him plenty of time to take care of business Saturday morning, afternoon, evening and night.

Unfortunately, Matt completely lost track of time Saturday night. After the rest of the gang left, he meticulously went over the features, timelines and operating budget of the system, over and over and over. When he finally looked up at the clock, it was 2 a.m. Matt got out of there shortly thereafter, but he was back early Sunday morning. Luckily, there were no phone calls, and there weren't even any messages on the answering machine when Matt arrived. The newspaper lay near the door, and Matt found the story about the system ... buried, as promised to Katy by Gene Simons, in the region section. A little publicity is not bad, but they weren't ready for the front page. If that would have happened, it would have been quite possible that Lansing, Ann Harbor and even Detroit could have been calling. What a mess.

At first, Matt was a little peeved that he arrived early for nothing. But his disappointment didn't last long because he remembered the importance of the day ahead — the final day before the launch. He had to make sure everything was in order. He had to find a couple of interns.

Drew and Sarina had the system testing well under control by the time Matt was going to leave.

"Matt, so exactly when will the site be available to the public?" Drew asked. "We're not going to do one of those midnight madness things, are we? It's bad enough when the stores do that around Christmastime. I'm not sure how Jessica and I get sucked into those damn sales."

"You know, we never gave anyone an exact time," Matt said. "What about noon?"

Sarina and Drew nodded.

"No way it should be any earlier," Sarina said. "I plan on being here late tonight. A little rest and a run in the morning tomorrow will do me good."

"Noon it is," Matt said. "So if anyone calls, that's what we'll tell them. I'm getting ready to head over to Tech for this intern meeting. When Katy and Kevin get in, tell them we'll have a meeting at 3. It's mandatory!"

Shortly after noon, Katy arrived. And right when she walked in the door, the phone started ringing. Most were simple calls: people who had seen the story in the paper, wanting to know the URL, and a few sponsors just double-checking to make sure the site would, indeed, be running on Monday. And this time, they were even given the noon start time!

Kevin appeared at 1:30. Katy, Drew and Sarina had decided that when Kevin made it to the office, they would not turn to look at him or greet him until he sat down. Usually after "dates," Kevin would immediately say whether it was good or bad, without a question being asked.

But Kevin didn't say a word. He went right to his desk, powered up his laptop and sunk into his chair. The other three took a quick peek at Kevin, then at each other. They did all notice he was wearing the same clothes as the day before, but that could mean a million things.

Drew was the first to speak.

"So Kevin, how's it going this morning ... er, afternoon?"

"Not bad man, not bad."

This was unusual, Sarina thought. The only time Kevin wasn't a blabber-mouth was when he was eating.

"Well?" Sarina said.

"Well what?" Kevin said.

"Are you going to tell us about the date?" Sarina said.

"Oh yeah, it went fine," Kevin said

"Fine? That's it?" Katy said.

"I mean yeah, it went fine," Kevin said. "We ate at a pretty good restaurant, we talked for awhile, we hung out for awhile. Overall, it was fine."

"I mean, are you going to see her again?" Drew said.

"Oh yes, I'm sure I will," Kevin said. "If one thing is for sure, I will see her again. Man, I gotta get my shit together or Matt's going to kill me! How is everything going with the system?"

Still perplexed with Kevin's answers, Drew decided Kevin's determination to switch subjects was a good move.

"Really good so far, Kevin," Drew said. "We're pretty much finished with the testing. We're still working on the FAQ for the site. I know you were doing a little research in that area."

"Yes, I found some pretty good items on Yahoo we can copy," Kevin said. "I'm guessing a lot of these people are going to have the same problems."

"I just hope they don't accuse us of a power outage or Internet connection loss," Sarina said. "I mean, we aren't playing God here."

"At least not yet!" Katy fired back.

"Oh Kevin, we almost forgot to tell you," Drew said "We have a 3 o'clock meeting to go over everything. Matt's over in Moxee trying to pick up a few interns. Not pick up like prostitutes, because he would have been back already, but to work on the system. Professor Jones gave him a list."

"Aw man, I forgot about that meeting," Kevin said. "I wish I would have known, I could have just gone over there."

"What like you would have driven over there this morning or something?" Sarina asked.

"No, I was over there this morning," Kevin said. "I could have just handled the meeting."

The jaws of Drew, Katy and Sarina dropped.

"You STAYED over at Jane's!" Drew said. "Are you serious?"

"Yeah, but ... there's a lot more to it," Kevin said. "I'll explain later."

"Since when do you 'explain' your dates?" Katy said. "What are you not telling us?"

"A lot, but there's no time right now," Kevin said. "Like I said, things went F-I-N-E."

"Oh, thanks for spelling that, I thought 'fine' was spelled with a 'y' and a silent 'q' " Sarina said.

Matt returned in plenty of time, as the 3 p.m. meeting went on as scheduled. Professor Jones had put together a nice group of people, and four of the students would be available for some type of work beginning in the next two weeks. A couple were even available on the weekends. Kevin suggested that he could definitely meet with any of the students next week, if necessary, because he would be making a trip over there. While everyone wanted to ask Kevin exactly why he would be going over there, no one did.

"So, what's everyone's estimation on whether or not we are ready to launch?" Matt asked.

"Well by no means will everything run smoothly," Drew said, thumbing through a couple of printouts of the .comU interface. "But we've got to start somewhere ... and now is probably as good a time as ever."

Sarina nodded in agreement.

"We've gone over this stuff like Cyndi Lauper, time after time after time," she said. "I like the fact that we'll have a couple of extra interns for help desk stuff, and to test new things."

"Besides, do we even know how many people are going to be on the system the first day, the first week?" Kevin said. "Maybe everyone will just go about their business as usual. It's not like we're advertising the system."

"True, we aren't, but the sponsors pretty much are," Matt said. "These businesses want it to succeed, and obviously, so do we. It's just that because we've been stuck in the office, we haven't been able to walk down the street and hand out flyers about it."

"I was thinking of getting a sandwich board outfit and standing outside for promotion," Kevin said. "Will that work?"

"Maybe if that's ALL you're wearing," Sarina said.

"Good idea!" Kevin said. Why didn't I think of that?"

"People definitely know about .comU," Katy said. "I've talked to way too many people the last couple of days. I guess they didn't tell me they were going to access the site all day Monday or anything, but I assume they will be there."

"OK, let's go over the plan for tomorrow then," Matt suggested. "Since we've decided the site goes live at noon, let's all be here by 10. Katy, does the newspaper know we are going live at noon?"

"Not sure, but I'll give them a call," Katy said.

"Good. All right, I'll be here a little earlier, and a couple of you should be here early too, just in case."

"In case of what?" Drew said. "Tornado drill?"

"Trick-or-treaters?" Kevin said.

"Tomorrow could be the day someone in this office wins ... 10 MILLION DOLLARS," Sarina said. "It would be a shame if Ed showed up and we all weren't here."

"Does he still make house calls like that?" Drew said. "He needs a stunt double or something. Man, that would be a good prank, to dress up like Ed McMahon and show up at somebody's house, saying they won the money."

"True, Drew, but where are you going to find a big check like that?" Kevin said. "The only place that makes them is *The Price Is Right.*"

"Another plan foiled," Drew said.

Matt was a little fidgety, but he didn't mind the occasional outburst of nonsense.

"Well, you never know who will call or show up tomorrow," he said. "Ed might have heard about the site too."

"If possible, I'd like to sleep in and get my run in during the morning," Sarina said. "It's not supposed to snow or anything, plus I think I'll need the run for later in the day. But I plan on staying late tonight."

"Me too," Katy said. "I need to get this stuff organized for tomorrow, so I'll be here late. I kind of figured I'd be here late tonight because I was out early yesterday."

"OK, I was thinking three of us in the morning," Matt said. "Is that all right with you guys?"

Kevin and Drew nodded.

"I promised Jessica I'd get out of here shortly," Drew said.

"I've got ... things ... to do tonight, that's for sure," Kevin said.

"What things?" Sarina said.

"Just things ... I told you I would tell you sometime soon!" Kevin said.

"Good, it's settled," Matt said. "Myself, Kevin and Drew will be here at 8 or so, Katy and Sarina by 10. Guys, get out of here soon because we have a long day tomorrow."

"What about you?" Sarina said. "I think you need to get out of here, too. You obviously haven't slept much the last few days. I mean, you left your four-color pen in the other room."

Matt looked down, and sure enough, he was using a regular ball point pen. He used his four-color pen for everything!

"I don't have much going on tonight," Matt said. "I think I will get out of here. But I'll take some stuff home with me, just in case."

"And if you get a chance tonight," Kevin said, "look on eBay and see if you can find one of those big checks. We might need it tomorrow."

***

It was 8 p.m., and Sarina and Katy were still at the office. But their grueling work had been replaced by gossip about anything and everything.

"So what do you think is going on with Kevin?" said Sarina, relaxing in her chair with her feet up on her desk.

"Ohhh, that's a good question," Katy said. "I would think if things had gone bad, then he would have said something about it. So maybe they are good ... considering they are NEVER good."

"Good possibility, but I wonder what the secrecy is all about. Maybe his sister found out something. It's hard to tell at this point."

"Yeah really."

"So Katy, what news do you have about Michael? Did anything happen last night?"

"Well ... it's no big deal."

"Sure it's a big deal! He's a lunatic."

"No, it's not like that ... I agreed to meet him for dinner. He was fairly cordial. I didn't tell you I was going to meet him because I figured you'd tell me not to. But everything went OK."

"Did you tell him to stop calling?"

"I told him that if he didn't stop calling, I would make sure he stopped."

"What, like you were going to cut off his balls?"

"Maybe ... I hope he got the hint."

"Guys never get the hint. And you're right, I would have told you not to go."

Sarina and Katy decided they had had enough. But as they got up to leave, they heard noises upstairs. Or were they just imagining things?

"Someone's up there," Katy said. "It's a Sunday, and there's no reason for anyone to be here."

As they exited the WAB and locked all the doors, they saw Butch at the rear stairwell.

"Butch! Was that you upstairs?" Sarina yelled.

Butch shook his head and walked slowly toward Sarina and Katy.

"Girls, I'm glad you're here," Butch said. "Or I should say, I'm glad you're the ONLY ones here. I was afraid I might get caught."

"That was kind of risky," Sarina said. "Why didn't you tell us you were coming down?"

"I thought no one would be here," Butch said. "I didn't see the guys' vehicles outside, so I thought I was good to go."

"What were you doing up there?" Sarina said, putting on her coat.

"Just setting up for the next meeting," Butch said. "It's next Friday, you know. Are you girls going to make it?"

"We should be there," said Katy, as Sarina nodded. "I'm still a little skeptical about all of this, though. I mean, it has been a month, and there really haven't been many new members. Six people seems a little small for a club."

"Especially when one of them is a guy," Sarina said. "Maybe we should come up with a different idea for a club like this."

"We can't give up yet!" Butch said. "This is not something I take lightly."

"You say this, but you are wearing a smiley face T-shirt," Sarina said. "How can we take anything you say seriously?"

"I'm just telling you, we are on to something," said Butch, unconvincingly. "We have an opportunity to start our own underground club, for professional women in the area. I'm already in the Yooper Club, but this is something totally different. It's like *Fight Club*, only we don't fight."

"So it's a club?" Katy said. "The problem isn't so much having a club like that ... it's the prerequisite of clothing that doesn't make sense. It is too damn cold to wear a miniskirt here."

"What if I wore a miniskirt in public?" Butch said.

Katy and Sarina shook their heads no.

"OK, I'll just keep it to the meetings then," Butch said.

"Well, I hope you find a few more people," Katy said, "or I'm dropping my membership. At least then I won't have to shave my legs the day before each meeting."

"I'll do my best," said Butch as the trio walked down the hallway. "Know this, girls: the Black Miniskirt Cult will survive, with or without you!"

Sarina and Katy looked at each other, then at Butch's smiley face T-shirt, and for some reason, they knew he was right.

{:p - Butch
:D, >:¢, {:p ... LOL

NINE

On an average Monday, Sarina tried to run a couple of miles before starting work. The run, Sarina said, makes you feel good even before walking into the office, like you had already accomplished something, like you had already conquered the day.

But on a day like today, Sarina thought she could run two marathons and still not feel content.

During each step through the lightly covered snowy sidewalk beside her apartment, Sarina could not shake the feeling of something missing from .comU. What would be the first complaint? People not able to login? People unable to access pages? People unhappy with the lack of porn on the site? The morning jog was good to clear Sarina's mind, but it worked terribly on this day. There was no way she could think about anything other than the site. That's probably why she completely ignored the DONT WALK sign two blocks away, almost causing a five-vehicle accident right before her eyes. Yes, she should have looked up and noticed the sign. Then again, the people installing the damn street signs should have made enough room to add an apostrophe in the digital printout. Now kids everywhere think DONT is a word.

Sarina decided she would run two miles at a decent pace. She had mapped out five different routes, all characterized by how long she would be running. The two-mile trek wasn't bad: turn left out of her apartment complex, up three blocks; take a right and head down the four-lane highway, away from the office, away from pretty much everything; take a right at the Malorett Park, and run pretty much all the way back to the end; then take another right, through the back entrance, then through a small neighborhood; and take a straightaway back to the apartment. The weather had been kind to Sarina as of late, with the exception of 7 inches of snow last week. Naturally, another snowfall was supposed to occur tomorrow afternoon, but that should give the road crew time to get the roads and sidewalks cleared for Wednesday's run.

She had fans along the way, too. Each morning, a couple of individuals, most right off the highway, greeted her on the run. There were a lot of older couples who lived on that road, and it was nice to see youth occasionally, especially that early in the morning. The older you get, the earlier you rise, Sarina's grandmother used to say. For this reason alone, Sarina was afraid if she ever broke 100, she might be getting up at 2 in the morning.

Not all of her fans were outwardly gracious. Many of them just stared at Sarina from their houses, some even through binoculars, as she ran by. It's not a common occurrence in Malorett, Michigan, to see a woman clad in only a sports bra, tight pants and a winter cap running through the cold winter. Somehow, she overcame the coldness; and as summer hit, she wore less and less, almost to the point where one time, she ran in her bikini. Kevin joked that maybe they could garner enough votes in the subdivision behind Sarina's complex to start a nudist colony. When she then asked Kevin for help on drafting a petition, he decided it wasn't really that funny anymore.

She had far fewer fans in the winter, but even still, there were some out this morning. As Sarina approached the end of main road, there was a short man standing right in her way. From 100 feet, it looked as if he were going to play chicken with her. She kept running, at the same pace, while he never budged. She moved to the inside of the sidewalk, and so did he. Sarina wasn't sure what was happening, but in order to avoid him, she took a step to the right, into the snow, to maneuver around the strange man. He stood his ground, and as Sarina attempted to go around him, he slapped her on the ass.

Sarina stopped, shocked, and didn't know what to say for a second.

"What the hell is your problem?" Sarina said. "I could call the police and have you locked up right now. But you are a pretty scrawny guy, so I'm not really that scared."

"I'm sorry about that," the man said, looking genuinely remorseful. "But I didn't know how else to stop you. You ran right through my pick!"

"Why did you want to stop me?"

"Well Sarina, I just wanted to ask you a few questions about the system before you made it into work."

"What do you want ... wait, how do you know my name?"

The man revealed his name badge from his pocket: Gene Simons. He was the reporter from the *Times*.

"I live right here on the corner, so I've seen you running," Gene said. "Then when I talked to Katy Terrill the other day concerning .comU, she gave me the URL to look at the site so far. I saw your picture on there as a member of The Developers, put two and two together, and realized who you were!"

"Wow, you are a fast one," said Sarina, gradually getting cold because she stopped running. "So do you really want to interview me?"

"Well, I'm going to call over to the office later. Or perhaps I might visit. Shouldn't you be getting ready for all the calls and stuff?"

"I'm going in at 10, then the site will be made public at noon. So we should have ample time to be prepared."

"Oh, that's cool. You guys seem to have a pretty cool operation going on down there. It's impressive to see a company with five full-time employees grab so much attention."

"What do you mean, so much attention? Nobody but people around here know anything about us."

"Nope, that's not true. We've gotten a couple of calls in the past few weeks around the state, and some from outside the state, asking about the system you guys are building. It sounds as if you are going to have people waiting in line to build similar sites for their cities."

"Are you serious? People know about us?"

"Yep, no joke. Well, you'd better finish your run. Maybe I'll talk to you later!"

"Oh yeah, the run. Thanks, I guess."

Gene walked into his house, while Sarina turned the corner and headed toward the park. People outside the state know about the system? What the hell is going on? Sarina couldn't help but smirk a little about this revelation. She was able to push herself to finish a little faster on the run too. And she had totally forgotten about the sexual harassment lawsuit she was ready to slap on Gene as well.

After a quick shower, and an even quicker bowl of oatmeal, Sarina was on her way to the office. She arrived just minutes after 10 and still managed to beat both Katy and Drew there. There wasn't much talking between Matt and Kevin when Katy entered the WAB.

"Hey guys ... have I missed anything?" said Sarina, powering on her computer.

"Except for a couple of calls around 9, it's been pretty quiet," Kevin said. "I'm not sure if that's a good thing or a bad thing."

"Yeah if no one goes on the site, then I'm not sure what I'll do with the interns," Matt said. "Three are coming in at 4 today."

Katy quietly entered the WAB. She appeared to have her own morning agenda, as she immediately flipped through her address book to make a call.

"Gene? Hi, it's Katy. I got your message. Yeah, 2:30 will be great. Do you want to come here? OK, yeah, just give me a call if you're going to come down. Thanks!"

"Was that Gene Simons from the paper?" Sarina said.

"Yep, he's going to work on a bigger story for Tuesday's paper," Katy said. "At least by then, he can get feedback from people who are online as well."

"That guy is a creep! He slapped me on the ass this morning during my run!"

"No way!" Kevin said. "What did you do to him?"

"Nothing," Sarina said.

"What!?!?" Kevin said. "If I did that, you'd probably knock my head off!"

"I was going to, but then he started going on about how all these people know about us," Sarina said.

"What people?" Matt said.

"People around Michigan, people outside the state," Sarina said. "Supposedly, people are calling the paper asking about us."

"Well that is interesting," Matt said. "Maybe we won't have to spend too much time advertising after all, at least, if everyone already knows about us."

"I just can't figure it out," Kevin said.

"What, why people know about us?" Drew said.

"No, why she didn't beat up that guy," Kevin said. "Sarina, I hope you let me know the next time you are in a good mood and don't mind something like that."

"Oh I will, possibly right after you tell me the news about Jane," Sarina said. "It's later ... so spill it!"

"Um, maybe not," Kevin said. "I've got ... some ... stuff to do."

Noon came fast. Surely, someone was going to be on the site, looking around, doing something. Matt and Kevin walked downtown to a deli and grabbed lunch. Katy had to finish making a few calls to advertisers, while Drew and Sarina worked on CellBook. Drew finally decided to pull up the administration side of .comU to see if anyone had registered. Sure enough, there were a few entries, 42 in all. I guess that's not bad for being up for 45 minutes, Drew thought. Apparently, no one was having trouble yet.

Not that there was an extreme amount of things for people to do on the site in the first place. From the home page, users had a few options and could run through a demo of The Profiler and input minimal material, but the full version wasn't available yet. The application was enabled to accept personals already, as the group believed that could be a useful feature for first-time users. The idea was that the personals area would be expanded to include anyone who wanted to be a user, just to make friends for other activities other than dating. Drew also instituted an idea called The Board, where people could post simple requests like "looking for a tennis partner" or "trying to find a carpool for the mornings." All of this was free to .comU users, obviously to get people onto the site.

When Matt and Kevin returned, all seemed quiet, so Drew, Katy and Sarina left for lunch. Not 10 minutes after they walked out the door, the phones began ringing. For the next 40 minutes, Matt fielded almost all of the calls. While Kevin tried to divert all the attention by answering some of the questions, most people HAD to talk to Matt. One lady even swore up and down Matt was her long lost grandson.

"Matthew, where have you been? Come home and eat your spinach."

"Is this for real?" Matt said into the phone, although Kevin swiveled around and nodded.

"People online are crazy," Kevin said. "Haven't you learned anything?"

Drew, Katy and Sarina returned, all looking fairly bloated. Amazingly enough, the phones stopped just as they walked in the door.

"Pretty boring, huh guys?" Katy said.

"Yeah, sure, whatever," said Kevin. "It was about as boring as Dave's Burger Bonanza."

"That definitely depends on whether or not you have crayons," Drew said.

The next few hours went smoothly. Kevin and Sarina continued working on .comU advanced user searches. Drew worked on installing a chat program, called Connect, that he had been toying with for the past few months. At this point, his interface was somewhat rough and still not nearly as good as mainstream messaging services. Drew, though, wanted to offer this particular application for city meetings and Q&A sessions that the group planned to offer through the site.

Meanwhile, Katy was on the phone with Gene Simons again. Katy got the sense that maybe Gene wanted a little more than just an interview. At times, Gene was talking more than Katy, and Katy was asking him questions. He hadn't quite asked her out yet. Then again, maybe he just had good taste in women and that was it. He did slap Sarina on the ass when she passed him running this morning, Katy thought. Wait a minute, didn't he ask Matt to have a drink with him before?

Oh, it was obvious. Gene was in love with The Developers. And who could blame him?

For the weekend story, Gene wanted to come down to the office and interview everyone. Katy agreed, but she wanted to tell Gene she would allow it only if he stayed at least five feet away from everyone and the equipment.

Katy cut the interview short. She had to help Matt with the interns. Matt decided the basic functions of an intern would consist of updating the events calendar and business list; responding to users who have questions about .comU features; and monitoring the message boards and user information. They would be responsible for reporting derogatory comments and lewd photos that ended up on the public site.

A fourth intern came barging into the LAB just as Matt and Katy began explaining their responsibilities. And of all people at Moxee Tech, the fourth was, indeed, Crissy Calhoun.

"Did I miss anything, guys?" said Crissy, wearing a decent amount of clothing for a trollop.

"Are you sure you are an intern?" Katy said. "Who approved you?"

"Dr. Jones, who else?" Crissy said. "I AM at the top of my class."

"Shouldn't you graduate soon?" Matt said.

"Well, I'm a grad student now ... going for my PhD in computer science," Crissy said.

"So now you can sleep with your students. How appropriate!" Katy said.

"Well if you're jealous, I could make room for you instead," Crissy said.

"This is getting out of hand," Katy said. "Let's get down to business."

Matt gave the group a simple schedule of when they should perform their duties. All four interns would have their own usernames and passwords, so they could log into the system and view and edit .comU users.

The interns seemed satisfied with their project. A few hours a week at this, and they would receive internship credit toward their coursework. Crissy, well, she was just in it because she always had to be in the middle of everything.

Katy walked the students to the front door. One of them almost hit his head on the top part of the door, but thankfully, it swung open just in time. As the group was leaving, Katy noticed a BMW pulling up into the parking lot. A middle-aged man got out and started walking up to the door. Katy thought he looked familiar but she couldn't remember where. Oh wait a minute ... it was Matt's new best friend, Doug Morris, the guy from the presentation who was in the room the last time Matt yelled at her.

"Hey Matt," yelled Katy down the hallway. "It's your buddy Doug."

"Doug?" Matt said, checking his watch. "I wonder what the hell he wants."

Doug made it to the door in one piece, avoiding slipping on some of the ice coverage on the steps. At least the snow was melting, with the sun out for about half of the day.

"Yo Katy! Yo Matt! What's happening!" Doug wiped his feet on the welcome mat, while Katy and Matt wondered if this was Doug Morris or Doug E. Fresh.

"Hey Doug," Matt said. Katy decided she didn't feel this conversation necessary, so she walked back to the WAB.

"What are you doing here?" Matt said. "Already out of the office for the day?"

"A lot of people were on the site at Foundation ... they love it!" Doug said. "I just had to run down here and tell you in person."

"Well that is a good sign, I guess. It will definitely be interesting to see how many people we rope in during the next few months."

"I concur. And this is only the beginning. I see Foundation Technologies partnering with The Developers in many upcoming projects."

"Are you serious? What do you guys have going on over there?"

"Oh this and that. Foundation is a decent-size operation. We have a few other offices around the country. You'll have to come down to take the tour sometime."

"Yeah, Doug, hopefully I can get down there sometime in the near future. I guess you are working on some advancements for government security, right?"

Doug opened his briefcase and handed Matt a plain manila folder.

"Actually Matt, that was another reason I came down here. I think they need a little more than a website. And I see some of the .comU enhancements fitting right in with their plans. Take a look at it and get back to me sometime soon."

"I will Doug ... this week is pretty much madness obviously, but maybe next week or something. I'd better get back in there, though, I've already fallen behind for the day."

"I hear ya Matt. I'll be giving you a call."

Matt started to open the manila folder to check out Doug's plans, but Drew interrupted him.

"Another phone call, Matt," Drew said.

"Who is it this time?"

"Beats the hell out of me. I stopped asking after the guy swore up and down that you were the Second Coming."

"Second coming of what?"

"Oh, John Denver, of course."

Matt walked briskly back to his desk. The rest of his day was hectic, which turned into an evening of even more work. There hadn't been any significant problems with .comU yet. A handful of people were trying to log into the system using the same username and password they used for their Internet access, and they never actually signed up for .comU. Another user had the caps lock on when entering his username.

"I really enjoy looking up people's passwords," Sarina said. "Although this guy might have the best username: groove_booty. What's that supposed to mean?"

"Maybe he's going to shake it online," Kevin said. "Here's my favorite so far: tacoman. What sucks is that I was going to use that exact same name. Now I'm going to have to go with burritoman."

"So does that make Jane the burritowoman?" Katy said.

"We can only hope so," Kevin answered.

All five Developers were still there at 6:30. Katy had pretty much taken care of the advertisers and media, and she also emailed another press release to the newspapers and TV stations in the region. As the clock neared 7, Drew seemed to be the most tired of the bunch.

"Guys, I think I'm going to head out," Drew said. "I'm going to have to sleep in to make up for my hallucinations I've been having at work."

"Get some rest," Katy said. "There weren't many problems today, so we should be fine early tomorrow. I mean, we are still in the testing phase."

"This is true," Katy said. "So what is going on tomorrow?"

"Sarina and Katy, why don't you come in early," Matt said. "Drew and I will come in late. Kevin, you decide whether you want to be here late or early. Or both."

"Do I have to decide right now?" Kevin said.

"No, just whenever," Matt said. "We have a couple of additional projects that we should discuss, now that .comU is off and running."

"Additional projects?" Sarina asked. "We're not finished yet?"

"I'm afraid not," Matt said. "With the way this is going, we may never be finished."

>:¢ + @:) + >:P + >8. + :D = $$$

TEN

Maybe it wasn't such a good idea to have Katy and Sarina operate the office by themselves Tuesday morning.

The good news was that the phones were silent. When Katy arrived at 8 a.m., there was but one phone call — from Susan Messer at the Malorett Chamber of Commerce, making sure the chamber members could have a preferred or extended listing. Katy learned long ago that neither .comU nor any project would be completed with zero customer questions.

Once Sarina arrived, they contemplated options on what they could do. They had already compiled notes the night before on future .comU functions, none of which would be launched this week. There were plenty of things to do: compile information from user inquiries to add to the Frequently Asked Questions page; generate reports for the current sponsors and advertisers to show how often their pages and ads had been viewed; brainstorm on pricing ideas for future system functions; the list goes on and on.

Because the two figured their afternoon would be full of work, Sarina and Katy figured a little play in the morning wouldn't hurt anyone, especially if they were playing on the system.

"I've been dying to know how many of these people made their information available in the personals section," Sarina said, clicking on various links, trying to remember just how to get to the personals.

"Come on Sarina, are you that hard up for a date?" Katy said. "Whatever happened to the guy at the gym?"

"Are you talking about Pete? My God, Katy, that was like three months ago. Oh, he was just interested in one thing: himself. Well, actually, I should say two things: himself, and himself in my bed."

"Well that's a little diversity for you, I suppose."

"What about you, Katy? I mean surely you still aren't sleeping with Michael."

"No Sarina, I'm not. I was trying to remember the last time ... it was a while back. I don't think I could ever be that desperate. Besides, we are too busy here at work."

"Oh, so now you are holding out for Matt? I see how you look at him. It's OK, I mean he's cute and all."

"Matt's yesterday's news too. Maybe you are on to something here. Did you find many people in the system?"

From the administration end, Sarina could immediately determine the number of people signed up through The Profiler and their interests. At this time, though, the only items available were the personals, community activity alerts and weather updates.

"Actually Katy, there are about 150 in here for the personals. Aren't we supposed to be monitoring these, and determining which should be live or not?"

"That's a good question. Maybe the interns are doing it. Can people perform searches right now?"

"I'll have to ask Drew, but I'm pretty sure in the infancy stage, it's going to be free. Now how long that's going to last, I have no idea. It seems as if I remember him saying something about a week or two."

"So how many of the 150 are guys? Are there any cute ones?"

"Hold on ... it's going to take a minute because I have to use the public search page. At least then we can see a thumbnail of some of the people in there."

Katy rolled her chair over toward Sarina's desk. Sarina called up all the available men — 95 in all — and sorted based on those with photos.

"I can't believe there are already this many guys in there. Are you serious?" Katy said.

"I don't think all of these are real, though," Sarina said. "Yeah, Drew and Kevin put a few guys in here as tests, and they didn't remove them yet."

"Boy, that's an old joke. Was that ever funny?"

"Maybe we should go ahead and delete these tests. It looks like the number of real ones is still like 75 or so."

"OK, let's delete them in a minute, but let's check out these guys. Wait a minute, go back to the last page. I thought I just saw Richard Simmons!"

Sarina hit the back button. Right in the middle of the page, the fifth guy down, had a ridiculously strong resemblance to Richard Simmons.

"You have to be kidding me!" Sarina said. "Richard Simmons lives in Malorett?"

"And his name is Rex Burns!" Katy said.

Sarina and Katy looked at the screen a little harder, like it was going to mysteriously change into something else. Sarina hit the detail button on Rex Burns. Not only did the guy look just like Richard Simmons — puffy, curly brown hair, like the Cowardly Lion from the *Wizard of Oz* — he was even dressed like him, with short, bright greenish-yellow nylon shorts and a red tank top! Rex, though, wasn't nearly as hairy as Richard, as he had just a few chest hairs protruding from the tank top.

"This HAS to be a joke," Sarina said. "There is no way some guy in his right mind would look EXACTLY like Richard Simmons. How is that possible?"

"Maybe he knows you have a thing for Richard ... he's on to you!" Katy said.

"Oh, for crying out loud Katy, that was a JOKE!!!!"

"I don't believe you Sarina. You meant it, whether you were drunk or not!"

A couple of months ago, after Michael and Katy broke up yet again, and Sarina was down in the dumps after another failed date with the guy at the gym, they decided to have a girls' night in. They rented some movies and drank a little too much. Of course, the subject of guys came up, and Sarina asked Katy to name a strange celebrity she would want to be with, just for a night.

Katy's answer was Paul McCartney. That wasn't entirely insane, even though by then, McCartney had to be at least 400 years old. So when it was Sarina's turn, she announced that she had been in love with Richard Simmons for the past 18 years.

"I don't know what it is about him," Sarina said. "But I'd sweat to the oldies with him ALL night long."

"That is disgusting!" Katy said. "Besides, does he even like females?"

"Of course he does. He even sent me an autographed tank top once before.

He signed it 'Hugs and Kisses, Richard.' "

"And how old were you at the time?"

"Oh, maybe 13? 14?"

"You, Sarina, are insane."

As Katy recounted this story, Sarina investigated a little further into this Rex Burns character. He was 36 years old and worked as a bank manager in Malorett. He apparently lived there all his life, although he didn't include much in his ad. His ad, actually, was more like a simple statement: "I'm looking for some adventure, some love and a whole lot of exercise."

"This is your guy!" Katy said. "You have to write to him!"

"I still don't believe it," Sarina said. "I mean, his screen name is sweatinrex. Whatever."

"All right Sarina, if you don't write to him, I will write to him for you. This is way too good to pass up."

As Sarina toyed with the idea, Katy went right for it. She immediately logged in using Sarina's screen name, runner4life, and wrote sweatinrex a little note.

> You seem like a really neat guy. I'm really into fitness, and I would like to get to know you better. Write me back if you have time. Thanks!

For a first note, Katy thought this was appropriate. Sarina didn't have her picture posted or anything like that, so they assumed it should be safe for now.

"If he writes me back, I don't know what I'll do," Sarina said.

"I know what you'll do," Katy said. "You'll meet him!"

"Oh gosh, if he's like Richard in person ... he might get a little freaked out if I jump his bones. I might not be able to control myself."

"I'm sure he won't mind."

***

"Well, the site's been live for a little more than 24 hours," said Matt while the other four Developers listened and shuffled a few papers. "I think we are sitting better than we anticipated at this point. What do you think?"

"Frankly, I'm surprised as well," Drew said.

"Frankly, who says frankly?" said Kevin, slouching down in his seat. "What is this, an old British cop show? I'm surprised as well, old chap."

Drew brushed the comment aside.

"Yeah, there's no way it could have been better at this point," he said. "Well, I mean, it could have been better, it could always be better. But at least from a user standpoint, it's obvious people are on the system."

"It might not be a bad idea right now to go over what we do have up and running and what everyone is watching," Matt said. "I know Sarina and Katy were concerned this morning about what areas were being moderated."

Matt approached the marker board, located on the back wall in the LAB.

"I'm just going to write down the main things we have going, and who is in charge of them," he said. "OK, let's start with The Profiler. What items are functioning, to this point, for The Profiler?"

"Well, of course, the registration works," Katy said. "Also, the personals, community alerts and weather updates. And Sarina and I tested the personals this morning, so they definitely work!"

"Picking another winner, eh?" Kevin said, spinning his focus Sarina's way.

"Well, I would have picked you, Kevin, but seeing that you weren't on there, and the fact that you are practically married to your little sister's friend, well, I decided to go with my second choice."

"All right, all right," Matt said. "The Profiler is in good shape. So with the community alerts set up, I'm assuming also that the events calendar is operational, right?"

"That is correct," Drew said. "At this point, there are about 40 people or businesses or groups or whatever who will be entering events. Some of these people have had the login information to add events for a week now, so we have something up already."

"Excellent," Matt said. "What's next?"

"Well, the business directory is pretty important," Katy said. "We imported all the data from the chamber members, and we've added most things in the phone book. We've also invited those companies who have email addresses and/or websites to add these things to the directory.

"Before I forget, Drew, where are we at with Connect?" Katy said.

"We're in pretty good shape," Drew said. "I think next week I'm going to have the interns play around with it. We should have a working product by next month, hopefully sooner than later."

"I chatted with a couple of the interns last night on instant messenger," Matt said. "They are monitoring the webmaster email, but to this point, there hasn't been too much craziness come through. They are also testing the product whenever they have time. They are getting credit from school, so they have to log basically everything they do. Crissy said she would make sure the kids give us a daily report of what they did and also what things they saw that needed to be fixed."

"So are they going to monitor the message boards, when those are launched?" Kevin said.

"Yeah, sure," Matt said. "What's the time table for that, next week?"

"Next week," Drew said.

"Also, I'm going to work on getting a couple of people lined up for online chats," Katy said.

"That definitely sounds like a plan," Matt said. "But let's focus on what we have so far. Sarina, what in the way of sports in functional right now?"

"The public school system has been very cooperative," Sarina said. "They are either updating their results through our system or are providing material through their site. The high school will be using the system, but the middle school didn't want to do the updates just yet."

"I was going to add my Nerf basketball results from when I kicked Matt's ass," Kevin said. "But I can't remember how to use the athletic updates."

"Thank God," Katy said.

"The schools seem to be really responsive so far," Matt said. "This is going to be key to keeping this system going."

"Maybe down the road, we can add a high school intern or two," Drew said. "The more people involved, the better."

"So Matt, what are these other projects that we are going to be working on?" Katy said. "We're not building a pyramid or anything, are we?"

Matt started to say something, then he looked down at his list. Matt was not the type of person to blurt out the wrong things, but he also rarely spent too much time thinking about what he was going to say. By his pause, the remaining group members knew that whatever he was bringing to The Developers was going to be a little more complex than just updating a website or building a simple database.

"Yesterday, Doug Morris of Foundation Technologies stopped by and gave me a folder that contained one of his company's upcoming projects," Matt said. "Now Doug has told me enough to know what Foundation does, but my total information on the company is very minimal. They are more like a consulting firm than one that actually has a production line or anything.

"Who do they do consulting for ?" Drew said.

"All sorts of businesses," Matt said. "While Doug is pretty open about sharing who Foundation works with, he says very little about what they actually do. Until now."

Matt pulled out the same manila folder that Doug dropped off the day before and opened a six-page report.

"I take it that's not a coloring book," Kevin said.

Drew perked up for a second, then realized he didn't have his crayons anyway.

"Apparently, Foundation is working on a deal with the US government for consulting," Matt said. "You would think in six pages, I would know something, but this document doesn't contain shit. I do know that it's a joint project through the US Department of Commerce and the Federal Communications Commission. Other than that, it's mostly a mystery."

"So what does this have to do with us?" Katy said.

"According to the letter included, Doug has invited me to discuss possibly partnering with Foundation on this project. Again, I'm speculating that Foundation has already begun working on this, but they would like to hone some of our expertise in databases or in some way with data management. Or maybe they just want an estimate on how much time some of the work will take."

"I'm not really sure I follow," Sarina said. "This Foundation Technologies, surely they have programmers who can do this stuff, right? Why would they be seeking our expertise?"

"Whether they have actual programmers remains to be seen," Matt said. "It's a decent-size operation ... they have a pretty nice renovated building just outside of town. At least, that's what Doug said. I would guess they have maybe 15-20 people working there. I know they have accounts all over Michigan, and from the way Doug acts, they are always busy. But he's never really gone into detail about the type of employees he has or anything like that."

"Or maybe it has little to do with programming and more to do with the marketing of our data," Kevin said. "There seem to be plenty of companies out there who can manage databases, and other companies who are advertising firms. But there aren't all sorts of businesses that can do both."

"That's a good point," Matt said. "Again I'm not really sure. I know that Doug has been very successful, and I don't mind aligning our business with other successful companies."

Katy wrote something on her scratch pad, seemingly as if she remembered something that had nothing to do with this particular part of the meeting.

"So when are you supposed to have this meeting with him?" Katy said.

"He wants to have it this Friday," Matt said. "I'm sure I can spare a few minutes to meet with Doug, and then I can bring back a report to you guys."

"Do we really have time to work on another big project?" Katy said. "I mean, I guess you don't have a timetable yet. But this seems kind of weird. We have this huge product we are developing, and now we are looking to help create other systems?"

"Katy, I don't know enough about this to know what we would be getting into," Matt said. "I don't think it could hurt to at least check it out. Hell, it might even be more lucrative than .comU."

"If it's through the government, I'm sure it pays well," Drew said. "But I agree with Katy. Unless this is far in the future, I think we should concentrate on what we have already."

"But what if this project takes us to a whole other level?" Kevin said. "Working with a government project ... that could make us known in more places than Malorett."

"Then again, we could also be known as coming up with this system for a small town and letting it become a flop," Sarina said.

"Guys, I'm not going Friday to tell Doug we'll start working on this immediately," Matt said. "But you can't help but wonder what's going on. I promise to report back everything that goes on. You won't be left out of the loop."

Katy gave Matt a "Yeah, whatever" look and wrote something else down on her note pad.

"So is there anything else that needs to be discussed in this meeting?" Katy said. "I'm sure there are voice mails piled up on the phone or something."

"Yeah, we're done," Matt said. "I think we have a pretty good idea of where we are for .comU. If you run into any roadblocks with your parts, just let me know."

Katy left the LAB first, followed by Sarina and Kevin. As Matt got up, Drew remained seated.

"Matt, I gotta tell you about the idea I had," Drew said. "OK, we want more people to fill out The Profiler, so they'll be in the system. But what's stopping people from inputting their friends, families or fake people?"

"I guess really nothing," Matt said. "I don't know what the point would be to input fake people though. You would have to be pretty bored to do that."

"True, but this is Malorett. I'm sure there are people bored out there."

"I'm getting bored just thinking about it."

"Well Matt, we're getting off the subject. The point of The Profiler is to try to create a database with all the people in town. Then all the people signed up can be eligible for special promotions and stuff like that."

"True, true."

"Which means that actually, people — I should say selfish people — would not want to enter other people into the system, so they would have a better chance to win a prize."

"That's probably true."

"So the trick is to get the people who are on the system to get people who aren't on the system to sign up."

"Drew, you have totally lost me. You have proven the opposite."

"Well, not quite. Let's say there was an incentive for getting others to sign up. Like there was a points system assigned to how many people were in the system."

"And what do the points do for you?"

"Well Matt, nothing right now. But they can be used in the future to classify people and what level they are within the system. Like if you gain 100 points, you can be considered a .comU Friend, with 500 points you could be a Preferred Member, stuff like that. We could use the point system to determine how people are eligible for contests, discounts at participating restaurants and possibly even portions of the site."

"Drew, I think you are on to something here. But I think it needs a little more thinking behind it."

"Wait, I'm not finished. I thought of a game we could play on The Profiler: Find the Missing Person. We could just pick a name out of the phone book and put them on the website. Whoever gets them to sign up wins like a hamburger at Dave's Burger Bonanza or something."

"What if we accidentally pick someone already in the system?"

"We can check beforehand, to make sure we don't do that."

"What if we pick someone who is dead?"

"If they sign up, we could contact *Unsolved Mysteries* or something."

Matt and Drew walked back to the lab, where they noticed Sarina and Kevin both huddled with Katy, staring at her computer.

"Check it out, guys," Kevin said. "We made it in the *Free Press!*"

Katy had pulled up the *Detroit Free Press* website, and sure enough, there was a small story about .comU. Even though it was a short write up, the five were impressed.

"Gene told me we also made it into the Kalamazoo paper," Katy said. "And we were on the front again in the *Times* today. I gave Gene a list of some people who were using the system, and he contacted them and got some quotes. Free publicity is great!"

"That's amazing, considering we're still beta testing," Drew said.

Drew, Matt and Sarina returned to their desks, while Katy went over a few changes to the sponsorship list with Kevin. It was only 1 p.m., and it seemed as if they had been at the office for a good three days straight. Despite the overload of work, everyone seemed to be in a good mood. The debate about whether or not they could handle another job would have to wait for another day. Until then, .comU would be the top priority of The Developers ... and hopefully, the system would stay on top of the local media sources as well.

ELEVEN

"I still don't get it," said Jane, adjusting the driver-side mirror in time to see a car passing beside her. "If a company is paying a fee to advertise on the site, shouldn't it get to choose exactly where it wants to advertise?"

"Well yes and no," said Kevin, watching ahead as Jane made her way onto the main strip in Moxee. "If they pay enough, yes, they can define where they want to advertise. Some companies even have sponsored sections of the site, so that's good. But then there are just some general advertisers, who show up anywhere. It's good to have a variety of advertiser types so we can fill all the spots."

"But you guys keep track of which of the ads are being looked at and clicked on, correct?"

"Oh yeah, we can tell the page the person is coming from when they click one of the ads. Probably what we'll do is just make available a report of the click-throughs so our advertisers will have the info. We're still looking for a few more sponsors, though. Any suggestions?"

"Um not really. Like I have time to think about that! I had a test today in calculus, then I have two more tests coming up Thursday."

"If I take your tests, then will you help me?"

It was already Wednesday evening. Kevin and Jane were on their way to the bowling alley. Kevin made the trip over to Moxee for the second straight night. They were beginning to spend a lot of free time together, and neither seemed to mind too much. Jane had played basketball Tuesday night; the team lost by 4, and Jane didn't have one of her better games. Kevin stayed with her for awhile, basically just watching her do her homework. Kevin needed a little break from Malorett, so he didn't mind. Jane was pretty beat, though, so Kevin took off before midnight. Before he left, Jane insisted he come back Wednesday to go bowling.

Why Jane wanted to go bowling, Kevin wasn't quite sure. But once they arrived at The Splits, the biggest bowling alley in Moxee, Kevin started to realize that maybe Jane was an avid bowler. She opened the trunk and pulled out a bright pink bowling bag. And that wasn't the scariest part. In big block letters on the side was "CHAMP."

"So, champ, do you come here a lot?" Kevin said.

"Not as much as I would like," Jane said. "I used to bowl a lot, back in high school. But with basketball and all, there's really not that much time. Are you intimidated because I have my own ball, shoes and resin bag?"

"Um, no. I've just never dated a girl who had her own bowling ball. This one girl had a field hockey stick, and another girl carried darts with her pretty much all the time. It's funny, she never let me touch them, though. They may have been poisonous for all I know."

The two entered the bowling alley and had little trouble acquiring a lane, even though there was a league in progress. Kevin was no match for Jane. She beat him by 50 pins in the first game and 70 in the next. But neither paid too much attention to the score of the games. They were more interested in each other's company.

Kevin was pleasantly surprised he had lasted this long. Jane seemed eager for Kevin to come over any time he wanted. Unfortunately, Kevin wasn't able to get over to Moxee as often as he would like. On Tuesday, Kevin worked with Katy until 7 p.m. on straightening out all of the advertisers and sponsors for the system and implementing the business directory.

Matt and Kevin also discussed giving out Site of the Month awards to local businesses. Although not as tasty as the Flavor of the Month at Baskin-Robbins, the Site of the Month winner would get a short write-up and featured listing in the directory.

On Wednesday, Kevin made it a point that he would get over to Moxee earlier than 8, but it almost didn't happen. Drew needed his help in devising the Find the Missing Person contest. Kevin composed a couple of promotional ads for it, while Drew made sure he could get the exact data needed to display on various .comU pages.

Drew worked to tie the referral points into a cumulative point bank within .comU. In the meantime, Kevin added text on the site to explain the concept. He also added a simple form where people could tell their friends about the site and start gaining meaningless points. Sarina also helped Kevin with the promotional pieces and came up with a simple logo for the contest. But the group wasn't positive as to what value the referrals should receive.

"Shouldn't we at least have something on the site that tells how many points are awarded?" Sarina said. "And on top of that, shouldn't we have something telling people what these points are for?"

"People like to collect points just to collect them," Drew said. "It's just like aluminum cans. Do people actually recycle those or just store them in a shed?"

"Do we have anything to give away at this point?" Kevin said. "I mean we can't very well promise something for these points and not have anything. Even if we said if you collect a million points, you'll win a pony, some crazy guy will manage to sign up half of Arkansas, and we'll have to give him a pony."

"Well, I'm not giving him mine," Drew said.

"What about these sponsors?" Kevin said. "You would think even Phil at Harris Hotels would spring for a weekend getaway or something."

"But why would someone from Malorett want to spend a weekend at one of the hotels in Malorett?" Sarina said. "I'm sure they have a good pool, but seriously. Oh wait, do they have one of those beds you can put a quarter in? Maybe it is worth it."

"I'm telling you, people like to collect points, even if they mean nothing," Drew said.

"We'll take your word for it," Sarina said. "But we'll also ask Katy tomorrow if she can find a few restaurants interested in this."

"I think it'll work," Kevin said. "At least, until all the missing people are found. Then people will have to find a new way to accumulate points."

By the time Kevin, Sarina and Drew put the finishing touches on Find the Missing Person, it was 5:30. Katy had left earlier to run by the *Times* and meet with Gene Simons. Matt, too, was gone, and no one was too sure where he was.

Kevin's eventful day was coming to a close now, but the car ride back to Jane's place was silent. It was definitely bizarre for them to come up with plenty of things to talk about before and during a date, but once it was almost

over, things got a little weird. Kevin thought he should say something, anything, to break the silence.

"I had a good time, Jane," Kevin said.

"Me too," Jane said.

Nothing else. That didn't work, Kevin thought. Maybe he should press a
little harder.

"I mean, I always have fun hanging out with you," Kevin said.

"Yeah, me too," Jane said.

Jane stared straight ahead, peering at the traffic, or lack thereof, on the
way back to her dorm. Kevin thought for a few seconds and decided to give
it one last try.

"Jane, don't you think it's time we had sex?"

This got her attention. She promptly slammed on the breaks, and luckily,
there was nothing behind her on the four-lane road.

"What did you say?" said Jane, as her car was motionless in the road.

"Uh, I said, 'Do you have a dime for some Chex?' "

"That's not what you said."

Kevin and Jane sat in the car, not saying a word for almost a minute. A
couple of cars buzzed by on the left side, while a truck nearly sideswiped
Jane's car, steering into the left lane while honking.

"Don't you think you should drive?" Kevin said. "Or at least get out of
the road?"

"Yes," Jane said. "But I don't feel like it, until you tell me why you said
what you said."

"No reason, I was just thinking of something to say. And that's what came
out. Are you mad?"

Jane released her foot of the break and gradually sped up to the speed
limit.

"From the time I met you, I always thought you were cute and cool, but I
figured you were just like the other guys. Well, and I had a boyfriend. Then
the last week, since we've been talking and going out, I thought maybe you
weren't like the others. That maybe you were different and actually cared
about me. But after a comment like that, I don't know what to think anymore."

Kevin sunk lower in his seat.

"It was a joke! I was just kidding," Kevin said. "I was just trying to liven up our ride home. That is all."

"Well you succeeded with that. But if that's all you're going to think about, then I would prefer you did it on your own time."

Jane pulled into the dorm parking lot and squealed past some students walking from the building. Kevin had parked at the back of the lot, but there was no sense in asking Jane to drive him back to the spot. She pulled in, immediately jumped out of the vehicle and started walking in. Kevin got out and stood next to her car.

"Jane ... don't you think you are overreacting? It could have been a lot worse."

Jane stopped and turned to face Kevin.

"And how could it have been worse?"

"Well, I could have started taking off my clothes ... or yours ... in the car!"

Jane threw her hands up in the air and kept walking toward the dorm. Kevin decided it was time to chase after her. She was only 50 yards in front of him, so a light jog made up the time quickly.

"Jane, you have to understand ... wait a minute, isn't this what happened on our first date?"

"What do you mean?"

"Well I distinctly remember a silent car ride, then me chasing you up to the dorm."

"But the circumstances seem a little different. I don't remember you asking me for sex on that date."

"Oh, I didn't? I meant to."

Jane wanted to walk away, but she just turned her head instead.

"Jane, come on. I know you aren't like the other girls. That's what I like about you."

"What do you mean I'm not like the other girls? Like I just don't have sex any guy I go out with? Yeah, not all girls are like that."

"Well, I've got news for you, not all guys are like that either. Some actually enjoy the company of a female lady friend."

"So that's what I am, a lady female friend?"

Kevin grabbed Jane's right hand and bent over to kiss it.

"Today dear, you are my lady female friend. Tomorrow, who knows what you will be. Maybe you will then be my lady."

Kevin let Jane's hand go, turned the other way and started walking slowly toward his car. Please still be standing there, please still be standing there, Kevin said to himself. After taking about 20 paces, he turned to see Jane, watching him walk. She blew him a kiss.

"Maybe someday you'll get your wish," said Jane.

Then she headed to her room. Kevin just stood there for a second, really wishing the moment did not have to end, and for the first time admitting that if there was The One, it had to be her.

***

Drew didn't mean to sneak up on Matt when he entered the WAB Thursday morning. He must have just been extremely cautious about opening and closing doors, because when he walked into the office, Matt nearly jumped out of his seat. There was no reason to not expect people in the office; it was 9 in the morning, but no one else had appeared yet.

"Sorry man, I didn't mean to scare you," Drew said.

Matt shuffled some papers and set them beside his computer.

"Oh, it's OK," Matt said. "I don't know what happened. I guess I was in a trance or something."

"Seriously, you should avoid hypnotizing yourself alone. It gets really tricky when you have to wake up."

As Drew booted up his computer, Matt called him over to show him the latest stats. The usage continued to climb obnoxiously, as there were 6,000 members, and the number of Profiler records almost made it to 4,500. But there were still plenty of people missing from the system, which of course, was expected for the first week.

Kevin was the next to arrive. He looked amazingly fresh for a guy who was dragging in the past few mornings.

"So you caught up on sleep last night, eh Kevin?" Matt asked.

"Yeah, you could say that," said Kevin, sitting down at his work station.

"No, something else is going on," Drew said. "Maybe he's in love. I can tell these things."

"I don't know about all of that," Kevin said. "But Jane is special. I can't stop thinking about her."

"Well that's good, I'm glad things are working out and all," Drew said.

"Jesus Christ, this sounds like a Hallmark commercial or something," Matt said. "I'm waiting for Oprah to walk in and console both of you."

"It sounds like you are the one who needs consoling," Kevin muttered.

"I'm doing all right, thank you," Matt said. "There's a lot of work to be done. No time for women."

"There's always time for women!" Kevin said.

"True, unless your woman doesn't wear a watch," Matt said.

Katy appeared at 9:30, and Sarina followed minutes later. The first order of business was adding Find the Missing Person to the site. Kevin showed the simple ads he and Sarina created, which Matt and Katy both approved. Everyone agreed it should be added immediately. Katy did have a few restaurants who would more than likely donate gift certificates for specifically this feature.

"Should we make them spot ads on the signup part as well?" Kevin said.

"No, we don't want people clicking away on the sign up," Katy said.

"Oh yeah, good point," Kevin said. "What the hell was I thinking?"

"You were thinking you were in love," Drew said. "So you weren't thinking."

"What, you really are in love?" Sarina said. "With Jen's friend?"

"Yeah Kevin, you told us you would give us the scoop," said Katy, acting more interested in the relationship than Kevin. "What's going on?"

"I hope Oprah saves all of you!" said Matt, returning his attention to his computer screen.

The other four looked at Matt for a second, agreed telepathically that Matt was crazy and turned their concern back to Kevin.

"Anyway, things are just going really well," Kevin said. "I think she really likes me. I know I really like her."

"So when are you going to have her come visit?" Sarina said.

"Oh, I don't know, that might be a little weird."

"How so?" Drew said. "She's a person, just like the rest of us. Well, at least most of us."

Again, the group looked in Matt's direction.

"If we weren't so busy, that would be one thing," Kevin said. "But there's just too much going on. Maybe in a week or two."

"I've got an idea!" said Matt, rolling his chair into the center of the group. "What if we all went skiing?"

Drew, Kevin, Katy and Sarina looked at each other. No one could tell if Matt was being serious.

"Uh, Matt, must I remind you that we are in the middle of controlling a website that eventually will be used by the majority of people in this city?" Katy said. "There's no way in hell we could all be out of the office at the same time."

"Well, it's a good thing this isn't hell, right?" Matt said.

No one got the joke, but Matt continued.

"First off, we can leave the site for a couple of hours, especially on a Saturday," he said. "Secondly, I talked to the guy at Ski Frenzy a couple days ago about building a website. He wants to give us the full tour and let us ski for free! He even mentioned he has a computer up there and high-speed access, if we did have to check on the site. What do you think?"

It sounded pretty convincing, but the group still thought it was a joke.

"So what if something really bad happens?" Drew said. "Then what do we do?"

"I guess if something bad happens, someone can come back," Matt said. "It's just 20 minutes down the road. I'm going to talk to Crissy and the interns, to see if they'll watch the site a little closer during that time," Matt said.

"Are you all right, man?" Drew said.

"Yeah Drew, I'm OK," Matt said. "And I have good news for you. You will be calling our first-ever .comU bingo!"

"OK, this has gone far enough," Drew said. "What the hell are you smoking?"

"I've scheduled an online midnight bingo for Saturday night," Matt said.

"People can either come down to the Knights of Columbus to play, or they can play via computer."

"We have a bingo game on .comU? Get out of here!" Kevin said.

"Unless Matt has installed a simple bingo module I created a year ago, just for grins, no we don't," Drew said.

"That would be the one!" Matt said. "Everything you have set up works great. People can play on the system, which ties directly into the setup they have at Knights of Columbus. They have a number of electronic playing cards, so all we have to do is enter a serial number into the system to give a user a set of cards. It's as simple as that."

"And how will they yell 'bingo'?" Katy asked.

"Through Connect," Matt said. "If someone has a bingo, they just send an instant message. Then they send the serial number. All someone has to do is input that serial number into the key to see if it's an actual bingo."

"You make it sound so easy," Drew said. "This is freaking me out."

"It will be fun, Drew!" Matt said. "So we'll go skiing from about noon until 5 or so, then we'll have dinner, then whoever wants to check out the bingo later can do so!"

Matt again returned to typing on his computer. The rest of the group just sat there, all with their mouths wide open.

"What just happened?" Kevin said. "Was that a nightmare?"

Just then, Butch appeared from inside the closet. He was carrying a new tub of cheese puffs.

"No, it really happened," said Butch, munching on a large handful of the tasty delicacies. "Unless I'm dreaming too."

Butch exited the room.

"So who all is invited to this ski trip?" Katy asked. "Can Kevin bring his date?"

"Sure, why not!" Matt said. "Everyone can bring a date!"

"Well I guess we'll get to meet her then," Drew said. "I'm sure Jessica would like to come. Especially if I have to call that damn bingo later, at least we will be able to spend some time together.

"What about you, Sarina?"

"I think Sarina is checking to find her date right now," Katy said.

Sure enough, Sarina was checking the .comU personals, to see if Rex Burns had written back. And sure enough, there was a message from sweatinrex.

Hi runner4life! You sound like my kind of woman! I really like girls who take good care of themselves. I volunteer at the nursing home a couple days a month to help the people there eat right and exercise. There are so many good people there. I almost get tears just thinking about it! I hope you don't think I'm saying this just to try to go out with you. I really want to meet you. Name the place and time and I'm there, sweetie!
- Rex

Sarina almost broke out into tears.

"OK, either this guy is the best imposter on earth, or he really thinks he's Richard Simmons," Sarina said. "I have to meet him just to find that out."

"Bring him along!" Matt said. "But remember, no pets."

Sarina immediately wrote him a message back.

Rex, it was good to hear from you! I would like to invite you skiing on Saturday. I'm going with some co-workers, and I would really enjoy your company. But let's meet before then. How about we meet for lunch Friday? Let's say noon at Buckeye's. If you can't make that, just let me know what would be better for you. Hope to see you soon! :-)
- Sarina

"This is great!" Matt said. "We are going to have all sorts of people going skiing. It's going to be fabulous."

"But wait a minute," Kevin said. "Who is going to be your date, Matt?"

"Well that's obvious," Matt said. "Katy will be my date. Right, Katy?"

Katy glanced over at Sarina, then at Drew, then at Kevin. No one had even a notion of what to say.

"I guess, Matt," Katy said. "I mean really, do I have a choice?"

:)> - Rex
:D ± :)> ???

TWELVE

Buckeye's is a popular lunchtime dining facility located in the heart of downtown Malorett. Sarina wondered if that sentence, written at the bottom of the menu at Buckeye's, was composed during a time when there was a heart of downtown Malorett. Judging solely on location, if this was the heart, then The Developers' office must be approximately the liver. That is, of course, assuming the Malorett man is lying on his back, facing the east. Also, according to these same coordinates, Sarina determined she must be sitting either at the edge of the left ventricle or somewhere in the middle of the aorta.

You guessed it! Sarina was extremely bored. She had been waiting for more than 20 minutes to meet Rex Burns. Surely he hadn't forgotten about the meeting. Surely he had read his email since the day before. Then again, Sarina didn't know where the guy lived, which bank he was manager at or really much of anything other than his similarities to Richard Simmons. Sarina had seen approximately 25 guys since arriving at Buckeye's, and not one even had an ounce of Simmons.

Sarina decided that if he didn't come off like the real one in person, then she had better things to do, like finding the heart of Malorett.

At least the water at Buckeye's was excellent, Sarina thought. Serving Malorett since 1922, Buckeye's offers a variety of items on the menu, from fresh fish to burgers to speciality salads. Buckeye's also offers a selection of wines and spirits for your dining pleasure. Reservations are welcome. She had read that part of the menu 32 times just today, and plenty of other times as well. But she hadn't read it enough that she could recite it during her morning run or even as a prayer.

Finally, just as Sarina had had enough, and had turned to grab her purse to leave, a man approached the table. He knocked lightly on the table top, and Sarina saw only his knuckles. They were hairy, but not too hairy. Then she gradually looked across at his stomach, up his shirt, and she immediately noticed sweat beads frolicking through his visible chest hairs.

"You are Sarina, right?" said the man, looking as if he wanted to sit down, but never actually making the move.

"And you must be Rex," Sarina said. "Have a seat! Where have you been?"

"Oh, I had to run a few errands for work," Rex said. "I thought I could still make it here in time, but then I remembered I had to do another favor for someone at work. I mean, it was no big deal, but I told Susie I would give her my recipe for Chicken a la Burns before she took off for the weekend. And I'm a man of my word."

"But wait a minute, if you're a man of your word, then why were you late?"

"You got me, Sarina. You got me."

Even though she waited for almost 25 minutes, Sarina could tell her wait was worth it. Rex was exactly how he described himself, exactly how he appeared in his picture and exactly what Sarina anticipated. After she ordered a chicken sandwich and fries, Rex ordered a chicken Caesar salad with light salad dressing and no croutons. When the waiter left, Rex leaned over the table and grabbed Sarina's left hand.

"Sarina! Fries? You can't eat fries and keep that great figure of yours," Rex said. "Would you like me to wave him down so you can get a baked potato?"

"No that's all right," said Sarina, taking another drink of water. "I like fries, and I want to eat fries. If I have to run a little more tomorrow, then so be it."

"Well, if you're OK with it ... then I am too! I'm sorry, I'm just extremely health conscious. Please don't take it personal."

"No problem, Rex. But speaking of personal — and I don't even know how to say this, but — has anyone ever told you that you look like Richard Simmons?"

Rex released his hand from Sarina's and folded his hands in his lap. He stared down below the table for an instant.

"No, Sarina, no one has ever told me that," Rex said. "But that is quite possibly the best compliment someone has ever given me!"

Rex stood, walked over to Sarina and kissed her on the cheek. Sarina turned away, then sat motionless, smiling and blushing. Rex returned to his seat, still beaming from Sarina's comment.

"Richard is my idol!" Rex said. "I wish I could be just like him. But I know that is impossible. There is only one Richard Simmons. Did you know he was born on July 12?"

"Actually, yes, I did know that," Sarina said. "I am a big fan of his as well. That is so odd. I never really thought I'd actually find something like that in common with a man."

"Well believe it, sister!"

Lunch went extremely well. Rex and Sarina sorted through each other's life stories, job duties, favorite pastimes, etc. By the time they had finished their meals, both wished there was more time to stay and chat.

"I really hate to cut this short, Rex, but I have to get back to the office," Sarina said. "We are in the process of trying to tie up all loose ends before the weekend."

"That's understandable," said Rex, dropping his napkin on his plate. "I, too, must get back before all my employees wonder where I am. Can we do this again sometime? I had a great time."

"I did as well, Rex. So do you want to go skiing with us tomorrow? I don't normally try to go on dates with new guys on back-to-back nights, but the people at work are getting together the trip and ... "

"That is fabulous! I haven't been in a month, but I love to ski!"

"Great! We're going to Ski Frenzy, and as far as I know, we're going to try to leave Malorett in the morning. Will that work for you?"

"I'll make it work, Sarina. I would definitely enjoy spending more time with you."

As they walked out of Buckeye's, Rex scribbled his home number on the back of a business card and gave it to Sarina.

"Call me there, or call my cell number, and just let me know what time to pick you up," Rex said, "if you want me to pick you up."

"Yep, that sounds fine," Sarina said. "I should know this afternoon what the plans will be. I'll definitely be calling you."

Rex leaned over to hug Sarina and gave her another kiss on the cheek. When he started to let go, Sarina was still holding him tight and pulling Rex back toward her. She lurched up and aimed a kiss on his lips. Rex gave Sarina a quick glance, held firm and then backed away.

"That was nice, Sarina," Rex said. "I can't wait to see you tomorrow!" With that, Rex got into his SUV and drove off.

Sarina wasn't sure exactly what to think about that kiss. Rex seemed somewhat abrupt in getting away, but then again, it was the first time they had ever met. Even still, Sarina had already fallen hard for Rex Burns.

***

Matt squinted at the address just above the door in front of him. It read 3216, which is the address Doug Morris gave him to Foundation Technologies. Matt turned around and checked the road as well. The sign definitely said Ohio Street. He turned back around, still unsure if he was where he was supposed to be.

Not that Matt had conjured up an idea of what Foundation Technologies was supposed to look like, but for some reason, this is not what it was supposed to look like. This building, 3216 Ohio Street, reminded him of a small dentist office, or a diner that seated 20 people and was frequented by passers-by in the wee hours of the morning. The place was one story, but it would be classified as a half story, if that were possible. There couldn't have been more than four rooms in the place, and if there were that many, at least one would have been smaller than a closet. The building was somewhat part of a strip mall because on the left side, Matt noticed a carryout Chinese restaurant, a dry cleaners and a liquor store. But this building did have 10-15 feet between it and the others, so it wasn't necessarily connected. They just shared a common parking lot, where Matt's truck sat with just one other vehicle.

Matt hesitated to even knock on the door, even though he finally noticed a sign beside the steps that read Foundation Technologies. This must be the place, he thought, even though there was no one around, and Doug said to be there by 11:30 a.m. Matt knocked, and almost immediately, a young man answered the door.

"You must be Matt from The Developers," the man said. "Please enter now."

Matt obliged, only to be led into what appeared to be a waiting room.

"Doug will be up in a minute to see you," said the man, scurrying back to a different room.

Matt sat down in a large wooden rocking chair and picked up a copy of *Time* magazine, although it was from seven years ago. Maybe people don't come in here and wait that often, he thought. Or maybe people don't come in here at all. Or maybe people who wait often feel nostalgic and enjoy the old issues of *Time*. Or maybe ...

"Long time, no see! Have you been waiting long?" Doug walked over to Matt and shook his hand. "Are you ready for the tour?"

"Sure, I guess," Matt said. "I mean, the tour won't take that long, for the size of this place, will it? I thought you said this building was renovated?"

"Ah yes, I knew you would think that. We didn't do too much to the up-stairs. But the downstairs, that is a different story."

Doug opened a side door, which actually was a large stairwell entrance. Matt looked down at what had to be at least two large flights of stairs, and he was flabbergasted.

"Yeah, the upstairs used to be some little diner that stayed open like 24 hours," said Doug, leading the way down the stairs. "Their speciality was breakfast, and some say there's still a ghost shaped like an omelette upstairs. Regardless, they had a large cellar that was originally built as some sort of fallout shelter. When I found out about it, I took a look, and sure enough, it was exactly the type of place I knew would work for us. Plus having an om-elette ghost guard the place, you just can't beat that."

Doug reached the cavernous entrance and unlocked the doors. He yanked the handle hard and the door finally gave way.

"When the funds for this project start flying in, I need to get this fixed," Doug said. He gave Matt a nod to enter, and the two made it inside.

Matt was instantly in awe of the massive room. It was approximately the size of three high school gyms, minus the bleachers, the concession stands and unfortunately, the cheerleaders. But there was only a small portion of the room that was being used. The center of the area contained 12 spacious cubicle-like areas, and all of the walls faced outward toward the rest of the room. It was like a cubicle castle, and the rest of the floor on the outside was a moat. Matt could see through to the center of the castle, which had a meeting room, equipped with chairs, a table, a projector and a large screen.

"This ... this is pretty slick," said Matt, walking closer toward the entrance into the cubicle castle. "But where is everyone?"

"Oh it's Friday," Doug said. "Everyone goes to eat up at Dave's on Friday. I had to stay behind to show you the place, so there would be no interruptions. I brought lunch with me. Would you like a pear?"

"No that's all right Doug, I'll eat later. So should we get down to business?"

"Of course, Matt."

They walked to the center area and took seats at the long meeting table. Matt still had the original folder that Doug had dropped off a few days ago, and Doug had a small briefcase, which he opened at the table. Most everything was still a mystery to Matt, so he decided to just shuffle some papers around until Doug started speaking.

"OK Matt, I see you are shuffling papers around," Doug said. "I'm not sure why because you basically have no information."

"That's why I am," Matt said. "I thought by shuffling papers, I could conjure up some knowledge."

"Good try! I have the info here. I'll give you a little more detail about the project, then you can ask questions, give opinions or juggle; you decide."

"Sounds good, Doug."

"Here it goes: We have won a bid from the United States government, a combined project from the Department of Commerce and FCC, to produce a loose backbone of Internet service, within the US, that will overlay the chaotic routing schematics that currently exist.

"The objective behind this routing technique is a little complex. OK, it's a lot complex. First, it's important to continue to allow all major and minor Internet service providers to continue, uninterrupted, from now until eternity. But these providers will, in turn, have to pay a fee to the government for usage. This could be equated to a universal connectivity charge for phone service. The charge hasn't been determined yet, but it will probably be at least

$1 a year per connection."

"But why would major ISPs like AOL or Earthlink want to do this?" Matt said. "They already have their own systems set up. They can just keep them the way they are."

"That's the thing, Matt. They won't be able to keep their lines the way they are. They are being phased out."

"Phased out? How so?"

"I have to stop for a moment, Matt, because this is classified information. I'm not even at liberty to say how this will be occurring, but as a main player in this system, you have to know this information."

"What information?"

Doug pulled out a piece of paper from his briefcase, and he also pulled out a pen.

"This is to protect us both," Doug explained. "This is a confidentiality agreement between Foundation Technologies, The Developers and the United States. This agreement will allow me to discuss in detail the rest of the plans. They have already run background checks on you, your employees and your company, and everything came out just fine. I trust you, Matt, but involving an outside business is no different, whether we're dealing with the Chinese carryout next door or the American government. Take a look at it."

Doug handed Matt the confidentiality agreement. It explained that what was discussed between the two organizations regarding this project would remain confidential and not be talked about with the general public. The client — the US government — would be in contact directly with Foundation and any additional companies used in outsourcing. Matt read over it thoroughly and signed, without asking questions. He handed the paper back to Doug and reluctantly grinned.

"OK, now tell me what the hell is going on here," Matt said.

"Now I can, with your trust on paper," Doug said. "There hasn't been an exact timeframe established, but the current connections used by all service providers will become virtually extinct five years from now. The engineers who have fortified the connection lines through the World Wide Web have been gathered to build what will be called the Super Information Portal, or SIP. All current routes will be absolved into the SIP and then improved and/or replaced by new lines. This is how the government will basically be able to place a toll on the use of the SIP."

"Damn the government!" Matt said. "Wait a minute, how do you pronounce this? Is it 'sip' or 's-i-p'?"

"Say it as one word, of course. But we can't damn the government here. We are going to be getting some of the funds earned from this."

"Oh yeah, never mind, good job government! But what are we getting out of this?"

"First off, the only way this is going to make everyone satisfied is if there is still a free market in the business of providing Internet service. Luckily, this system doesn't take away from that at all. For instance, Company A and Company B can still compete freely even though they are paying for their electric from the same company, or paying the same state taxes.

"Secondly, five years from now, after SIP has been fully implemented, every Internet connection will have this charge associated with it. I would assume that for AOL, the charge will basically be built into a monthly statement. This might not even be directly announced to the public in a large fashion. I mean an extra dollar a year won't be much to complain about.

"At the same time, think of what an extra buck or two from every computer connected to the SIP could do for Internet-related funding. It would be like setting up a toll booth that everyone has to walk through once a year."

"But there is a slight problem with that thinking," Matt said. "For networked computers, you have only one main Internet connection. Then you have wireless Internet and routers, where providers can cluster large groups into one. So how will that affect the cost of these charges?"

"That's a good question, Matt, and I don't have all of the specifics. But I'm guessing businesses will be charged the SIP fee based on computer usage or something like that. For networked users within a household, I don't think there will be an extra charge. I'm not really too concerned with that, because that's not the part that we will be doing anyway."

"OK, now I'm really confused," Matt said. "I thought we were going over the part in which Foundation Technologies won the bid? So what are you doing?"

"Don't get me wrong, our technicians will be working closely with the network specialists to determine the best way to lay out the SIP," Doug said. "Actually, most of it will be wireless, with main hubs near large cities. It's sort of like when you go to an airport, and they have wireless access, but you have to login to actually use the Internet. What I need from you, though, is your database expertise and your ability to track users throughout various websites and, in effect, the entire World Wide Web."

"You're going to track all of these users?" Matt said. "Isn't that illegal?"

"It is right now, but it won't be," Doug said. "This isn't complex tracking, at least to start out with. It will be, more or less, finding out the number of users visiting sites, the time spent on the site, that sort of thing. We won't be examining individual times; we'll be looking at grouping these users based on where they are from and what service provider they are using. It's similar to what search engines do by tracking how often people hit certain pages. That's what moves sites up in the listings, more than anything."

Matt had a stupefied look on his face, even though he understood everything Doug was telling him. Matt didn't necessarily think this was a bad idea, but he wondered just how this would help the Internet in general. Having a unified, central service would be good if there wasn't a chance of the system ever being down. But if there was a problem, would that mean everyone in America would not be able to access the Web? The tracking mechanism also seemed somewhat fishy, although it didn't seem as if it would be too difficult to construct, especially with everyone in the same system.

"Matt, I know I've left out plenty of specifics," Doug said. "But I had to start somewhere. The basic concepts have been laid down, and now, it's just a matter of putting the pieces together. Our contact from Washington will be in Wednesday, so I'd like you to come back and sit in on the meeting."

"Does he know that we could be involved?" Matt said.

"He is aware that The Developers are Foundation's first choice to code-velop some of the work here," Doug said. "He has looked over some of your work, and he is impressed with it."

"Well, that is a good sign. I'm always looking for the best thing for our company. If a partnership with you and the government could pay off big for The Developers, then I am all for it. I'm sure the guys and girls back at the office would agree."

"I guarantee you two things," Doug said. "First of all, your employees will agree with you because they will see how big this project can be, and will be. You have hired smart people with great work ethic. Secondly, and most importantly, there's no doubt in my mind that this will pay off big time for both of our companies."

***

Although keeping the lights off could have been an option, Katy thought it was in the best interest of everyone involved that the lights should be left on. Not only was it difficult to hold a meeting in a pitch-black room, but it was possible the electricity could generate at least a little bit of extra warmth.

None of the rooms on the second floor had names like the first-floor LAB and WAB. In fact, there were just five total rooms on the second floor. The meeting room, as Katy and the others called it, was obviously the most spacious, and it was slightly larger than the WAB. Of course, four of the rooms upstairs were once used as bedrooms, while the fifth was, and still is, a bathroom. The other rooms were most likely empty, although for all Katy knew, they could have been used to store Butch's used cheese puff canisters.

"Ladies and ... ladies. As president, I will lead us, just as we do in every meeting, by reciting our mission statement."

"We pledge to uphold the law, as citizens of this great nation and of Malorett, Michigan, to be true to form, display our best efforts and continue to proclaim our keen fashion sense as members of the Black Miniskirt Cult."

"Let us now take roll call. Of course, I, Butch Hodges, president and club founder, am here. Now, please say 'aye' if I call your name."

"Sarina Metcalfe?"

"Aye."

"Patty Benningfield?"

"Aye."

"Katy Terrill?"

"Aye."

"Ginger Winfield?"

No response.

"Ginger Winfield, are you here?"

"Butch, it's pretty obvious Ginger is not here," Katy said. "There are only five of us in the room."

"Good point, Katy. Let's move on. Last but not least, Ethel McMahan?"

"Aye, sonny."

"Glad you could make it tonight, Ethel," Butch said. "I couldn't remember if this conflicted with bingo."

"It did, but that's OK," Ethel said. "I let Jimmy Dickson take my troll with him, so maybe I'll get a few bucks off pull tabs or something."

If only the guy Developers knew about these meetings, they would probably be standing outside, looking through the window with the binoculars. At least, they could look at Sarina, Katy and Patty, who all had gorgeous legs, thighs and butts, especially when nestled inside a black miniskirt. Ethel, well, any lady who would still want to put herself in a miniskirt at age 104 has to be given some credit.

It was generally a tossup as to which was more perplexing: Ethel, the walker and the miniskirt, or Butch, the smiley face T-shirt and the miniskirt. What was even more dumbfounding was that Butch never seemed to show any regret whatsoever that he was showing off his legs, shaved at that. At first, Katy and Sarina suspected he was just in it to see the girls in their skirts. But after five months, they never caught him looking at their legs. He simply liked dressing in women's clothing.

"OK girls, let's get down to business," Butch said. "We are looking at potentially doing some activities in the upcoming months. One idea was a bake sale. Another was Katy and Sarina performing a striptease out on the street."

"Who suggested that?" Katy demanded.

"It was me," Ethel said. "I would do it, but by the time I took all my clothes off, everyone would have gone home."

"Anyway, these are the ideas on the table," Butch said. "Well, if we had a table, they would be on the table. So what should we do?"

"Hold on a second," Katy said. "Let's be realistic here. We are basically an underground club. How can we have a bake sale? How can we do any of these things? We would blow our cover!"

The others thought about this for a second and nodded in agreement.

"Maybe we need to rethink our policies or something," Sarina said. "Or maybe we could change our name."

"No way!" Butch said. "This is the Black Miniskirt Cult! We cannot change our name!"

"Well then we might as well cast ourselves off into oblivion," Ethel said. "Butch, we all know you and I can't wear these things in public."

"Yeah, I've tried WAY too many times," Butch whispered.

"But maybe we can keep the name and not wear it all the time," Ethel continued. "Plus, we have a few girls who can wear these garments."

Ethel pointed to the other three girls in the room.

"Another problem is the weather," Patty said. "When it's 20 below, and we have to come to the meetings here in this room, with little heat. I think maybe we should change the format somewhat."

"Not only that, but we have just six members!" Katy said. "Maybe if we could get a few more folks to join, we could do some of these other things."

"Excellent point, Katy," Ethel said. "Does anyone know a person or two who could join?"

"What about Drew's wife, Jessica?" Sarina asked.

"What about all the guys?" Butch asked.

"No way, we can't get those guys involved," Katy said. "They would never be able to live by the mission statement. But Jessica might be a possibility. Maybe we can ask her at the ski trip tomorrow."

"Good idea," Sarina said. "I could ask Rex if he wants to join."

"Who is Rex?" Ethel said.

"He's just a guy I met, and he sort of resembles Richard Simmons," Sarina said.

"OH MY GOODNESS," Ethel said. "Let's get him in here! I just love those *Sweatin' to the Oldies* tapes! They get my heart a-pumping!"

"There are a few girls at the bank I could ask," Patty said. "I didn't know we were opening up enrollment."

"Yes, the only way we will survive is with at least a few more members," Butch said. "Once they get in here, maybe we can decide on what avenues we need to take to make the cult thrive like it once did."

"I hate to break the news to you Butch, but the cult has never thrived," Katy said. "I mean, you just started it a few months ago."

"Good point," Butch said. "All right girls, then it is settled. We'll try to find some new recruits and get them in the cult. Now all we need to determine is some sort of initiation into the club. We can't make it that easy for them."

"I'll come up with something really good," Ethel said.

"OK, meeting is adjourned," Butch said. "Let's go out and find some new members! And Katy and Sarina, if you are still willing to do that striptease, just let me know."

Butch smiled, grabbed a half-full canister of cheese puffs from the floor and bolted toward the door. Before he left, though, he gave his miniskirt a swift tug on the bottom, because it was riding up on him again.

THIRTEEN

"Are you sure we are going the right way?" said Jessica, barely able to see the road through the windshield because the snow was piling up rapidly.

"This has to be the way," said Drew, trying to keep the windshield clean. "Matt said it was just outside of town, on Highway 22. I'm sure we are almost there."

As soon as Drew said this, both he and Jessica saw the sign for Ski Frenzy. The ski area just north of Malorett should be packed, they thought, as the current conditions were favorable for excellent paths. It was almost noon, and The Developers were supposed to meet at the front entrance in just a couple minutes. Luckily, the roads were still in pretty good condition because the snow had started only an hour earlier. The accumulation was supposed to be under a couple of inches, which was nothing in the Upper Peninsula region this time of year.

Drew was extremely happy to get out of the office for a few hours. The project had been toying with his mind the last few days. He couldn't seem to concentrate long enough to completely fix any of the minor problems, but he was able to plug up a few holes long enough to think in more detail at a later date. The progress, and the vision of expanded progress, was putting Drew on the verge of a mental breakdown. This short vacation, along with the bingo later in the evening, would surely ease some of the tension.

"OK, now remind me again who is going to be here?" said Jessica, lugging her skis from the car.

"Well you know Matt, Katy, Sarina and Kevin," Drew said. "At least, you know who they are ... do you remember what they look like?"

"Not really. I just remember Kevin as the guy who ate everything and Sarina being the runner. And of course I know Matt, but I'm not sure I remember who Katy is. Does she have blonde hair?"

"Yes, well, it's kind of a dirty blonde."

"She's a dirty blonde?"

"You would have to ask Matt about that."

"I'll leave that between you two. Tell me about the others."

"I don't really know that much about them. Kevin is bringing some girl he is dating who is friends with his sister. And Sarina is bringing a guy she met online. He supposedly looks like Richard Simmons."

"And this is a good thing?"

"I guess for her, it is."

"So Matt and Katy ... are coming as a pair?"

"Your guess is as good as mine."

Drew and Jessica made it to the entrance, where Matt and Katy were waiting. Kevin and Sarina were nowhere to be found.

"Hey guys," said Drew, leaning his skis next to a bench beside Katy. "Where are Kevin and Sarina?"

"Kevin said he would meet us inside," Matt said. "He had to pick up Jane this morning, but in reality I think he was leaving from Moxee to begin with. How are you Jessica? I haven't seen you in a while."

"I'm fine Matt, thanks," Jessica said. "It has been awhile, hasn't it? I guess that's what happens when you're busy all the time."

"That's for sure," Matt said. "Sorry to keep your husband from you for so many hours each day."

"Yeah, it gets really bad when the two of them snuggle all the time," Katy said. "Talk about not getting any work done!"

Everyone had a good laugh, then everyone's attention turned toward the parking lot. They saw Sarina, bundled up with jacket and winter hat, standing next to a man who appeared to be wearing shorts! Surely this was not her date, the group thought. Surely he had enough sense to wear long pants to go skiing. As they approached, the group realized that he was wearing long pants, but they were almost flesh-colored and somewhat resembled long underwear. Above those, though, he was wearing bright red nylon shorts. If there was ever going to be a fashion statement made on the slopes, this could be the day.

"Hi guys!" Sarina said. "I would like you to meet Rex Burns." Sarina adjusted her cap and grabbed Rex's skis for a moment. Sarina had been skiing on a few occasions, but she didn't have her own set. Luckily, Rex had an extra set to loan. "This is Matt, Katy, Drew and Jessica."

"It is so wonderful to meet you!" said Rex, enthusiastically shaking their hands, although all were wearing gloves.

"So Rex, Sarina has told us a little about you," Katy said. "But she never mentioned if you like to ski or not."

"I like to ski from time to time," Rex said. "I usually don't have too much time to do so. We occasionally try to take the club skiing at least once a year. It's something to at least break up the monotony, and of course it can be excellent exercise."

"I'm sorry, Rex, but what club are you talking about?" Drew said.

"Oh, my mistake," Rex said. "The Malorett Weight Watchers Group. I don't actually work there, but one of my friends runs the club. I occasionally try to help him out. He knows I watch my weight and eat healthy and exercise. He counts on me to be motivation for some of these people who might need it."

Matt started to ask, "Who do you think you are, Richard Simmons?" but Katy elbowed him in the stomach. She knew he was going to say something like that, and she didn't want to cause a scene this early.

"So what do you do for a living?" Drew said.

"I work as a bank manager ... nothing extremely spectacular," Rex said. "But there are a lot of good people there."

"What's up with the shorts?" Matt said. Katy couldn't stop him this time.

"I just HAVE to wear these shorts," Rex said. "It's like my calling card, something that's always with me. I mean, I don't wear them to work, just participating in athletic activities. Would you like a pair? I got them at ... "

"Uh, maybe later," Matt said. "I guess we should go ahead and start skiing. I'm supposed to meet with the owner here in a few minutes."

The caravan entered Ski Frenzy. It contained four cross-country skiing trails at different levels of difficulty. Although no one was an skiing expert, Drew and Jessica had more experience than the others. Initially, they decided to go around the easy loop twice, predicting Kevin would show up within that time frame. The loop was less than a mile, which would give them the opportunity to see Kevin if he appeared.

Rex was a hit with the group. Everyone had questions about his philosophies on staying in shape, eating right, etc. He seemed to speak genuinely about his views, and on top of that, he had no problem explaining each point intricately. He broke down the types of sugars and their purposes for Jessica and also devised a quick 20-minute workout routine for Drew based on his favorite activities.

Matt enjoyed the conversation, but was still somewhat skeptical. Or maybe it wasn't the skepticism, but the feeling that this Rex guy was just trying to be Richard Simmons. Even his voice, which was definitely a cross between an effeminate man and Rod Stewart, sounded as close to Simmons as humanly possible. But why would anyone go out of their way to imitate him? This point alone seemed reason enough to believe that Rex respected Simmons and honestly wanted to be like him, but not an exact duplicate. Of course, Simmons didn't work at a bank, but he might if they gave out sugar-free lollipops at the drive-through.

As the group returned from its second trip through the loop, they saw Kevin and Jane near the head of the trails. Matt was the first to approach the couple.

"Glad you guys could make it!" Matt said. "What took you so long?"

"The roads are a little slick out there, so we were just being careful," Kevin said. "But it's nothing too bad. Just some flurries most of the way here. I'd like everyone to meet Jane."

"Hello Jane!" Rex shouted.

"He speaks for all of us," Sarina said.

"Well hello to you," Jane said. "I'm not that great of a skier, so I hope if I fall down, you won't make fun of me."

"Jane, you must be positive in your abilities!" Rex said. "That is the only way you will exceed in life!"

Kevin glanced down at Rex's getup.

"And who are you, Richard Simmons?" Kevin asked.

Rex, still in his skis like the others, scooted over toward Kevin, leaned over and attempted to kiss him on the cheek. Kevin flinched, basically because he had no idea what the hell was happening. Rex missed, picked up too much speed and gradually passed beside him. While the others looked shocked and laughed a bit, Rex returned to the back of the group, next to Sarina.

"Richard is my bud," Rex said. "Thank you so much for the wonderful comment. I hope I didn't startle you."

"Um, I'm not sure what you would call it," Kevin said. "But that was different. I guess I'm not used to guys trying to kiss me. Now girls ... " He leaned over and put his head on Jane's shoulder. "Girls, I'm a little bit more used to." Kevin gave Jane a quick peck on the cheek.

"Well guys, I'm sorry I'm going to miss the end of this Lifetime movie, but I have an appointment with Jim Sanders, the owner of some of the trails up this way," Matt said. "It'll probably last an hour or so. I guess you can just take one of the trails, then I'll catch up with you later."

"Let's take the Bear Trail," Katy said. "It's an easy trail, plus we have to take part of the Wolf Trail to even get over to it. If we make decent time, we'll be back in an hour."

"Sounds good to me," Drew said. "I want to ski as much as possible while we're here!"

"All right guys, I'll see you in a little while," said Matt, sitting on a bench and removing his skis.

The remaining seven members of the group started toward the Bear Trail. Drew and Jessica stayed near the front with Kevin and Jane, and Rex stayed just behind them. In the meantime, Sarina and Katy moved slower and slower behind to talk.

"So what do you think of Rex?" Sarina said.

"Honestly? Besides the whole overbearing thing about health and fitness, he seems like a nice guy," Katy said.

"You think it's overbearing?"

"Well maybe not for you ... because you are the same way!"

"Oh, thanks for the vote of confidence there. So I noticed that you and Matt seem to be a little closer than normal. What's going on there?"

"Nothing Sarina. When everyone else has a date ... we're just kind of stuck together for today, I guess."

"Maybe you should have invited Michael!"

"I hope I don't have to talk to that guy ever again. You know what he told me the other day? He said that he might stop by the office some day. Why would he stop by the office? Some guys just never understand."

"That's an understatement. Hey, they are getting really far ahead of us. We should catch up."

Sarina and Katy pushed forward a little faster to get back to the rest of the group. Up at the front, Jane and Jessica discussed their vitamin intake with Rex, while Kevin and Drew talked briefly about work and .comU.

"Can you believe that right now, there are hundreds, possibly thousands, of people using a system that you basically built by yourself?" Kevin said.

"No way, I didn't do that anywhere close to by myself," Drew said. "Everyone put in their efforts. I just happened to do a lot of the programming.

"But even still, yeah, it's hard to believe. But what's harder to believe is people can be using that system while we are out here skiing."

"Then again, it is Saturday. Maybe no one is using it at all."

"Well if they are, and if they are having problems, I just hope the Tech students are helping them out."

"I'm sure as we speak, Crissy is making friends on her webcam. So are you looking forward to the bingo tonight?"

"Yes and no. It'll be interesting to see if the system works out OK. But it is work. I just hope that while the bingo is occurring, something else doesn't break. The people at the bingo would never forgive me for that."

The trip along the Bear Trail went by fast. The group returned to the chalet close to 2:30. Matt wasn't there, but everyone agreed it would be good to take a little break. Kevin and Jane went inside to grab hot chocolate for the others. The snow had tapered off, and the sun was out, turning a rather drab day into a somewhat comfortable one. The temperature had reached 20 degrees, and there was relatively no wind. Combine that with a good deal of exercise, and no one appeared to be too frozen.

Kevin and Jane returned with trays of hot chocolate. The group members had removed their skis and had entered a resting area within the chalet. It wasn't directly heated, but it was about 15 degrees warmer than it was outside, probably because it was connected to the snack bar. Just as everyone found a seat, Matt appeared in the doorway.

"Good timing!" Sarina said. "We just made it over here, and here's an extra hot chocolate for you."

"Thanks," Matt said. "The meeting went well. I need to write up a pro-posal for Jim, but there's a good chance we'll get something together for him in the near future."

"Cool," Kevin said. "Besides, we don't have that much time to work on a humongous project like that anyway. There's plenty of stuff left to do for .comU!"

"You guys aren't done skiing, are you?" Matt said.

"I could go around again on all the trails, at least three times!" Rex said.

"Calm down, my boy Rex," Matt said. "How about we head over to the Wolf Trail and see how long we last."

"Sounds good to me," said Drew, as Jessica nodded in accordance.

Everyone finished their hot chocolate, reattached their skis and headed back out to the trails. When they were in the breakroom, Jane had mentioned she played basketball at Moxee Tech, and Drew was extremely interested in how the team was doing. While they talked, Kevin told Jessica a little bit about his relationship with Jane, traveling back and forth between Malorett and Moxee and other odds and ends. Rex and Sarina took off down the trail, apparently racing to see who could get to the end the fastest.

That left Matt and Katy behind the parade, each appearing as if they had something to say, but neither saying too much of anything.

"It's amazing how they can keep the snow groomed so well," Matt said. "I wonder how they do it?"

"I think they use power tilling, which packs the snow down better," Katy said. "But I really don't know that much about it."

"It would be cool to ski more often than once a millennium."

"Yeah ... there's just not enough time in the day to get everything accom-plished."

"Katy, are you happy with everything at work right now? Sometimes you seem kind of distant and stuff."

"Distant? I don't think I'm distant. What makes you think that?"

"Nothing in particular. Or maybe it's just that ... never mind."

"What?"

"Maybe it's just that I think more about you than the others. It's like my nature to do this, just because of our past."

"But that's what it is. It's a past."

"Is that ALL it is to you?"

Katy really wasn't in the mood to go through this again.

"What do you want from me, Matt?" Katy said. "I spend so much time at work that I don't really have much time to have a life of my own as it is. So why are we even discussing this?"

"I don't know," Matt said. "I guess I just miss you sometimes. It's weird to miss someone you see every single day."

"Well that's definitely true. But you know good and well it wouldn't work out. Not under these circumstances."

"What circumstances?"

"The fact that we work together the way we do. The fact that any personal relationship shouldn't interfere with the project, at this point. The fact that we tried before, and it didn't work!"

"So you are saying that if we didn't work together, this would work?"

Katy shook her head and started skiing a bit faster. Matt gave two good pushes and caught her immediately.

"You're missing the point," Katy said. "There's no reason to discuss what-ifs. A personal relationship between us can be only platonic right now. Trying to find out where I stand on anything else would be a complete waste of time."

"I don't think so," Matt said. "I value your opinion on a lot of things. But don't you ever think about me, I mean other than just work-related things?"

"Well yes, but ... "

"Well if that's the case, then that steps out of the work realm."

"But that doesn't mean too much. I mean, Sarina and I hang out outside of work. Does that mean I want to have a sexual relationship with her?"

"So now it's about sex? That's not what I was getting at."

"For crying out loud Matt, that's what it is ALWAYS about."

Matt wasn't sure how to answer that. He wasn't going to deny sexual feelings for Katy. But he didn't want this conversation to escalate any further. It was apparent that their current status would not change overnight.

"All right Katy, you win," Matt said. "I guess the only point I was trying to make is that I still think there could be something between us, and I don't want to give up just because we work together. If you don't see it, then tell me now."

"We have to be just friends," Katy said. "No matter how you look at it, that's the way it has to be."

"But we can still meet up for fish every once in awhile, right?"

"Sure Matt, we can still have dinner. Only if you are paying!"

Matt and Katy realized the group was far ahead, so they decided to go a little bit faster. They sped past a few other skiers, laughing when Matt ended up off the trail and fell to the ground after scooting down a small incline. When they finally made it back to the trailhead, the others were standing there waiting.

"Were you guys making out on the trail?" Kevin said. "Because there are some good spots for that, right Jane?"

Jane slapped Kevin on the back.

"No, we were just going really slow," Katy said. "And then we realized you guys were too far ahead."

"Yeah, we've been waiting here for about 10 minutes," Drew said.

"Where are Rex and Sarina?" Matt said.

"Oh they took off to the loop," Kevin said. "They just went past a minute ago. I think they both had at least 15 cups of coffee this morning or there was too much sugar in their cups of hot chocolate or something. They're even starting to talk faster."

"But he still sounds like he is trying to sound like Richard Simmons," Jessica said.

About that time, Rex and Sarina appeared, both sweating profusely.

"I won! I won!" Rex shouted, pumping his fists.

"I let you win," Sarina said. "There's no way you could beat me again!"

"Oh, do you really think that?"

Sarina unlatched her skis, and while Rex was attempting to take his off, she ran over and tried to jump on his back. Fortunately for Rex, she missed, and fell into a newly shoveled snow pile. Rex stood up and reached over to help Sarina out of the pile.

"Babe, watch out," Rex said. "You are going to hurt yourself!"

"But Rex, I love you!" Sarina said. "You are great!"

Sarina followed that with a passionate kiss, as the others looked on. Kevin tugged on Drew's jacket, and Drew leaned over toward Kevin.

"That's something you don't see every day," Kevin said softly. "A guy with shorts on over pants being romantically attacked."

The crew removed its skis. It was 4:30, and everyone was pretty hungry.

"Who's up for Dave's?" Matt said.

Although no one explicitly shouted, Matt noticed a fair amount of nodding heads.

"Then it's settled," Matt said. "Let's go to Dave's, have a hearty dinner, then for those of you who are going to the bingo, let's get rested up."

"Doesn't a hearty dinner kind of sound like we are having dog food?" Kevin said.

"I always eat a hearty dinner!" Rex said. "Does this place have low-fat salad dressing?"

"I don't think Dave's has low-fat anything," Drew said. "Even the straws have calories. But if you can't finish your food, I'm sure Kevin would love to help you out."

"Not only would I like to finish off extra food, but I really enjoy it when people leave their saliva on their hamburger," Kevin said. "It's like extra seasoning. It is delicious!"

"Well I thought I was hungry, but now I'm grossed out," Katy said.

"I can't eat hamburgers! Way too much grease!" Rex said. "Do they have turkey burgers? What about a veggie burger?"

"Just get a burger WITHOUT the burger," Kevin said. "And get an extra glass of water to use as a dipping sauce for your fries."

"Fries?" Rex said. "NOOOOOOOOOOO! I can't eat fries."

Kevin walked over and put his arm around Rex.

"I tell you what Rex," Kevin said. "You can sit right by me, and I'll eat whatever you don't want to eat."

Rex nodded, and the others rolled their eyes. The Richard Simmons lookalike handing food to the George Foreman wannabe was about as symbiotic of a relationship as you could get.

FOURTEEN

"May I have your attention please?" Drew announced to the crowd accumulating at the Knights of Columbus Hall. "I have an unfortunate statement to make. The Freeze machine is broken. They are working on the problem as I speak, and they hope to have it fixed before halftime. Sorry for the inconvenience."

"BOOOOOOOO!!!" shouted the overzealous crowd, although most of them had probably never even tried a Freeze. Like most bingo halls, the Knights of Columbus concession stand was the spot to be just before the real games began. It was 11:30 p.m., and a light lingering snow had not deterred the attendance for .comU's first public event. Gene Simons added a short story in today's paper, and apparently, it had worked. The main room was packed, and the auxiliary room, set aside for non-smoking, was running out of room as well. Drew estimated there must be at least 300 people just in the bingo hall and probably 75 in the non-smoking area, and others were still entering.

Sarina, seated to Drew's left on the caller stage, checked the status of the online participants. The group had virtually no idea how many people within .comU would be playing along. The turnout was astonishing. According to the statistics, Sarina showed another 1,000 people ready to play. The system emailed users a registration form earlier in the week to participate in the midnight bingo. It stated that if the turnout was successful, there was a chance that it could become a weekly event. There were close to 1,400 people who registered, so Sarina expected more bingo players were rushing to their computers now. Let's face it: Would a true bingo player turn down a free bingo, even if it occurred at midnight?

The prizes were donations from various businesses; most were $50 gift certificates, but most impressive was the coverall prize. Phil Harris of the Harris Hotel Enterprise managed to put up a weekend getaway in New York, including airfare and hotel accommodations. This alone gave the hotel guru top billing on .comU and in the newspaper story and advertisements.

There were a few differences from this bingo and a normal Malorett bingo. There would be just 10 games and each player had only three cards. Most sets come with cards in packs of nine or 18, but for simplicity's sake, and for the sake of the online players, the cards were limited to three apiece. Everyone who entered the hall had to give their .comU username to show they participated in the event. Besides being able to win prizes for this particular outing, users also earned 25 points for the system, which could be redeemed in some fashion at a later date.

One thing would remain the same about this bingo session: It would have Malorett's most-renowned caller behind the balls. Drew had attained a god-like status among the local bingo crowd. To make matters worse, some of the players at St. Pius often refused to attend on days when Drew wasn't calling. Ethel McMahan summed it up the best when she called Drew the best caller since the Civil War. Considering there were only a couple of years between the end of the war and Ethel's birth, she could justify a statement like that.

Most of the St. Pius crew got to Knights of Columbus early and sat near the front. Ethel, Jimmy Dickson, Dale Washington, Chet Marshall and Martha Singleton grabbed the first row closest to the calling stage. As the clock grew closer to midnight, and the crowd continued to file in, Ethel tried in vain to get Drew's attention.

"Hey Drew, do me a favor and lick G-49 for me," Ethel said.

Drew set his nachos down and stood up from his seat.

"Lick G-49?" Drew said. "Why on earth would I do that?"

"I needed that damn number three times last week. I don't want to see it here. If you lick it, the ball will stay on the bottom and not come up."

"Well I did not know that. Thanks for the info."

"No problem, honey bunny."

The place was packed. They didn't have to turn anyone away, but it appeared there were people standing in the back as Drew called game one. Sarina gave Drew the tally online — 1,287 made it to the system. Including all the people at the hall, that had to be pretty close to 2,000. Sarina and Drew estimated that had to be close to 40 percent of .comU subscribers ... and a large chunk of Malorett's population. Anything this large had to be considered a success.

Sarina instant messaged Matt, who was back at the office, to alert him that the bingo was beginning. Matt wanted someone to be in the office, just in case something went wrong, a server had to be rebooted, anything like that. He had also answered a few emails from people preparing to play online.

Luckily, the format was pretty simple. The cards were generated for each game, and when Drew called a number, Sarina entered it into the online administration. If online users wanted to call 'bingo,' all they had to do was message Sarina and send their user ID and their generated bingo card ID. Sarina then would enter the 12-digit bingo card ID into the administration, which would spit out the same card, using the same algorithm, and also fill in the numbers called. The system that Drew had built was not complex and not extremely automated, but it made it possible for live and online users to play at the same time.

Someone in the hall won the first game, while an online user picked up the second one. Both Ethel and Dale Washington had cases in the second game, but they were denied. Becky Washington, Dale's granddaughter, was working the crowd as a bingo helper. Drew asked Becky again if she would be interested in helping him test part of .comU, and she said yes. Drew thought he could definitely use her help, if he ever had a chance to finish some of the things he was supposed to finish. When that was going to happen, he had no idea.

The two maintenance workers told Drew after game three that the Freeze machine was back in business. The crowd roared in delight once Drew reported this, and there was a 10-minute delay before the fourth game due to the concession stand rush. Martha Singleton bingoed using the four corners, which everyone thought was appropriate for the fourth game, and an online player took game five. Game Six would be coverall, but there would be a short intermission before the game began.

"Hey Drew, do you want more nachos?" Sarina said, heading toward the concession stand.

"No, I'm OK, Sarina," Drew said.

"Well I'm going to run over there and get a barbecue sandwich. I'm starving! I just sent out a blanket message to the site saying we were going to have 15 minutes until the next game."

"Good idea. Thanks for doing that. Is Matt having any problems at the office?"

"He seems to be doing OK, getting some paperwork finished. He mentioned that we would have a quick meeting at 2 p.m. tomorrow, just for us to report how everything went tonight."

"Did he tell Kevin and Katy too?"

"Yeah, I think he told them right after dinner. I know Kevin was going over to Jane's tonight, but I'm not sure where Katy went. She should have come down here and hung out with us!"

I think she made the right decision, Drew thought. Although he did manage to take a quick nap after dinner, he was getting pretty tired. The bingo was supposed to be over by 1:30, but after the Freeze incident, and with the coverall looming, Drew was doubtful he would leave before 2. He decided to call semi-speed bingo to help make up for some of the lost time.

Everyone concentrated on their cards for the coverall. No one moved toward the bathroom or the concession stand. They knew what was at stake — a trip to New York City. Before the game, Ethel mentioned the last time she visited New York, Truman was president and she didn't even know what bingo was then. Everyone at the St. Pius table gasped, almost as if they thought SHE had actually invented bingo. Ethel quickly explained that although bingo was around before her time, she did invent strip bingo. The table then grew quiet for Drew's 18th number.

"I-17," Drew said, as Sarina input the number into the .comU bingo processor. Just then, the overhead lights began to flicker. Drew looked up, then at the crowd, then over at Sarina. Everyone seemed to be hesitant to daub their cards, but the lights suddenly commanded full power again. Sarina gave a sigh of relief, while Drew went ahead and grabbed another Ping-Pong ball.

Then the Knights of Columbus Hall went pitch black.

"Ladies and gentleman, please stay calm and quiet," Drew said. "Everything is going to be OK."

The announcement was too late. Chaos had begun. Some people were flinging their bingo cushion seats in the air, trying to figure out exactly where they were. Other people were scrounging around for their daubers and screaming that thieves were taking their cards and their Lime Freezes. A few folks even rushed to the exit, that is, if you can actually rush anywhere while using a walker. A handful of flashlights clicked on, as apparently smart bingo players carry crisis instruments in case something like this occurs.

The maintenance men who fixed the Freeze machine told Drew they were going to check the breakers in the basement. There was some light in the front because a full moon shined through a large window near the front entrance.

"Where am I?" Ethel said. "Am I dead? Am I asleep? I thought I was playing bingo?"

"You are, hot stuff," Jimmy Dickson said. "This is what I like to call bingo mood lighting. Are you in the mood yet?"

"I'm always in the mood," Martha said. "In the mood to play bingo, that is!"

"Everyone ... everyone please stay seated!" Drew's comments weren't helping the situation. Two women in the back fought over their daubers. Another gentleman started an argument with a trash can. A few more people produced flashlights, but it was still difficult to see in the back of the room. The bedlam appeared to be escalating.

Meanwhile, Sarina was sending messages furiously to online participants, alerting them to the situation. Her computer was using its battery supply, which would last for maybe another 20 minutes.

"Drew, what should I tell them?" Sarina said. "That we'll come back on when the power comes back on? I'm getting too many instant messages, and my power might die soon. This is crazy!"

"Yeah, tell them we'll be back up in a minute," Drew said. "Hopefully the maintenance guys will fix the situation."

"Some of these people are irate because it's not effecting them. Power appears to be good throughout Malorett, so let's hope they get that breaker fixed."

"It shouldn't be long. Tell them ... wait a minute, I have an idea."

Drew reached for the ball he had set down five minutes earlier, when the power went out.

"The next number ... O-70," Drew said.

The place was silent for a moment. Then everyone scurried back to their seats. Those people in the front adjusted their seats to use the natural light from the moon, while those seated in the back shared their flashlights with one another. It was like magic ... all of the arguments stopped, except for the man yelling at the garbage can. Finally, one of his friends pulled him back to his cards.

Sarina hurriedly entered the number into the system and warned the at-home players the game would be continuing. Drew gave everyone a little extra time to find their numbers, and find their cards. A couple of people threw theirs away, but they were able to gather them together in time to continue.

It appeared to be calm again at the Knights of Columbus Hall. All eyes were on the playing cards, and all ears were tuned to hear the bingo-calling voice of Drew Davis. He reported number after number, yet no one seemed to be closing in on a victory.

"B-10," Drew announced as the 50th number, and a slight grimace fell over the crowd. B-10 was the last B to be called. Drew had worked up a reputation of calling a lot of B's, except in games like the Four Corners, when B's are essential. At this point, Drew was definitely ready for the game to end.

Just as Drew reached for another ball, Sarina received a message that someone online had a bingo. She announced the bingo to the crowd.

"Damn the online users!" Ethel said, flipping her cards. "Those fools probably made their own cards!"

Sarina verified the bingo. Some players in the crowd got up, as if they were going to leave. It made sense, Drew thought, considering the time and the light problems. And as if on cue, the lights came on. The maintenance guys came through the basement door and issued Drew a thumbs up. The audience noticed the maintenance men's return and gave them a standing ovation. One of the guys approached the stage.

"Yep, it was the breaker," the maintenance man said.

"Why did it take so long to turn it back on?" Drew said.

"We just had a hard time getting to the breaker box. I have no clue when the last time someone was actually in that basement. I'm not sure what overloaded it ... possibly the extra lights in the non-smoking room. I don't think that room gets used too much."

"Well I'm just glad you were able to correct the problem. We did manage to finish one game while the lights were out."

"While they were out? How did you do that?"

"Some people had flashlights. The moon is pretty bright when all the lights were off. We were OK."

The maintenance man started to walk away, then he spun back toward the stage.

"That's kind of funny, playing bingo in a bingo hall with the lights out," the man said.

"How so?" said Sarina, standing to stretch her legs.

"Well, you have all these people gathered here, and they can see each other. Then you have all the people at home who can't see each other, but they know there are other people playing.

"It just seems like sometimes, the Internet is like a big room that doesn't have much light. You know there are other people out there, but you have no idea what they look like, or really, who they are. You know only what their current actions are, and if you are interacting with them, you know that potentially, you both share a common goal."

With that, the maintenance man left to join his partner at the concession stand. Drew and Sarina looked at each other, mesmerized at what the man just said. It may have been the greatest comment ever made by a Knights of Columbus maintenance man.

"Come on, ya fool!" Ethel said, pelting Drew with one of her trolls that wasn't extremely lucky. "We still have four games to go, and all of us old folks get up at 6 o'clock."

"OK, Ethel, you're right," Drew said. "Let's finish these games and get the hell out of here, or else we may have to eat nachos for breakfast. Not that it would be the first time I ever did that."

***

The late-night bingo charade was evident at the office Sunday early afternoon. Matt, usually an early riser for every occasion, arrived at noon. The rest of the clan got there sometime after 1:30 since the meeting was scheduled to start at 2. Matt didn't get too much done beforehand, considering he didn't get to bed until 4. The bingo ended around 3, but the snow started piling up a bit before then. Malorett received 6 inches of new snow, but according to the weatherman, there was supposed to be a heat wave, with temperatures in the low 40s, for the upcoming week.

"Sarina, did you bring your blow-up pillow?" said Drew, extending his right arm across the boardroom table as his forehead still lay on the table.

"If I did, I would be using it," said Sarina, slouched back in her chair. "Unfortunately, I was way too tired to remember it."

"Well maybe we should go ahead and get the meeting started," Matt said. "Why are we having a meeting again?"

"That was your idea, slick," said Katy, writing notes as if she had to transcribe Jane Eyre by the end of the hour. "I've got some things, if you can't think of anything."

"OK Katy, why don't you lead the meeting," Matt said. "I'll just lie back ... er, sit back and listen."

"That sounds excellent," said Katy, standing while shuffling her papers. "I know we've all been busy as of late, but it seems as if the bugs are working themselves out, and also, we will soon be able to launch the second phase of .comU. I've made a short list of those items that were to be part of phase two, so I want to see how far ... what, Kevin?"

Kevin raised his hand, although it wasn't extended too far in the air.

"Can we move this meeting to Dave's or something?" Kevin said. "I'm freaking starving."

"Buckeye's is closer," Drew said. "Maybe we should just go there."

"Maybe you guys should eat before showing up at a meeting!" Katy said.

"Well some of us were working late!" Drew said.

"Yeah, and some of us were up late ... doing ... other things!" Kevin said.

"All right guys, calm down," Matt said. "We need to go over this stuff. Then we can eat afterwards."

"Thank you, Matt," Katy said. "The first thing on the list is The Profiler information. I know Sarina and Drew have been working on this. Where do we stand?"

"The actual database work and the page work is pretty much complete," Sarina said. "We're still waiting on some of the data though."

"It composes about 80 percent of Malorett," Drew said. "We just want to have the whole enchilada."

"Mmmmmm ... enchiladas," Kevin said.

"They're just not sure what to do," Sarina said. "So that's why we are officially waiting."

"Well thanks for the update," Katy said. "What about CellBook?"

"I have what should be a final meeting with the local wireless providers Tuesday," Matt said. "This should launch sometime the week afterward. Sarina has the lists from the companies, and they are willing to release the numbers if there is an incentive behind it."

"That's great news," said Matt, having a hard time sitting up straight in his seat. "Katy, where are we with company ads and sponsorships?"

"We're now up to 17 ... Kevin confirmed another yesterday," Katy said.

"Yeah, I had a little chat with the manager at Dave's," Kevin said. "He figured as often as we go there to hold meetings, he could advertise on the site, and maybe make a few more customers. Speaking of which, maybe we should head on down there now."

"Good try," Katy said. "Now we're almost finished anyway. How close are we to having Connect going?"

"That is an excellent question," Drew said. "I really haven't devoted nearly as much time lately to it as I would have liked. I would like to get the forums running first, definitely."

"So when will the forums be running?" Katy said.

"I say next week," Drew said.

"And I say let's go to Dave's!" Kevin proclaimed.

"If I'm going to stay here much longer, I'm going to need some food," Drew said.

"OK, that sounds good," Matt said. "Ladies, are you hungry as well?"

"Um, I need to get out of here and get my run in," Sarina said.

"And I just ate before I came in," Katy said.

Drew, Matt and Kevin exited, while Katy and Sarina stayed in the LAB. Katy walked around the table and sat down next to Sarina, but before she said anything, they heard a slight commotion outside. Katy got back up, ran to the door and looked down the hallway. Butch had met the guys at the door, and Katy suspected Butch was asking Matt again for the rent check. Katy returned, and a minute later, Butch entered the LAB.

"So ladies," said Butch, wearing his favorite, the purple smiley face T-shirt. "Did we pick up any new members for the cult?"

"Well ... possibly," Sarina said. "Jessica, Drew's wife, really isn't sure about it. She doesn't know if she can make all the meetings."

"Tell him why you're not sure if she's sure or not," Katy said.

"Well, I didn't really tell her what our cult was," Sarina said. "Why should I bring her into the identity crisis?"

"Oh, good gravy," Butch said. "How are we going to get people to join if you don't tell them what the club is?"

"The good news is she did find at least one enthusiastic member," said Katy, nudging Sarina.

"Yeah, Rex is pretty hyped about joining," Sarina said.

"That is great news!" Butch said. "Does he know what the club is about?"

"Yep," Sarina said.

"So what's the problem here?" Butch said.

"He just seemed ... too enthused," Sarina said.

"But he's too enthused about everything," Katy said.

"That is a good point," Sarina said.

"All right, now we just need an initiation day," said Butch, pulling out a blank notepad. "Hmm, Thursday looks good for me."

"Dude, that's a blank notepad," Sarina said.

"OK, if you want to be specific, every day looks like a good day," Butch said. "But Thursdays always seem the best."

"Thursday is fine with us," Katy said. "And he'll definitely have to wear a black miniskirt, no matter if we change our identity, for the initiation."

"Let's just hope he doesn't make it a habit to wear it every day," Sarina said.

FIFTEEN

Kevin wasn't sure how to react to Matt's Sunday night phone call, telling him to arrive at work at 8 a.m. sharp. If something needed to be fixed immediately, surely he would have just asked him to fix it, Kevin thought. Or if it was a meeting with everyone, maybe he would have told him. But Matt didn't tell him a damn thing. On top of that, Kevin was in the middle of enjoying a snack from Taco Bell: a gordita, two soft tacos and some nachos. Matt, though, assured him it was important, and could not wait until Monday morning.

As Kevin navigated through the melting snow, he still had no idea what could be happening. Kevin stayed in Malorett on Sunday night, as Jane was busy studying for a calculus test. Besides, they had been together the previous three days, including the ski trip Saturday, so it was probably best for both of them to return to their regularly scheduled programs. Kevin had an enormous amount of work with .comU, and with the way Sunday's meeting adjourned, it appeared everyone else had just as much.

But no one seemed to mind the long hours. They appreciated the system and each other's dedication to resolving any issues that came up during the development.

Kevin made his way through a half-shoveled pathway, up to the office front door. The sun was out, and temperatures were already above freezing, which was a good sign that the melting process would continue all day.

Matt was intently studying what appeared to be a pamphlet of some sort when Kevin walked into the WAB.

"Where is everyone?" said Kevin, taking a seat in front of his work station. "Are we having a meeting this morning, or what's going on?"

"We are having a meeting," Matt said. "But it's just between you and me, right now."

"Am I in trouble? Did I forget to do something? I think I did everything

... but I was pretty hungry yesterday. You know I get a little delirious when I'm hungry."

"No, no, it's not that. I just thought I could talk to you about something, and you would be completely honest about it. I think your opinion could really be valuable."

Kevin stood up and paced toward the opposite side of the room.

"This is about Katy, right?" Kevin said. "I know you still like her. You guys just need to get it out of your system and sleep together. It would make everything better."

"No, this isn't about ... what?" Matt said. "That's illogical, but no, this isn't just about Katy. This is about our company, and a potential new job that could exceed .comU in terms of responsibility and revenue."

"Exceed it in revenue?" said Kevin, taking back his seat. "Well I'm all ears. I thought .comU was our main generating resource. I didn't know there was something else."

"No one knows there's something else. You remember that guy Doug Morris, from Foundation Technologies, one of the .comU sponsors?"

Kevin nodded.

"Well, his company is on the verge of something gigantic," Matt said. "I've been trying to read through this literature, and I don't have it completely figured out. I met with Doug on Thursday, and he proposed that The Developers become part of this grand project his business is performing for the government."

"How is the government involved?" Kevin said.

"This is pretty much how Doug explained it. The government is in the process of building something called the Super Information Portal. From what I've read, this entails laying new lines and creating wireless entities that will allow larger bandwidth and faster connection speeds for everyone connected to the World Wide Web. His company is compiling the schematics for the process, and, along with a few other companies, they will develop this throughout the United States.

"A few years from now, all Internet service providers will be required to be on these new lines. But all computers connected to this new line will be required to pay government access to use it, Doug says. Although the charge is relatively small, if every business and home computer owner is charged a fee per computer to have access, that will total a bunch of money."

"That sounds like an interesting theoretical project, but I can't imagine that actually happening," Kevin said. "Why would the big service providers want to invest in this when they have their own lines?"

"I wondered that too, until I started reading the white pages on the system," Matt said. "Apparently, these companies have engineers who are building the SIP lines. They may even be running this thing jointly, I don't know. Surely they think this will help squelch out the smaller competition. Of course, the smaller competition won't be disallowed; those businesses will have to use the new lines and pay the fees as well."

"What is the time frame on all of this?"

"It is already being built, and they are hoping to have the system in the US finished in five years. I'm sure there will be a little leeway time in moving over to the new lines, though. There still seems to be a lot of speculation on how this will work, but Doug has assured me those guys in Washington know what they are doing. On top of that, the officials Doug has been working with will be in town Wednesday, and Doug wants me to join him in a meeting."

"Wait a minute, though ... how are we going to be part of this plan? We can't build lines or anything."

"That's the same thing I asked Doug. What he wants is for us to build a mechanism to track all of the users."

"Track the users from all ISPs? Matt, I don't think that's legal since most people have contracts through their ISPs to not release their information."

"Yeah, I know, that's what I told Doug, but he said this would change as well. I'm not sure how all this will change. I guess we would be tracking this information for the government. I don't know, maybe the Washington contact can answer some of these questions we have."

"So what's in it for The Developers?"

"For our tracking systems, we will receive recurring revenue, at least according to this outline here. We'll receive a certain percentage based on the amount of money collected through the SIP."

"OK, let's think about this for a second," said Kevin, grabbing a notebook and a pencil. "Let's see, by the time this is done, the population will be well over 300 million in the US. Of course not everyone has a computer, but some people have multiple computers ... especially companies that have tons of computers. But not all will be on a network, and besides, there might be some group rate or something. Let's start at 200 million households, which at a $1 a year, that's 200 million dollars right away for the SIP."

"Right," said Matt, watching Kevin calculate. "And that's probably conservative, considering we don't know how the business connections will be handled, and the fees could be more."

"But this is just the revenue generated from the new lines," Kevin said.

"Yep, kind of like a toll booth."

"So with our tracking system, we should be able to compile some of the work done by the Census Bureau, right? The government already compiles the Current Population Study every year, so it seems as if they could replace the paper altogether."

"But there would be people without computers."

"True, but is this the beginning of something else? Like, for instance, this tracking also tracks those without computers ... because if you have data for everyone on a computer, and you have the data for everyone, can't you determine, by process of elimination, who doesn't have a computer?"

"Holy shit, that's a good point. So Kevin, how are these users updated?"

"I guess paper form, or kiosks, or automated telephone calls, or ... "

"Or what?"

"Well, what if this information is stored in another fashion, like through when you buy something at Wal-Mart or when you create a bank account?"

"How would that ... "

"Easy. If every computer is on this system, and information can be captured through any single part of it, then any person who has contact with a computer terminal could be divulging information to be processed. There would be no way to get around it, at this point."

"Which would mean this system would be similar to .comU, only that .comU is voluntary."

"And in the SIP world, Matt, there would be no way to not give your information."

"So you really think this is what this system is all about?"

"I mean, you know more about it than I do. All I know, though, is simple calculations show that this is on its way to being a multi-billion dollar revenue-generating project. The security on this system would have to be massive."

"And Doug never mentioned to me about the security aspect. I have no idea if we'll even be a part of that. But do you think this is something we want to be a part of anyway?"

"Just looking at the sheer numbers ... and realizing if this is the way the Internet goes, this will probably be the most important addition in the history of the Internet thus far. We would be dumb to pass it up."

"Even though .comU is such a high priority?"

"This even exceeds .comU. It practically makes it obsolete. With this type of information, every town can just create their own .comU."

"Kevin, I don't know about that."

"I think it would be foolish not to entertain the idea of joining forces with Doug's company," said Kevin, scribbling a few numbers down. "Even if we receive a tiny percentage of the total revenue, we'll potentially be pulling down a million or so just to build what we basically already have. This is simple. I bet Drew could put this together in his sleep."

Matt set down the SIP booklet on his desk.

"That's probably true, but I don't want anyone else to know about this yet," Matt said. "It's too risky, with the rest of the projects going on."

"Are you kidding?" Kevin said. "Everyone would want to work on this, immediately!"

"I'm not so sure. I don't think they would be as upbeat as you are. After we meet with the guy from Washington, then we can open it up. We should keep this to ourselves for now. If we speculate on the SIP, we may never get .comU up the way we want it to be. And that system is already bringing us revenue. There's no guarantee from the new one."

"True, but I don't see how it could go wrong. There is a lot to be made there, and I think we are the ones that can do it."

"I just don't want it to affect what we have already done."

"But Matt, this takes what we've already done to a whole new level."

***

Temperatures outside rose above 45 degrees, which was very uncommon in northern Michigan during March. The parking lot turned to slush as many visitors and clients came in and out of the WAB.

Gene Simons from the *Times* was the first lucky guest. Katy hadn't heard from Gene since Friday, when he wrote a short piece about the bingo. This week, he wanted to highlight a few more things in the system. Katy passed him off to Drew, where Gene heard about the forum system that would be released the following week.

"So let me get this straight," Gene said. "People can go on and ask anything they want, and you guys will respond?"

"It's just like any Internet message board," Drew said. "It's not really something that needs any tinkering. But we are going to be looking for local celebrities to answer questions on a routine basis. We'd like to have these chat sessions start soon."

"Who will be your first celebrity?"

"Right now, people can write in and let us know who they would like to be our first guest?"

"Were there any good ones?"

"Yeah, but we had to go back and specify that the first person would have to be someone local. And someone alive. And a real person. People selected Arnold Schwarzenegger, Margaret Thatcher, Buddy Holly, Bojangles, George Jetson and God."

"I read somewhere God was from around here."

"Maybe farther north, but not Malorett. I think Snopes had an article about that chain email awhile back."

Phil Harris paid The Developers a visit as well. He was more than satisfied with the turnout at the midnight bingo. Matt assured him that he would be first on their list of corporate sponsors when they ran other interesting events.

Of course, the day wouldn't have been complete, or even 34 percent complete, without a visitor from everyone's favorite building landlord. Today, Butch was actully wearing a new shirt — a red and yellow tie-dyed smiley face T-shirt.

"Hello all!" Butch said, poking his head in the door to the WAB.

"No, we don't have a check," Drew said.

"No, we don't have any cheese puffs," Katy said.

"Geez guys, is that all you think I ever want?" Butch asked. "Actually, I have a computer question for someone. Some days it works, and some days it doesn't."

"What kind of computer is it?" said Matt, only half listening while trying to answer email.

"What kind?" Butch said. "It's the kind you type things on."

"Um, right," Kevin said. "Like is it a PC, Mac or what?"

"Oh, beats the hell out of me," Butch said. "Why don't you ask it? It'll talk to you."

"Your computer talks?" said Drew, swiveling around in his chair.

"Sure it talks," Butch said. "It tells me what to do sometimes."

"Like to come down here and bother us?" Katy said.

Butch thought for a moment.

"I don't recall it ever saying anything like that," Butch said. "It told me that it couldn't read the CD I had in the CD tray. I didn't even have a CD in the tray!"

"What the ... and it really told you that?" Kevin said.

"Yeah, you would think computers would be a little smarter than that," Butch said. "I set the canister top of my cheese puffs in the CD tray, and the computer thought it was a CD. Then it tried to take the top, but it only got half of it. Maybe it won't work because I pried the other half of the top out of the computer."

"Good God," Kevin said.

"Just bring it down here, Butch," Drew said. "I don't know if we'll be able to fix it, but I guess we can try."

"Thanks a lot fellas," Butch said. "At the very least, get it to not be so dumb and say stupid things."

While Butch exited the building, it sounded to The Developers as if someone was on the way in. It was close to 5 p.m., and the group wasn't expecting anyone else.

And the group definitely wasn't expecting this guest. Michael Fletcher, Katy's ex-husband, poked his head in through the doorway and gave a gentle rap on the door.

"Hi guys," Michael said.

Matt, Drew, Kevin and Sarina turned toward Michael but didn't know what to say. Katy didn't have to turn around to know who it was. Michael stood there, no one saying anything, no one making a move to do anything, either.

"This won't take long," said Michael, looking toward Katy's turned back. "I just want my Tiffany poster back."

"Guys," Matt said, leaning toward the middle of the room, peering over at the others. "We'd better vacate the premises for awhile."

They stood and started to leave.

"It was good seeing you again, Michael!" Kevin said in jest as he walked out the door.

Michael took two steps forward in the WAB, then stopped suddenly. He started to speak, yet nothing came out. In the meantime, Katy still had her back turned and was continuing to work on other things.

"Katy, would you hear what I have to say?" Michael said.

Finally, Katy turned around, still looking over financial documents for .comU.

"Yeah, yeah, what do you want?" Katy said.

"OK, here it goes," Michael said. "I've been trying to tell you this for awhile, but you keep blowing me off. I am engaged."

"You are engaged?" Katy said. "We've been divorced for five months. How is that possible?"

"Well, I've been seeing someone. Someone I'm very much into. Someone ... just like you."

"Just like me? Are you sure that's a good idea?"

"Um, I'm not positive if she's JUST like you, but she seems like you. At least the two times I've talked to her."

"You've talked to her only twice? And you are engaged? Have I met this girl in person?"

"I doubt you have. I mean, I haven't even met her just yet."

Katy was about ready to go ballistic. She stood up and flung her papers to the floor.

"You WHAT?" Katy screamed. "You haven't even met her? What the hell are you talking about?"

"Well, she is one of those mail-order Russian brides," Michael said. "We've been corresponding through the Internet and through regular mail. She is really a great girl. Her name is Martina."

"Are you absolutely nuts? You are engaged to a girl you've have never met. What on earth were you thinking?"

"I just came down here to tell you this, Katy. I didn't come for a lecture. Anyway, why are you so concerned?"

That was a good question, Katy thought. Maybe I should be happy for him. Maybe I should let him figure out his own life. He is my ex-husband ... but of just five months!

"You're right, Michael," Katy said. "It just seems bizarre what you are doing here. You've basically been trying to contact me for absurd reasons, like you still want to talk to me and stuff. And now you are going to get married to some Russian bimbo you've never even met."

"She is not a bimbo," Michael said. "In fact, we are in the midst of a great online chess match, and she is beating me."

"You don't know how to play chess. Remember, I beat you in three moves before?"

"Oh good point ... maybe that wasn't such a good example. Besides, I love her."

"How can you love someone you've never met?"

"That's what I asked myself when it first happened. But now I know it is possible. I must be with her, and it must happen soon."

"So when are you getting married then? Later tonight or something?"

"If Martina can obtain her Green Card, it could happen by the end of next week. I'm flying her over here the first chance I get. We were meant to be together."

"Puhlease. That's the same sort of crap you said to me."

"But this time I really mean it!"

Katy had had enough of this conversation. She walked over to where her papers landed, picked them up and began working again.

"Fine then. Go and find your Russian bride," Katy said. "Let me know how the wedding goes."

"Seriously, can I get my Tiffany poster back?" Michael said. "Martina is a big Tiffany fan. She saw her a few times touring at malls over in Russia and ... "

"I don't have your Tiffany poster! Get out of here!"

Michael exited, and moments later, the rest of the gang re-entered the room. Everyone sat down before saying anything to Katy.

"So, did you give him the poster back?" Kevin said.

"This is insane," Katy said. "He came down here to tell me he was engaged to a mail-order Russian bride he met on the Internet. Can you believe that?"

"But Katy, why do you even care?" Sarina said. "The last time we talked about Michael, you wanted him out of your life for good. Wouldn't this be the perfect solution for that?"

"I was thinking about that as well," Katy said. "I guess I just didn't expect it like this. I guess I'll miss his 26-ring phone messages and his lame excuses to see me. I can't even believe I'm saying this, but I will miss him in a way."

"Well don't forget," Matt said. "You still have me ... I mean, us!"

The group, including Katy, knew this wasn't an innocent slip. But Katy couldn't take two men she once loved messing with her head at the same time.

SIXTEEN

Sarina awoke, a little more disoriented than usual. At first, she thought it was a Monday, just by looking out the window. Mondays seemed to be the dreariest in Malorett. Then again, every winter day looked a little dreary, Sarina thought. Or maybe it just seemed like a Monday because she didn't do her normal couple of miles running the day before. She decided to hold off until Tuesday because she was still recovering from the late night at bingo Saturday.

But even as Sarina got out of bed to begin looking for minimal attire for the morning run, something still seemed unusual. She checked her clock; it read 8:30 a.m., but she didn't remember the alarm sounding. Everything in her bedroom appeared to be in order; of course, there was a small scattering of workout clothes near the closet, and her favorite pair of tennis shoes took a little while to locate. Probably the oddest thing in Sarina's bedroom was the fact that she was wearing a top, since oftentimes she slept in absolutely nothing.

Sarina started to think for a moment about Monday night, and if there was anything peculiar about it, but she was interrupted by a THUD! in what could have been another room in her apartment. Maybe the maintenance guy was here, she thought, or maybe an ornament from her Christmas tree fell off. Sarina had been meaning to take the tree down, but she figured if she didn't think about it, maybe it could potentially disappear on its own. And if that didn't happen, she theorized, it could be used next year, without the hassle of setting it up again.

As Sarina walked out of her bedroom, she didn't seem too concerned, until she noticed a shadow moving in her kitchen. Surely the maintenance man would have knocked or something. If he were going to check the fire alarm, he should have already done it and left. Sarina backed up a few steps, back into the entrance of her bedroom. The hallway from her bedroom to kitchen was about 30 feet, and an additional bedroom and a bathroom existed across from each other near the hall's midpoint.

There was more noise coming from the kitchen, and Sarina was on the verge of freaking out. Whoever was in there wasn't planning on leaving any time soon. Now the intruder was using the microwave! Sarina thought this was ridiculous, but at the same time, she wasn't sure if she should confront the person in the kitchen. She began looking for some sort of weapon in her bedroom, tossing over her clothes and old pairs of shoes. The best she could find was an old thermometer. Although it didn't have a sharp point, it could still be poked in many orifices, and on top of that, it contained Mercury.

While Sarina inched out the doorway and slowly down the hall, she heard the Microwaveable Bandit humming. Obviously he was having a big party of microwaving random items in Sarina's refrigerator and pantry. Sarina held the thermometer firmly in her right hand, ready to strike. Then thoughts crossed her mind: What if the bandit had a gun? What about one of her big kitchen knives? Or even worse, what about her sharp spatula?

Sarina decided her best plan of attack would be to run down the hall, pass the kitchen entrance while taking a look at the bandit then make a run through the living room and out the door. In case of a chase, she thought, she would still have the thermometer. Sarina counted to three and took off. She zoomed passed the kitchen, glanced quickly but didn't miss stride. She hurdled her coffee table, popped the door open and was outside in seconds. She broke into an all-out sprint for about 15 steps, then she stopped.

That wasn't the Microwaveable Bandit. That was Rex.

"Honey?" said Rex, peering out the front door. "Are you starting your morning run without me? Can I at least finish my honeydew?"

Sarina turned around. She wasn't positive how to answer that, partly because she had no idea Rex was even at her apartment, and partly because Rex was wearing one of her running T-shirts. It didn't fit very well, she noted, and his body hair was jumping out at all openings that existed.

She started walking back toward Rex, with her head down, partly in embarrassment, and partly so she didn't have to look at the over-the-cuff puff of chest hair protruding from her favorite workout shirt.

"Rex ... this is so strange," said Sarina, walking back inside her apartment.

"What did you ... how could ... where on earth ... "

Rex slowly rubbed Sarina's back and let her rest her head on his shoulder.

"Sarina, Sarina, slow down," Rex said. "You were definitely out cold when you fell asleep last night. We were talking, and all of the sudden, you were out! Those Fuzzy Navels we had must have really gotten to you!"

"Oh my goodness Rex, now I remember," Sarina said.

Everything came back to Sarina. After work, she met Rex for dinner, and after that, they came back to her place. They watched TV for a little while and also played German Scrabble. Neither had more than a couple of years in high school and college in German, but fortunately, Sarina did have an English-German dictionary to look up questionable usage. The game didn't last long, though, because Rex was a whiz at using umlauted vowels.

Then Sarina grabbed a couple of Fuzzy Navels out of the fridge, and the fun really started. While Sarina was in the kitchen, Rex decided to be nosy and check out her living room closet. When they first returned from dinner, Sarina placed each of their coats in the closet. Rex thought he remembered seeing board games on top of one of the shelves, and after opening the closet again, he was correct! Rex grabbed Life and set up the game before Sarina returned.

They played Life for awhile, but Sarina really wasn't sure how long they continued the madness. All she remembered was having another Fuzzy Navel, laughing and wanting Rex so badly to put the moves on her. She thought he was flirting, but she expected him to be a little stronger in showing that he wanted to sleep with her. After that, Sarina really couldn't remember anything, other than waking up this morning.

"Or maybe I don't really remember," Sarina said. "We were playing Life and then ... "

"And then you were really wasted!" Rex said, removing hot water from the microwave. Evidently, Rex was preparing hot chocolate or some sort of hot cider.

"So, I was wasted," Sarina said. "Is that really a surprise? OK, it should be because I don't drink that much. So what happened after that?"

"After what?"

"After we played Life?"

"We went to bed."

"We went to bed?"

"Well yeah! What else were we supposed to do? You were pretty much too drunk to do anything else."

"So you slept with me?"

"What the?" Rex set down his hot drink and took a bite of his honeydew. "Slept with you? What do you mean?"

"So we had sex?" Sarina said. "That's impossible. I would have remembered that."

"Oh, no no no," Rex said. "I never said that. I wouldn't have sex with you like that. How insane. I laid in your bed until you were asleep, then I slept on the couch."

"Oh ... OK. I guess that makes sense. So did you try anything?"

"Try anything? Like try on your clothes? With the exception of this great shirt, no I didn't."

"No, not try on clothes. Like try to ... touch me? Look at me?"

"Sarina, I respect you. I would not do that." Rex walked over to where Sarina was sitting in the living room. He bent over and kissed her on the cheek. "I wouldn't take advantage of you. You had a little too much to drink, that's all. So are we going to eat and run or what?"

Sarina stood and joined Rex in the kitchen. They were going to eat a little fruit and drink some sort of exotic concoction Rex always has before a morning run.

"This, my dear, puts hair on my chest," said Rex, taking a huge gulp.

"Well then maybe you should stop drinking it," Sarina said. She took a drink and wasn't particularly fond of the taste. "What the hell is in this shit?" she said as she spit part of it in the sink.

"Let's see, there's hot water, honey, lemon juice, a touch of milk — I usually use half and half — and pineapple juice that you had, but any fruit juice will suffice. Just drink the rest, it won't hurt!"

She thought for a minute and took another sip. It wasn't great, but it wasn't too bad. It could be worse, she thought. She could have had to lick it off Rex's chest. But actually, she contemplated doing other things to Rex and thought that maybe that would be a better scenario at the present time. It was already getting late in the morning though, so they should do their run and maybe play strip German Scrabble later tonight.

***

Sarina sensed trouble the moment she made it into the office. Kevin paced in and out of the WAB. Drew glared at his monitor and shook his head. Katy shuffled through papers, but that wasn't anything out of the ordinary. Matt seemed the most calm, discussing something on the phone with an apparent .comU user.

"Yes ma'am, we are working on a fix," Matt told the woman on the phone. "No, it shouldn't be down too long. No, none of your information should be lost. No, we don't have any pizza, it's 10 a.m.!"

After looking over Drew's shoulder, Sarina began to see the problem. Apparently, the main .comU server had locked up sometime the night before. It must have occurred after 1 a.m., though, because one of the Moxee Tech students had been monitoring the site up until that time.

The server had been set to reboot automatically due to a lockup of more than 30 minutes, which could occur for a variety of reasons, but for some reason, the server did not reboot. On a reboot, Matt would have received an email alert to his phone that the server went down. But because there was no reboot, he never knew there was a problem.

The first indication of a problem came immediately when Drew arrived in the office Tuesday morning. There had been numerous emails come through to The Developers, saying they couldn't access their accounts. One person went further to say that he thought the server was down because of the strange errors he was receiving. Another person demanded a full refund for his Viagra, but he was obviously confusing email addresses.

Drew didn't have too many problems rebooting the server. But Drew wanted to investigate a little further to find out why .comU went down in the first place. It didn't appear as if anyone actually went out of their way to infiltrate the server or do anything malicious. Drew checked the anti-virus software on the server, and everything appeared in place. The other alternative was a power outage, but there wasn't a true indication of that, either. Possibly there was a blip in electrical services to that machine, but there was no fuse blown.

He checked the server time, and it showed it went down at 3:47 a.m. Drew managed to get everything back up by 9. Everything appeared to be functioning normally, but Drew wanted to double check to make sure. He reviewed database-generated pages. He also checked random records and tables within the database, and again, all appeared quiet on the computer front.

Kevin, meanwhile, went through the emails directed toward the site's technical support address to make sure people were able to login. He was extremely surprised at the number of people who had written, asking why nothing worked. With .comU down for just a couple of hours, they didn't really expect that many patrons to run into problems. So the good news was there were people using the system at all times of the day; the bad news, though, is that now there were a few individuals who were a little displeased.

"Sir can you just check it now?" said Matt, talking to yet another user. "Everything should be functioning fine. Right, just use your login information. Well, you might have lost some of your changes, but if you put them back up, I promise they'll work this time. If not I'll enter the information for you. What? Fill out a personal for you? I think I'll pass, mister. But have a nice day, and good luck finding that special someone who shares your affection of armadillos."

Katy wasn't sure if she should be helping the others, and if she should be, exactly what she should be doing. Instead, she was in normal Katy mode of organizing everything she possibly could. She had also prepared a short paragraph for Gene Simons, in case he wanted to add something to the newspaper for those people inquiring about .comU's availability. Katy sent the brief to Kevin so it could be posted on the website.

"Well guys, I think everything is back up," Drew said. "I'm still not positive what took it down, though. It had to be some sort of power surge or just a short power loss."

"So did we lose any data?" Matt said.

"None that I can find," Drew said. "But I guess if we lost it, then I wouldn't be able to find it anyway."

"Man, all this talk of computer problems is making me hungry," Kevin said. "Can we run to Dave's?"

"I don't think Dave's is open for breakfast," Sarina said. "And it's just after 10."

"But they open at 11 for lunch," Kevin said. "So maybe we should make plans to head down there. Don't forget, they are paying our bills. They are an advertiser!"

"Today would be a good day to go to Dave's," Matt said. "Especially that everything seems to be working. But we should go closer to lunch time. Is that OK with everyone? What about you, Katy? You are really quiet today."

Katy looked up momentarily and glanced at the other Developers.

"Sure, that's fine with me," Katy said. She then proceeded to continue looking at her files.

"Well OK then," Kevin said.

"All right, let's just concentrate on filling in the cracks and anything else that needs to get done for the system," Matt said. "After lunch, we need to work on the kids area. I've had a couple of calls and emails recently wondering when we were going to have that part of the site running. So maybe now would be a good time to do this."

"I'm just glad we're waiting until after lunch to do any additional work," Kevin said. "You know I can barely breathe on an empty stomach."

Katy stood and walked over to Kevin's desk. She handed him a Tic Tac.

"Here, this should hold you over," Katy said.

"Wow Katy, thanks!" Kevin said. "A whole two calories!"

***

While none of the five Developers had children of their own, they had had plenty of experience, both business and personal, with kids. So in building .comU for Kids, the group utilized its expertise in the area while also gaining information from local schools, churches and nurseries.

All groups recommended the system have as many educational tools as possible. Drew and Sarina built quizzes testing skills in math, science and English for various levels of kids. The public school system also considered using some of the quizzes as an extra incentive for their students to obtain extra credit during the school year.

Of course, children would more than likely want to do more than just take tests on school subjects. So The Developers also built information sections on a variety of subjects, including animals, hygiene, astronomy and history. Sarina worked with Kevin to develop animated graphics for many of these sections.

Older kids had many more options within the system. Whenever they logged in, features would come and go based on age and also personal configuration. Most forums would be available to teenage users, as well as general city information and the directories.

Drew and Sarina wanted to complete as many of the sections as possible before releasing it to the public. They still needed to finish the music, art, sports and technology areas. Matt worked with Sarina on the literature for the technology area, while Kevin and Katy compiled links and graphical elements for the remaining sections.

By Tuesday evening, The Developers had very little left to do for the kids site. Drew, who was the first to arrive and first to work on the server issue, was also the first to leave. He told the others he had planned a quiet night with Jessica.

Kevin followed suit just a couple minutes later. He had planned to attend Jane's basketball game, and of course, he needed to put something in his stomach before he drove to Moxee Tech. Sarina was also anxious to get out of the office, just so she could give Rex a call and see if what had happened this morning, and the night before, actually happened. Because if it did, she thought, she could hardly wait for a repeat performance tonight.

That left just Matt and Katy still inside the WAB. As the evening wore on, both seemed content working individually. At this juncture, Katy was definitely viewed by The Developers as second in command. Even though Drew had been partners with Matt since day one, and he was extremely talented at programming .comU and adding features, he was never meant to be in a leadership role within the group. Katy always seemed destined for this, and she was willing to work with Matt on any project. At the same time, though, their relationship had its volatile moments, mostly stemming from their physical relationship. Fortunately for the group, and everyone's sanity, the two spent just about all of their time conversing about work.

While Katy gathered her belongings to head home, she noticed Matt mulling over a packet of information that didn't look familiar.

"Hey Matt, is that the stuff from Susan Messer?" Katy said. "She was going to send some papers over and I think contracts from chamber companies who were planning to use the advertising capabilities in .comU."

"Nope, this is something separate from that," Matt said.

"Oh ... I've just been waiting for those contracts," Katy said. "Should I go ahead and try to find someone for the first online chat through the forums?"

"Um, I guess it wouldn't hurt," Matt said.

Matt continued paying more attention to the mysterious papers than Katy She thought it was strange that he didn't tell her where the papers came from, but then she noticed a Foundation Technologies folder sitting near Matt's machine.

"Oh, so it's from your good buddy Doug, huh?" said Katy, putting on her coat. "Is he trying to sell us something?"

"No, not really," said Matt, grabbing the folder and putting it into his briefcase. "Why are you so interested about what I'm reading?"

"I figured it was for work," Katy said. "And I know we don't keep secrets about work around here, right?"

"Right ... what secrets could there be about work? I mean all of us spend so much time in here already. It would be hard to keep secrets."

"Well, then why aren't you giving me any details about why Doug sent you a folder with all sorts of information in it? I mean it just seems like there's a little more to it than a short story or a coloring book or something."

Matt glanced down at the papers, looked at his briefcase and then stared at his blank monitor. Katy could tell Matt was somewhat agitated, but she was unsure if he was perturbed at his questioning or at what he was reading.

"Sorry Matt, I guess it really wasn't any of my business," said Katy, starting to walk toward the door. "For all I know, Doug's sending you dirty pictures or whatever. I'll talk to you later."

"Wait a minute, Katy," Matt said. Katy stopped near the doorway. "Doug has ... a favor to ask of us. Potentially. I have a meeting with him tomorrow, so hopefully I'll understand a little better then what is really going on."

"What do you mean? Is the job complicated?"

"I really don't think it will amount to anything. That's kind of why I haven't told you about it. We don't need to be bothered with other things while this .comU project is taking off."

"Then again, if it's too good a deal to pass up, you should keep your options open."

"I'm glad you said that, Katy. There are a lot of uncertainties here, but I'm glad you trust me to make the right decision."

"But Matt, do I really have a choice? You are sort of the owner of the business."

"That's a good point. Hey, what do you say we have dinner? I hear Buckeye's has trout as their special this week."

"Really? Yeah, I could use a little to eat. It's already 8 o'clock for crying out loud."

Matt grabbed his coat and put his laptop in his briefcase.

"This is a lot of eating out for one day," said Matt, turning off the lights in the WAB and heading down the hallway to the front door. "I'll have to make this up by fixing you dinner soon."

"Well don't feel obligated," said Katy, opening the front door. "You don't see me offering to cook you dinner or take you out to eat."

"That's a good point. Maybe you should do that! Or you could give me back MY Rod Stewart poster. I mean Tiffany? Who likes Tiffany?"

"Oh please don't remind me of that lunatic."

"Rod Stewart is not a lunatic. He's not the greatest singer, but he's not a lunatic."

"No I'm talking about Michael."

"Oh, OK then, that guy is a lunatic. Maybe he'll show up at dinner with his Russian bride."

Matt locked the door, while Katy, standing right behind him, was giving him the if-that-happened-I-would-jump-out-the-window look. But by the time Matt turned around, and gave Katy a mischievous yet sexy smile, she decided to leave visions of Michael walking down the aisle with Natasha from *Bullwinkle and Rocky* for another day.

SEVENTEEN

"Man, you must have taken a wrong turn," said Kevin, stepping out of Matt's vehicle. "I thought you had been here before? Oh, well at least there's a Chinese restaurant. Let's go in and get something to eat."

"Hold it right there, buckaroo," said Matt, grabbing Kevin's arm, although Kevin was still moving. "First of all, we have business to do. Second, Chinese restaurants aren't open for breakfast."

"Why is that? Don't they eat breakfast? Pizza places can serve breakfast pizzas. Mexican places can serve breakfast burritos. What's wrong with breakfast egg rolls? Breakfast Kung Pao Duck? Or maybe just Rice Krispies?"

"OK Kevin, how about we focus a little on ... the business?"

"Sure, that's easy to do. Let's see, what do we know? Jack shit! All of this could be bogus, for real."

Matt and Kevin approached the entrance to Foundation Technologies.

"I don't think Doug lies," said Matt, knocking on the door. "Then again, maybe he does. Maybe this whole place is a lie, and really, it's all a front for Malorett's huge drug ring."

"Drug ring, I didn't know about that!" Kevin said. "Are you sure we have the right place? This looks like an old diner or something."

The door opened, and the same man who answered the door the last time was there again.

"Good morning, Matt!" the man said. "Please, come in."

Things looked different from the last time Matt entered the building. The furniture had been changed, and the carpet had been exchanged for a hardwood floor. Even the old magazines were gone, replaced with newer ones, although they were still a few years old.

"You guys have been doing some redecorating, huh?" said Matt, thumbing through *Newsweek* from just 19 months ago.

"Uh, sorry, but I'm sort of new here," Kevin said. "Isn't this supposed to be an office building of some sort? I realize your operation isn't huge, but where do you file your employees?"

"Sorry, I didn't tell him," Matt told the Keeper of the Waiting Room. At least that's what it said on his name tag, minus an actual name. "I wanted it to be a surprise."

"A surprise?" Kevin said. "Does it come with a fortune cookie?"

"Right this way, gentlemen," the Keeper of the Waiting Room said.

Matt and Kevin were led down the stairs and into the lower level of the operation. Once the doors were open to the underground lair, Kevin understood.

"This is pretty impressive," said Kevin, walking with the others to the middle of the room. "Why don't we have an office like this?"

"I think Butch had already rented out the underground model," Matt said.

The Keeper of the Waiting Room motioned for Matt and Kevin to be quiet as they entered the castle of cubicles. They walked past one of the smaller offices and emerged in front of the large conference room. Doug Morris saw them immediately and motioned for them to enter.

"Welcome, gentlemen," said Doug, scurrying over to greet Matt and Kevin. "Let me introduce you to the others. This is Blake Smith, with the FCC's Office of Engineering and Technology. And this is Rusty Snopek, one of the engineering managers."

Doug, Matt and Kevin took their seats around the table. Blake and Rusty were dressed sharply and appeared focused on the task at hand. Kevin, on the other hand, was contemplating additional items on the Chinese breakfast menu. A breakfast wrap with rice noodles, eggs and bacon would be good, he thought. Crab rangoons could probably pass for breakfast food already. Sweet and sour sauce could be just the kick for any item! Kevin then decided that maybe he should pay attention or Matt may never let him leave the office again.

"Matt, I know Doug has filled you in on bits and pieces of this project, but I'm sure there are still a lot of holes," Blake said. "I want to spend some time trying to fill in those cracks and also determine if your company is qualified for the job."

"Qualified?" Matt said. "So is this like a job interview or something?"

"I guess you could look at it like that," Blake said. "As you may have guessed, this project is fairly large and will be extremely lucrative for those companies involved. If one piece of the puzzle doesn't fit just right, that could spell doom for everyone."

"I understand," Matt said. "Since I'm sure you know what our company does, why don't you explain what you're trying to do here."

"Fair enough," Blake said.

Blake stood and turned on the projector. Doug walked over to the light switch and dimmed the overhead lights. A map of the United States, with different color shapes located in numerous places, appeared on the far wall. Matt and Kevin figured these denoted cities, but there wasn't a clear pattern as to what the different shapes meant. There were red boxes, blue diamonds, green triangles and yellow circles. Kevin thought maybe they were Lucky Charms, but he didn't see any purple horseshoes. They did notice that Malorett was a green triangle.

"Here's the plan," Blake said. "The Super Information Portal will stretch across the entire continental US within an 18-month span. The four types of shapes denote the order in which the connection lines and hubs will be intact. The order is green, blue, red and yellow."

"So Malorett is slated for a first-run hub?" Kevin said. "I noticed there aren't too many green triangles up there. Actually the green triangles don't seem to stand for cities at all."

"They do," Rusty said. "It's just that some of the cities are pretty small. We didn't want to start out with too many big cities immediately. And the big cities we chose are within a certain range of somewhat smaller cities.

"For instance, you'll notice that Green Bay is also a triangle. This is because it will be within range of the hub located here. Baltimore will also be close to a group of hubs, plus it will be critical for government lines in and out of D.C."

"So what will a hub entail?" Matt said.

"The obvious next question," Blake said. "A hub will be nothing more than a server cluster. These will feed the new lines that are being put in currently all over the country.

"New lines?" Kevin said. "Won't that take forever?"

"Actually, he should have said modified lines," Rusty said. "The majority of areas are just needing upgrades of their fiber-optic lines. There are some new lines that need to be added, but all of that will be completed by the end of this year anyway."

"Wait, this can't be," Matt said. "Most of the lines installed at least three years ago do not have the capacity to carry the bandwidth necessary for high-speed access. There must be some kind of mistake or ... "

"What you say is true," Doug interrupted. "But what you are missing is that these lines won't be carrying all the data packets."

"Uh, could you say that again," Kevin said. "For a minute, I thought you said ketchup packets. I'm getting hungry."

Rusty scooted toward the end of the table to the laptop running the presentation. He pressed a button, which generated an overlay on blue, yellow and black lines that were entangled across the country. Blake pulled out a laser pointer and walked toward the projector screen.

"You'll see the blue lines here, as Matt suggested, are the fiber-optic ones built not too long ago, but ones that do not have full bandwidth capacity," Blake said. "The yellow lines are the new lines being installed. You'll see they fill in some of the blank spots from the blue lines and have maximum capabilities. Of course, they do not overlap the blue lines, though.

"The black lines, which are the longest, are not actually lines, but bounce points from hubs. Using 802.11g technology, and server clusters as sort of checkpoints, this opens up another realm of data transfer. This will give us the ability to pass information from point to point and also bear some of the burden of the simple fiber-optic lines."

"This sounds really, really nice," Matt said. "How on earth will the data, if sent separately, understand when and where to go?"

"I told you this guy knows his stuff," said Doug, pointing at Matt while looking over at Blake and Rusty. "You're not going to get anything by him."

"Matt, to answer your question, this is actually a process we've been designing for awhile," Rusty said. "At the same time, it's a process that has been used to send data for years. By assigning a key to a data file, we can break it apart, but still keep the key intact within each packet. The mini files can be sent through separate channels, but as long as we can keep them in order, we can piece them back together in the proper form.

"Basically, we are extending existing lines to T3-speed-plus lines. You will have your speed, on top of the bandwidth capacity of a T3. This should be 300 times faster for those people just on T1s, and seemingly an infinite time amount faster than those people on a 56k."

"OK, so let me get this straight," Kevin said. "You are saying that Joe Blow still has a 56k modem here in town. When he connects to the Internet, once this SIP system is applied, he'll have T3 speed, even though he still has his rinky-dink modem?"

"Yes, that will be the case," Blake said, "but not immediately. It will depend on his Internet carrier. The providers will be phased into the new system. America Online, EarthLink, Microsoft and Yahoo, the four largest national competitors, will usher in this project. The providers who are regional suppliers will get into the ball game soon thereafter, we would expect."

"So this will give a huge advantage to these national providers," Kevin said. "And it may cause some people to switch over to them."

"What are you looking at as far as pricing goes?" Matt said. "Doug originally mentioned that there would be a certain tax added to the Internet access."

"We've worked out the deals, if they were to happen today, as follows," said Blake, passing out papers with the pricing structure to the other members in the meeting. "You'll notice that the current broadband pricing for the four ISPs is on the sheet, with the additional upgrade cost. As you can see, the price won't increase that much, and almost certainly fewer than a couple dollars a year.

"And don't forget, these people will not be forced into the initial SIP upgrade," Doug said. "This will be for only those people who wish to boost their speeds substantially."

"But Doug, didn't you tell me that the other plans would be phased out eventually?" Matt said.

"True," Blake said. "We foresee this process taking a year or two to happen. This also includes the time for regional providers to be added to the system."

"What additional fees will be added there?" Kevin said.

"These will be added on a case-by-case basis," Rusty said. "The rates will be standard, and the regional ISPs can handle the fees however they want. Of course, the engineers and planners who are building the system infrastructure are from the four service providers, so the pricing won't be to the smaller company's advantage."

Matt and Kevin looked at each other with perplexed expressions. Matt wondered how the coordination of this grandiose SIP could come to fruition in such a specific time frame. There had to be a lot of planning going on behind the scenes, he thought. They still weren't giving him all the details, but that really wasn't necessary for him to know anyway.

"Well, your plan does look innovative," Matt said. "There are specific details with which I have some doubt, but I also realize there are things that aren't really much of my business anyway."

"Here, Matt, maybe later you can take a look at this," said Rusty, sliding Matt a binder full of papers. "This shows more of a detailed look at the configuration of the SIP. I'm guessing that some of the answers might be in there."

"Thanks, Rusty," Matt said. "So let's get on with this. You need our help, but what is it that you need from us, exactly?"

"We just need a little data, in a nice order, and a bit of security on that data," Rusty said.

"You make it sound like a simple process, like putting a password on a spreadsheet," said Kevin in a cynical tone of voice. "Almost simple enough that you could do yourself."

Blake chuckled.

"He has a way of making the complex stuff sound like it's simple," said Blake, referring to Rusty. "But that's why we've brought this project to you. Doug has assured us of an expedient return on the more difficult junctures of the development."

"Whoa, hold on," Matt said. "You are giving me a time table before I even know what the hell is going on. Seriously guys, that doesn't make any sense."

"Maybe we should have gone to the Chinese restaurant," said Kevin, nudging Matt. "I bet they're open by now."

"I'm sorry Matt, we're not trying to assume anything here," Blake said. "But I know you guys have the ability to build the system we need. I've seen .comU, and there are many, many things that correlate to our project."

"For instance ... " Kevin insisted.

"The stored information, for starters," Rusty said. "A lot of this is similar material that will be stored for users of the SIP."

"Yeah, but it's the same information stored in a lot of systems," Kevin said. "It's not like we invented the database or anything."

"Your development company offers a lot more than just database functionality," Doug said. "This hasn't been spelled out yet, but you asked earlier why they, meaning the government, I presume, couldn't just build the system. That's just it. The government could, theoretically, build the system. But in this particular situation, as with many others, an outside contractor decreases development time exponentially. Your particular part of the project would take, by Blake's estimates, up to two years to complete by government technicians."

"Thank you, Doug," Blake said. "Also, keeping the project under wraps is of great interest to people above me. Situating in Malorett, Michigan, was perfect for that reason as well."

"I knew it would eventually come in handy to be in the middle of nowhere," said Kevin.

"This doesn't have to be something like Area 51," Blake said. "People need to know what's coming. But allowing the builders ample time, without being ambushed all the time with questions, will expedite the project just as much."

"Have you guys discussed this with anyone else, like your wives, friends, anything?" Rusty said.

"Wives?" Matt said. "No, we aren't married. And we haven't discussed it with anyone, not even people at work."

"Oh well that's good," Rusty said. "Just take it from me, it's better not to go around talking too much about it. At least our engineers can just tell people we are upgrading systems or correcting issues when they are out on the job. If you told someone you were building a database or testing security on a system, they would surely ask about it."

"You keep mentioning security, but you've never really said what exactly we are keeping secure," Kevin said.

Rusty pulled up a flow chart on the screen.

"Through the SIP, we will be able to gain basic information on ... just about everyone," Blake said. "If all users with Internet access will be in the system, we might as well have a comprehensive database to list them all. I know what you're going to say ... this is illegal, right?"

Matt and Kevin looked at each other, then back at Blake and nodded.

"The US Code addresses confidentiality and privacy issues," Blake said. "But you'll notice in the SIP booklet that Title 13, which deals specifically with the census, outlines who can review this material. Basically, the data can be used only for statistical purposes; has to be in published format; and can be reviewed only by sworn officials within the census. This can be circumvented, however, by slightly altering the code so that government officials could allow any department or bureau to utilize the information, plus potentially allowing outside contractors — like the ISPs — to be considered as part of a specific agency."

"Could all that really be changed?" Kevin said.

"Most people don't even realize the US Code exists, let alone how it applies to them," Blake said. "Furthermore, by capturing the data online, it will be much, much faster and easier to collect. People will receive mail to go onto the website to verify information. If they don't do it, we still have their info regardless. We'll still have to do it the old-fashioned way with those people without SIP access, but this number will surely dwindle as time passes. Second, we fully expect legislation to pass so that it will become increasingly difficult for anonymous users to access the Web."

"Hold on a sec," Matt said. "I'm not sure that's going to be easy to do. Not allowing anonymous users on the Internet ... that's like asking for IDs when people enter Wal-Mart."

"I think what Doug means is through the SIP, all connections will be made in a fashion so that they are attributed to a record in the SIP database," Doug said. "Therefore, if people jump on the Internet through the public library, the 'user' will be the library. So there will still be plenty of anonymous users ... just fewer anonymous connections. And again, this is an indirect part of the scope of work from both Foundation and The Developers."

"Yes, we hope all security holes can be plugged," Blake said. "We don't want anyone to think we're Microsoft and have to create security updates every other day."

"Matt, that binder I gave you specs out the security that will be involved," Rusty said. "And the database schema is in there, too. Of course, we know you guys will have a good handle on that and perhaps create additional information."

"Yeah, we'll have Drew take a look at it when we get back to the office," Matt said. "He is our main database programmer."

"So Matt, what do you think so far?" Doug said.

"This is definitely an interesting project," Matt said. "You guys have mentioned many of the same things Kevin and I discussed a couple of days ago, so it seems like we're all on the same page. Now, it sounds to me like you are expecting this job to be done in the near future. Is this true?"

"With the collaboration between Foundation and The Developers, we would assume that within a month, you guys could compile a comprehensive report on where we stand and probably some demo work, and within two months maximum afterward, the job would be nearly complete, with the exception of full testing."

"On the database end, this seems reasonable," Matt said. "On the security end ... "

"Don't worry so much about that, Matt," Doug said. "Foundation plans to implement the majority of this and use you guys as more of a consultant. Obviously when we combine these two objects, we'll need massive overlapped testing."

"Even still, we have to account for the security within the database," Matt said. "There are certain things that need to be in place almost immediately, or else we will be backtracking if we wait until the end of the project."

"Also, what about the administration side of this SIP?" Kevin said. "I mean Blake said he's seen .comU in action, but he hasn't seen the administration side of things. It seems like that would be a major part of this system."

"Most definitely we would need an admin side," Blake said. "I guess I just assumed that would be part of the database development. How could you build the system without it?"

"Oh that's pretty simple," Kevin said. "We could just set it up so that you have no idea what information is being stored, and it's just sitting there, collecting dust on the World Wide Web. It's pretty fun, actually, because then you can go in and look at it sometime far down the road and reminisce about the good times you had building it."

"What is he talking about?" Blake said to Rusty.

"Blake, he's just joking," Matt said. "It probably has something to do with hunger."

"It has a lot to do with hunger," said Kevin checking his watch. "I mean, I've gone almost three hours without any grub. My metabolism doesn't allow me to do such things on a normal basis."

"OK, fine, I'll get Bo to go grab us some Chinese takeout," Blake said. He picked up his cellphone and dialed a number, apparently Bo's.

"Who is Bo?" Kevin said to the others.

"He's the guy upstairs," Doug said. "He brought you down here."

"But his name tag said 'Keeper of the Waiting Room,'" Kevin said. "If his name is Bo, why not put that on his name tag?"

"He just doesn't like unknown people calling him by his first name," Doug said. "Bo has this complex about anyone saying his name. It's OK for us to say his name, as long as he's not around. The doctors call it the Rumplestiltskin Effect. Apparently there's no cure, except by giving him a different name."

"But shouldn't you give him a normal-sounding name?" Kevin said. "So there isn't so much drama in what his name really is?"

"We could, but Bo really likes drama," Doug said. "That's actually one of the main syndromes of the Rumplestiltskin Effect."

Blake finished placing his order with Bo, while Kevin, Matt and Rusty tried to discern what Doug had just said about the Keeper of the Waiting Room. Fortunately, Blake wasn't paying attention and managed to get the conversation back on track.

"So as I was saying, the admin side was a given," Blake said. "Actually, some of the reports and layouts are outlined in the binder you have, Matt."

"It sounds like there's a lot outlined in that binder," said Matt, glancing down at the SIP bible.

"There really is a lot of information in there," Rusty said. "I think some of the specifications of the process and development are a bit boring, but overall, that should give you a complete understanding of what this project really entails."

"But in general, it's pretty straight forward," Blake said. "I think after you glance over it, you'll be able to decide quickly whether you are in or out."

"So we're hired?" Kevin said. "The decision is ours to make?"

"I think we've heard enough," Blake said. "We have to move fast on this though. If you do decline, we'll be scrambling a little."

"Thanks for the pressure, Blake," Kevin said.

"When do you want a decision?" Matt said. "On top of that, what type of revenue are we looking at? We haven't really discussed it, and obviously, this will determine the amount of time we actually have to spend on a project like this. I mean we are still developing .comU right now."

"Of course I didn't think I'd get out of here without discussing your payment thoroughly," Blake said. "But in all honesty, I cannot really discuss the contracts with you unless I have a good indication that either you are definitely in, or, if you are contemplating being out, this discussion will not leave the room. In fact, if you guys are out, this conversation never even happened, and you, indeed, never even met us."

"What the ... " Kevin said.

"The way you make it sound, Blake, we don't really have much of a choice," Matt said.

"You definitely have a choice," Blake said. "There's a right choice and a wrong choice. It's just that the wrong choice, well, maybe you should think about making the right one."

Matt was pretty pissed off. While the discussion had seemingly been fairly good overall, there was an overlaying tone that Blake, and even Rusty and Doug, would be running the show. Matt didn't like to operate like this, which is one of the primary reasons he started his own company. Furthermore, it appeared that backing out, or even showing signs of disapproval, could potentially make matters worse.

"I just want to make sure I understand what's happening here," Matt said. "You want me to decide whether my company should press on with a project that needs to be completed quickly, yet I have no idea how much time it will take, nor do I know what I will be paid? Surely I'm missing something because no one does business like that."

"Maybe we should approach this from a different standpoint," Blake said. "Normally if you go meet with a client, you can come up with a broad figure of how long it will take you to do a job, plus you probably attach a price to it, correct?"

"That's true," Matt said. "But it looks like I'm going to have to read this binder to determine much of anything."

"Do you, by any chance, have an audio book of the binder?" Kevin said. "I could listen to it when I sleep tonight and get back with you tomorrow."

"The info in there is comprehensive, including an amount of time necessary to complete the project, at least by our count," Rusty said. "Of course, our count is an approximation because we won't be building it. We assume you will dive in and investigate the time more thoroughly."

"I helped Blake and Rusty put together a safe boundary of hours," Doug said. "Not that I completely understand what you guys do all the time, but I think the buffer I built in is sufficient."

"Matt, go ahead and check out the last tab in the binder, labeled 'Schedule,' " Rusty said.

Matt flipped to the back pages. Sure enough, there were time estimates for the various sections of the project.

"Do you think that's workable?" Blake said. "Assuming that everything in the binder is succinct and there are few intangibles?"

"Yeah, I think the time is about right," Matt said. "Just like any business, sometimes it falls below the range, and sometimes above. So again, does this lead to our discussion about the price being placed on something like this?"

"We want you guys to work on this project," Blake said. "At D.C., they are pretty strict on what we can and cannot say when we are in negotiation for a contract. But obviously, this isn't a normal, cut-and-dry contract. We realize we are going to have to give a little. Matt, what if we tripled your current hourly rate for development?"

Kevin's eyes lit up, thinking that was the most overpriced estimate ever given by The Developers.

"Triple?" Kevin said. "You can't be serious. You could acquire three other development teams and pay them far, far less."

"But are these other development teams any good?" Rusty said. "We are looking at only the best, and we are not as concerned with the price as we are with the quality."

"If it takes longer than the anticipated time frame to complete, then we're looking at paying you for the extra time," Blake said.

"There must be some mistake," Matt said. "Unless you are trying to buy out the system and not allow us to benefit from the profits you make on this."

"Matt, Matt, it's understandable you want to cover all the bases," Doug said. "All of us here realize how big the SIP will be. And none of us will be left out of the success."

"Precisely," Blake said. "The huge upfront cost should show you how serious we are, not that we are trying to snatch up the database you will build and run. In fact, we have some incentives built in that should make this even more tantalizing of a deal."

"I'm assuming these deals are also in the binder," Kevin said.

"Yes, they are, but I can tell you the logistics of them," Rusty said. "First off, if you meet the deadline, you will be given a $250,000 bonus. Secondly, as a system subcontractor, you will be guaranteed at least 5 percent of the profits generated. Now, what those profits will entail, we do not know just yet. And assuming all goes well, we will keep you on staff as a contractor for upgrades and technical support at double your hourly rate. Of course, this is dependent on the number of hours you will be doing development."

"Don't forget the best part, Rusty," Blake said. "A provision about your current .comU development that's not listed in the binder."

"Oh yeah, because the development of our database goes hand in hand with the development of .comU, we plan to be a major contributor of the site," Rusty said. "Through the Foundation, which we know has a substantial invested interest in the system already, we are going to match their total contribution."

Matt completely forgot the earlier tiff about not having enough information about the project and the project revenue.

"Well, I have to admit guys, I had planned to take this back to the shop and get everyone's opinion on what we should do," Matt said. "But I don't think anyone would want to back out of something like this. The idea of generating that much revenue will not only allow us to hire more team members, it will allow us to virtually do anything we want to do."

"I agree," Kevin said. "There's no way they would talk us out of this."

"So is it settled?" Blake said. "You guys are going to be our guys?"

"It appears that way," Matt said.

Rusty handed Matt a couple of contracts to sign, and as Matt read over them, the Keeper of the Waiting Room appeared with lunch. Kevin immediately grabbed a sack of food and found an order of sweet and sour chicken. Kevin started eating before the others had even made a move to the food. Kevin heard Blake and Matt discussing the contract, but he chose to ignore the talk because the food was so good.

"Man, do you have to eat all the time?" said Rusty, pulling out an order of beef and rice.

"I think this room makes me hungry," Kevin said.

Matt and Blake finished their discussion and began to eat with the others. While Blake had no trouble enjoying his food, Matt was already anxious to get started on the system. Even though Matt had anticipated this could be big, he never could have dreamed it would be as big as this. No longer was .comU the system that would put The Developers on the map, Matt thought. That was just to be the stepping stone that would leave his company as potentially the leading development firm in the nation.

@8) - Doug
@:) + >:P --> TTFN

EIGHTEEN

It took Katy a while, but she finally realized at some point that Michael was a strange character ... and definitely too strange to think the two of them should continue to be together. Unfortunately for her, though, those strange characteristics had been magnified tremendously since they separated almost a half year ago.

So it didn't really surprise Katy that Michael wanted her to meet him at Nate's Pawn Shop, which was on the north side of Malorett. And it didn't surprise her that Michael refused to say exactly why they should meet. But she was shocked when Michael showed up with a bunch of her old clothes.

Katy immediately jumped out of her car once she realized Michael had T-shirts, sweatshirts and random other things practically falling out the back of his vehicle. After they split for good, Katy took as much stuff as she could, and after awhile, she decided not to go back to get any more. Every time Katy returned to pick up anything else, Michael tried fervently to get her to stay; and after she refused repeatedly, Michael would make claims that Katy was taking his stuff instead.

"Michael, why do you have all my old clothes in your car?" Katy said. "Are you crazy?"

"I wanted to give you the option of taking them," Michael said. "Or else I'm going to sell them at the pawn shop."

"Dumbass, the pawn shop isn't going to take this stuff," Katy said. "Either you should give it to me, give it away or throw it away. You're not going to get any return for these items."

"But what about this curling iron?" said Michael, picking up Katy's old hair accessory. "I bet I could get a dollar or something for this."

"This is ridiculous!" Katy said. "Besides, it's cold out here."

It was Thursday evening, and the winds were starting to pick up. Michael motioned for Katy to get into his car, instead of standing outside as they spoke through his rolled-down window. She got in, rubbed her hands together and noticed that he had brought just about everything that used to be hers.

"This is madness, Michael," Katy said. "What has prompted you to try to clean out all of this stuff right now?"

"I'm trying to make room for Martina," Michael said. "I spoke with her last night on the computer, and there's a good chance she will be here next weekend. I need to make room in the house for her, and I also need to complete all the wedding invitations. Since I see you all the time, I'll just give one to you when I get them done."

"So you really are going through with this?" Katy said.

"Oh most definitely. Martina and I are in love."

"What are you saying! You've never even met her!"

"Well I'm sure there will be an adjustment period. For instance, she doesn't know a whole lot of English. But love knows no language boundaries!"

"So what is she going to do after you get married? Is she going to get a job?"

"I guess so. I have a couple of ideas of where she could work. She currently works at a shop in Russia right now anyway. I also thinks she likes to sew. It's not important what we like and don't like. We love each other, and I'll do whatever it takes for me to be with her, even if that means her parents are coming with her."

"Her parents?"

"Oh yes, they want to be here for the wedding. And it is a long trip, so I think they might stay for a little while afterward. Martina wants them to move in, but I think she is just kidding. I bet they won't last that long."

"So where will they stay?"

"Oh, that crazy Martina. She's thinking they'll stay at the house with us. I mean, there's not enough room for them and their dogs."

"Dogs?"

"I keep forgetting, you've never met her so you don't know about her family and her pets!"

"You've never met her, either."

"Right. Anyway, she has three Terriers, so I'm building a pen for them in the backyard. It will be really nifty."

"So you are telling me not only is Martina coming here, but she's bringing her parents and three Terriers? Are you absolutely insane?"

"What do you mean?"

Katy opened Michael's car door and jumped out.

"Stop being so dense," Katy said. "I'll take this stuff back if you want to get rid of it."

Michael turned off the car and got out to help transfer Katy's items. There were a couple of bags of clothes, some loose garments and various other items, including the curling iron. Both Katy and Michael made two trips apiece. As Katy organized her things, Michael walked back to his car. He waved goodbye, and Katy did the same.

But Katy had much more important things to do before the day was complete. Luckily, the last two days at work had been about as smooth as possible. On Wednesday, Drew and Sarina decided to go ahead and implement Connect, the .comU chat and forum component, within the system.

They even found their first "celebrity" to feature: Phil Harris of Harris Hotel Enterprise would be on to speak about future promotions through .comU. Phil was well-known within the community, so not only would people ask him about his business, but they would surely be interested in more fun and games within the system. After the bingo success, Phil had been working with Kevin on developing more interest and to find out what the people wanted. Most users listed music as one of their biggest hobbies, so the group proposed some sort of concert or dance for .comU members.

Thursday was mostly a restful day for The Developers. The group met in the morning to discuss modifications and improvements to the .comU business directory. While the directory was meant to be inclusive of all local companies, the Malorett Chamber of Commerce sought an exclusive deal for its members. The chamber's Site of the Month contest appeared to be the answer, but there were still issues with the system. Katy asked the others for ideas, but the only thing she got was Kevin babbling about being in love with Jane.

As Katy drove away from the pawn shop, she thought about how she never seriously thought it would work between him and Jane. But since Katy met her at the ski trip, and saw their interaction, she thought maybe it wasn't such a bad thing. And on top of that Sarina had even found someone, even though he was a bit bizarre. Now if only she could iron out her past. Or even better, find someone to take her away from her past, because Michael's antics were becoming unimaginable. At least the remainder of her evening would definitely take her mind off personal problems.

***

"Isn't there something else I can do, besides this?" Rex shouted to the group of individuals standing roughly 30 feet to his right. "I can't ... I can't see ... ANYTHING! And it's cold! I want my teddy bear!"

Rex was situated at the peak of one of the tallest and fastest ski slopes in the Upper Peninsula. Dubbed the Mudslide, this trail shot straight down the hill at a steep angle for the first 150 feet, turned slightly to the left, then trailed off back to the right all the way to the bottom. This also included a medium jump, one that Rex had bragged about hitting three straight times on his last trip to the slope.

Of course, Rex had never taken the run at midnight, on a night when the hill was closed, in the dark. And he had never done it wearing just a black miniskirt.

"Seriously, it's cccoooooooooolllllldddddd!" said Rex, wavering back and forth on his skis. "Can I at least put on my favorite shorts?"

"Sorry Rex," Butch said through a bullhorn. "The Black Miniskirt Cult strictly enforces initiation rituals. This is the way it works, pal."

"Do you mean you guys had to do this as well?" Rex said.

"Actually no," Butch said. "You are the first to be initiated."

"You can't change the rules?" Rex said.

"We don't change the rules here, Rex!" said Ethel, donning her bright red parka with a bingo card on the back. "You play by our rules! We gotta see that chest hair flowing through the night before you can join our club!"

Rex did have two things to his advantage. First, being hairy made the below-zero wind chill feel like it was about, oh, 2 degrees instead. Also, he could see a little bit of the hill: Ethel and Butch held lamps near the top, while Katy, Patty and Ginger waited at the bottom in Patty's car, with her headlights on. Sarina paced back and forth, wondering if maybe they were pushing Rex over the limit.

"Hey Butch, perhaps we could give him his ski mask," Sarina said. "At the very least, he could shield his face from debris. You never know what could be on the trail."

"Yeah, what if a Bigfoot shows up?" Ethel said.

"Bigfoot?" Rex said. "Does he really live in these parts?"

"Stop your whining," Ethel said. "You act like you're 4. Take it like a man, bee-yatch!"

"OK, Sarina, very well ... let's give him the ski mask," Butch said. "It's only fair. I mean, he already doesn't have a shirt or pants on."

Sarina unzipped Rex's duffel bag, which contained the clothes he shed before getting into his costume, and pulled out his ski mask. Rex was shivering even more horribly as she approached him with the mask.

"Oh thank you, thank you so much Sarina," said Rex as he quickly grabbed the mask and put it on. "Geez, I still can't see, but my eyes sure are a lot warmer!"

"Rex, you don't really have to go through with it," Sarina said. "I had no idea they would make you do a stunt like this. I thought it would be something simple, like walk around town in a skirt or something."

"That would have been a lot easier," Rex said. "I mean, I've done that plenty of times already!"

"You've what?" Sarina said.

"Just kidding, honeybun," Rex said. "I'm trying to liven the situation a bit."

"You are standing at the top of the most monstrous ski slope in the area," Sarina said. "There's no need to liven the situation any more."

"Oh, good point," Rex said.

"So are you really going to go through with it?" Sarina said. "This is insane."

"Do you want me to do it?"

"Do I want you to? Um, this has nothing to do with what I want you to do."

"So you won't hate me if I don't go down this hill without wearing a shirt and without being able to see anything?"

"Rex, I would never hate you. This has nothing to do with our relationship. This is just about joining our little silly club. You are fascinating Rex, and I would never, ever hate you for something like this."

"Would you love me for something like this?"

Sarina thought for a second about just how to answer a loaded question like that.

"No," she said.

"No?" Rex said.

"That's right, no," said Sarina, walking back toward Butch and Ethel. "I can't just love you if you do the run because I love you already."

"Are you ... did you ... how can ... " said Rex, basically speechless, which was definitely different. He finally collected himself. "Sarina, all I can say is WOW! That's the best thing I've heard in a long time!"

On that note, Rex took off. It wasn't without a loud 12-year-old girl scream, though. With his hair, both on his head and his chest, flailing, Rex almost lost his footing immediately out of the gate. He regained his balance by shifting weight to his right leg midway down the initial drop and recovered nicely. As the trail veered to the left, Rex could see very little. About the only thing he could make out was the bright light coming from the bottom of the hill, where Patty's car was parked. But the trail moved farther and farther away from the bright spot, and Rex's visibility eventually became zero once he was two-thirds down the hill.

He wasn't worried at first because he knew just when the trail readjusted and bent back to the right. He made it past the bend but overcompensated slightly and lost his balance again. This time, though, he couldn't stay up. Rex crashed to his right and tumbled the rest of the way down the hill, this time screaming more like a 3-year-old.

Sarina, Butch and Ethel could barely make out Rex as he dusted down the trail, but once they saw the snow flying upwards in clumps, they knew something had gone wrong. Immediately, Sarina took off down the mountain. Ethel and Butch weren't quite as mobile. Luckily, it was just a short walk to where Butch had parked his car, so they walked up the trail to the road that encompassed the ski resort.

Since Rex tumbled practically to the bottom of the trail, Patty, Ginger and Katy arrived first. He was sprawled out, mostly covered with snow, lying on his back, smiling.

"Rex, man, are you OK?" said Katy, also carrying a handful of blankets for the mostly nude skier.

"Oh yeah, I'm just great," said Rex, still motionless. "I feel just great."

"Well are you going to move?" Ginger said.

"I could move," Rex said. "But this is pretty comfortable. Aren't you guys having fun?"

"Uh, I guess so," Katy said. "You've got to get up, Rex. You're probably getting frostbite. You've been outside shirtless for at least a half hour!"

"But bears never wear shirts, and they never get frostbitten!" Rex screamed. "Just think of me as a human bear."

"Oh God, it's worse than we thought," Patty said. "He has lost his mind."

"Nope, that's just normal Rex," Katy said. "He's pretty ridiculous most of the time.

Sarina finally arrived, running full speed down the hill. She actually ran past Rex, and in an attempt to stop, she fell into the snow as well.

"Sarina, baby, is that you?" said Rex, trying to look around. "Are you making a snow angel?"

"No Rex," said Sarina, standing up and brushing off the snow. "I'm coming to see you. Are you OK?"

"Just fine, never been better here," Rex said.

"Well then get up!" Katy said. "Sarina, he won't move."

"I'll get him to move," Sarina said. She walked over to where Rex was lying and jumped on top of him. She then proceeded to give him a large smooch on the lips.

"WOW times two!" Rex said. "No, WOW times infinity. No, WOW to the infinite power. Sarina, you are a fabulous kisser!"

"Well you can have another if you get up now!" said Sarina, standing up and backing away from the scene of the crime.

"Actually I have some news," Rex said. "I don't think I can get up. I think I broke my leg."

"Are you serious?" Katy said. "I can never tell when this guy is being serious or what."

"Yep, it hurts," Rex said. "But don't worry about me! Just leave me behind! Just go on without me!"

"You are a freak, man!" Patty said. "I think Butch has a stretcher in his car. I'll go get it."

Patty ran to the parking lot, which was just a few yards away. Butch showed up just as Patty reached the area. While they managed to drag the stretcher out of the car, Katy, Sarina and Ginger moved as much of the snow around Rex as they could. He grimaced a little as they removed the skis from his feet.

"Whoa, easy down there," said Rex, sitting up on his elbows. "Remember my left leg is sort of out of commission. Hey, what happened to those blankets? I think I'll take a nap here."

Sarina and Ginger pushed Rex onto his left side while Patty and Butch started to slide the stretch beneath him. Katy, meanwhile, tried to keep Rex's legs straight and also used one of the blankets to tie his injured leg to the other. The group successfully rolled Rex on the stretcher. Butch lifted Rex from the top of the stretcher, while Katy and Ginger carried the bottom. Sarina stood on the right and held Rex's hand as they headed to the car.

"Hey Butch," said Sarina as she sloshed through the pile of snow Rex had created during the crash. "Do you always have a stretcher in your car?"

"Why yes, of course," Butch said.

"And what's the reason for that?" Ginger said.

"Doesn't everyone have a stretcher in their trunk?" Butch said.

No one answered, so Butch assumed that maybe they didn't.

"Well I was a Boy Scout," Butch said. "And the motto is 'Be Prepared.' So isn't that a good reason to keep a stretcher in your car?"

"There's only one problem with that logic," Sarina said. "I mean, do you have to be prepared for everything? What else do you have in your car?"

"OK, let's see, I have a stash of food in case I'm stranded," Butch said. "I have an extra swimsuit in case I fall off a bridge ... or if I landed near a swimming pool. There's a fishing pole in case there are fish nearby; there's some glue if I need to put something back together; oh, I almost forgot about the stapler."

"Why would you ever need a stapler?" Katy said.

"In case someone had a huge gash, and they needed to be stapled back together," Butch said.

"That's disgusting!" Ginger said. "Shouldn't you use needle and thread instead? That's what the doctors would do."

"Yeah, I would, but I never earned my sewing merit badge," Butch said. "I earned only my stapling badge."

The group finally made it to Butch's car, where Ethel had tried to create room in the back seat for Rex. She had moved the empty cheese puff tubs to the trunk, and Rex didn't wail too much even though his arms were crammed up against Butch's seat.

"Well, our first Black Miniskirt Cult initiation was definitely a success!" Ethel said.

"This is a success?" Sarina said. "My man is hurt!"

"Yeah, but he's not dead," Ethel said. "If he were dead, then it may have been a success, but that's debatable."

"Rex, I'm sure this is the moment you have been waiting for," Butch said. He grabbed a small brochure from the front seat and handed it to Rex.

"This is our code," Butch said. "You must memorize it to be a full-fledged member. But I hear by announce that Rex Burns has earned the right to be a part of the club."

Everyone clapped, except Rex, who was still trying to get his arms out from being sandwiched between the car cushions and his body. Finally, Sarina helped him get better situated.

"That is wonderful news!" Rex said. "It almost makes me forget about needing to go to the emergency room. Wait, no it doesn't. I'm still in pain."

"Maybe it wouldn't be such a bad idea to remove the miniskirt before we get to the hospital, eh?" Katy said.

"Good idea," Sarina said. "Here are his lucky shorts."

"My lucky shorts!" Rex said. "I feel better already."

"OK everyone, before we go, let's recite the code."

"We pledge to uphold the law, as citizens of this great nation and of Malorett, Michigan, to be true to form, display our best efforts and continue to

proclaim our keen fashion sense as members of the Black Miniskirt Cult."

"Wonderful," Ethel said. "Now let's get the hell out of here! If we hurry home, we can still catch the last few minutes of *Matlock*."

NINETEEN

It would have been quite impossible for Drew to prepare for the email the group received Friday morning.

After a vacation week — vacation, in the sense that he worked fewer than 50 hours at the office, and had just one bingo-calling night — Drew was ready to get back into some heavy-duty items. He had made a list of things that still needed to be completed in the system.

So he basically had his day set up, until he opened that first email, titled, "Another .comU." Drew almost sent it immediately to his junk mail, thinking it was one of those spam emails about optimizing your site for search engines or writing a site in Swahili. But he decided that the subject was enticing enough to warrant a click.

> Hello, my name is Bob Clarkson, and I am a board member of the Green Bay Area Chamber of Commerce. I recently checked out your website, .comU, and I found it to be extremely appealing, both the components and the structure. We have been debating for almost a year now here in Green Bay about putting something together extremely similar to what you have built for Malorett. Unfortunately, the plans keep falling through because we cannot seem to find the right developers who would be willing to work with us. Would you be interested in building a system that parallels .comU, for the Green Bay area? I look forward to hearing back from you!

Drew had envisioned the day would come when other cities may want something like this for their city, but not this soon. Matt, Katy and Kevin arrived at the office, and all noticed Drew just sitting and staring at his screen. They didn't think too much of it, until they booted up their machines and noticed he was still just sitting there, staring.

"Hey man, did you see a ghost?" said Matt, pointing his four-color pin Drew's way. "The light upstairs wasn't on when you got here, was it?"

"I think once you guys open your email, you will see what I'm talking about," Drew said. "We received an interesting inquiry last night."

"All right, another website with hours and hours of beastiality footage!" Kevin said. "I'm on target to receive about 100 of those this month. I never knew they could get zebras to do things like that."

"You actually visited the sites?" Katy said.

"Oh ... of course not," Kevin said. "I heard it from a friend, who heard it from a friend, who ... "

"Come on, stop messing around," Drew said. "Just check out the email from Bob Clarkson."

Drew waited in anticipation much as a 4-year-old waits on Christmas morning for his parents to get out of bed.

"I thought the system was really only for smaller communities," Katy said. "It seems like Green Bay would be way out of the question. I move that we just tell him thanks but no thanks."

"Hold up a minute," Matt said. "So now, all of a sudden, we aren't interested in taking on new clients just because they are too big? When has that become our mission statement?"

"It's crazy that someone from an actual city would even take a gander at .comU," Kevin said. "Maybe he has some long-lost relatives here."

"Or maybe all his exes live in Malorett," Drew said.

"I guess the question becomes what can we actually get accomplished with this possibility," Matt said. "We still have plenty of things to add. So do we just give them what we have, then promise to continue development?"

"A really important question to ask is the time frame," Kevin said. "I think we could probably get more out of them with a short-term development contract. With Malorett, we just pretty much build what they ask for, and worried about the revenue later."

There was a loud thud in Katy's corner.

"What the hell are you guys talking about!" Katy said. "We can't possibly move with this right now. Do you see this stack of papers? These are the sponsors for .comU. OUR CLIENTS! How would you like it if you went in for your doctor's appointment, and your doctor couldn't be there, all of the sudden, because he had to work on a different patient?"

"Of course that would depend on how cute the nurse is," Kevin said.

"Yeah, sure, like the nurse would be under 80," Drew said.

"You know what they say about older women though," Kevin said.

"ENOUGH!" said Katy, standing with papers in both hands. "We are behind here. We need to get things done before we start making more things."

"Is there anything I can do to help?" Matt said. He definitely could sense this was something that had been bothering Katy for more than the last few seconds.

"For starters, you can take care of YOUR clients," said Katy, handing Matt about 20 sheets of paper. "Here are the advertisers that are waiting for one thing or another. The .comU system is adequate, but advertisers are never satisfied."

"What do you mean adequate?" Drew said. "We've gotten great responses from the users."

"Sure, from the users," Katy said. "That doesn't always translate to the actual client, the advertiser. If they don't see an increase in revenue, then they won't just keep advertising."

"What about the guy who sponsored the bingo?" Matt said. "Phil ... "

"Harris, Phil Harris," Katy said. "He's a sponsor for crying out loud, and you can't even remember his name!"

"Katy, come on now, calm down," Matt said.

"This isn't a time to calm down!" Katy said, storming out the door. Just as she reached the door, she almost ran right into Sarina, who was just coming in for the day. Sarina watched Katy exit for a moment, then proceeded to take her coat off and take a seat.

"I guess I missed something good, didn't I?" Sarina said.

"Actually, I'm not positive what just happened," Matt said. "But Katy wasn't too hip on the whole thing."

"It definitely wasn't too rad for her," Kevin said.

"Yeah, the plan just couldn't be groovy enough," Drew said.

"Interesting choice of descriptive words," Sarina said. "What was the plan anyway?"

"Oh, this guy from Green Bay wrote in and wanted to know if we would be interested in putting together a .comU system for their city," Matt said.

"That's totally tubular!" Sarina said. "She was against it?"

"I guess she — I mean we — have too much stuff to do," Kevin said.

"Besides, depending on what they want with the system, we can always hire extra people," Drew said. "Who's to say we couldn't have a Green Bay office?"

"As long as I could still run outside in a sports bra and people wouldn't look at me funny," Sarina said. "Oh, never mind, they look at me funny here too."

"Don't worry Sarina, we'll keep you here," Kevin said. "Now Katy, we might have to think about shipping her off, if she's going to act like this."

Matt thought that was somewhat of a bold statement by the youngest member of the group, but at the same time, he was beginning to wonder why all of this was weighing so heavily on Katy. Maybe it was the job, maybe it was that damn Michael ... or maybe it was something else. Matt made a mental note to discuss some things with Katy later tonight. She was a vital part of the group, and she was definitely a vital part to Matt's life.

***

Kevin missed only the first three minutes of Jane's basketball game, which was an improvement over the last time, when he got there with three minutes remaining in the third quarter. Jane started the last two games and posted career highs in points and rebounds earlier in the week. Kevin followed some collegiate and professional sports but never really thought too much about women's sports. Now that he had an official girlfriend, and she played basketball, Kevin couldn't be happier to support her and the team. He still wasn't wearing a No. 1 foam finger, but perhaps he would bring it along for the next game.

Kevin saw his sister, Jen, a couple rows up in the closest section, and there was plenty of room for him. Kevin made his way up the stairs, narrowly avoiding a small group of kids munching on cotton candy. He took a seat next to Jen and a couple of her friends, some of whom were cute and had never been seen by big brother. Under normal circumstances, Kevin would pull out his game and see how far he could get, but since his romance with Jane, his game had been collecting spider webs.

"Hey Kev, glad you could make it, almost on time," Jen said. "This team they are playing isn't too great. I think Tech already beat them earlier in the year by like 20."

"Why are they playing again then?" Kevin said.

"Because that's what's on the schedule."

"That's dumb that they have to go by those things. It's obvious it's a mismatch. Maybe the other team will surrender."

"This is a basketball game, not the Battle of Antietam."

A rather boring game ensued. As Jen had predicted, Moxee Tech led by 15 at halftime, and by the beginning of the fourth quarter, the only excitement occurred in the crowd. Crissy Calhoun decided to spice things up by removing an article of clothing every time the visitors hit a 3-pointer. They hit two in a row to begin the last period, prompting Crissy to remove her jacket and top shirt, but the team missed its last six 3-pointers, losing by 26. A few guys shouted for her to take her clothes off anyway, so she gave them her number and an invitation to a private postgame interview.

Kevin and Jen waited near the locker room for Jane. She scored 12 points and added eight rebounds in perhaps her best game of the year. Jane finally emerged from the locker room, as most of the other girls had already exited. Kevin walked over to Jane and gave her a hug.

"You were great, hon!" said Kevin, taking Jane's duffel bag in one hand and her left hand in the other.

"Thanks," Jane said. "I'm glad you could make it ... and be on time!"

"Yeah, I didn't miss too much," Kevin said. "And luckily, Jen saved me a seat."

"So, where are we going to eat?" Jen said. "I heard they have some specials over at The Barn."

"The Barn?" Kevin said. "Man, I haven't eaten there since I was a student here."

"Uh, that was just last year," Jane said.

"It sure seems like longer," Kevin said. "When you get out of school, and start working in the real world, every day is equivalent to at least three weeks."

The Barn was on the edge of campus, and it was one of the main Tech hangouts. The place was packed on Friday nights, especially right after basketball games, because they had special prices on everything from buffalo wings to drinks to desserts.

The group had to wait a few minutes until other patrons vacated, but after 10 minutes, they found a booth. Jen and Jane both said hi to a few of their school friends while heading to the table, and Kevin scanned the room, but didn't see any familiar faces.

"I remember the days when I would come in here and know just about everyone," Kevin said. "Those were the days."

"Yeah, again, you are so freakin' old," Jane said.

"You might want to order off the senior citizens menu," Jen said. "Anyway, you are in really good spirits. Is this a special occasion?"

"Great company, great food, what could be better?" Kevin said.

"I think he meant to put the 'great food' portion first," Jen said.

"That's what I was thinking, too," Jane said.

"Come on," Kevin said. "No actually, work is going really well. Almost TOO well. We had a guy write us from Green Bay last night, and he wants a .comU system too!"

"He wants one by himself?" Jane said. "That would probably be pretty boring. I mean, I guess he could find himself on the personals site."

The group had a short laugh, and a waiter stopped by to take their orders.

"But the crazy thing is that the Green Bay deal might be just a drop in the bucket compared to the other things we might be doing," Kevin said. "We are working on this deal potentially for a database that's going to be used nationwide. It's kind of top secret right now, but I figure it doesn't matter too much if I tell you guys. That is as long as you aren't going to go around and tell everyone."

"Yeah really, who would we tell?" Jen said.

"So what will this database do?" Jane said. "Or is it really just a big black book of all your former girlfriends?"

"Yeah, like I really need a database for those," Kevin said. "No, really it's going to be used to track everyone."

"Everyone?" Jen said. "Everyone in the country? How would that be possible?"

"We're still trying to get a good grasp on all the details, but apparently this other company is contracting with us for the project," Kevin said. "They are building a more powerful Internet connection all around the country, and maybe around the world. Like five years from now, everyone is going to be on the new connection, so everyone will be in the database."

"So what happens with the information?" Jane said. "It will be protected, right?"

"I guess it will be some sort of census data," Kevin said. "Or maybe advertisers will have access to it."

"They'll be able to get to all of it?" Jane said. "That can't be possible. Then the government would just be tracking everyone. Are you guys trying to recreate *1984*? Maybe that explains why you have so little information ... 'Ignorance is Strength.' I like you Kevin, but that's the wrong sort of Ministry of Love to be involved in."

"Kevin, I think the job has finally gone to your head," Jen said. "Maybe you should take a little break."

"See, that's what Matt thought too, but the guys seemed pretty confident that the confidentiality policies would be rewritten," Kevin said.

"Rewritten?" Jane said. "Who's stepping in to do that, the Department of Homeland Security? You must be on crack."

"OK so I don't know exactly how it will happen," Kevin said. "But if we build this system, they are planning on paying us a huge amount for the database and then upkeep. I just went with Matt to the meeting the other day, and I may have missed some things. There was a Chinese restaurant right outside, and the aroma was sooooooo good."

"Chinese food," Jen said to Jane, "is probably Kevin's worst weakness. Superman has Kryptonite, Bob Barker has Plinko and Kevin has Chinese food."

"I don't think Bob Barker had a problem with Plinko," Jane said.

"Oh definitely," Kevin said. "Look at all those times he had to beat on the damn thing because the chips got stuck. I bet the dude could have just built a better one, just like he did with the golf game."

Kevin, Jane and Jen enjoyed their wings and tea. They discussed more about school and less about work, which was a relief to Kevin. He did like telling about what he did, but he wasn't positive how in-depth he could go about this potential project. There was so much uncertainty, and besides, Drew, Katy and Sarina didn't even know anything about it. That is, unless Matt finally spilled the beans to them. Kevin thought any more speculation could wait.

They left the restaurant talking about calculus, cafeteria food and Crissy. The girls weren't interested in seeing Crissy's postgame "show," so he decided to take Jen and Jane home. They walked to Jen's room first. It was almost 11, and she had to get up early for a class project. Jane, on the other hand, had the morning off but had study table in the afternoon. Kevin and Jane walked back to her room, on the other side of the residence hall. They sat on Jane's couch, and while Jane flipped through the channels on TV, Kevin thumbed through her schoolbooks.

"So Jane, you don't have any homework to do tonight, do you?" Kevin said.

Jane shook her head no.

"That's great! I wasn't really in the mood for any problem sets. But I am in the mood to give the star player a massage."

"Well I can't refuse that," said Jane, lying on the couch. Kevin stood up and moved to sit next to her hips, on the edge of the couch, and began to massage her back.

"Hey, that feels really good," said Jane, in total relaxation.

"No problem," Kevin said. "It's kind of fun."

"Just kind of?" Jane said.

"OK, REALLY fun," said Kevin as he leaned over to kiss Jane on the back of the neck. Jane turned slowly, and when Kevin didn't retract to his seat, Jane returned his kiss, this time on the lips. They engaged in a longer kiss, and Kevin casually maneuvered to lie halfway beside Jane and halfway on top of her as they made out.

"I wish I didn't have to stop kissing you," Kevin said.

"Who says you have to?" Jane said. "I'm not telling you to stop."

"Well yeah, but the minute your roommate comes back, I'll have to get out of here," Kevin said. "So you just get me all excited and then BAM! It's over."

"What if I told you that tonight, my roommate isn't going to be coming home?" Jane said. Kevin sat up for a minute.

"Really?" Kevin said. "So I CAN kiss you longer! That is just great!" He started to move in for another kiss, but Jane held her head back.

"What if it were more than just kissing?" Jane said.

"What do you mean?" Kevin said.

"Like other things ... besides kissing."

"Like ... "

"Like, you know ... things that don't involve clothes and such."

Kevin sat up on the side of the couch.

"I thought those kind of things were out," Kevin said. "It's no big deal, it's just ... "

"Well I changed my mind, I think," Jane said. "I really want to be more with you."

"Are you serious?" Kevin said. "That is ... that is ... that is awesome! But we don't have to do it or anything, unless you want to."

"Yes, I do," Jane said. "I'm ready, and I want to be with you."

Kevin really wasn't prepared for this, but on the other hand, he had always been prepared for it. He had had feelings for Jane for awhile, and to hear that she had similar feelings made him forget about work altogether. And that never happened.

"Well, you aren't going to hear any complaints here," said Kevin, still trying to take in what was actually happening. "And I'm going to go out on a limb when I say that in the morning, I don't think you'll be making any complaints, either."

***

Matt could have left the office long ago, but he just couldn't put down the binder.

Five hundred pages full of the method the government would be using to create the most massive undertaking on the Internet since the damn thing began. And as luck would have it, Matt's company was not only in the middle of it, but was depended on making it happen. Was it luck? Was it timing? Was it being in the dinky little town of Malorett, or was it something even more meaningful than that?

Regardless, Matt had to figure out how to set priorities. It would seem that .comU should be the main thing for The Developers. Then there's the potential for another .comU. Then there's the SIP. What's a girl to do, Matt thought, then he remembered he wasn't a girl, so therefore, it didn't matter what a girl would do.

There really wasn't a good way to go about understanding the methodology in the binder, either. Matt realized the basics of what he should supply — the database, the ability to administer it and produce reports in every fashion necessary, adequate testing and some security features. In theory, it wouldn't be too difficult, but for the money involved, Matt and the group would have to put forth its finest.

Then the other matter was springing it on the rest of the group. After the way Katy reacted earlier in the day, Matt assumed she would definitely be against it. Drew and Sarina, meanwhile, might be a little more open to it. With four people gung-ho about the SIP, Katy could be persuaded. But Matt still couldn't determine if he was, indeed, really wanting the job. He told Doug and the others he was ready because at the time, it seemed like the right thing to say. But something just didn't seem right ...

Matt couldn't figure it out, so instead, he began scribbling on a notebook with his pen. The key to scribbling with a four-color pen was utilizing the right colors, at the right moments. Matt could almost produce a perfect spirograph, with symmetrical colors, with his eyes closed. He appreciated the green ink much more than the red, blue and black, but at the same time, he tried to draw with each ink in an equal amount of time. At the present time, Matt arduously drew small circles in green and blue triangles around an ocean of red and black rectangles. Fortunately he found a refill for the black ink just two days previously. The drawing represented absolutely nothing. But at least it gave Matt a piece of mind, instead of trying to figure out the problems of the world, or even just Malorett.

It was drawing near midnight, and the binder could wait, Matt thought, until Sunday. Matt started to put on his jacket when he noticed headlights outside. Matt looked out the window and noticed Katy walking toward the door.

"Hey Matt, what are you doing here?" said Katy, entering the office and wiping off a light dusting of snow.

"Oh, nothing too crazy, just reading over some things," Matt said. "A better question, though, is what the hell are you doing here?"

"I left a bunch of my information here," Katy said. "I was just in a hurry to get out of here."

"In a hurry? That's an understatement. It was as if you were out to fight the world or something."

"I wasn't too happy with much of anything, but I feel better now. I just needed to go home, take a nap and recuperate."

"Is there anything I can do to make anything better?"

"No, I don't think so. Everything will be OK, that's all."

"So this really isn't about work, but about Michael?"

Katy stopped stacking her papers and glared at Matt.

"Why does it matter what the problem is?" Katy said.

"Oh, I guess it doesn't," Matt said. "I just want to help."

"I'll let you know if there's anything you can do," Katy said. "But right now, there isn't."

At this point, Matt figured the best thing to do would be to just drop it and work on other things. He didn't like leaving her there alone, however, so instead of leaving immediately, he flipped through his email again.

Just for fun, Matt also checked the .comU webmaster email to see if anything exciting was happening on the site. The Moxee Tech students had been doing a fabulous job responding to the users, and now there were 10 students taking turns with responses. None of the group realized how taxing it could be to keep up with the thousands of users, and thankfully, Professor Jones supplied his students for the system.

There appeared to be more messages than usual, however, tonight. Matt went ahead and opened one, and the user, named BrownClown, complained that portions of the site were inaccessible. FreakyDeakyDoo and Pants129 echoed the same problems, primarily within The Profiler area. Matt opened a new browser window and tried to access the site, but he was unable to get to anything.

"Hey Katy, something's wrong on the site," Matt said. "I'm not sure what's going on, but I can't get to it. Is our connection down?"

Katy quickly tried the site.

"Our connection can't be down, I was just online," Katy said. "Yep, I can't get to it, either."

As Matt started to check the responses from the students, his phone rang. It was coming from Tech.

"Hi Matt, it's Crissy. Everything is down, it looks like. Can you restart the server or something?"

"Yeah, I'm here at the office," Matt said. "I'll go ahead and restart it. Thanks for keeping up with everything."

"Oh, no problem," Crissy said. "I'll check back in a couple of minutes and just write an email to all the people who were waiting."

"Thanks for your help, Crissy," Matt said.

Matt walked over to the server to see if he could figure out the problem. The computer was frozen, so he tried to reboot it. That restarted the machine, but as Matt waited for the system to come back up, nothing happened. Matt tried to be patient and give it a little more time, but after five minutes, he restarted it again. Still nothing. He figured it would just be best to leave it off for a few minutes and maybe that would correct any sort of problem occurring.

"What's happening?" Katy said. "Did you get it fixed?"

"I'm not sure," Matt said. "But .comU is definitely down."

TWENTY

"Maybe we should call Drew," said Katy, still trying to access the site from her computer. "I mean if the damn thing won't even come on, we have definite problems."

"Yeah, I don't want to call him ... unless I really have to," Matt said. "I'm sure he has more important things to do, like sharpening his extra bingo daubbers."

Matt checked the connections from the server to the nearby router. The Developers had two servers, one exclusively devoted to .comU, and the other hosting various other websites. The servers produced backups to each other on a daily basis, but to reload the one for .comU would take at least an hour to perform. What's worse is that the backups run in the middle of the night, which meant if Matt were to rely on the most recent backup, he would lose all new data from Friday.

Matt contemplated this as he unplugged and plugged the machine back into the router. Although Friday was seemingly slow for site traffic, there was no reason to delete the data, if he could get to it.

"The site is still coming up unresolved," Katy said.

"Well I would like to think so," Matt said. "The server is not even on right now!"

"Well what are you doing over there, trying to coax it back on?" Katy said. "If it doesn't work, I'll call Drew."

She picked up her phone and began to dial.

"Katy just give me a few more minutes," said Matt, powering on the machine. "You can't rush a technician. Unless you want me to blow up something."

"Yeah, like you can really blow up something. You are not MacGyver."

Suddenly, the screen came on, and the system finally powered on. Matt examined the normal startup screen, willing it to show a sign that it was, indeed, working. Katy glanced toward the computer, and after actually seeing something on the monitor, she walked over behind Matt.

"We are closer," Matt said. "But I'm still not sure it's going to boot."

"This is better than a couple of minutes ago, when the power button didn't even work," Katy said.

"I'm still not sure what the problem is, though," Matt said. "The only difference was instead of doing a hard restart, I did a hard shutdown and powered up from there."

"Whatever works," Katy said. "Fortunately, this is happening late on a Friday night. Who's on the system on a Friday night?"

Finally, the startup script began on screen. The machine ran a short diagnostics test and found zero errors. The server loaded all of its necessary components and completed the reboot. Katy walked back over to her machine and checked the site again. This time, it loaded.

"Matt you did it!" said Katy, walking briskly back over toward Matt. She gave him a bear hug and a pat on the back.

"Yeah, I did it," Matt said. "I unplugged the machine and plugged it back in. Man, I AM a genius! Maybe I deserve something more!"

"Well what about this?" said Katy as she proceeded to kiss Matt. Although Matt was definitely surprised, he wasn't complaining. He pulled Katy closer to him and continued kissing her. After a couple of seconds, Katy backed away.

"Um, that's not what I was thinking, but that was surely something more," said Matt, still trying to catch his breath. "Where did that come from?"

"I don't know," Katy said. "I guess I was just caught up in the moment."

"The moment? The only thing that happened was the server came back on. It's not like someone smashed the box and I carefully pieced it back together, using masking tape and honey. Now that would have been a moment, a MacGyver one at that."

Katy sat down and looked over a couple of papers sitting on her desk. Matt couldn't tell if she was dismayed about what happened or if she was just trying to finish the work she began earlier. Matt checked the server, and everything appeared to be normal again. He then moved toward Katy's desk.

"Hey are you OK?" said Matt, rubbing Katy's back.

"Yeah, I guess so," Katy said. "I just need to get this stuff completed. There's too much to do."

"True, but if there's something on your mind, maybe you should talk about it and not avoid it. Maybe that would help you focus on things that are more important, you know?"

"That's easier said than done. I'm just not sure what to think about a lot of things."

"Like what?"

"Not that I'm hung up on Michael at all ... because I'm not. But he is just such a maniac that I don't know what to do. I mean the guy tried to sell my old curling iron at the pawn shop! Now he's running off with some girl he has never even met before. If I act like I don't care, he might do something really stupid, but if I act like I do care, I'm afraid he's going to get the wrong impression. I've had enough of his shit, but I still care about him. I don't want to see him get hurt."

"Katy, you have done so much for that guy. I mean back when you guys first started dating, it never seemed like he appreciated you. Then he finally figured out you were unhappy and tried to change. But he was interested only in the chase. Right now, he doesn't have you, so maybe he thinks he is trying to win you over again or something. But you can't live his life for him. He has to make the decision."

Katy looked around at Matt, smiled and held his left hand.

"That's right, Matt," Katy said. "You always have good advice for me. I'm glad you are my friend."

"So that's what we are, right?" Matt said. "We are just, I mean, still friends?"

"What do you mean?" Katy said.

"Well, that kiss, what just happened there?" Matt said.

Katy dropped Matt's hand and turned away from Matt in her chair.

"I told you, I got caught up in the moment," Katy said.

"So it meant nothing?" Matt said.

"You fixed the site. That deserved some sort of celebration. I think we should just leave it at that."

"I know, but it's not like that was the first time we ever kissed or something.

I mean, we HAVE a history, if you recall."

"And again, that's what it is, Matt. It's history. You know, like the Magna Carta or the French and Indian War. It has to be that way."

"But why does it have to be that way? The Indians got cheated over and over, but can't I avoid that same fate with you?"

Katy wasn't happy at all with Matt's pressuring questions. She began to gather her papers into her briefcase. Matt, on the other hand, wasn't sure why Katy was being so defensive. He was just trying to figure out why she kissed him and played it off like nothing occurred.

"Matt, I should get going," Katy said. "I can work on this stuff at home."

"Wait Katy, we need to talk," Matt said. "It's something really important."

"I'm finished talking about us. There is nothing more to say. I've told you this numerous times, and it doesn't appear to be getting through your thick skull."

No, it's not about us. It's about The Developers and a new job. We have got to figure this out."

"I told you earlier what my feelings are. Now if everyone else thinks it could work, with building a new .comU, then maybe we should go forward, and I'll deal with it. I'll go with a consensus, after a thorough discussion, of course."

"Um, no, not that new job. A different new job."

Matt handed Katy the SIP specs binder. Katy looked puzzled, and Matt motioned for her to take a look.

"You know Doug, over at Foundation?" Matt said. "They want us to help them with a gigantic project. One that could bring us so much revenue that we won't know what to do."

"So what exactly does this project entail?" asked Katy, flipping quickly through the binder, not reading anything in particular.

"It would take a little while to explain," Matt said. "But we would need to focus a lot of time on it. It might take over some of the .comU development."

"What?" Katy said. "We are going to focus on another project? How would that be possible?"

"It would probably move up as a greater importance. It would mean more, not only to us, but to the community and to the country as a whole."

"The country?"

"Yeah, Foundation is actually doing consulting through the United States government. We would be one of the project leaders."

"Honestly Matt, you know what I think?"

"What?"

"I think this is a bunch of bull shit. And I can tell you that none of the others will want to do this. Working for the government, in general, is not something appealing to our crew. Is it appealing to you?"

"Not necessarily, but ... "

"Well if you don't want to do it, why would you think anyone else would want to?"

"I'm not saying I don't want to do this. I'm saying that my feelings about working on this government project are ... well, I don't think you would understand unless you read the binder."

"That's crazy, I'm not reading this damn thing," said Katy, handing the binder back to Matt. "If you have a good reason for scrapping .comU and starting on something else, by all means, tell me now."

"That's the thing, we aren't scrapping .comU. In fact, the guys who are heading this new project have informed me they would even become a sponsor of what we already have. And for the amount of money they are willing to pay us to build the system, we could probably afford to add staff and work on the projects simultaneously."

"So you already have people lined up you want to hire?"

"Well ... I can go back through the most recent resumes. But I don't have anyone in particular in mind, no."

"And when will this other project begin?"

"I guess the sooner the better. Because the sooner it's started, the sooner they'll start funding it. And the sooner it's completed, the sooner we'll reap the benefits."

"So it's really all about the money, right? It's all about what we get out of it, regardless of what the system really is?"

Matt retreated to his desk after Katy's remark. He wasn't sure how to defend his opinion because it was, indeed, a lot about the money. But explaining to Katy it wasn't the main driving force, that it was actually the idea of creating some sort of legacy for The Developers on the World Wide Web, was so far-fetched that there was no way she would believe it. What's more, though, is that he wasn't sure he should even be discussing specifics about the system with her at this point anyway.

"It's not all about the money," Matt said. "What it's about, though, is too complex to explain."

"OK, if it's too complex to explain, then how on earth are you going to convince us this is what we should be doing?" Katy said. "You aren't convincing me now, and you keep avoiding details of what is going on. You are beginning to sound like a typical politician. Are you building a system that will replace government officials? They could be programmed to say sound bytes like, 'I cannot answer that question at this time,' or 'We are heading in the right direction and are doing the will of the people.' That sure would save taxpayers some money. So maybe that's not a bad idea."

"Well that's not what we are supposedly going to build," Matt said. "At least, I don't think so."

Katy gave Matt an evil look, then walked back to her desk.

"I also think it's rather rude to tell me 'it's too complex to explain,'" Katy said. "What the hell is that supposed to mean? I don't have the comprehension skills to get it? I hate to tell you, Matt, but we have virtually the SAME degree from the SAME school, so unless you've learned things that they didn't teach us in school, like the meaning of life or the meaning of synchronized swimming, then I suggest you leave personal comments out of this."

"No, I'm not saying it's too complex to explain to you," Matt said. "I'm saying to anyone, it's too complex to explain to anyone, unless they understand the ultimate plan of the government and the system. And there is no meaning to synchronized swimming. It's a sanctioned Olympic sport, but so is curling, and let's face it, clearing ice in front of a big concrete ball is pretty silly."

"Don't try to change the subject!" Katy said. "You aren't making any sense. And on top of that, you are trying to come on to me. I think you are going about this all wrong."

"Going about what all wrong?" Matt said. "You are appropriating two totally different things and trying to combine them into one. I shouldn't have even brought it up. I knew you would try to find a way to turn everything against me."

"What?" Katy said. "How can I turn something against you that I know nothing about?"

"I don't even remember what we are arguing about anymore," Matt said. "It's almost as if we are arguing about what we are arguing about."

"Oh no no no, that's not how I see it," said Butch, entering the room while eating a small container of sherbet with a wooden spoon. "It's obvious Katy is distressed, Matt, because you refuse to reveal information about a project, but you seem to think the project is the way to go."

Matt and Katy gave each other shocking glances as Butch entered the room and spoke.

"It's like one in the morning," Matt said to Butch. "Why on earth are you here?"

"I can get a lot accomplished at night down here," Butch said. "I was just upstairs cleaning and all. But it's difficult to get things done when there are people downstairs YELLING and SCREAMING about the most ridiculous things EVER! Curling is a lot of fun, by the way, and if you guys would ever like to play, I can take you to cousin Leo's matches. They play up in Green Bay every Thursday."

"Butch, did you steal that sherbet from a church picnic dinner or something?" Katy said.

No, I didn't steal it," Butch said. "I do like to collect sherbet cups from picnics and eat them later, though. I have a nice little stash right now. Sherbet is nothing like my favorite delicacy, cheese puffs, but it's not too far behind."

"Are we really having this conversation," Matt softly told Katy, "or is Butch sleepwalking and eating sherbet?"

"Another good place to get sherbet is at Leo's matches," Butch said. "You wouldn't believe the amount of sherbet people eat there. They even had sherbet night, where everyone got a free scoop of sherbet in the container of your choice. The catch, though, was you had to bring a container. Do you know how difficult it is to get a tiny scoop of sherbet out of a huge cheese puff tub? It's not fun."

"Butch! You are rambling again," Matt said.

"Indeed I am," Butch said. "But if you would give me your rent check, I wouldn't bother you."

"We already paid for the next month!" Katy said.

"Oh, OK then," Butch said. "I guess it's just a habit to ask for it. I'll leave you two lovebirds alone. Just don't be so LOUD! It makes me gnash my teeth, more than eating sherbet with a wooden spoon."

Butch left the WAB and returned to his cleaning and renovation duties. Matt and Katy started to pack up their stuff, again, and tried to ignore each other. Matt figured maybe Katy was trying to beat him out the door, while Katy assumed the same about Matt. The race, though, ended in a dead heat, as Matt and Katy were practically face to face walking out the WAB. Katy walked out first, so Matt locked the door. Katy picked up the pace down the long corridor to the front door, but Matt caught up as she made it to the entrance.

"Katy, wait a minute," said Matt, tapping Katy on the back. "We can't just leave like this. Look, I'm sorry for ... I mean, I didn't mean to offend you. I was just trying to explain something that I couldn't explain."

"Well I still don't get it," Katy said. "And I don't understand what all this mystery is about. Are you going to have a meeting to explain it? I don't think anyone will be particularly interested in reading the binder."

"I think I'll hold off for a little bit on that," Matt said.

"It's about time you said something that made at least a little bit of sense," Katy said. "It's late. We should really get going."

"Yeah ... so are you still mad at me?"

"Ask me again tomorrow. Maybe by then, I'll be over you."

"Over me?"

"It, over it, that's what I said."

Katy made it through the door, and for once, the top part of the door actually opened with no problems. Matt walked through and locked the door behind him, watching Katy scramble down the ice-covered path to the parking area. He wasn't positive what her last comment meant, if it was a Freudian slip or why Katy would need to get over him anyway. It was a shame he couldn't conceal his feelings for Katy any better than that. But from her reactions this evening, she couldn't hide her feelings, either. While being in the middle of quite possibly the most crucial point of his relatively young business — with the success of .comU, the possibility of one for Green Bay and the SIP project — this was not the right time to get wrapped up in a girl, especially one of his employees.

But another thought crossed his mind while watching Katy get into her car and drive away. What if the right time never occurred?

***

A knock at the door woke both Kevin and Jane. While Jane jumped out of bed, trying fervently to find clothes before answering the door, it took Kevin a few minutes to finally register exactly where he was. It seemed as if last night was only a dream, Kevin thought, but realizing he was still at Jane's place must have meant it actually happened! Kevin lay motionless in Jane's bed while she answered the door.

Even though Kevin hid under the sheets, he could tell that Jane was talking to his little sis at the door.

"You want me to come down for brunch right now?" Jane said to Jen. "Um, I'm really not that hungry."

"How is that possible?" Jen said. "You are ALWAYS hungry! Don't tell me you ate again with Kevin after I left! He is a bad influence as far as eating goes."

"No, I didn't eat anymore, I'm just not ... "

"How long have you been up, anyway? It's almost noon. I mean by now, you are usually up and out doing something. You must have been pretty tired."

"I was. I don't even remember when I went to bed. It was pretty late."

"So how late did my brother stay?"

"It was pretty late, Jen. I mean really, I don't even remember when I actually went to bed."

"I know it's none of my business, but I was just curious. Well I'm going to eat. I'll save you a seat if you want to meet me down there in a minute. See ya!"

Jane shut the door and came back into the bedroom, where Kevin had pulled the covers over his head.

"Yikes!" Kevin said. "I never thought I would be scared to see my little sister. Wait a minute, I also never thought I'd be awakened by her after being in bed with one of her friends!"

"It's not a big deal," said Jane, sitting on the edge of the bed. "I'm sure she just wanted to know how I was doing, considering how tired I've been the last few days."

"So are you going to tell her anything? I mean, what are you going to tell her?"

"I guess eventually I will. She is my best friend. But I don't anticipate I will just blurt out something about last night in casual conversation with her. I'll be a little more careful than that."

"So you aren't mad about anything, are you?"

"Why would I be mad?"

"I just wanted to check," said Kevin, getting out of bed and putting on his socks. "I had an awesome time with you and I really didn't want it to end!"

Kevin stood, walked to the other side of the bed, where Jane was sitting, and kissed her on the cheek.

"Thanks, Kevin," Jane said. "I had a great time. I'm really glad we are together. Everything was perfect!"

"That is just great, Jane. I guess I should get going, and you can meet Jen down at the cafeteria. Is there an easy way out of here?"

"You mean, like jumping out the window?"

"At least we are on the ground floor, so that shouldn't be too bad."

Kevin finished getting dressed, and he and Jane walked out to the parking lot. They were careful, though, to walk out a side door, and along the far row of cars, just in case Jen happened to be watching out the dorm. Even though Jen knew they were pretty much a couple, they agreed that maybe slowly explaining what happened might be the best way to handle it, instead of letting Jen know immediately.

They made it to Kevin's car and gave each other one last kiss goodbye.

"So what does your schedule look like this week?" Kevin said.

"I've got a couple of tests ... I've got a game Wednesday, away, and also Saturday, so I probably won't be able to hang out too much," Jane said. "Except for tomorrow. Are you busy tomorrow?"

"I'm not sure yet, but I have a feeling I'll have something going on," Kevin said. "Tuesday we have another meeting with the government guys about the Super Information Portal. I'm guessing we could start working on that in a matter of a few days."

"Give me a call tonight and let me know if you want to do something tomorrow. I wish I could come down and visit you, but I'm just swamped with schoolwork and basketball right now."

"That's no problem, Jane. You guys have so many good restaurants, and it makes me feel like I'm in college again and stuff. Speaking of food, I really need to eat SOMETHING! And Jen's waiting for you. Tell her I said hello ... no, wait a minute, don't tell her anything!"

"Good idea, Kevin. I'll talk to you later!"

They hugged, and Kevin got in his car and left. Jane watched Kevin drive away, and she expected the drive back today would be nice, considering it was sunny and 40. Although she truly hoped Kevin would be able to come back Sunday, there was supposed to be a fairly sizeable snowstorm preparing to hit the area, dropping close to a foot of snow on most of the Upper Peninsula. Jane reasoned that even if he couldn't come back, at least they could chat on the phone, and that would just have to do.

Jane found Jen in the cafeteria with no problem. Jen had practically finished her meal, but she still sat with Jane as she ate.

"So come on, Jane," Jen said. "I think you are leaving something out of the story. You HAVE to know when Kevin left last night, or when you went to bed or something. It just sounds so suspicious."

"Suspicious?" Jane asked. "How so?"

"It just seems like you're hiding something."

"He is your brother. What is there to hide?"

"I don't know. But you guys are boyfriend-girlfriend now, right?"

"Why, should I not trust him or something? Now I'm getting paranoid."

"No, you can trust him. Just know you can still talk about things with me, even if it is my brother. That's no big deal. If you get in a fight, if you have sex, if you fight while having sex ... you can still talk to me about it."

"Thanks Jen, I'll definitely keep that in mind. But unfortunately, this bacon and eggs has not helped remind me what time I went to bed!"

They finished their breakfast and agreed to do homework, then go to the gym later on. Jen did not try to intrude any further into the happenings of the night and the morning, with Kevin, much to Jane's delight. Eventually she would have to tell Jen, but she wanted to hold out at least for 24 hours.

When Jane returned to her room, there was note attached to her door. She opened it, and inside there was a card with a large heart on the front. Jane opened the card and read inside.

Hey babe! I thought I was hungry for food, but I was really hungry for more of you! As I drove away, I already started missing you, so I wanted to let you know, before I called you later. Have a great day. Whoa, now the hunger is for real.
Love,
Kevin

Whether it's for real or surreal, Jane thought, it sure was nice having someone to love again. Even if that love was oftentimes confused for a burger or a burrito.

TWENTY-ONE

"Whaddya mean this isn't a bingo? Look at all the numbers I got!"

The relatively young, burlesque man wasn't giving in easily. Drew imagined the man, who somewhat resembled a hefty Charlton Heston, was about 60 years old, which left him in the toddler section at the bingo hall. He must have been a newcomer to St. Pius, unless he usually sat in the back, because Drew had never seen him. Not that he would have really stood out anyway — he wore a simple green-striped polo shirt and khakis — but as Drew listened to the man talk about winning the last game, Drew knew a Heston lookalike, even though he wasn't dressed as Moses, would not have gone unnoticed.

"Sir, I realize you have covered all the numbers," Drew calmly explained. "But O-65 was not called."

"What do you mean it wasn't called?" the man said.

"It was still on the monitor," Drew said. "The number had not been called, and that young lady over there called bingo on N-31, which was the final number."

Drew pointed to the young lady, Ethel McMahan, who had been on a tear recently, bingoing the last two nights Drew had worked. Evidently, not only was the man a newbie to St. Pius, but to the game of bingo itself. He had called bingo when his final number in the coverall was shown on the monitor. Most bingo halls in Malorett have TV screens that show the next number to be called, so players have time to scan through all their cards. Some play two full packs of cards, and each pack contains 18 cards. In fact, when Ethel is feeling frisky, she'll take on two 18-packs and a nine-pack, just to prove her worthiness. The others call her a show off, but being 104 doesn't allow too much longer to show off, so they accept it and buy her a Coke Freeze on the days she loses.

"But if it was on the monitor, then it was fair play?" the man said.

"No, you had what's called a monitor bingo," Drew said. "If Ethel wouldn't have hit the bingo, you would have won. But she did win, so you are left with nothing."

"What, no consolation prize?"

"You just had a case. I'm sure a lot of people were one number away from winning."

"So what should I do now?"

"We still have plenty of games left. I highly recommend the nachos from the snack bar as well."

"Nachos? Can I get chili on them too?"

"Usually they have meat, but I'm not sure about today."

"And peppers? I really like peppers. Is the cheese good?"

"Oh, most definitely. Why don't you go ask them. I need to get back up to the calling stand."

Drew rarely had problems at the Sunday afternoon bingo, but when non-regulars show up and almost bingo you never know what is going happen. The biggest change for Drew, though, was he felt completely refreshed, both from a physical and mental standpoint. He left work at a reasonable time Friday night, and Saturday he spent the whole day with Jessica. Saturday was Jessica's birthday, so they had a relaxing day at home, followed by a drive to Moxee, dinner and a musical produced by the local dance theater.

Jessica enjoyed the experience, but Drew may have enjoyed it even more, getting away from the office and spending an extended amount of time with his wife for a change. Drew had looked for any opportunities to see her more, and with the .comU production winding down a bit, he finally saw the light at the end of the tunnel.

At least, that's what Drew thought before Friday. After bingo, he dropped by the office to begin working on a proposal for the Green Bay version of .comU. He figured there would be plenty of peace and quiet at the office Sunday evening, at least from outsider phone calls. But after just 30 minutes, Drew saw Doug pull into the parking lot. Drew walked down the hall to meet Doug at the door.

"Hello Drew!" said Doug, wiping his feet and shaking snow off his coat. "I came to drop off some contracts for Matt, but I don't see his truck. Any idea when he'll be here?"

"Not really," said Drew, closing the door behind. "You can come down and just wait for him in the WAB. I'm just working on a proposal."

"Really ... what are you guys going to build now?" Doug said.

"There was a guy from Green Bay who was interested in .comU," Drew said.

"That's splendid!" Doug said. "It's good to hear that's really taking off."

As they walked down the hall, Drew tried to remember the last time he heard someone say the word "splendid." Without consulting a dictionary, Drew thought maybe the word had been removed from service. It was definitely an antiquated word, so possibly the last time he heard it was watching *Leave it to Beaver* on Nick at Night. That was Jessica's nighttime viewing choice, and even if the show was periodically funny, the wording needed to be updated in some fashion. Drew had imagined even updating the show to the '80s, where Eddie Haskell could proclaim things as "rad" and June and Ward Beaver could teach Wally about safe sex practices instead of just baking cookies.

That was for another time, as Drew needed to work on the proposal, but the Beaver himself was sitting in Sarina's chair, glancing over a few papers from a folder. Actually, Doug Morris looked nothing like Jerry Mathers: He had medium-length brown hair — slightly gelled — dark eyes and zero freckles. Even on Sunday, he was dressed like he could attend a business meeting if necessary, wearing what resembled a Catholic grade school uniform (dark trousers and a plain blue-collared shirt). Drew then realized the common ground between Doug and the Beaver — both always had plenty of questions and plenty of answers, but the two rarely seemed to match.

"So Drew, do you enjoy working with Matt and the other developers?" said Doug, thumbing through the papers he held. "I was just wondering how everyone got along, and how everyone worked together."

"It's definitely a team atmosphere," Drew said. "And so far it has worked pretty well."

"So are you pretty excited about the new project?"

"It's hard to say. Green Bay is a big city, and I'm not convinced .comU is really ready for it. But it's worth a shot."

Doug stood and scooted Sarina's chair toward Drew's work station.

"No, I'm talking about the OTHER new project," Doug said. "The one you are working on with us."

"With who?" Drew said.

"With us ... Foundation and the United States government."

"Oh yeah, Matt mentioned something about that a few days ago. I think it sounds like a pretty good deal if we have time to go through with it."

"I'm afraid I don't understand what you mean. Matt is supposed to be signing these contracts today."

Doug handed Drew three contracts.

"On Wednesday of this week, we came out with a handshake to start on the system," Doug said. "Actually, I figured you would be working on the system today, considering we have about a month or so before the preliminary database should be completed."

"Database?" Drew said. "We don't even know the specifics of the system yet! I think somewhere along the line, you have been given some bad information."

"Maybe you have been misinformed," Doug countered. "At the meeting, Matt gave all indications you guys were in. Kevin seemed equally ecstatic about the job."

Drew turned his chair back toward his computer and went back to looking over the Green Bay .comU proposal. He was bewildered by Doug's comments, but the more he thought about it, the more he thought Doug might be telling the truth. Did Matt tell Doug this was a go? Why was Kevin at the meeting? Had Doug ever tried the nachos at St. Pius?

As Drew contemplated these things, the phone rang. It was Matt.

"Hey Drew, Doug should be stopping by in a little while," Matt said. "Could you tell him I'm not going to be able to make it down there right now? I think I had some bad fish last night. I'm in pretty bad shape."

"Actually, he's here right now," Drew said.

"Oh ... just tell him I'll catch up with him tomorrow or something."

"Sure Matt, I'll tell him."

"Thanks Drew. You da man."

Although Drew was becoming more and more infuriated by what had transpired in the last few minutes, he decided it was better to question Matt at a later time, and get Doug the hell out of there.

"Well Doug, that was Matt," Drew said.

"Oh, why didn't you just let me talk to him?" Doug said. "Then we could have straightened all this out."

"He didn't have time to talk because he was sick, I guess. He just wants you to leave the papers, and he'll send them back to you tomorrow."

"Oh, well all right then. I knew I was right! I knew it, I knew it, I knew it!"

Doug jumped around the room on one foot, which looked like an amputee playing hopscotch. Drew played it cool and let Doug continue his Dance of Joy. But after 30 seconds or so, Drew had had enough, and Doug seemed to notice.

"I guess maybe I should calm down," Doug said, finally standing on two feet, breathing a little too heavy for a person in a Catholic school uniform. At least he didn't opt for the plaid skirt, Drew thought.

"Here are the papers," Doug said. "Just tell Matt to give me a call tomorrow."

"I'll give him the message," Drew said. "Good luck with the dance video!"

"Ha ha, very funny!" Doug said. "I'll be talking to you again soon."

With that, Doug left, but as he walked out, Katy and Sarina entered. They were surprised to see him, but they became more suspicious when they walked into the WAB to see Drew holding a folder, shaking his head.

"Oh geez," said Sarina, grabbing her chair from the middle of the room to move it back to her work station. "That Doug guy creeps me out. Not as much as the newspaper guy who grabbed my ass, but almost as much. What the hell did he want?"

"It's hard to explain," Drew said.

"Here we go again," Katy said. "What is it with you guys? Why is everything so hard to explain to females? We are not inferior to you!"

"Drew, just ignore her for right now," Sarina said. "Matt messed with her head, and it's her time of the month, so she's a little off right now. But we'll go into that later. How about you try to explain it."

Drew shrugged and pulled out the contracts.

"Remember the other day when Matt said he was contemplating taking on this new job through Foundation?" Drew said. Katy and Sarina nodded. "Well I guess it's more than just contemplating. Doug came here so Matt could sign the contracts."

Drew handed the contracts to the girls. Sarina looked dazed, while Katy still looked furious.

"We talked about this yesterday," Katy said. "I told Matt he was going to have a hard time convincing us to go along with this project. So he must have decided to just go along with it without us!"

"Not really," Drew said. "He decided this a while back, according to Doug. He said they agreed on this Wednesday. And on top of that, Kevin was there!"

"What?" both Sarina and Katy shouted.

"So you all aren't in on this right?" Drew said.

"I'm not," Sarina said. "But I'm not sure about Katy, since she's in love with Matt."

"That is ridiculous," Katy said. "And no, I'm not in on this. Where is the bastard anyway?"

"He won't be down here today, that's for sure," Drew said. "He called while Doug was here to say he wasn't going to make it. He told me he had some bad fish, whatever that means."

"He had FISH ... without me?!?!?!?!" Katy said. "It just keeps getting worse!" Katy jumped up and down for a minute, but not as lively as Doug, then ran into the hallway.

"She's pretty unstable right now," Sarina said. "But it doesn't help that's she's dealing with Michael and Matt at the same time. Other than that, she's just great, though. So you didn't know about any of this either?"

"Sarina, I honestly don't know what to think about this," Drew said. "Maybe we misinterpreted what Matt asked the other day, or maybe I didn't understand exactly what Doug was saying. It looks like Matt has at least a little bit of explaining to do."

"Yeah, and don't forget Kevin," Sarina said. "He hasn't said anything about this either. At least not to me."

"You're right," Drew said. "The first thing we should do is confront Kevin about this. Maybe Doug is playing us. He surely is a silly fellow."

Katy came back into the room, with her eyes red and nose running. She looked at Sarina with a mean look, then shot an even meaner look at Drew. She appeared to be a charging bull, except she was wearing a coat and didn't have a nose ring.

"So it has come to this," Katy said. "It has come to Matt trying to coerce us into just following his lead, regardless. Did anyone sign up for that?"

"Hold on Katy," Drew said. "We don't know ... "

"Oh yes we do," said Katy, flopping down the papers. "Did you look closely at those contracts? We are supposed to have this stuff done in April? Don't we have other obligations?"

"Yes, that's why it doesn't make sense," Sarina said.

"The other night, when Matt and I were here late into the morning, he wanted me to read a binder that Doug gave him about this new product. It explains the whole process, and Matt has it at home, probably sleeping with it or something."

"Don't be jealous," Sarina blurted out.

"Huh?" Drew said. "Did I miss something?"

"Oh nothing, except the fact that Katy kissed Matt the other night while they were here together," Sarina said.

"SARINA!" Katy said. "You weren't supposed to tell ANYONE!"

"I'm sure he would find out eventually," Sarina said.

"This really is turning into a Lifetime Original," said Drew, trying to ease back over to his computer. "Can I have Beau Bridges play my part in the movie? Judith Light has to be one of you, but I'm not sure who the other actress should be."

There was a moment of silence, but no one was actually thinking who would play their parts if a motion picture was made.

"OK, let's concentrate for a minute," Katy said. "What we need is a plan of action."

"Yeah, we already decided that while you were out pouting," Sarina said. "We're going to confront Kevin about this craziness. If he denies it, and it didn't happen, then Doug owes us an explanation. If he doesn't deny it, then Matt needs to tell us what the hell is going on. If he avoids the question and starts talking about food ... well that would be expected, but I think we'll know if something's up."

"This trust issue is killing me," Drew said. "Matt has never intentionally deceived me. I mean, about work-related things. He did try to keep things undercover with a certain female in this room though."

"Can we get past it now?" Katy said.

"It would be a lot easier to get past if you weren't going around kissing him," Drew said.

At that moment, Rex somersaulted into the room. Time seemed to stop for the moment as Rex appeared at the doorway, gave a quick wave and a short nod, jumped slightly, ran forward and completed an almost-perfect somersault. Glares of shock, awe and disbelief appeared on the three audience members.

"Hello everyone!" Rex shouted.

The others were still paralyzed for a few seconds.

"Maybe you deserve an award of some sort for that," Drew said. "Let me look through my desk drawer for a trophy."

"That's OK Drew, I don't need a trophy," Rex said. "It was really fun actually."

Something has gone badly wrong with today, Drew thought. First the monitor bingo incident, then Matt, now this. At least he wasn't stuck in "Groundhog Day," having to relive this day over and over and over. At least, not yet.

Sarina skipped over to Rex and gave him a kiss and hug.

"Babe, you have to be careful with your leg," Sarina said. "You don't want to re-injure yourself, or make it any worse than what it is."

"What happened to you?" Drew said.

"Oh, just a minor flesh wound, skiing," Rex said. "I thought I had broken my leg the other night, but the X-rays were negative. It was just badly bruised."

"Skiing?" Drew said. "I thought you were the skiing pro? How could you have been injured?"

"Well it wasn't under normal ... circumstances," Katy said. "Actually it was midnight, and the Mudslide was sort of closed."

"You guys snuck onto the slope in the middle of the night?" Drew said. "I do work with the most insane people on earth."

"It was part of the initiation," said Rex, forgetting that this information wasn't widely announced.

"Initiation?" Drew said. "I sure am learning a lot today. Do you care to explain?"

"No," Rex said.

"Isn't that surprising," Drew said. "Does anyone want to make any sense today?"

"I'll tell you about it," Sarina said. "Katy and I are members of a secret club that meets every so often. We invited Rex into the club, and he was the first initiated member."

"A secret club ... very interesting," Drew said. "Is it like *Fight Club*? I almost started one of those, then I remembered I didn't like to fight."

"I guess it's like the Fight Club in a sense that, well, it's a club," Katy said. "Other than that, it's a little different."

"So why have I not been invited to join this club?" Drew said.

"It was sort of a girls-only type thing," Sarina said. "But we made an exception for Rex."

"Hey, that's no problem, my feelings aren't completed smashed," Drew said.

"We've been looking to bolster club membership," Katy said. "Jessica said she might be interested in it."

"What is the club called anyway?" Drew said.

"It's called the Black Miniskirt Cult," Rex said. "We have seven members now, and Butch is the president."

Drew laughed and continued to shake his head.

"Are you guys playing a prank on me?" Drew said.

"Sorry, no," Sarina said. "So do you think Jessica would be interested in joining? I bet she has sexy legs and could show them off sometimes."

"Come to think of it, some of this IS starting to make sense," Drew said. "I thought you girls were insane for wearing black miniskirts, or maybe you were trying to impress Kevin and Matt or investors or something. So if I join, do I get to wear a miniskirt as well?"

"They have them in all sizes down at Wal-Mart," Rex said. "Or you could just borrow mine, if you want."

"Oh brother," Drew said. "I think for now, I'm going to pass, but Jessica will probably want to get in on it."

"Great!" Katy said. "That would push enrollment up to eight people. Maybe Ethel could get a couple more people from the bingo or something."

"You're not talking about Ethel McMahan, are you?" Drew said. "She wears a miniskirt? Maybe I will join after all. And if she could get Big Martha in the club, it could get really interesting."

"I think she asked Martha before, and she declined," Sarina said. "But maybe you could talk her into it, over some nachos?"

"It's worth a shot," Drew said.

"It will definitely be nice to watch someone else have to go through the initiation process," Rex said. "I would recommend, though, that the others wear a coat, or at least a shirt, going down the slopes."

The group mulled over other possible types of initiations of the Black Miniskirt Cult. At the same time, it appeared as if another group was starting to form. On Monday, Kevin and perhaps Matt as well were going to have to come up with a few good answers to avoid this type of schism within The Developers.

TWENTY-TWO

Monday had been marked for quite some time as another milestone in the short lifespan of .comU. Phil Harris of Harris Hotel Enterprise was set to be the first celebrity chatter on the system. Unfortunately, it was still somewhat of a mystery as to what types of things Phil would be asked.

Drew at first envisioned users sending their questions during the chat, but the consensus was to allow questions beforehand, too. The group took forever to decide whether to have it during the day or at night, on the weekend or during the week, and they simply decided any time would be OK, as long as it didn't interfere with *The Price is Right* viewing. This also made it possible to someday invite Bob Barker on the show, but Sarina mentioned the show was taped at night and played during the day, so it became a moot point.

Katy, Sarina and Drew arrived at the office early, not only to prepare for the evening event, but to agree on a story about the Doug Morris project.

"I'll be standing behind the door with a bottle, and when Kevin walks in, I'll smash it over his head!" said Drew, scanning the room for a bottle, which he didn't find. "Then Sarina, you can sit him down in a chair while I tie his hands, and Katy, you can interrogate him so we can get to the bottom of this. If he doesn't cooperate, we'll burn his eyelids off!"

Drew continued to search the room for a bottle, and now, a lighter or matches of some sort.

"Sure Drew, that sounds just perfect," Sarina said. "I'm glad you came up with the sensible plan. "We might as well tar and feather him nude, too."

"We must leave the nudity out," Drew said. "Sarina, I don't want you and Katy enjoying this too much. We must be serious."

"I'm not really interested in that nudity part, but I'm sure if it involved Matt, Katy would be," Sarina said.

Katy looked over from her corner and snarled at both Sarina and Drew. She was paying attention!

"I've got a great idea, and maybe this would make you both happy, so you will stop talking about Matt and Michael and whomever else you come up with," Katy said. "I'm going to go on .comU and post a simple personal. Here's what it will say: 'Sex-starved 20-something looking for immediate action. Must like a woman who always wants more, who rarely wears underwear and who always pleases. Send me your photo and I'll send you mine, so you can see ALL of me.' Then will you guys stop hounding me about all this nonsense?"

Drew and Sarina gulped.

"Katy, are you wearing underwear today?" Drew said, prompting Katy to throw a folder filled with paper at him.

"What the hell?" said Katy, standing up and walking over to Drew's seat. "If you must know, here you go."

While Drew was still staring at his email on screen, Katy, standing to his right, unbuttoned her pants and guided them down with her thumb just enough to reveal solid black underwear. Drew knew she was standing next to him but didn't realize what she was doing until Sarina quipped "Katy, what are you doing over there?" Drew spun around to see Katy's bare midriff inches from his face.

"See Drew, I'm wearing underwear," Katy said.

Drew quickly turned his chair back facing his screen.

"OK, OK," Drew said. "I hope I'm not turning you to it."

"Well did you see it?" said Katy, still holding her pants open and waiting for a definite response. "Or do I need to just strip all the way down?"

"Hey, that's a great idea!" said Kevin, entering the room. "I guess I should start getting to work at 8 instead of 8:30!"

Katy turned away from Drew and the door, buttoned herself back up and walked back to her seat.

"Oh, you didn't have to stop on my account," said Kevin, removing his coat at his desk. "Or is everyone going to get a turn?"

"I think it's in everyone's best interest to not address Katy in a sexual fashion for the rest of the day, perhaps until 2058," Sarina said. "Besides, we have more important things to discuss, including one that involves you."

"Well, if you think I'm going to start talking about Jane, forget it!" Kevin said. "Things are going well, and I don't want to screw it up!"

"Lucky for you, it's not about Jane," Drew said. "It's about our friends at Foundation Technologies. You know, that crazy fellow Doug Morris?"

"Oh yeah, I remember him," Kevin said. "He's somewhat of a weirdo, like combining a car salesman with Brainy Smurf, only without the brain."

"Huh?" Sarina asked.

"Uh, never mind, I don't think that analogy worked," Kevin said. "So what do you want to know about him?"

"Well he stopped by here yesterday evening with some contracts," Drew said. "Do you know anything about these contracts?"

Drew threw them to Kevin, and he thumbed through them.

"I know Matt talked about this potential project and stuff, but you guys were here," Kevin said.

"Doug also mentioned to Drew that you and Matt were at a meeting re cently at Foundation with him," said Katy, still aggravated with the earlier underwear escapade but also outraged at what was transpiring. "Was this a true statement?"

"Oh, I know what he's talking about, duh," Kevin said. "Last Wednesday, Matt and I were out, and he wanted to show me Doug's hangout. It's actually pretty cool ... it doesn't look much like an office, but it's all underground, and it's freakin' huge. Anyway, we discussed some stuff for a few minutes and that was about it."

"So Matt didn't agree on signing these contracts and working on this new system?" Sarina said.

"Well if he did, I wasn't paying attention," Kevin said. "Besides, the other day, didn't he ask us what we should do, and if we should work on the system? Why would he ask us if he had already decided what we were going to do?"

"That's basically what we're trying to figure out," Drew said. "But Doug said he brought them over to be signed immediately."

Kevin glanced at the contracts, then walked over to Drew and flung them on his desk.

"I've got an idea," said Kevin, walking back to his workspace. "What if I leisurely bring up the topic to Matt today, just so we can really know what's going on here, without placing blame on him, or Doug, or any other random person?"

"If we placed blame on Chubby Checker, that would be a random person," Katy said. "But Doug and Matt are major players."

"But should we really believe Doug over Matt?" Kevin said. "Drew, did you ask Matt why he wanted the contracts signed already? Did anyone bother to ask him this?"

Drew, Sarina and Katy were silent. The computers, in the meantime, hummed their own variety of "The Twist."

"Exactly," Kevin said. "No one has even asked him. So we should, instead of getting your panties in a twist. I'm assuming that was the cause of the earlier strip show."

Katy glared at Kevin, and he decided to wipe the smirk off his face immediately. The Developers noticed that Katy had, indeed, become a grizzly bear. If you left her alone, she went about her business, gathering papers, clients, berries, etc. But the minute you come near her, and make a reference to her, she pretty much wanted to tear off your arm and roar. Oh, and she liked fish, but no one ever witnessed her in the stream, catching one with her paws.

"So it's settled," Kevin said. "I'll speak to Matt this afternoon about it."

"If he even comes in," Drew said. "He was sick yesterday, so he might just work from home."

"And if we don't hear from him, I might just call him later tonight," Kevin said. "I don't need to be here for the chat thing, right?"

"No, we have it under control," Drew said. "Sarina and I are going to take care of it."

"Sweet," Kevin said. "Because I want to go visit Jane tonight."

"Is she going to give you a strip show?" Katy said. "Well, I hope it's better than mine."

"Well I haven't seen all of yours," Kevin said. "And don't take this personally, Katy. But she does, indeed, have a killer strip show."

***

Kevin didn't have a moment to lose. At a time like this, there was only one thing he needed to do: take a pit stop at McDonald's.

But this time, it wasn't a stop just for him. Kevin ordered two Big Macs and two large fries, Fresh Prince-style. Jane would be heading back to her dorm from class for lunch, so he wanted to surprise her with some grub.

Kevin pulled into the dorm parking lot and immediately dialed Jane's number. As the phone rang, he noticed Jane fighting the wind and cold to make it to the building. While the flurries had all but disappeared, the wind gusts appeared to pick up just in time for Kevin to make a dash out of the car. He grabbed the food sack and held it under his right arm, then he pulled out the soft drinks. After shoving the door shut with his backside, Kevin remembered it was freaking cold outside. Kevin barely made it to the sidewalk, and just before Jane made it to the door about 30 feet in front of him, he called out to her.

"Wait up!" said Kevin, as the McDonald's sack begin to slide out from under his arm and the condensation on both Cokes turned to ice and began to coat his hands. There was a momentary delay — apparently the wind had slowed down the speed of his voice — but then Jane turned around. She bounced back toward Kevin, caught the food just before it fell and again made her way back to the dorm. Kevin followed.

"Holy shit, it's cold!" said Kevin, jumping up and down in a frugal attempt to warm up in the dorm room foyer. Jane removed her wool cap, which revealed more of her long brown hair.

"Cold, honey?" said Jane, giving Kevin a peck on the cheek. "Just be glad YOU didn't have to walk to class today. It wasn't fun. I saw a little girl get blown away earlier. I would've stopped to help, but these football players were walking in front of me, shielding the wind, so I figured that was my best chance to make it over to campus."

Kevin and Jane made it down to Jane's room. While Kevin grabbed two TV trays, Jane checked the food, and because it wasn't too hot, she pulled out a couple of plates and nuked it.

"So how were your classes today?" Kevin said. "Any calculus tests?"

"Nope, no quizzes, no tests," Jane said. "I have a paper due in Psych later this week, but it's nothing too complex. How was work today?"

"Well, I witnessed a strip show," said Kevin, watching Jane divide the food and almost dropping it on the floor.

"A strip show?" Jane said.

"Well, Katy has gone mad or something. She has some real relationship issues. Anyway, I got there too late to see anything. Besides, I told the gang that your strip show was better."

"You WHAT?"

"It was just a joke. Actually, it was an eventful morning. Matt hasn't really told the others about the big government job, and I didn't know what to tell them."

"What do you mean he hasn't told them? I thought you guys talked about it the other day?"

"We did. It's just that they think everything is still up in the air, but I thought Matt was going to sign the contracts and start development. But now I'm confused about the whole thing, like I don't think it's my job to tell them what we're doing. I don't make the decisions."

"That's pretty weird. So what did you tell them?"

"I said I would mention something to Matt, just to make sure everyone is on the same page. Drew wasn't too happy with that answer, but Katy and Sarina kind of went along with it."

"Hmm ... maybe the others don't want to work on this project," said Jane, finishing off her Big Mac. Jane was the first girl Kevin ever met who could polish off a McDonald's meal faster than he could. He thought that was extremely sexy.

"But what about .comU, and the Green Bay project?" Jane said.

"Those will just take resources away from the bigger project," Kevin said. "It's hard to tell what the timelines are on these projects anyway. What time are your classes tomorrow?"

Jane shrugged, then she opened up her backpack and pulled out her planner.

"Looks pretty normal for a Tuesday," Jane said. "Oh yeah, my 9:30 got canceled. That's my Psych class, and our teacher is giving us that day to do research."

"Well then, how would you like to do your research in a different atmosphere ... like at my place?" Kevin said.

"On a school night?" Jane said. "I don't know if that's such a good idea."

"How much homework do you have left?"

"Not too much, and I should be able to get it finished at study table tonight."

"When will you get out of there?"

"We practice early Mondays ... at 5:30. Then study table at 7:30, but I guess I don't have to stay for all of it."

"OK, what about this: After study table, you come down to Malorett, and I'll make you dinner. Then you can work on any remaining homework OR you can work on that fabulous strip show of yours. What do you say?"

Jane thought for a minute and stared into Kevin's begging eyes.

"If you have something really good for dinner," Jane said, "I MIGHT be able to make it."

"It'll be good!" Kevin said.

Jane and Kevin talked for a few more minutes, but Jane had to make her way back to campus for American Literature class. Kevin drove her back to campus, then left for Malorett.

As Kevin sped back toward the office, he determined that perhaps today wouldn't be so bad after all. He was still a bit leery of what to make of the whole Doug Morris situation, but that was outweighed by the prospects of seeing Jane later in the evening. Kevin tried to think what would be the best thing he could make for dinner ... maybe steak? Chicken? Seafood? And what about sides? What about dessert? Even though Kevin had just eaten, he was getting hungry thinking about these great possibilities. He definitely needed to get his mind off his stomach and get some other things straightened out. He dialed Matt's cellphone number.

"Hello?" said an obviously weak Matt.

"Yo, Matt, what's up," said Kevin, just reaching the outer limits of Moxee. "You don't sound so good, really. I guess you're not doing any Elmer Fudd impersonations, huh?"

"Actually it's much easier, but it's not quite as funny," Matt said. "That's probably why Elmer never got sick on the cartoons because his voice is immeasurably boring in that context."

"I see," Kevin said. "I did have a reason to call you this afternoon, so I hope it's not a bad time."

"I'm at home and sick. It's a bad time, but considering I'm not sitting on the pot or standing over it, now is fine."

"When I was in the office earlier today, I was interrogated about the Super Information Portal stuff. Doug hinted to the crew that the work should go on as planned. The crew didn't seem too ecstatic about it."

"Were they mad? They didn't want to work on the system?"

"I'm not really positive, but I don't think they were thinking this was a done deal, nor something they would be working on immediately. Are we going to be working on this immediately?"

Matt hesitated for a second, because he was uncertain about a lot of things: Were they to start on this immediately? What did Doug tell the others? Was Elmer Fudd gay, and just trying to create a hot-tub atmosphere for Bugs Bunny with a cauldron and floating carrots?

"Kevin, I think this has turned into a little bit more of a complex issue than I anticipated," said Matt. "I'm kind of pissed at Doug for talking to everyone before I did. So what did he tell them anyway?"

"That the contracts needed to be signed, or at least that you were going to sign them," Kevin said. "And then he went on to tell Drew that the work would be starting soon."

"It's about time for me to give Doug a call. Then we can ... "

Before Matt could finish his sentence, Doug was beeping in.

"Hey, that's Doug now," Matt said. "Let me take his call, and I'll get back to you."

"All right," Kevin said. "Later."

Matt flipped over to talk to Doug.

"Hello?" said Matt, trying to sound stronger.

"Hey good buddy! It's your friend Doug Morris!" Doug, was never void of energy, Matt thought. "I dropped off the contracts last night, and Hugh said you were at home sick."

"Hugh?" Matt said. "Do you mean Drew?"

"Oh yeah, Drew," Doug said. "Drew, Hugh, Pooh, it's all the same. Anyway, are you really sick? Or were you out on the slopes playing with a ski bunny or two?"

"No Doug, I am pretty sick. I thought it was food poisoning, but I've been sick all of yesterday and today. Maybe it's stress-related."

"Well, I can just call you back tomorrow and reschedule our meeting."

"The meeting? I should be back up and running tomorrow. But I was going to call you about the contracts."

"Matt, if you just bring them tomorrow, that will suffice. They should still be at the office."

"That's what I need to talk to you about, Doug. What did you tell Drew anyway?"

"About what, the contracts?"

"Yeah?"

"I just told them they needed to be signed before we started working, and since that would be soon, they should probably be signed soon."

"Well I hate to break the news to you, but the others did not know the whole plan was a go yet. I hadn't told them."

"You hadn't?"

"No! You guys said the other day not to talk to too many people just yet, until we started working on it."

"Gee willikers, Matt, I had totally forgotten about that. So will this be a problem?"

"I won't know until I get into work, but supposedly they aren't happy about me going behind their back."

"But Matt, you're in charge, so you should tell them what they are going to do."

"It doesn't quite work like that at my office."

"Well maybe we should start looking for another company to work with, if this is going to be a problem."

Matt was caught off guard by this conversation, since Doug was trying to play it off as if Matt had been the one who had done something wrong.

"No Doug, we are still in," Matt said. "In fact, I seem to be feeling better already. I'll be up for that meeting in the morning. Kevin will most likely be coming along as well."

"That sounds like the Matt I know," Doug said. "Then tomorrow, we can discuss any other details that need to be ironed out before you sign the contracts. We need to get started on this stuff, or else we're going to lose the government contract."

"That won't be a problem at all," Matt said. "I will see you at 9 tomorrow at your office."

"Sounds good, Matt," Doug said. "I'll see you then."

As Matt hung up, he started feeling even worse. He was ready to start the work on the SIP, but now he wasn't sure of the best way to confront the rest of the group. Hopefully they would understand, once it was apparent how much this job would help the team as a whole.

Matt wasn't quite ready to throw up, but he was also starting to feel a migraine in the works. He figured the best thing to do would be to sleep until the meeting. He still had to check in with the others, so he took the easy way out and called Kevin back.

"Hey Matt ... did you get it fixed up?" said Kevin, answering his phone.

"At least for now," Matt said. "We're meeting with Doug and the government guys again tomorrow morning at 9. Do you want me to pick you up, or do you want to meet at the office?"

Kevin wasn't expecting anything that early, except maybe a little rough-housing with Jane, if they hadn't gotten enough in the evening.

"You can just pick me up," Kevin said. "I'm having company tonight, but I'll try to be ready."

"OK, I'll see you about 20 till 9," said Matt. "I'm going to bed, so tell everyone not to wake me up, unless it is absolutely urgent."

"Will do," Kevin said. "Get some rest. We definitely have to be on our game tomorrow."

***

Drew had to explain to Phil Harris that for the first .comU chat, he didn't have to answer EVERY question. But Phil went ahead with the inquisition and determined that he was there, it was 7 and he had to say something to anything thrown at him. As Drew retrieved the newest email messages, Sarina posted the few Phil answered.

Phil, can you mix in some country with rap every once in awhile on your show?
– **TuPac**

Dear Tu-Pac, I do like rap, but mostly old school, like NWA, Tribe Called Quest. Unfortunately, I don't have a show, but if I did, I would play some of this stuff. I KNEW you were still alive!

Mr. Harris, I had some problems the last time I stayed at one of your hotels. I was having my way with a fine-looking local co-ed, and just then, the phone in the room rang. It was my wife! Can't you screen the calls so something like this won't happen?
– **Pissed Off**

Dear POed, You can always tell the front desk to hold all calls. You can even ask for room service at specific times, in case there is a bad time for you. Thanks for the question, I think.

Phil! Why don't you ever call anymore?
– **Martha**

Dear Martha, Do I know you?

Luckily for all involved, the questions did get a little better, and began to pertain to why Phil was there in the first place. In future months, Phil had hoped to put together an array of events for .comU users. Some would be online only, but others would be taking place around town. The next big upcoming event would be the St. Patrick's Day party, which Phil himself would be hosting at his platinum hotel, The Royal. Up until the day of the party, Phil would give away a weekend package for two for The Royal and tickets to the party. And obviously, it wouldn't be a party without hordes of green beer and other random green things, including a vacation getaway to Greenland.

The chat went according to plan. They wrapped up the chat around 9:15, after Phil wrote that he was not a Hilton and did not have any dateable daughters. Phil thanked The Developers for having him online and took off. Drew reviewed the current system activity, Sarina finished posting the last couple of questions and Katy did her usual of tracking the advertisers and generally keeping the office organized.

Normally, Drew would call Matt and let him know everything went as planned, but tonight wasn't normal. Earlier, Kevin let the others know Matt was still sick and might not make it in the morning either. Kevin also assured the others that Matt would address the group about the SIP project.

"Man, Matt must really be sick," Katy said. "He didn't call here a single time all day. That might be a first."

"Yeah, I hope he gets better and gets back here," Drew said. "We need him here to discuss this other project."

"But in the meantime, it seems like we can take care of things ourselves," Katy said. "It was nice to be able to breathe a little without having to worry too much about other things that WE don't even know about."

"Come on now Katy, there's no reason to be negative," Sarina said.

"I'm not trying to be negative," Katy said. "I'm just making the point that we did this without the others."

Katy, Drew and Sarina grabbed their coats and headed for their cars. The wind had died down, and it was remarkably calm outside. Rain was in the forecast for Tuesday, which meant a little more snow that was on the ground would disappear. While The Developers agreed a new snow could make an old Malorett downtown look breathtaking, an old snow made it look even more decrepit than it actually was. Regardless of its appearance, less snow was welcomed most during the winter months, at least for those who need to get around town. This included Katy, who needed to run to a few advertisers and to the newspaper as well tomorrow afternoon.

"Katy, we'll see you after your errands tomorrow," Drew said. "Everyone, be careful on your way home tonight. These roads look a little slick."

"Yeah, you all be careful," Sarina said. "We have another big day ahead. Let's hope we get the answers we need."

"And if we don't," said Katy, getting in her car, "we can take matters into our own hands."

Katy shut the door, and Sarina and Drew looked at each other and sighed. While Katy had her moments of getting a little big-headed, they thought maybe this time, she had a right to be.

@:) = :-& ... :-(

TWENTY-THREE

Matt spent most of Monday night flipping through the SIP binder. But it appeared that his attempt to be as knowledgeable as possible about the project was backfiring. Not only did Matt's stomach continue to feel as if he were stuck in a magician's box, being sliced with knives, he managed no more than 30 minutes of interrupted sleep until 5 a.m. He finally went to sleep for good, and his alarm woke him up what seemed like mere seconds later, at 6:30.

Matt staggered into the shower, then tried to determine if this really was food poisoning or something else. He was aware of the potential coup at the office. He was also aware that if he didn't move on this project, Doug would find another development company. As The Developers president, Matt couldn't just sit back and play the unassuming fool. The problem was, Matt thought, that was what it appeared he was doing: not explaining things, not giving definitive answers, calling in sick, etc. Then again, as a government contractor, maybe this type of leadership would bolster his chances as a future politician.

That part made Matt cringe, or maybe it was the feeling of sharp jabs into his abdomen. There was no way he could cancel this meeting today, but Matt wondered if he would even last through all of it. He had already told Kevin that he would drive to the meeting, but on second thought, it might be best if Kevin drove. Matt started to call and reveal the new plans, but he remembered Kevin had company. So instead, Matt planned to drive to Kevin's and just leave his 4x4 there.

As the morning progressed, Matt felt adequate, and driving 10 minutes to Kevin's apartment didn't seem too bad. Matt knocked on Kevin's apartment door. The door swung open, and Matt's sickness immediately disappeared as he was confronted with a gorgeous, tall brunette. Briefly, Matt shook his head and took a step back to check the number on the outside. It was, in fact,

Kevin's.

"Hi, you must be Matt," said Jane, who, unlike movie stars, had matted hair and a pale complexion in the morning. "I remember you from Ski Frenzy."

"Oh ... yeah, that's me," said Matt, suddenly remembering his sickness, and meeting Jane. "Is Kevin ready to go? I think I might ask him to drive. I'm not feeling too well."

"He's in the other room, and should be out any minute," Jane said. "Kevin mentioned you possibly had food poisoning. Doesn't that usually go away after a day or so?"

"That's what I thought," Matt said. "Maybe once I get through this meeting, the feeling will go away."

"Yeah, we can only hope so," said Kevin, entering the living room while adjusting his tie. Jane recommended Kevin wear the solid purple tie as opposed to the forest green and light gray one. Actually, Jane recommended neither, but since Kevin had just two ties, and the recommendation didn't come until five minutes ago, it was too late to make a more suitable suggestion.

"Kevin, you don't mind driving, do you?" Matt said.

"No, that's cool," Kevin said. "My car isn't in too bad shape ... just a couple of old food containers, but nothing serious."

Matt stepped back outside, jingled his keys and turned toward Jane.

"So what are you going to do, hang out here?" Matt said.

"I have some studying to catch up on," Jane said.

"And then I'll come back here for lunch, maybe like noon, before you have to go back," Kevin added. "How long do you think this meeting will last, an hour or two?"

"With these guys, who knows," Matt said. "But surely we won't be there until noon. I don't know if I'll even make it to 10."

"Speaking of which, we need to get out of here," said Kevin, checking Jane's watch. He gave her a peck on the cheek and headed out the door, just behind Matt. "See you later, hon!"

Matt went over to his vehicle and retrieved his briefcase. As Kevin waved goodbye to Jane, Matt slowly opened the passenger-side door and practically fell into the seat. Things seemed to be a little hazy to Matt, and Kevin was concerned as he pulled out of the apartment parking lot.

"Dude, are you going to be able to make it to the meeting?" Kevin said.

"Yeah, yeah," Matt said. "Just keep driving."

"I think it would be in your best interest for me to stop up here, so we can get medical attention," Kevin said.

"No, that's OK," Matt said.

But it was too late. Kevin had pulled into McDonald's. Even though Matt was dizzy, he was pretty sure this wasn't a hospital.

"Uh, Kevin, this is McDonald's," Matt said.

"Well DUH!" Kevin said. "What are your symptoms again?"

"Why?"

"Just tell me what they are."

"OK, I have a pain in my side, a splitting headache and I see about seven steering wheels right now. No, make it eight."

Kevin pulled up to the drive-thru menu.

"I would like a cinnamon roll, an Egg McMuffin and two orange juices, please," Kevin barked into the microphone. He then turned to Matt. "With those symptoms, it's apparent you need a cinnamon roll. With that and a little OJ, you should be cleared up in no time. However, make certain you don't bite into the plastic fork. That could compound your problems."

At this point Matt wasn't sure if this was actually happening, or if he was just hallucinating. Regardless, when Kevin obtained the food, Matt figured it would be worth it to try the cinnamon roll and see what happened. In the meantime, Kevin unwrapped his Egg McMuffin. Foundation Technologies was just a few miles down the road, so even though it was already 10 till, neither worried about being late.

As they arrived, Kevin finished his orange juice, got out of the car and made his way to Matt's side, to give him an extra boost. Luckily, the cinnamon roll and juice did appear to give Matt at least a little bit of an energy burst. Kevin extended his hand, but Matt declined, jumping out of the car. He then took a couple of hops, stretched and took in a breath of air.

"Maybe that little stop did do some good," said Matt, peering over at the Chinese restaurant, just beside Foundation. "I think I'll be able to outlast this meeting after all."

"I know, I know, the doctor is in," Kevin said. "But I have a feeling our day is about ready to get a whole lot more interesting. Let's hope it doesn't make us ill."

***

Matt and Kevin watched anxiously as Rusty Snopek completed the construction of the miniature SIP on the Foundation's boardroom table. Rusty was the engineer who had met with the group the week before, along with Blake Smith, from the FCC, regarding the project. The presentation was pretty good last time, but never in their wildest dreams could they have envisioned an actual model of the system.

The thing was, the model was extremely cheesy. The biggest pieces of the model were the substations, or the server clusters. Rusty positioned those on a partial United States map. It wasn't a complete map because the West Coast was destined for later SIP construction. Of course, unless it fell into the ocean first. Blake and Doug reasoned that inside Phase II, California and the Silicon Valley would be highlighted, which would give the region the upper hand in new hardware and software. In addition, the cost to connect the West to the nation's capital with their current setup would be highly expensive so early into the project.

So for the model, Rusty slid a server cluster to the Upper Peninsula, one near D.C. and a handful of others in the South, Midwest and New England regions. The miniature map did resemble the map Matt and Kevin had viewed previously, with the exception of the color-coded triangles. Apparently all of the substations in this model were first-run hubs, and that was the only concern for this meeting.

Doug and Blake entered the boardroom. While most of the pain from Matt's stomach had subsided, he still wondered how useful another overview would be.

"Matt, my man!" said Doug, shaking Matt's hand like a frantic stalker trying to shield his identity. "How are you feeling? Are you ready for a big day?"

"Yeah, I'm feeling better, Doug," Matt said. "I think maybe this morning was the end of the sickness."

"Well that is really good to hear," Doug said. "By the way, did you bring the contracts with you?"

"No I didn't, Doug. Can I just get them to you tomorrow? They are back at the office."

Doug started to speak, but he noticed Blake glaring at him. Matt noticed, too, but he wasn't sure what to make of it.

"Oh Matt, that's no big deal. I have copies here," Doug said. "After the meeting, we can get things taken care of."

"Well ... OK," Matt said."

Rusty appeared to be finished setting up the model; at least, he stopped building and took a seat on the other side of the table. Blake took his place next to the model, farthest from the doorway; Doug sat to his left, and Kevin and Matt to the right; and Rusty sat next to Kevin, nearest the door. If anyone else showed, there were plenty of seats available, Kevin thought, as the boardroom could probably seat 20 people, assuming there were a few more chairs and the fire marshal obliged.

"All right, it's time to get down to business," Blake said. "We have the go-ahead from Washington to get the SIP under way. Of course, there are a lot of heads, and a lot of manpower, involved in such an intensive project. The main item we need to discuss today is what has been done and what we need from Foundation Technologies, and of course, The Developers.

"As you can see by this model, there are five hubs within Phase I of this plan. The one flanking Baltimore is being set up as we speak, and the one here will be starting construction this week. We have ordered the majority of the hardware, and it will be installed beginning Wednesday.

"In the meantime, the database system to be used is the next obvious crucial piece for the project. Matt, I'm assuming you've immersed yourself within the SIP specs, correct?"

Matt was taken aback that he was being called on like school, but he was paying attention.

"Yes, I've looked over the binder a couple of times," Matt said.

"And did you see anything unusual, out of the ordinary or something your group could not handle?" Blake said.

"There were a few minor questions, but nothing too terribly difficult," Matt said.

"Well now is the time to address those minor questions," Rusty said. "It's now or never."

"I guess it comes down to the storage of some of this information," Matt said. "It just doesn't seem like this is really legal at this point."

"So are you saying it cannot be done, or that it isn't legal?" Blake said.

"Of course it can be done," Matt said. "I will, though, need to defer to Drew regarding additional secure methods, because he's up on that type of stuff. But I don't see any reason why it wouldn't work."

"That's the best answer," Blake said. "If we are paying your group to produce a certain product, we would expect nothing less. So what were the other questions?"

Matt gulped, and wondered if that was a good enough answer for his first question.

"As far as general items, that's the main thing," Matt said. "I'll have to review my notes for anything else. Again, they were simple items."

"There was one thing I was curious about," Kevin interrupted. "How concerned should we be with the number of users on the system? Will we have enough bandwidth if everyone in the region is using it? I know this is basically out of scope for our part, but it would be useful to know how this works."

Blake nodded to Rusty, who rose from his chair and moved toward the miniature set.

"Kevin, thanks for the fantastic lead-in to the rehash of the system," Blake said.

"Did you say rehash, or hash browns?" Kevin said. "I knew I had forgotten something at McDonald's."

Blake stepped back and dimmed the overhead lights. On the table, the substations slowly started to glow, and had somewhat of a blueish hue to them. Matt and Kevin glanced at each other, not realizing that both of them thought exactly the same thing: This was way better than a field trip to the planetarium.

"Like we discussed last time, the hubs in this model represent the server clusters," Rusty said. "But let's take this a step further here."

He picked up each of the substations and pressed a small red button located on their undersides. Each emitted various colors of light, so Rusty had to position them correctly on the map for them to make any sense. After close to a minute of Rusty meticulously adjusting the models — with the rest of the group eyeing each move — the connections from cluster to cluster illuminated the room to the point where Kevin almost pulled out his sunglasses.

"Now Kevin, to answer your question, here's what we have," Rusty said. "As you can see, each server cluster will provide a backbone to the adjoining clusters. That way, we have redundancy throughout the system, creating somewhat of a circle around the sites.

"Obviously, all will not be connected immediately. The most important thing will be to connect the Baltimore hub to the Indianapolis hub to the hub here. From there, we plan to branch down through St. Louis and Atlanta to provide the redundancy. Then we'll stretch back up to Cleveland, Boston and New York, which will provide basically a third level of backup power, should any of the others fail."

"Well then what does the rollout schedule look like?" Matt said. "Because if there are going to be as many users on this as it appears — meaning most of the United States east of the Mississippi — I mean, we've never built a system that large. I'm not saying we can't, I'm just saying we'll need a lot of testing."

"That's understandable, and part of the plan," Blake said. "The important thing will be gathering the data, and putting it into the system. Once we have the information, and once everything is connected throughout, then we predict there will be more people putting a strain on the respective servers."

Matt and Kevin basically had the same question: What the hell was going on here? Both sat steadfast and determined not to let on to their potential ignorance, and possibly it would just tail off and disappear, like the aftertaste of a cheap, warm beer.

Doug, on the other hand, gleefully watched the light show and appeared apprehensive about making some sort of provocative comment.

"Blake, this system is going to be FABULOUS!" Doug said. "I cannot wait to see its fruition. How about we break for lunch, then come back and discuss the database scenario?"

The clock showed 11:15, which seemed early for lunch, Kevin thought. The time had passed so fast that Kevin had completely forgotten about Jane, back at his apartment. She was probably taking a bubble bath or lying in his bed, naked, waiting for him to jump in. Unfortunately, that did not appear to be on the card for today, as the meeting was far from over.

As Bo, the Keeper of the Waiting Room, took orders for Chinese (Where else could they eat without driving at least five miles?), Kevin hurriedly tried to reach Jane on his cellphone. He wasn't sure she would answer his phone, but then again, she knew they would need to make lunch plans at some point.

"Hello?"

"Jane, how are things going?"

"I've gotten a lot done this morning, Kevin! I finished up my homework like 30 minutes ago, so I've just kind of been hanging out, watching TV, nothing too crazy."

"Really? Well that's great. Actually, I ... "

"Yeah, and I still have three hours before I need to go back to class. So when will you be back? I'm still in bed, waiting for you, Kevy."

Kevin thought that a business meeting was the last place he should be aroused. But there really wasn't a way to get around that, with his girlfriend turning into a phone sex operator.

"Jane, that sounds really good. I mean, really, really, really, really good. But I can't."

"You can't? What's wrong? You had enough already?"

"No, no! It's not like that. We are still at this meeting. We haven't even gotten to our part of it yet."

"How is that possible, you've been gone for like three hours."

"Yeah, this is what it's like in the business world, at least our business world. One hour of a meeting equals about five minutes of important information. For this project, we need about 30 minutes of important information, so we have a long way to go."

Jane didn't respond immediately.

"Jane, babe, are you OK?"

"Sure, Kevin, I understand. I'll talk to you later."

"Are you mad?"

But she had already hung up. If sitting in a meeting wasn't bad enough, Kevin now wouldn't be able to see the hottest girl alive until ... hmm, that was a good question, he thought. It wouldn't be tonight, probably not tomorrow. Now, for the rest of the meeting, instead of trying to concentrate on the biggest proposition of his career, Kevin found himself contemplating any plan feasible of making this up to Jane. He just hoped she would accept the apology because the thought of losing her seemed like the emptiest feeling he had ever felt. Even comparing it to not eating for a day seemed silly. In fact, Kevin decided that Jane had become his favorite thing, topping a Big Mac. He almost fell out of his chair when he decided this, and it was at that time, 11:26 a.m., that Kevin Gentry knew he was in love with Jane Wilson.

***

As Matt half-heartedly listened to Doug's explanation to the group concerning Foundation's part of the project, he wondered if this particular moment in history would be remembered for anything more than the most senseless meeting that ever took place. Matt even contemplated asking The Keeper of the Waiting Room if there was a dictionary nearby, to see if there was a picture of this meeting next to the word "pointless." He knew this would take up some of his time, but he was fairly certain they would be out of there by lunch, or soon thereafter. With the rest of the team working back at the office, he hoped that the email he sent to Drew, Sarina and Katy this morning would suffice. In the email, Matt said he was meeting with Doug and others to once again go over the SIP system. He had hoped this would buy him enough time to make amends with the others but win them over more gradually.

Unfortunately, when dealing with these fellows, there wouldn't be anything gradual, if they didn't want it.

Because of the earlier exchange, Matt knew he wouldn't be able to get out of there without signing on for the project. During lunch, Rusty had even tried to get Matt to sign because "everyone would feel much more at ease about the project," Rusty explained. Matt wavered, buying a little more time, and Kevin changed the subject by telling everyone he was in love. Of course, what he wanted to say was, "My girl's in heat, and I'm stuck here with you crazy asses. This is bull shit." Kevin thought better of it, though, and decided to leave some of the details out.

"And that, my friends, is exactly what we're going to do with the setup," said Doug, waltzing around the room, discussing the hardwiring of the server clusters. "We have many things in place, and starting Thursday, we'll have a full force working on the project."

"That's beautiful," said Blake, turning his attention to Matt. "So Mr. Severson, let us discuss your end of the solution."

"Well that's the best thing I've heard all day," Matt said. "I was starting to wonder if you even needed to keep track of anything in database format anymore."

The group gave a small chuckle, similar to a sitcom laugh track.

"As the system has been specified, the database itself doesn't look bad at all," Matt said. "We have already developed this with .comU. Creating the database is the easy part. More importantly though, is the issue of security. From what we discussed before, Foundation will be in charge of the security for the hardware. But we may also be interested in implementing an additional feature with the main database."

"Is that really necessary?" Blake said. "The system will already be utilizing the Advanced Encryption Standard, Rijndael."

"That might be enough, but let me explain," Matt said. "What if, instead of one database, there were multiple databases set up on multiple servers. A certain person's system record would actually be a conglomeration of multiple system records. And they would all be connected through a different key, so the database could easily construct a complete record for viewing. Many programs do this already, but we want to make it possible for different servers, at different locations, to be able to handle a wide variety of functions."

"That sounds nice, in a futuristic, Jetson's sort of way," Rusty said. "But that couldn't work, not with the load being placed on the server."

"Yep, that's the same thing we thought at first," Matt said. "But Drew has come up with a way, at least on paper, to make this happen so seamlessly that it would be impossible to tell any sort of lag of system resources."

"So even if a hacker gets in, and finds a database, or finds all the databases, he wouldn't be able to match up the info properly?" Rusty said.

"Drew used to hack into various systems in college all the time," Matt said. "He'd leave files in different locations, then access them later and connect them all together. Now implementing it on a larger scale ... well, he did some preliminary testing back then, but not to the extent we need to do here."

"Excellent," Blake said. "I thought maybe we needed to discuss the database side more today, but I think that part is in good hands. Honestly, what we really need to do is just get started on this thing."

"I'll second that!" said Doug, whose grin was growing faster than a sea monkey. "All that's left, Matt, is for you to sign on."

Doug handed Matt the contracts. Kevin looked on and shrugged as Matt put the ink to the paper. He didn't seem too reluctant, Kevin thought, but he also didn't seem too eager, either.

"I guess if the others at work have a problem, we'll have to come up with something else to do," said Matt as he shook Blake's hand on the deal.

"And if that happens, there will be plenty other things your people can do," Blake said. "Of course, they'll be fired and working someplace else, but still they can find something else!"

Doug, Blake and Rusty laughed at the notion. Kevin told Matt not to worry, but at this stage, it was hard not to. Matt had made a decision, he was sticking with it and the others would have to accept it. At least, that would make things the easiest.

***

"Go to the bingo, topless?" said Jessica to the Black Miniskirt Cult on Tuesday night. "This is a joke, right?"

"Let me tell you what a joke is," said Rex, holding up his crutches. "This club, it's not for the weak-hearted. But the rewards are many."

"Really, there are rewards here?" Butch said. "I guess I'm still waiting for mine. Then again, I didn't have an initiation. Then again, I'm in charge. Motion to reward me with ... rewards?"

There was silence.

"OK, motion declined," Butch said. "Let's move on to more pressing business, shall we?"

Jessica, Butch, Rex, Katy, Sarina and Ginger all piled into Rex's blue 4runner. Tuesday had been a fairly odd day down at the office. The work seemed fairly normal: Katy collecting two new advertisers, one for the next chat session and one for The Profiler; Sarina compiling new names and numbers for the cellphone directory; Drew making database and site modifications to the entertainment and education sections; and even Crissy "working" on her webcam while answering a good deal of user questions. Site usage had even jumped 5 percent from the previous day, but there were still no major problems.

The odd part was the fact that Matt and Kevin never made it in. Matt had sent an email telling the rest of the gang about a big meeting discussing the SIP, but there was no contact the rest of the day, at least until 4 p.m. Matt called and spoke with Drew, telling him the meeting went well and since a storm front was supposedly moving in that evening, they were just going to work from home.

But even though Matt and Kevin were missing all day, no one really missed them because there were more important things going on that night. Of course, Drew just thought he was going to celebrate his birthday fairly low key by calling some numbers, and maybe the parish would make him a cake or something. Jessica had told him she was going out with friends and might try to swing by the bingo hall later, just to see what was going on.

"Your 49th number, G-54," exclaimed Drew, alerting the crowd that if a coverall occurred in more than 49 numbers, the actual jackpot winnings would be reduced.

"BINGO!"

Drew heard it, but he couldn't determine where exactly it was coming from. There seemed to be some commotion coming from the non-smoking section, but he wasn't positive that's where the call came from. Just then, he saw Jessica: black miniskirt, bright white tennis shoes and the necklace he gave her last Christmas, rounding the corner and heading up the middle aisle. The crowd in the main hall gasped as it finally hit Drew why he could clearly see the necklace. He appeared to be stuck in a high state of shock: not the highest state, like witnessing a horrible automobile accident, but more like witnessing a dog driving a truck. Jessica approached the caller stand, walked up the steps, still jiggling as she threw Drew's face right into her exposed breasts.

"Happy birthday, honey," Jessica said. She then turned to the crowd and waved. They stood and cheered, while Drew continued to be motionless. Jessica gave Drew a quick kiss then bounced down the stairs, exiting out the back door. The group proceeded to sing "Happy Birthday" to their favorite caller. Drew was 32, a step closer to the ageless patrons of St. Pius and a step farther away from the hip people on the Internet. Yet at this moment, the Internet had become a fad, while his wife had been so real, so beautiful ... and so nude.

"Wasn't that a great birthday present?" Butch yelled from the back corner. He carried the cake, as the others followed.

"Um, that was different," Drew said. "Who was that girl? She was hot."

"She WAS hot!" said Jimmy Dickson, overhearing their conversation. "How much for 30 minutes with her?"

"You want 30 minutes?" Ethel McMahan said. "You couldn't even last five."

"I'll give you 35, Jimmy," Martha Singleton said. "But I need more nachos."

Jessica returned to the group, this time clothed more appropriately. As the group stood on the stage during the bingo halftime, Rex noticed someone else approaching the caller area swiftly.

"Does anyone know that guy, he looks like he's in a hurry," Rex said. The group turned and let out a sigh. It was Michael.

"Katy, I saw you turning into St. Pius, so I followed you in," Michael said.

"Um, that's stalking," Sarina said. "But if you want to call it following, well OK."

"Michael, what do you want?" Katy said. "We're in the middle of something here."

"Yes, yes, I see that," Michael said. "That's what I want to talk to you about. I want to be a PART of something. Like this, this party. One of the fellows in the back said it was an initiation of some sort. I've always wanted to be in a club with an initiation!"

"Is this guy serious?" Rex said.

"Sadly, yes," Sarina said.

"What happened to your Russian love?" Katy said.

"Oh Martina, I'm not sure," Michael said. "I guess she's still coming here. But I ... we want to be a part of something."

"You don't even know what this is," Drew said. "And trust me, you don't want to know."

"Oh yes, definitely, I do!" Michael said. "Please let me into your club. I won't do any harm. I'll help with the bake sale, the car wash. Just let me know!"

"Sorry to break the news to you," Rex said. "But there are no guys allowed."

"Huh, no guys?" Michael said. "What are you?"

"What does it look like?" Rex said.

Michael refrained from answering, especially because Rex was wearing his new pair of sweat pants, which were pink, still covered at the top by his favorite pair of shorts.

"Uh, OK, well what about you?" said Michael, pointing to Drew.

"I'm not in it," Drew said. "I just call the bingo and mind my own business."

"Well what about you?" said Michael, pointing to Butch.

"I've seen you before, down at the office, and I have one thing to say," said Butch, scratching his abdomen. "You aren't of our kind. You's a be needin' to run along, son. A black miniskirt isn't in your cards tonight, buster."

Defeated, Michael left the stage, and walked in the door. Meanwhile, the cult — plus Drew and the bingoers — had one hell of a time in the church cafeteria.

TWENTY-FOUR

The chatter between Drew and Sarina halted abruptly Wednesday morning when Kevin walked into the WAB.

"Hey guys," said Kevin, powering up his computer. "Did I miss much yesterday?"

Neither Drew nor Sarina seemed too interested to answer.

"Same shit, different day," Drew said. "Well, I shouldn't say the exact same shit, considering we were missing two people."

"Yeah, we got caught up over at Foundation much longer than antici-pated," Kevin said. "Those guys never shut up. I wonder when they ever get any work accomplished."

"Speaking of work," Sarina said, "are we having a meeting about this SIP thing soon? I mean, I don't know when we're going to fit it in, but we've got to come to a consensus about what to do. I guess Matt will go over it when he comes in?"

"That makes sense," Kevin said. "But he didn't say as much to me. I sup-pose we'll find out when he gets here."

"He's not still sick, is he?" Drew said.

"No he's good," Kevin said. "Although, I figured he'd be here by now. It's already almost nine and ... "

Before Kevin could finish, they heard a vehicle in the parking lot. Matt hopped out of his 4x4 and briskly walked toward the door. The storm the night before had been grossly exaggerated and left just a dusting of snow along the Malorett streets. But even with the sun out this early, most of the snow that covered the city landscape wouldn't be melting today, nor tomor-row and probably not any time before the summer, which was approximately four decades away.

"Good morning, everyone," said Matt, positioning his laptop in place and removing his jacket.

"Hey, I remember you," Sarina said with a partially sarcastic tone. "Didn't you use to work here?"

"Ha ha," Matt said. "I don't know if I was sick because I was working too hard, or working too hard because I was sick. A couple of good nights' rests and a good rest in a meeting has put me back on track."

"So by saying 'back on track,' you mean we're going to discuss the next .comU, the new features for it, as well as the SIP?" Drew said. "After we discussed it yesterday, we really feel that the need to move on this Green Bay thing should take precedence. I've already started on the proposal, based on what we have for the system already."

"Good work, Drew," Matt said. "I'm just wondering, though, if we should focus so many resources on that project. I mean we don't even know what type of budget they are dealing with, and furthermore, how the system would run in a city that size."

"On the other hand, we already have the product," Sarina said. "And from the beginning, we designed it in a way to use for other cities."

"True," Matt said. "But this SIP project sounds like a real winner. Maybe there's a way we can work on both. Drew, the guys at the meeting really liked your idea keeping the information in separate server locations."

"Huh?" Drew said. "You talked to them about that?"

"Yeah, and they thought that's exactly the type of thing that could be used in the new system," Matt said.

Drew was a bit confused at to why Matt would bring up something that big without discussing it further beforehand. He had toyed with running database calls in multiple locations in college, but the issues of making it work on this large scale was purely theoretical, if not asinine. While the SIP appeared to be something that could warrant a more serious discussion, the idea would have to be mulled over more carefully.

"Matt, we need to take a step back here," said Drew, taking a deep breath and swiveling around in his chair to face his boss. "I have no clue how long it would take to make it work, and even if it would."

"That's OK," Matt said. "I just think maybe today we could spend a little time maybe outlining the possibilities of making it work."

"Would this meeting include a trip over to Dave's?" Kevin said, never missing a moment to mention his inner grumblings. "I could go for Cheezie Wheezie about now."

"That's not a bad idea," Matt said. "Today is the first time I've felt like eating in what seems like a century. Can everyone attend? Where's Katy?"

"She had to run some errands this morning," Sarina said. "I think she had to go to the newspaper, but she should be back pretty soon."

"OK, that's cool," said Matt, with the SIP contract still lingering in his head. He assumed maybe lunch would be the right time to bring up the fact that the work on the SIP system needed to begin immediately. Matt wanted to ease into this, but the chances of that appeared dim.

Katy returned, just in time to give Matt the cold shoulder as she made a quick move to her desk. During the last couple of days, Katy had taken on the bulk of administrative work, with Matt being on the disabled list. This didn't seem to be a burden. But at the same time, Katy really didn't consider herself as having the power to make group decisions. But with the uncertainty looming with the SIP system, Katy was nearing the point where she was just going to have to put her foot down.

"Katy, how is everything in your world?" said Matt after more than 20 minutes had elapsed since her return.

"Hey, Matt, sorry I don't really have much time to talk right now," Katy said. "Phil wanted me to prepare a new contract for his sponsorship role in the system. He has gotten a lot of good feedback from the contest and the chat, so he's trying to figure out other ways to get involved."

"That's really great," Matt said. "What ideas does he have?"

"Well, Phil knew the annual Tootsie Roll drive was coming up, so he wants to put a spin on things, and apparently, the Knights of Columbus are interested," Katy said. "He said they are going to try to make a model of the city out of different sizes of Tootsie Rolls. I'm not sure how exactly that will work, but it seemed like a good idea."

"A whole city, out of Tootsie Rolls?" said Kevin, wiping his eyes. "That's beautiful!"

"That's definitely interesting," Drew said. "Maybe they can use the small ones sort of like those small Lincoln Logs. I guess they could soften them up a bit, to put them together."

"He's supposed to meet with the Knights later today, so I wanted to give him an idea of what we can do here," Katy said.

"Cool," Sarina said. "I'll look over what we have coming up soon. I'm supposed to meet with the interns later today as well."

"We can discuss it over lunch, and lump it together with a myriad of other things," Matt said.

"Yeah, tell me about it," said Drew, finally discovering a file folder containing his notes on the information-splitting database system. If remembering where his notes were located took 30 minutes, Drew wondered if he would even remember what the whole damn thing was about in the first place.

"Let's head over to Dave's a little after noon," Matt said. "Everyone write down a few things you'd like to bring up so we can put everything on the table."

"As long as they give me crayons, that's OK with me," Drew said.

***

It had been nearly three weeks since the entire group met at Dave's. That was a drought for The Developers, who practically held weekly meetings there for a while. The last time, though, the group was reaching a consensus on a common goal for the .comU development. This time, The Developers seemed headed for a crossroad.

Matt wasn't sure what to say about the SIP contracts. Kevin knew about the contracts, but decided to focus his effort on selecting the proper toppings for his burger. Katy was up to her neck in paperwork and exes, which was pretty usual. Sarina was trying to figure out how to get all the Tech interns on the same page while her co-workers didn't even know their priorities. Drew was busy sketching the new split database structure with a broken green crayon.

"So Drew, let's discuss this secure database structure," Matt said. "From what I recall, the information for a single person, or record, will actually be housed in multiple locations, and then pieced together when necessary."

"That's the essential basis of it," Drew said. "When a component calls the record, the databases could talk, put the pieces together in the proper order and send the correct information."

"Why is this more secure?" said Katy, sipping on her Coke and noticing Kevin already needed a refill on his iced tea.

"It's more secure because you would need all the databases to get one full record," Drew said. "If a hacker just found one of the databases, he would have a hard time using just that piece."

"Well, unless that piece included social security numbers or credit card numbers," Sarina said.

"But it would be encrypted, and even still, you wouldn't have the names to go with it," Matt said. "Most e-commerce solutions utilize this to keep credit card numbers and names separate, but most names are still associated with addresses, phone numbers, etc."

"That's correct," Drew said. "Which means that dividing the information to this extent may also restrict spammers from grabbing both email addresses and names within the same record. That way, even if they did get the emails, there would be no names, and therefore, that sort of mail would probably show as junk."

"Everybody talks about how bad junk email is," Kevin said, "but those people would probably also not receive any email if they didn't get junk mail. I mean I'm thankful for those people who are going to give me 27 million dollars because they are from Nigeria and they want to move to America. And also I'm thankful for those great offers to get out of debt and make money from your very own home."

Matt started to continue, but then he realized he couldn't tell if Kevin was joking. After hesitating, Katy spoke up.

"You are kidding Kevin, right?" Katy said.

"Oh ... of course I'm kidding," Kevin said. "I mean, um, junk email is bad and stuff. Yeah, I'm going to look for that waitress to get some more tea."

The others looked on as Kevin stood and started walking around the restaurant, finally bumping into a waiter.

"Did I miss something, or was Kevin just saying he was pro-junk email?" Drew said.

"Must be that girl on his mind," Sarina said. "Or maybe a burger ... or who the hell knows."

"He's one crazy mutha," Matt said. "So Drew, do you think it will be hard to implement this database structure?"

"Well that depends on whether or not it actually works," Drew said. "And to determine if it could work ... it could take months."

"Surely it wouldn't take months," Matt said. "If we determined the fields, and worked on it exclusively ... "

"We're not working on this exclusively though," Drew said. "At least not until next week. I still have to finish that proposal."

"We definitely can't do everything at once," Matt said. "But we have to get this in working order, by the beginning of next month."

"Next month," Katy said. "What if it doesn't even work?"

"Yeah, this is all speculation," Drew said. "There are no definites involved."

Matt was getting increasingly frustrated, but before he could say anything, the waitress arrived with their food. He tore into his burger and decided to give it a few minutes before continuing the discussion. Matt had hoped the others would realize the importance of this speculative work, but instead, they had apparently changed the subject completely.

"Kevin, what do you think is the sexiest burger topping?" Sarina said.

"The sexiest burger topping?" Kevin said. "That's a tough one."

"I would have to vote for the tomato," Drew said. "It's juicy, it's red, it's delicious. Also, when I think of tomatoes, I think of Julia Roberts for some reason, and she is hot."

"That's a good observation," Kevin said. "But I'm not that big on tomatoes."

Katy wasn't in a particularly good mood, which seemed standard for the past week or so, but she thought this was peculiar enough to voice her own opinion.

"I think I would vote for the pickle," Katy said.

"Hmm, that is interesting," Sarina said. "What about lettuce? It's soft and leafy and could always be used for edible underwear."

"What, during the Olympics?" Drew said.

"OK, I figured out my answer," Kevin said. "It would have to be pepper."

"Pepper?" Drew said. "Is that an actual topping?"

"I always get pepper on my burgers," Kevin said. "If they have fresh ground pepper, it's even better. Pepper just makes everything hotter, makes your mouth water and once you get a little taste, you gotta keep getting more. And if you get too much of it, it comes out your nose."

"Huh?" Katy said. "What does that have to do with being sexy?"

"You know, if your mouth waters, then ... " Kevin started to say.

"No, the part about it coming out your nose," Katy said.

"Oh, I see," said Kevin. "You'll just have to use your imagination."

Katy decided it would be in her best interest just to finish her sandwich and not try to figure out what Kevin meant by the sexual reference. Meanwhile, Matt thought now would be a good time to again revisit the SIP situation.

"Well Drew, I understand what you mean by the database split not being the easiest task in our short history," Matt started. "And while it is important, it isn't crucial to the first build of the SIP. It's not a project stopper if it's impossible."

"That's a good thing," Drew said. "Because who knows how long something like that will take."

"At the very least, we still have the new .comU system to put together," Sarina said. "Possibly while working on that, we can come up with some ideas about this database dilemma."

"And maybe the Green Bay and SIP projects can be developed simultaneously," Matt said. "But Doug requests that we move quickly on his project. In fact, he wanted to have a preliminary system up by next month."

"I guess it could happen if we essentially use what we already have," Katy said. "But don't they need all sorts of additional functionality?"

"It's hard to tell," Matt said. "It's going to be a little different, and most of it is outlined in the binder, I think."

"Oh the binder, of course," Katy said. "Matt, didn't you spend time the other day reading it for the fifth time? I was actually working on a project to translate it into Latin."

"Should we put a lock on it, like a Gutenberg Bible?" Drew said.

"I've read through some of the binder," said Kevin, with a piece of lettuce hanging out of his mouth. Kevin had been quiet, which wasn't too unusual during feeding time. "The plan they have is pretty good, and from what I've heard, we're going to be reeling in the dough pretty fast."

"I've heard that before," Drew said. "And usually when someone talks about reeling in the dough, it ends up in some disaster that has to be rebuilt like 342 times. We definitely need time to do it right."

"Sure, we need time, but everything we build takes time, right?" Matt said.

"It's just that we can't continue to divide our focus," Drew said. "If we build the system for Green Bay, we can continue to knock out kinks, make advancements, etc. But if we throw in this other project, how can we keep the two straight? I highly recommend focusing on Green Bay, then going back to the SIP."

"But Drew, we don't have a choice like that," Kevin said. "The government doesn't wait on anyone. If we don't work on it, they will find someone else who will."

"If that's the case, then I'm out," Drew said.

Matt didn't like the way the conversation had turned, but it was pretty much expected. At some point, though, he was going to have to break the news to the group that they really had no choice. How Matt was going to explain the agreement was anyone's guess. It was increasingly evident, though, that whatever method he used was not going to be well-received.

***

When The Developers returned to the office, the place was virtually silent. The computers were humming, the hard drives spinning and the fans blowing at the usual levels. Occasionally the howling wind could be heard, possibly from a new storm brewing. But there was absolutely zero conversation between the bunch.

Matt still hadn't determined the appropriate time to give the news. Drew was working on the Green Bay proposal, and Matt decided that hopefully his time spent doing that would be necessary for the SIP project. Matt also had to take off for a 4 p.m. meeting with the Malorett Chamber of Commerce.

Katy and Kevin worked together on a few items dealing with the sponsors, primarily those dealing with the schools portion of .comU. There was a list of features that had to be added, so Kevin decided he would think about it a little more that evening. More importantly, he needed to go see Jane and try to explain the events of yesterday.

Sarina looked over Drew's information before preparing to meet online with the interns. They were also going to discuss the education additions as well as various other system improvements. Sarina expected all four interns to all be available for the chat, and as she checked on Instant Messenger, they had already started a group chat. As the oldest and most experienced intern Crissy Calhoun (sexy_crissy) had conversed with the other three — Mike Dalton (mikeyd), Edgar Saprelli (esap48) and Amie Ortiz (amelieu) — regarding ideas and suggestions about what they should be doing for .comU.

runner4life: Hey, I finally made it here. How is everyone?

sexy_crissy: we were wondering exactly when you'd make it on for the chat :-) we have already gone over a multitude of things ... so you had a couple of things for the schools area right?

runner4life: Yes, we are expanding the Malorett public school system section, and we'll need some help in monitoring this new area. Basically the teachers will have their own areas, so they can upload files and assign and collect homework more efficiently. But we need an intern or two to be available on weeknights for a basic tutorial service.

mikeyd: what types of ?s are the kids going to ask? What grade levels?

runner4life: We're going to start it out for the high school levels, since those are the kids mostly likely to be utilizing the computer for help. If it's successful, we might expand it to other levels.

esap48: cool idea. I should be available Mondays and Wednesdays. What times are we going to do this?

runner4life: We were going to start 6-8 Monday through Thursday. As long as there are two or three people answering questions, we should be OK.

amelieu: I'm good for Thursdays ... might be available another night

sexy_crissy: I can Tuesday and Thursday for now.

mikeyd: not sure yet, but I should be able to pick up a day or two. What about the other project? What are we going to do for that?

runner4life: Which other project?

mikeyd: the govt one ... Jane was telling us about it, but she didn't know too many details. It sounded pretty cool.

runner4life: The government project?

mikeyd: Yeah, Jane said Kevin and Matt signed off to build the system, and that's why Kevin left her at his place for so long.

runner4life: Signed off? It's all just speculation, I don't think we're definitely going to do it.

esap48: When she was telling us about it, everything sure sounded definite. Kevin made it sound like he probably wouldn't be able to leave the office because you guys would be so busy.

Sarina was trying to not show that she was bewildered and pissed at the same time, but that was nearly becoming impossible. Fortunately, neither Matt nor Kevin were in the office, so she couldn't lash out at them immediately.

runner4life: Well I'm going to check on this stuff immediately. If for some reason we are supposed to be doing something with this now, then maybe we aren't starting this tutoring service. No one tells me anything!

sexy_crissy: Let us know something soon. Until then, we'll just chill and work on other things.

runner4life: OK, I'll let you guys talk about that stuff, but I gotta get going. ttyl

Sarina turned toward the others. Drew was still analyzing the proposal, and Katy had her head buried in something that looked halfway important.

"Interesting news from the interns," Sarina said.

"What now, Crissy is televising an erogenous zone body piercing?" Drew said.

"No, she did that last week," Katy said.

"Apparently, the SIP work is a go," Sarina said. "Mike said that Jane said that Kevin said that the contracts were signed and everything."

"You just said the word 'said' like 200 times," Drew said. "Of course, I just said it twice, make it three times now."

"Sarina, what did you say?" Katy said. "The contracts have been signed?"

"That's what they said," Sarina said.

"OK, there's another, you're going to have to stop using that word," Drew said.

"Well I've had it," Katy said. "I'm going to pay Matt a visit tonight. If he really went behind our back, we're going to have to deal with it in a harsh fashion."

"Like what, fine him?" Drew said.

"I'm serious, this is crazy," Katy said. "We should be able to have a say in what happens here, and if not, then I don't want to work with him anymore."

"I've got a job opening," came from the hallway, but it was obviously Butch. Besides, who else would be standing out in the hallway anyway?

"You have a job opening?" Drew said to no one, until Butch entered the room. "Doing what?"

"I need someone to take over my duties as the president of the cult," Butch said. "It's consuming too much of my time."

"What, like two hours a week?" Katy said.

"Yes, but that's two hours I could be doing something more productive, like refilling my tubs of cheese balls," Butch said.

"I think that's the kind of productivity Henry Ford had in mind with the assembly line," Drew said.

"Henry Ford?" Butch said. "You know him? I played Little League with that guy. He would come up to bat, and I would say, 'Hey Ford, have you driven one lately?' "

"Right," Drew said. "Anyway, back to a more important task in hand, which is trying to figure out what we are doing here at work. Does anyone know?"

Butch raised his hand and jumped up and down frantically, looking like a child who needed to go to the bathroom.

"If Katy is going to Matt's, then let's wait here and see what happens," Sarina said.

"Why are we going to wait here?" Drew said.

"If they are working on something else, I say we just don't let them into the building, until they have a full explanation," Katy said. "And if we don't like the explanation, then we can still keep them out."

"That seems a bit radical, but at least it will get the point across," Drew said. "If you go over there in a few hours, we'll wait around until we hear from you. And if you don't come back, we'll assume the worst and just hold down the fort."

"It's hard to imagine the office as a fort," Katy said. "But if a war is what it takes to get this figured out, then we'll have a war."

"Dem's fightin' words!" said Butch, skipping out the doorway and fumbling down the hall.

***

Matt, still peering over the SIP binder, needed a short break, so he decided to heat up baked salmon he had made two nights before. The meeting with the chamber went well, and while Matt felt completely over his sickness, the SIP development loomed even more so than ever. A schism had taken form within The Developers, and it was looking harder and harder to turn around.

Thursday, Matt had scheduled a meeting with Blake and Rusty to give them a better estimate on the time to implement at least a skeleton system. It was 7:30, and Matt was already dreading entering the WAB the next morning. He had a copy of the .comU database structure on his laptop, so he thought it would be helpful to maybe determine the usage and conversion to SIP.

But as time ticked away, Matt's guilty conscious seemed to grow and grow, almost as if the SIP was becoming his own tell-tale heart. The problem had to be remedied before the morning, he thought. He couldn't talk to Drew, but maybe there was another way. Maybe Katy would be willing to listen ...

Matt picked up his phone, dialed the first five digits of Katy's number, then hung up. He knew he had to say something, but he didn't know what to say. It would be better to collect his thoughts, explain he had been handcuffed and that in the long run, everything would work out. He started to dial the number again, but before he pressed a button, there was a knock at the door. Matt thought it was strange, but there had been a recent report of Jehovah's Witnesses staying out late at night in his neighborhood, so it wasn't unreasonable. He opened the door and saw Katy, looking like she was full of a noble gas and getting ready to burst.

"What the hell are you doing?" said Katy, barging through the door and making her way up the two-step landing, into the living room. "How could you do this to us?"

"Do what to who?" Matt said.

"Why are you acting like you don't know what I'm talking about?"

"Should I know what you're talking about?"

Katy already wasn't a happy camper, but after this exchange, she was on par with a couple who had just had their kids swallowed by mountain lions.

"We found out you had signed the contracts for the SIP," Katy said. "From the interns. From the interns!" Why are they privy to this information?"

"Yeah, I've been meaning to talk to you guys about this," Matt said.

"And just when were you going to do that?" Katy said. "After the system was built?"

"Katy I had no choice. The government guys, they put so much pressure on me to get going with this project. One minute, we were just speculating what to do, the next minute, I was already in. It was an hypnotic experience."

"Well that's great Matthew, but we aren't interested in your excuses. We are down for some serious business because you can't just make decisions on a whim without consulting the group."

"There was nothing I could do! I tried to buy time, but it wouldn't work. They are promising all this money up front and ... "

"We aren't interested in the money. We are interested in working as a team. And even though you are the president or whatever, we're thinking about cutting you out of the team."

"You can't kick me out," said Matt, laughing. "Just how do you think you can?"

"Sarina and Drew aren't letting you back into the office until we get this straightened out," said Katy, vehemently pacing around the room. "What do you have to say about that?"

Matt didn't know how to respond. He composed this team, and now they were turning on him, all because he had to give the government an immediate answer?

"Surely you jest," Matt said.

"Do you want to place a bet on that?" Katy said.

"Um, not really," Matt said. "So how can we rectify this? If we don't build the SIP, I'm guessing there will be repercussions, considering I've signed the contract."

"Then the only way is to ... is that salmon I smell?" said Katy, sniffing curiously.

"Yes it is, I had fish earlier," Matt said. "There's still some in the kitchen. Would you like to finish it off?"

"Well, I haven't had dinner yet," Katy said.

The two proceeded into the kitchen, where Matt removed the remaining piece of fish from the dish in the oven. Matt grabbed a plate, and Katy started to realize just how hungry she was. Katy sat at the kitchen table, and Matt added a scoop of cole slaw to her plate. She smiled and began to eat ravenously.

"Thanks, Matt," said Katy, her mouth half full. "I was freakin' starving."

"No problem, it's just leftovers," Matt said. "I think I'll fix us both a glass of tea and maybe we can discuss other things when you finish dinner."

Matt turned toward the refrigerator to grab the tea, but before he turned around, Katy had moved behind him and had grabbed hold of his waist. Stunned, Matt turned around as Katy gave him a huge open mouth kiss.

"No, really, Matt," said Katy, wiping off her mouth. "Thanks for everything. I can't go on like this for too much longer. You have been a really good friend, and with Michael trying to work his way back into my life ... I've been thinking a lot about you. About how maybe we should get back together."

"You're not serious, right?" Matt said. "That has to be the fish talking."

"I'm serious Matt," Katy said. "I think tonight is a good night to start again."

Katy landed another big one on Matt, and even though he was surprised, he wasn't about to turn it down. Katy was the one girl, throughout his entire life, who had meant everything to him. He had told her this so many times that it had become fruitless, but he always thought there might be a chance, somewhere in the future. And if the future was now, in the heat of a fish dinner, Matt had no choice but to surrender. Considering the amount of stress he had succumbed to in the last few days, there was no doubt in Matt's mind that the best thing for him to do was to swim upstream tonight.

>:¢ + @:) ... :-#

TWENTY-FIVE

Katy awoke and heard her phone beeping voraciously. Most nights she changed the ring to silent, so no one could wake her up. Last night, though, she must have forgotten because "Girls Just Want to Have Fun" was blaring in the bedroom. No, this wasn't Katy's favorite song; Sarina had tinkered with the phone one day and managed to install the Cyndi Lauper hit, if you can call it that. Katy had one of the older cellphone models so actually, the tones supposedly associated with the song made it sound more like old Atari music than anything.

After realizing the noise was coming from the floor, and after swaying her hand back and forth on the ground to locate her phone, Katy hit the button and said hello in a groggy manner.

"Katy! It's Sarina. I thought you were going to let us know about your 'talk.' Drew and I are already down at the office, and Kevin is outside."

"Sarina, what ... what time is it?"

"It's 8:20. We got down here at 8 just in case anyone got here earlier. Kevin just pulled up. Butch is even here if we need him."

"Uh, maybe we should, I don't know what ... "

"Katy, are you on your way to work now? Where are you?"

As they were talking, the realization set in that she was still at Matt's. She couldn't tell Sarina this, but what could she tell her? The plan was to come to a compromise, but the compromise never seemed to involve sex, even when it was 1850, and Missouri was involved.

"Sarina, yes, I'm on my way into work," said Katy, noticing that maybe it wouldn't be a good idea to wear a T-shirt and nothing else into work. "I still have to get ready, but I'll be there shortly."

"And what do you recommend we do about Kevin?" Sarina said. "Should we let him into work?"

"Absolutely not!" Katy said. "Tell him Matt said for him to go home. He might believe it."

"We'll give it a try," Sarina said. "See you shortly."

Sarina hung up, turned toward Drew and shrugged.

"Maybe we should have come up with a better plan than this," Drew said. "How can we stop him from coming in? It's not like we're the British Royal Guard in front of the queen. At the very least, those guys could throw their furry hats at troublemakers."

Sarina and Drew heard the front door open, and they waited in anticipation for Kevin to enter the WAB. Still, neither of them appeared to know what their actions would be, but in the end, they would need to convince Kevin to leave.

"Hey guys," said Kevin, strolling into the office. "Did you notice that smell in the hallway?"

"What smell?" said Sarina, trying to take deeper breaths to determine what he meant. "I didn't notice ... "

Before Sarina could finish, the fire alarm in the kitchen erupted. The group was perplexed, so Drew decided to check it out. But before he could make his way to the WAB entrance, Butch appeared.

"We've got a little problem in the kitchen," said Butch over the ringing alarm. "I accidentally put tin foil in the microwave again. We need to exit the premises. Kevin, you lead the way."

"Um, OK," grimaced Kevin as he walked out. Butch, his smiley face T-shirt singed, winked at Sarina and Drew once Kevin had exited. They followed Kevin to the door, but as he walked out, Butch grabbed the top portion of the door and swung it shut. Before Kevin could see what was going on, Butch lurched forward to grab the bottom handle as well. Kevin knocked a couple of times on the top half, but Butch had managed to lock them both from the inside.

"That'll keep him out," said Butch, smashing his hands like cymbals.

"Well, that was a good end result," said Drew as Kevin continued to pound on the door. "But there's a slight problem. He has no idea why you just did that."

"Say what?" said Butch, scratching his head. "I thought you wanted him out? I came up with the foil-microwave trick myself. Oh no, I just remembered, that tin foil is HOT HOT HOT!"

Butch raced through the hallway and back into the kitchen, while Drew and Sarina stood solemnly in front of the door. Sarina could still see Kevin's arm through the peep hole, and as his knocks grew with intensity, Sarina's sense of urgency grew.

"What the hell?" said Kevin, muffled through the thick Dutch-style door. "Let me in. I left my doughnuts on the table!"

Sarina faced Drew, who was now pacing between the door and a small window on the left side of the foyer. He could see only Kevin's back leg from that vantage point.

"I'm going to get his doughnuts," Drew said. "You need to tell him ... something."

"OK," said Sarina, as Drew marched back to the office. "Kevin? Kevin, can you hear me?"

"Just barely," Kevin said. "I must have my doughnuts! Let me in or I'll slash your tires with my pointy teeth!"

"No need to be drastic," Sarina said. "Matt called earlier and wants you to go back home."

"Go home?" Kevin said. "Why?"

"Something to do with work," Sarina said. "I think it's a meeting you are supposed to attend. He's going to pick you up there."

"Why wouldn't he just pick me up here?" Kevin said. "And why would you lock me out? Let me in, damn it!"

Sarina braced herself as Kevin pulled on the front handle. The bolt began to slowly indent the door's wooden casing, much like a beaver gnawing on a log. As the fibers began to break up, Sarina backed away from the door. Finally, the door swung open and Kevin, stumbling backward a bit, regained his footing and approached the door.

"Ah ha!" said Kevin, dusting the wood shavings off his blue jeans. "I knew this door would never stand for a little force! It's a good thing, too, because I didn't want to slash your tires, Sarina. And I don't care how good of gas mileage your Metro gets!"

Before Kevin went any farther, though, Drew strolled down the hallway with a small package of powdered doughnuts. Kevin ran to greet him.

"My babies, my babies!" said Kevin, tearing open the wrapper and inhaling the first one. "I thought I'd never see you again!"

"First off, you should chew with your mouth closed," Sarina said. "But while eating powdered doughnuts, maybe you should look the other way because smoke is coming from your mouth."

"Smoke? Did you say smoke?" said Butch, running down the corridor. "The tin foil is out. I repeat, the tin foil is out!"

"Why did you lock me out, Butch?" asked Kevin, still gobbling the powdered delicacies.

"Um, I misunderstood Drew and Sarina," said Butch, looking down at his shirt to finally realize his favorite shirt, the tan smiley face, had been seriously damaged. "I thought it was a .comU game."

"But really, Matt just wants you to run back home," Drew said. "I think he's going to pick you up at 10."

"Oh, that's no biggie," Kevin said. "This certainly was a silly ordeal, then, if that's what it's all about."

"This ain't no 'Hokey Pokey,' " Butch said. "That's what it's all about."

Kevin got in his car and started the ignition after polishing off the sixth and final doughnut. But just as he pulled out of the parking lot, he thought something seemed a little strange, even though Butch is capable of anything. Instead of returning home, Kevin headed for Matt's place. It was only 9, so if Matt were at home, there was still plenty of time before he would be at Kevin's. Kevin was determined to report this bizarre behavior to Matt before he got wind of it.

***

"Be vewwy, vewwy quiet ... I'm hunting wabbits!" said Matt as he dove underneath the blankets. He touched Katy's tummy for a moment, and although she was extremely ticklish, she didn't seem to be laughing as hard as she normally did.

"Katy, baby, what's a matter?" Matt said.

"Oh nothing," said Katy, inching out and facing away from Matt. "Just thinking about us ... and about US."

"You mean the United States?" Matt said. "I know what you mean. Should they abolish the death penalty? Should they start nationwide health insurance? What about privatizing Social Security?"

"No, dumbass!" said Katy, flipping off the covers and standing next to the bed. "I mean US, as in you and me, and US, as in The Developers. We have a problem."

"We do?" said Matt, still lying in bed. "Honestly, I don't remember what it is. I've slept since then. Although with you in bed, I didn't sleep AT ALL last night. Do do-do do."

"Enough with the jokes!" Katy said. "We still have a major problem at work. We, as in myself, Drew and Sarina, are not prepared to work on the SIP yet."

"But I can't go back and not sign the contracts," Matt said. "So what can we do?"

"I think it's pretty apparent what we can do," Katy said as she began to get dressed. "You and Kevin can work on that SIP thing, and we will work on .comU. We can just split the company down the middle."

"We can't really split the company down the middle, we have an odd number of people," Matt said.

"Yeah, and since I'm on the side with more people, I'm not backing down from our stance," Katy said. "Plus I have the main developer, and I'm one of the main client contacts. It appears my side is definitely the strongest of the two."

"This is ludicrous!" said Matt, jumping out of bed. "You can't just take my employees and lock me out of the office. What authority do you have?"

"I don't need authority; I have the backing of two of the three other employees. Democracy rules in Malorett."

"Get out of here Katy, you're not making any sense," Matt said.

"I think I will!" said Katy, grabbing her coat. "So while we're at the office working, what are you going to do, have a Big Mac-eating contest with Kevin?"

"Hey, we've got business of our own," said Matt, moving toward Katy and slowly nudging her closer to the door. "We shall see which side wins."

"Yeah, it's pretty obvious which one will," Katy said.

As she started to open the door, Matt clasped his hands around Katy's waist. She fell back into him, and slowly turned around. Matt brushed back Katy's medium-length straight hair and began to kiss her. Matt swirled his tongue around Katy's and had lost all sense of being. He could not think of anything — anything at all — as the two were lip-locked for what seemed like an eternity. His heart raced faster than ever before, but at the same time, he felt calm, almost to the point of being numb, throughout his body. They stood at the door and goose bumps came over both of their bodies. Finally, as time neared its end, they separated, opened their eyes and stared at each other in astonishment.

"Wow," Matt said. "That was really good."

"Yeah, that was ... great!" Katy said.

Matt, still dazed a bit, tried to think of something else to say, but he couldn't stop staring at the beautiful woman with which he had just shared this precious moment.

"I'm not sure, but wow, that was amazing."

Before Katy could answer, they noticed a car pulling into Matt's driveway. It was Kevin's.

"I guess that was it," said Katy, backing away from Matt and heading out the door. "I'll see you ... later?"

"Will you come back tonight?" Matt said.

"Yes," said Katy, walking down the steps toward the driveway. She hurried to her car, and as Kevin was getting out of his, Katy jumped into hers. Matt had a spacious enough driveway so Katy backed out unscathed while Kevin and Matt spectated.

Kevin approached Matt at the front door.

"So she came over here to tell you about what they did to me," Kevin said. "They told me you wanted to talk to me about something, but it all seemed suspicious. I almost didn't get my doughnuts!"

"I think we're going to have to go to plan B," Matt said to Kevin as they walked back inside. "We need to meet again with Doug and tell him what we can do, at least at this point. It's starting to get ugly."

"Man, this is pretty ridiculous," Kevin said. "And furthermore, I can't believe Katy came over here to rub it in your face."

"The thing is," Matt said, "with a girl like Katy, you can never get enough of that rubbing in your face."

***

"Matt, my man, this is so not cool," said Doug, pacing in his office while Matt and Kevin sat in chairs and tried to determine why there was a cardboard cutout of Kermit the Frog in a grown man's office.

"What should we do, frog, I mean, Doug?" Matt said. "The deal can't be off. I know we can do this, just Kevin and I."

"Yeah, we talked about it on the way over," Kevin said. "We have the database, we have the code. We can still connect to the server and grab anything else that's necessary."

"I think the two of us could start out doing a lot of the work, and we could coerce the others eventually," Matt said. "They have their own thing going on, and we might be spreading ourselves a little thin, but I think it will work."

"It doesn't sound like you are spreading yourself thin by choice though," Doug said. "It sounds like mutiny!"

For an instant, Doug remembered his days as a pirate, sailing the seas, looking for booty — both the money and the girls variety. He took a deep breath and could smell the saltwater breeze lingering around him, just as a deckhand hoisted the ship's flag nearby. Ah yes, Doug thought, the pirate's life is still the life for me. Then he opened his eyes and realized he had never been a pirate, and that his vision was just a rehashing of a dream he had after watching *Pirates of the Caribbean* on DVD three times in one night.

"I don't think I can make a decision on this without consulting Blake," said Doug, regaining composure. "Let's give him a quick buzz and see what he thinks."

As Doug dialed, Matt and Kevin conversed quietly in the corner.

"Should we just throw in the towel?" Matt said. "Maybe we can't do this."

"No way," Kevin said. "Remember it's only temporary. We'll get the crew back into this in no time. Once they see we're not really changing that much, and the money is coming in, how will they think any differently?"

"Yeah, I think that's what I thought last week when I signed the contracts," Matt said. "And look what happened!"

"Hello, Blake Smith?" said Doug as Matt and Kevin halted their conversation and inched toward Doug's desk. "Yes, this is Doug Morris from Foundation. We have a very, very minor issue, but I'm going to put you on speaker and let Matt explain."

Doug pressed a button and set the receiver back in its base.

"Matt, how are you?" Blake said.

"I'm good Blake, but we do have something to address," Matt said. "Apparently my .com-padres are not seeing eye to eye about the SIP project. But I don't see a problem with the schedule because Kevin and I are in it for the long haul."

"So you still think next week, we'll have something to try out?" Blake said.

"Most definitely," Matt said. "We are going to be working as much as possible from now until then. I have a laptop, and I think Kevin might have an older computer at home he can use."

"Yeah, I got the doughnuts but not the laptop," Kevin said.

"Well then, it's settled," Blake said. "Guys, get in touch with me tomorrow regarding your progress. I hope to see something by Monday or Tuesday or else we're going to have to look at other options."

"That's understandable," Matt said.

"We won't disappoint you," Kevin said.

"I would prefer if you didn't," Blake said. "Because up here in D.C., we don't like to be disappointed. Gotta jet. Bye."

Doug pressed a button on the speaker phone to turn it off.

"Then again, who likes to be disappointed?" said Doug, sitting down and swiveling in his chair. "What's worse is finding out a treasure map that has been forged."

"Huh?" Matt and Kevin said.

"Uh, never mind," Doug said. "You'd better go. From the tone in Blake's voice, you might want to get started this very moment."

***

Of all the days to show, and of all the people to show, Katy noticed Gene Simons' car in the parking lot just as she pulled into the office. Then again, those newspaper folks seem to have a nose for a story, especially if it is a risque one. Katy walked inside to see Gene calmly sitting at her desk, ogling Sarina's way.

"Katy darling, glad you could make it," Gene said. "They said you would be in shortly, but I guess that translates to any time before 10. Anything new to report?"

Although a lot was indeed going on, Katy wanted to make sure it didn't turn into a circus.

"It seems pretty calm today, Gene," said Katy, ruffling through papers. "We're planning an upgrade to the education portion of the site, but we're probably a good week away from that. Maybe I could give you some info and you could promo it at the beginning of next week."

"That sounds like a plan," said Gene, scooting his chair toward Sarina. "What about you, Sarina, anything you'd like to report?"

"I think I'll pass, Gino," said Sarina, gradually inching away from Gene. "Why not ask Drew? I bet he has some amazing stories to tell."

"I'm sure he does, but does he go running without any clothes on?" Gene said.

Before Sarina could return a clever comment, Butch barged into the WAB.

"Hey, how did you get in here?" Butch said to Gene. Startled, Gene rose out of his chair and backed away from Butch.

"Why does it matter?" Gene said. "And who are you anyway?"

"I'm the owner of this here office," Butch said. "And we're having a problem with trespassers."

"He's OK," Katy said. "Well, as long as he's not hitting on Sarina."

"Well you're going to have to give me a list of who's not allowed right now," Butch said. "So we've got Kevin, Matt ... what about that odd fellow who is Matt's friend? That guy drives me crazy."

"Wait, Matt and Kevin aren't allowed here?" Gene said.

"We've had a little ... incident," Drew said. "Just a minor disagreement over priorities, that's all."

"That's big news," said Gene, so excited he could barely turn to a blank page in his notebook. "When did this happen? What projects are you discussing?"

"Gene, you can't put this in the paper," said Katy, taking a swipe at his notebook. "There's not a story here."

"It's my job to tell the public what's going on," Gene said. "Your site has become an integral part of the town. So it's only right to also explain when there is trouble brewing."

"Maybe you can throw in a brief or something to explain that The Developers are diversifying," Drew said. "That would be innocent and shouldn't cause too much of a stink."

"That does sound like a good way to put it," Gene said. "I'd better get back to let them know we have a little something extra for tomorrow's paper. Call me if you want to say anything else."

Gene made his way past Butch, who sneered, and Sarina, who scowled. After he left the room, they breathed a group sigh of relief and returned to business. Butch decided there were more interesting things in the kitchen and exited as well.

"Well that was a close one," Sarina said. "I was afraid he was going to tell the world we were shutting down."

"Yeah, he sure is nosy," Drew said. "By the way Katy, you really haven't told us very much about your meeting with Matt. In fact, you haven't told us a damn thing about what he said."

"He didn't really say much," Katy said. "But he wouldn't back down regarding the SIP. He mentioned it would be bad to renege on the government. So at least he admitted to signing the contracts."

"So you didn't get anything, huh?" Drew said. "That can be expected. He can be stubborn sometimes. I hope you didn't do anything silly like kiss him or anything."

Katy turned toward her desk and Drew and Sarina both noticed the avoidance to the question.

"I can't believe you!" Sarina said. "I thought we, us three, were in this together!"

"We are," Katy said. "It was dumb, but I couldn't help it. Anyway, I'm not going to talk to him again until this is over."

Just as Katy finished, her cellphone rang.

"OK, after I talk to him right now, I won't talk to him until it's over," Katy said. "I'm still with you 100 percent on .comU."

Katy answered her phone and left the room.

"Well at least she knows the guy she's kissing is straight," Sarina said.

"You mean to tell me that masculine hunk of yours, Rex, might not be straight?" said Drew, barely containing himself. "What first tipped you off?"

"It's sort of driving me crazy," Sarina said. "I really like him, and he's a lot of fun to be around, but he's becoming one of the girls."

"That's what happens when your perfect guy resembles Richard Simmons," Drew said. "I like the guy, but that could be annoying after awhile."

"And you haven't seen the half of it. Yesterday, he got his hair permed ... AGAIN. Monday, he cooked dinner for me, which was great, but I started to realize he reminded me of my mom."

"That's never a good sign. Did your mom have a perm?"

"Her hair was naturally curly and thin, just like Rex's."

"Wow, you have a problem on your hands for sure."

"He's supposed to be coming down here any minute, so I'm going to tell him we just need to be friends. I hope everything goes OK."

After 40 minutes, Rex entered the room with Katy, who had apparently just finished talking to Matt.

"Oh yes, this new fingernail polish would look great with your complexion!" Rex said to Katy, gently caressing her right hand as they strolled into the office. "I gave some samples to Sarina that someone from work had given me. I'll see if I can get some for you too."

"Thanks Rex, you're a real ladies' man!" said Katy, sitting back at her desk. Drew wondered if Katy really meant ladies' man, or just a manly lady, although with a head of hair like that, Drew hoped Rex would never seal the deal with an operation.

"Hey, honey!" said Rex, bending down to peck Sarina on the cheek. "What did you need to see me about? I need to meet the ladies from work down at the bazaar downtown. I think we're looking for antiques. I'm so excited I just can't hide it!"

"Rex, how about we step outside the office so we can talk?" said Sarina, realizing that if Rex had had a pink headband, he could have been just another Pointer Sister. Sarina nudged Rex closer and closer to the door as Drew and Katy looked on.

"Did I do something wrong?" Rex said as they moved into the hallway.

"No, you didn't do anything wrong, Rex," Sarina said. "It's just that ... I'm having a hard time knowing where you stand."

"Where I stand about what?"

"Where you stand about us."

Rex took Sarina's hands into his own.

"Babe, I told you that I loved you!" Rex said. "Am I not a good boy-friend?"

"Rex, you might be — no, I think you are — the greatest thing that has ever happened to me," Sarina said. "But it just seems like you are interested in just being friends."

"I feel as if we are best friends. Sarina, that's what I like so much about you! I would do anything for you."

"Anything?"

"I would give you the world, if I had it, or if it were on sale at Kmart."

Sarina figured this was how the conversation would go. Rex just didn't seem to get the fact that masculinity was important to Sarina, but she really didn't want to give up the friendship the two had currently.

"Maybe we should stop seeing each other," said Sarina, gently removing her hands from within Rex's reach.

"Stop seeing each other?" Rex panted. "Why?"

"I just need a little time to think about all this," Sarina said. "How you are, and what we would become."

"Well if you need time, sugar, I can give you that," said Rex, reaching over to hug Sarina. "Let me know what I need to do because I don't want to lose you."

They hugged, but Sarina was fairly certain she would have to address this issue again. Drew peeped out the door and peered toward the couple.

"Sarina, you gotta see this," Drew said.

Rex and Sarina walked back into the WAB. They noticed Katy was on the phone and trying desperately to explain something to the person on the other end.

"Katy is talking to Phil Harris from the hotel chain," said Drew, grabbing his chair. "Apparently Gene called him up to ask if he had heard about the splitting factions down here."

"What?" Sarina said. "Why would Gene call him?"

"That's what Katy is trying to find out," Drew said. "I've just overheard a little of the conversation so far. I think he's threatening to back out of his contract if the company is not in full force."

"I must be missing something," said Rex, scratching his head.

"Long story short, Matt and Kevin are trying to work on some other project," Sarina said. "None of us agreed to work on it. And we are busy as hell already."

"So what's the verdict?" Rex said.

"We're working on our part, they're working on theirs," Drew said. "That is, until we can come up with a better alternative."

Katy finished her phone conversation with Phil and turned to the group.

"He's pissed," Katy said. "The funny thing is, he wasn't mad at the service or anything. He just felt like if there was going to be some major change in the business structure that he should be notified."

"Well WE just found out about it yesterday!" Drew said.

"That's what I tried to explain to him," Katy said. "But I don't think he was buying it."

"So are we losing his sponsorship?" Sarina said. "That would be a gigantic blow to .comU."

"It sorted of sounded like that, but I told him I would get back in touch with him later today and come up with an amicable solution," Katy said.

"What would even give him the idea that we weren't going to be able to follow through with our plans?" Sarina said.

"Guys, I think I know why," said Drew, moving the mouse on his screen.

Sarina, Katy and Rex filed behind Drew to take a look at his monitor. Drew had pulled up the most recent edition of the *Times* and had clicked on a breaking news story.

Local Technology Company Headed for Split

The Developers, the Malorett-based Internet solutions provider, is apparently in turmoil over conflicting business interests within the company.

Matt Severson, president of The Developers, announced today that he and co-worker Kevin Gentry would be taking an indefinite leave of absence to complete another project not associated with the group.

"We feel that, at this time, it is in our best interest to follow through with a contractual agreement and put other items on hold," Severson said. "This could just be a few days, or this could take a little longer."

Katy Terrill, acting Developers manager, claimed that the group is just diversifying, and there is no reason for alarm.

We will have more on this story in tonight's full Internet report.

"That Gene is a fast cookie," Sarina said. "I mean I try to sprint by him and he still somehow manages to touch me."

"I cannot believe this," Katy said. "Why would Matt have gone on record saying something like this?"

"We're going to have to come up with something fast because we've run out of time," Sarina said, "Hey Rex, where's that time you were going to give me? I need it now."

Rex pulled out his pockets, both in his shorts and also in the pants underneath his shorts, and they were even void of lint.

>:¢, @:), :D, :)> = :-\

TWENTY-SIX

Drew opened his email to discover a handful of messages regarding the system status. Most people wanted to know if they were shutting down the .comU entirely. Drew started to respond, but he wasn't sure what to say.

"I'm at a loss for words here," said Drew, staring at his monitor while the others stood behind him, still trying to determine a solution. "That story was posted less than an hour ago, and there have already been 22 emails pertaining to the demise."

"Maybe we should have a chat session or something," Sarina said. "Then we could let everyone know our plans."

"But what are our plans?" Drew said.

The group contemplated options. They had to let the people of Malorett know something, at the very least as a rebuttal to this news story. But at this point, they could not guarantee the project surviving.

Katy recommended shutting the system down for the weekend. This could halt rumors from starting, she thought, but Drew argued that having the system running wouldn't be that much of an effort.

Drew thought they should continue as if nothing was wrong, and maybe post a message on the site that the story was erroneous. The problem with this method, Katy thought, was they didn't know what else Gene had in store to publish. Another option was to give Gene an interview and let him know things were OK but that they would be operating on a skeleton crew of sorts for the next few days. The dilemma with this procedure was not knowing exactly what Matt and Kevin were doing, or what they would be releasing.

Rex thought the best thing to do would be to go door to door and give all .comU members a hug and tell them to be patient. The group glared at Rex, and Sarina told him that if he really wanted to do that, he had full reign, but the rest of the group wasn't interested. On that note, Rex remembered he needed to go catch up with the ladies at the bazaar.

"I'd like to stay and figure out what to do, but I need to run," said Rex, already halfway out the door. "Sarina, call me tonight so we can sort things out. I'll do anything for you, babe!"

Rex gave a half-hearted wave and dashed for the door.

"What did you tell that guy?" Katy said. "He gets stranger by the second."

"Did you break up with him?" Drew said. "That is, if you were dating in the first place?"

"I didn't have the heart to tell him," Sarina said. "Then again, I wasn't sure what to tell him. Besides, we have more important things to discuss. Whatever we do, we need to give a report to Gene, or else this will turn into an even larger debacle."

"Right," said Katy, creeping over to her desk to grab a pen and notebook. She sat in her chair and scooted toward Drew's machine, where he and Sarina were already seated.

"Now we just need to conjure up what we want printed," Katy said.

"How about 'Two-headed father gives birth to baby Elton John,' " Drew said. "That'll grab their attention."

"I think we're looking for something less provocative," Sarina said. "And something that has to do with what's happening."

"Good point," Drew said. "So are we in favor of shutting the system down for a period of time?"

Sarina and Katy paused for a moment.

"It just seems like we could take the site down for an indefinite amount of time, and then bring it back when needed," Katy said.

"Wait, I think I have an idea," Drew said. "What if we announced the site would be down over the weekend for upgrades. That would give us time to figure out this mess."

"What sort of upgrades do we have?" Katy said.

"For starters, we do have the education section just about ready," Drew said. "I don't know, maybe we can think of something else between now and the end of the weekend."

"I think it's worth a shot," Katy said. "It's better than anything else we've thought of at this point. So what do we do now?"

"If you want to shut it down tonight, one of you will have to do it," Drew said. "I've got bingo calling duties."

"I can come back here and do that tonight," Sarina said. "It might be good to run up and get this and Rex off my mind. Unless you wanted to do it, Katy."

"If you want to Sarina, go for it," said Katy, thinking in the back of her mind about having another late-night meeting with Matt. "I'm still not sure what exactly I'll be doing later, but I'm more than likely going to be trying to get all of us back on the same page."

"Well if you talk to Matt, try to stay on business, and no fish!" Drew said.

"You can count on me," said Katy, thinking it was pretty sad that Drew had to specifically comment on her worst vice. "Now I think I'll go ahead and contact Gene. Maybe we could talk him into coming down here tomorrow, for a full interview. That could buy us even more time to finalize the plan."

It was already late in the workday, and Katy noticed a trickling of snow outside as she dialed Gene's number. Katy told Gene the group's plans, and he obliged to write a small brief for tomorrow's story plus announce there would be more information to follow after the morning briefing.

But just as Gene finished his conversation with Katy, he immediately dialed Matt's cellphone, to see what was happening on the other side.

"Matt, it seems we have a little conflict with our stories now," Gene said. "I've been told the remaining Developers are having some sort of announcement tomorrow about serious upgrades to .comU. Is this true?"

"Upgrades?" said Matt as he paced around his living room. He and Kevin had been there since the earlier talk with Doug, outlining the SIP system. "There are always a couple of things we are adding here and there, but I don't think they have any major upgrades."

"Well apparently it's big enough to shut the system down over the weekend," Gene said.

"They are shutting it down?" said Matt in disbelief. "OK, that is bizarre. I cannot imagine anything that big, without my input."

"So are you calling it a bluff?" Gene said.

"Well, it's hard to be 100 percent sure," Matt said. "It's just unimaginable they would do something like that."

"I want to report the truth, and you are the president of the company," Gene said. "So which is it?"

"I don't think they would lie, so let's leave it at this," Matt said. "How about once we hear what they are doing tomorrow, we'll also announce the top secret project Kevin and I are creating."

"Sounds fascinating," Gene said. "They have scheduled an interview with me at 10 in the morning."

"Tell you what, we'll be down there at that time, too," Matt said. "You know, just in case their interview is long enough for them to tell you they have no idea what they are doing!"

"Sounds good, Matt," Gene said. "I'll talk to you tomorrow."

"See you, Gene," Matt said.

As Matt hung up, Kevin noticed he seemed somewhat troubled by the phone conversation with Gene.

"Hey man, are you OK?" Kevin said. "What's going on over at the office?"

"It appears they are going on without us," Matt said. "At least, that's what they want everyone to believe. Who really knows anymore."

"So you think it's going to be tougher to convince them to work on the SIP now?" Kevin said.

"I don't know, but if so, we'd better get cracking," Matt said. "We still have a ridiculous amount to do before Monday. What should we start with?"

Kevin picked up the SIP project binder and flipped to the center.

"I was reading something in here a minute ago about an administration structure," said Kevin, still thumbing through the pages. "Here it is. I think we need to devise a simple interface to pull out names and perform searches."

"Well we already have that set up in .comU," Matt said. "So I cannot imagine it would be any different. I can still access all the files of .comU and put them on the machine to test. Although Drew can change the superuser password, I doubt he'll do it. We trust each other."

"Even with what's going on, you think he still trusts you?"

"At the very least, when it comes to security, he wouldn't sell me out."

Kevin's phone rang, and he noticed it was Jane calling. Kevin hadn't talked to her since Tuesday's unfortunate incident of depriving Jane of his manly body. She had called yesterday, but Kevin never had a chance to call her back. He knew he would be in for mild berating.

"Hello?" Kevin said.

"So you are answering your phone today," Jane said. Kevin noticed her tone was worse than he could have even imagined. "Are you just going to forget about me, and forget about the Big Macs we've shared?"

"No way, honey," Kevin said. "There have just been too many crazy things going on here. I'm sorry I haven't been able to get in touch with you the last two days. The others are working on a different project while me and Matt try to put this thing together for the government. We have to have something to them by the first of the week."

"I see how it is," said Jane, growing even more huffy. "So you'd rather work on that project than see me. I should have known this would happen."

"That's not it at all!" Kevin said. "We made a promise, a contract, and we have to fulfill it."

"Well if you're going to fulfill that, then you can forget about feeling this," Jane said.

Kevin, puzzled, said, "Jane, I have to tell you something really important. Even though work has taken a majority of my time recently, I still think of you every second of the day. You are the most wonderful girl I've ever met, and I've actually been thinking it would be great to spend the rest of our lives together. Jane, will you marry me?"

Kevin heard nothing on the phone.

"Hello?"

There was just static, then a dead line. What a dumb thing, to try to propose over a cellphone, Kevin thought.

"What was I thinking?" Kevin said.

"What were you thinking about what?" said Matt, entering back into the room after returning from the kitchen.

"Now I'm really in a quandary," Kevin said, standing and gathering a couple of papers. "I just tried to propose to Jane."

"That was vewwy, vewwy stupid," Matt said. "Who ever heard of proposing over the phone anyway? I guess it would be OK if your girlfriend was a phone sex operator, or maybe a telemarketer, or Catherine Zeta-Jones on one of those cellphone commercials."

"OK, I realize it was dumb!" Kevin said. "I've got to go see her. Right now."

The snow was starting to accumulate outside, even though the temperature was barely below freezing, and the storm front had virtually passed.

"This is no time to take off," Matt said. "We have to work on this project or it's never going to get done. Doug was beeping in while I was talking to Gene, and I have to give him a status report."

"I'll take the work with me," said Kevin, grabbing his computer. "I'll be back in the morning, and I'll meet you at the office. Then I can work the rest of the weekend, 24 hours a day if necessary."

"I doubt that will be necessary, but is that for the record?" Matt said.

"Jane means so much to me, I don't want her to be angry," Kevin said. "She is worth everything, and if that means I don't get any sleep the next few days, it'll have to be done."

"What if you don't have time to eat much, either?" Matt said.

Kevin thought about the prospects of not eating too much.

"Yep, she is worth even that too," Kevin said.

Kevin left, trying to keep balanced on the icy steps to his car. He had just a little of the powder on his windshield, which he swiped away, and he made out of the driveway without incident. Kevin actually noticed more powder residue from the doughnuts in his front seat than on the car. Matt watched from his front window, then decided to give Doug a quick call to see what he needed.

"Hey Doug, it's Matt. Sorry I missed your call, I was talking to the newspaper. What's going on?"

"Actually, that's what I was calling about, Matt. I noticed on the website that your remaining clan is announcing tomorrow system upgrades. How will they be able to do this if they are going to be persuaded to work with you?"

"I think the upgrades they are talking about have already been completed."

"But you don't know for sure?"

"No, I'm not positive, but I'm fairly certain."

"You don't think they have other plans, so they would not be available for the SIP project?"

"I don't really think so Doug."

"How can you be sure?"

"I really can't be sure, Doug, but Kevin and I have everything under control."

"Are you sure about that?"

"Doug, who are you, Regis Philbin? Why do you ask me if I'm sure about everything? Kevin and I will be fully prepared for you to test out the system come Monday."

"OK then, so what is the big announcement you are planning to make tomorrow?"

"The announcement?"

"It says in the story here you are also making an announcement. You aren't going to give the secrets away, are you?"

"I'm planning just to tell the newspaper we are developing a system that will be used for the government. I think we have to tell them something or else they'll think we're making all of this up."

"Is that your final answer?"

"Doug, why don't you meet us down there tomorrow as well. If you have anything to say, you can add it as well."

"All right, Matt. I don't like the sound of it but you're the boss. You're the Bruce Springsteen. You're the Tony Danza."

"OK, Doug, I'll talk to you later."

Matt set down his phone and thought maybe the best thing to do would be to just go to bed. Then he could hope to wake up from the nightmare. In the meantime, though, he hoped Katy would drop by tonight to help clear things up a bit.

On the other hand, Doug was somewhat irritated with Matt's nonchalant attitude. Doug decided he needed to get to the bottom of this for himself, maybe even before the morning.

***

St. Pius was practically empty for its Thursday night bingo. That didn't affect Drew too much, although time seemed to pass quicker when he was performing for a larger crowd.

Tonight, he hoped the time would be swift. Too many things with work loomed on the horizon, and he wanted to get home at a decent time to see if Jessica had any suggestions for approaching Matt. His work partner had never been the type to stab him in the back, and it didn't completely feel like he was here. In fact, Drew didn't understand what he felt toward Matt right now, which was odd considering the amount of things they had been through already.

"Wake up, ya old bastard," screamed Ethel McMahan, waiting impatiently for Drew to call the next number. "I'm working on three cases, and Game Six is always my game. Call my number like a REAL man."

"I'll show you a real man," Jimmy Dickson said.

"Where, where?" Martha Singleton said as she peered around the room.

Same old crowd, Drew thought. Even Dale Washington and his grand-daughter, Becky, were in attendance. Becky told Drew before the games that she had been spending a lot of spare time on .comU recently. When Drew told her about the new education portion they would be launching next week, Becky thought a lot of kids at school would be interested. He also mentioned that they might try to use tutors for younger grades from the high school ranks, and Becky said she would be interested.

Of course, all of this was speculative, Drew thought, considering that when they shut the system down, it might be down for good.

***

Katy had a difficult time trying to figure out what she should wear to Matt's. As she thumbed through her clothes, she realized at no other point in her life had she felt so torn over a guy. Matt had always been there for her — during the periods with Michael, during their times as a couple and even now, on opposing sides of a huge business decision.

Part of Katy just wanted to not see him, and not talk to him, because that would be the easiest thing to do. But the compassionate side thought it would be difficult to be without him, no matter what happened with The Developers.

After hours of decision-making, Katy decided not to flaunt too much. But as she started out the door, with a notecard of things to tell Matt — both personal and work-related — she grew about as nervous as humanly possible.

***

Matt worked away, blasting off page after page of code to be used for the SIP. He had determined the simplest modification process for .comU pages and had knocked out a good portion by 9 p.m. He wanted to get as much done as he could before Katy arrived. He didn't know when that would be, but he assumed Katy would work late and come over after that. Besides, the roads were getting worse, still passable though, so that might encourage her to meet him sooner.

And it might also encourage her to stay longer, possibly until the morning.

Matt wasn't mad at Katy, Drew or Sarina for making the decision they made. He wasn't really mad at Doug or Blake or anyone, for that matter. He just wished there was a little more time to sort it all out. Unfortunately, they needed to tell the public what they were really going to do. He had avoided cellphone calls from .comU clients and investors because he was uncertain what to tell them. Tomorrow would be a different story, as both sides would have to lay their cards on the table.

But before then, Katy was just as pressing of an issue as The Developers were. Could they become a couple again? Would that be possible? He dreamed of just leaving it all behind and heading to a tropical island. As he glanced outside, and saw the headlights of Katy's car, he realized there would be little chance of that in a snowstorm like this.

***

Fortunately, Kevin dodged the heavy snow when he arrived at Moxee.

That didn't calm his nerves, however. After several empty attempts to reach Jane on the way to her place, Kevin thought of nothing else but trying to make sense out of everything. He had no intentions of ignoring the girl of his dreams, but how was he supposed to act?

Kevin had never been in this situation before, which was probably one of the reasons he slipped on the ice and fell just as he shoved the car door shut. It serves me right, he thought, although it's a good thing there's not a taco in my back pocket. As a child, Kevin had a strange habit of keeping a taco in his pocket, just in case he ever got hungry. The problem was, by the time he actually wanted to eat the taco, it was ingrained in his pants, so eventually he came up with a better idea: eating food when he received it.

But for Jane, he would wait, so the satchel of McDonald's steamy Big Macs and fries was tucked safely inside of Kevin's heavy coat. The warmth of the bag reminded Kevin of Jane's touch, so delicate, so hot and oftentimes, included a packet of ketchup.

This surprise trip, though, could be different, if Jane didn't answer his calls soon. He decided his best bet was trying one of the dorm phones. If that failed, Kevin might be stuck between two Big Macs in his car on a dark, snowy night in Michigan.

***

Me, afraid of a little snow? That's funny, Sarina thought as she ran in a black sports bra and nylon running pants through downtown Malorett. The snow fell faster, but she didn't seemed fazed; if anything, it made her run faster.

The office was almost three miles from her apartment. As she glided through the last half mile, Sarina pondered how long she would have to be at the office. It would be close to midnight before she could verify that .comU was shut down. By 12:30, she could be on her way back home, unless something unforeseen happened. Or, unless Rex called while she was there.

Sarina had been thinking about Rex, and his hairy chest, a lot since they parted ways earlier in the day. She had expected him to call, but when? Surely he wasn't part of a gardening club that met in the middle of a winter night, but then again, that guy was a part of every club known to man.

***

Rex skipped his Upper Peninsula Evergreen Friends meeting Thursday night, partly due to the weather, and partly due to Sarina. He had to figure out just what to do if he wanted to win her back. Rex was the type of guy who girls always thought would be the best boyfriend in the world. Of course, the type of girl who always said this wasn't interested, which always left Rex in a strange predicament.

But Sarina was different, and he had to find out why. The snow had subsided slightly near the bank, so Rex took a stroll downtown after stopping by to pick up a few items. He noticed a second floor light was on in The Developers' building, but he didn't even think about knocking on the door. He pulled out his cellphone to call Sarina, but he couldn't handle that, either. Rex thought maybe he could gain the nerve after getting "wasted" on hot apple cider, so he stopped at Buckeye's and contemplated his next step.

***

As Doug watched the snow flicker off his porch light, he determined he must do something else this night besides watching his *Hawaii 5-0* DVD collection. The *Pirates of the Caribbean* had already gotten to him, and since he started watching his favorite show again, Doug donned a lei around the house.

Downtown wasn't too far away, he thought, and there wouldn't be much traffic out at this time, with the weather as it was. At least the BMW wouldn't get scratched, and possibly he could find some answers down at The Developers' office. Doug grabbed his keys and was so fixated on preventing a meltdown of the SIP system that the lei made the trip with him.

TWENTY-SEVEN

Jessica didn't fully understand Drew's work scenario, but as she nibbled on her takeout Chinese food, she listened to the explanation.

"Matt has been talking about the new system we are going to build for the government, something that will bring The Developers a pretty sizable contract," Drew said. "But we have other more pressing projects, and Matt went behind our back to sign the contract with the government deal!"

"So what has Matt said about all of this?"

"I've barely talked to him this week. We've been busy, plus I'm too angry to address him. Katy has been talking to him the most."

"But shouldn't you talk to him? You could get right to the bottom of the situation. You started it together, not as two separate entities."

"Maybe you're right," Drew said. "So you think I should call him tonight?"

"It's not 11 yet, so I would call him now. With the way the snow is coming down right now, he couldn't go anywhere."

Jessica left the room. Drew knew she was right; he and Matt could figure this out, over the phone, and stop the madness. But there was no guarantee they could agree on the best thing for the two sides to do. It's possible, Drew thought, that Matt had been brainwashed by Doug and his government connections. Drew recalled the time that Matt claimed he had seen a UFO and had even taken a picture of it. Even though after viewing the picture closely, the UFO turned out to be a disc from a local Frisbee Golf tournament, Matt had always shown an appreciation for the paranormal. So Drew reasoned that brainwashing might work if Matt were involved.

Drew called Matt, but he didn't answer.

At Matt's, Katy thought she heard a phone ringing. But she was paying little attention to the surroundings around her, considering she had no clothes on, and Matt was on top of her.

She had forgotten how great it was to be with Matt. He knew just where to touch her, and his firm, gentle hands were the best things she had ever felt. Katy entered into a state of sheer bliss as Matt continued to kiss and stroke her neck. Now wasn't the best time to talk about the other reason Katy came to visit, she thought. But for Matt, it was weighing too heavily on his mind.

"Katy we have to stop this," said Matt, kneeling beside Katy. "I really, really, really want to be with you, but we have more important things at hand."

"Oh are you hungry?" said Katy, grabbing her clothes sitting beside Matt's couch. "Do you have any more leftover salmon?"

Matt was a little irritated, but it was hard to be mad at an irresistible female.

"Katy, you know what I mean," Matt said. "We have to make some real decisions before tomorrow. We don't want to make it look like the company is falling apart."

"But isn't it, Matt? Isn't the company falling apart?" said Katy as she turned away from Matt to put on her underwear and bra. "It seems there has been a split down the middle. Well, again, as close to the middle as you can get when you have five people."

"True, but we can still work together," Matt said. "I just don't understand why you guys can't work on the SIP project first."

"And we don't understand why YOU guys can't work on the .comU items first," Katy said. "That was the initial project anyway!"

"It's not as easy as that. Doug has worked out a sweet deal, and the contracts have been signed and ... "

"No one told you to sign the contracts. The deal seems a little shady and backhanded to the rest of us."

"But Katy, I can't change that now! We need to move forward, as a unit."

"The only way that's going to work is if you concede to work on .comU first and foremost and worry about the other projects at a later time."

Matt knew there would be resistance, and Katy was perhaps the most stubborn female he knew. This was a bad time, he thought, to realize that was a turn-on, but he still believed there was some way around it.

Meanwhile, Katy had decided she would not budge for anything nor anyone.

In theory, the group could work on both projects at the same time; that is, if there were about 49 hours in a day. In practicality, The Developers needed to focus their resources if they were going to continue to be successful. The sponsors around town were already catching wind of the dissimilation within and were contemplating other advertising ideas — without the system.

"Katy, honestly, I'm having a really, really hard time with this," said Matt, appearing as if he might cry, which hadn't happened since he saw "Titanic" in the theaters. "I want us to work together, but we have to fulfill this obligation to Doug and the government. It's our duty as United States citizens."

"So what, we need to recite the Pledge of Allegiance every morning before work?" Katy said. "I could even wear my Benjamin Franklin wig to the office. You shouldn't have made the promise. You surely had chances to rescind, and now, this is where we are."

Matt had an idea.

"Instead of us bickering back and forth, what if we decided this a different way," Matt said. "How about a competition?"

"A competition?" Katy said. "Like what?"

"What about Yahtzee?" Matt said.

"Uh, Matt, you're saying you want to play Yahtzee to determine the fate of your company?" Katy said. "Seems pretty risky."

"At least we could come up with a solution," Matt said. "And the sooner we decide that, the sooner we can get back to us."

Katy thought it was peculiar that Matt would want to hurry and get something with work out of the way in favor of a personal life. Then again, maybe he was changing into someone Katy could, indeed, be happy with forever.

"It's a deal," said Katy, reaching out to shake Matt's hand. "But as you know, I was Yahtzee champ five straight years in grade school."

Matt grabbed the game from his bedroom closet and met Katy in the living room. He thought possibly he could take advantage of Katy's competitiveness to finalize the standoff between the company sectors. Of course, the idea would work only if he won.

Even though Katy started out strong with a large straight and sixes for four of a kind, Matt fought back with a Yahtzee and three straight turns with fours of a kind, setting him up to gain the bonus points. While Matt started to realize he was sure to win the match, Katy's face slowly tinted with frustration, then anger.

"I think we might have to reassess this method of company focus," said Katy, shaking the red cup full of five dice.

"You're just saying that because you're losing!" said Matt as he glanced over the scorecard. "You have at least three throws left though, so there's always hope."

Matt grinned, but Katy glared back and set down the dice cup.

"I don't care what the score is!" Katy said. "We aren't changing our direction."

"What? We said whoever won would decide the fate of the business plans," Matt said. "It's not like I'm using eight-sided dice, although I might have some of those around here ... "

"You are hopeless!" Katy said. She picked up the cup, shook it and threw the dice on the table. Without looking, she stormed into the bathroom.

Matt stood to chase after her, but before doing so, he noticed Katy had just rolled five threes.

Matt raced into the bathroom, where he noticed Katy, hanging over his sink and drying a few tears.

"Katy, what is wrong?" said Matt, handing her another Kleenex.

"This just won't work," Katy said. "You, me, The Developers, this town ... I just can't take it anymore. I want to be with you, but not if it's going to cause me this much pain."

"Well, maybe we should just go our separate ways," Matt said. "I love you, and I don't want to hurt you. But you are right, things are getting ugly here."

Matt took Katy in his arms.

"Tomorrow, each side should just speak and we'll see what happens," Matt said. "Maybe the answer will come to us."

Before Matt could say anything else, his phone rang. Kevin was calling, and it was close to midnight, so Matt hurriedly grabbed it, thinking his buddy might be in trouble.

"Kevin, are you OK?" Matt said.

"Physically yes, mentally no," Kevin said. "Jane won't answer my calls."

"She won't answer ... are you sure she's even there?" Matt said.

"No, not really," Kevin said. "I can't find my sister either, so maybe they are out somewhere. It's pretty late though, and I seriously doubt they are hanging out at a party or something."

"So what are you going to do?"

"I guess I'll keep looking. I don't think the roads are good enough to come back tonight."

"Give me a call if you run into more difficulties. Don't forget about the press conference in the morning."

"All right, I'll talk to you later."

Kevin stood near the phones in Jen and Jane's dormitory, but he decided he might as well take a seat for awhile. Jane didn't stay out late on Thursday nights, usually because she either had a game or homework.

There's really not much to do but wait, Kevin thought. The food was still lukewarm, but it wouldn't stay that way much longer, even under Kevin's jacket. Just as he had finally conceded to eat his portion, Crissy appeared through the doorway and immediately noticed Kevin.

"Kevy baby, what are you doing here?" said Crissy, wearing a conservative red turtleneck and khaki Capri pants. "Oh, and by the way, I'm not wearing any underwear."

"Thanks for the info," Kevin said. "I can't find Jane nor Jen, and I just figured they would be around here somewhere."

"I think I heard Jane earlier saying she was going bowling tonight," Crissy said. "I don't know if Jen went with her. I haven't seen her in a week or so. Hey, so what's happening with .comU? Is it shut down for good?"

"No, I don't think it's down for good, but we're having a press conference tomorrow to determine what will happen to it," Kevin said. "So you think Jane is at the bowling alley?"

"Yeah, do you want to walk over there?" Crissy said. "It's the one near campus. What is under your jacket? It smells like McDonald's."

"It is," Kevin said. "I figured Jane would want a snack."

"Well let's eat, and then walk over to the bowling alley," Crissy said.

Kevin agreed, and he figured at this point, Jane wouldn't want to eat her favorite food if it were mashed under his coat for this long.

Kevin and Crissy ate quickly. The walk wasn't too bad because most of the roads around Tech had been cleared. The sidewalks were covered with about a half foot of snow, but there were hardly any cars out, so Kevin and Crissy walked the entire route on the road.

The bowling alley was pretty crowded for a Thursday night. Kevin remembered Jane saying something about a rock 'n' bowl at the alley near campus, but he didn't even know what that meant. Kevin and Crissy entered the establishment to see virtually nothing. All of the lights were off, and spotlights flared around the lanes, lighting up pins occasionally. As a random Def Leppard song blared over the loudspeakers, Kevin tried to locate Jane among the crowd of college coeds.

"This is my kind of place!" Crissy said. "Come on Kevy, let's grind!"

"Sorry Crissy, but I'm in no mood to dance or pour sugar on anyone," Kevin said. "Remember, we are looking for Jane."

"Well, you look for Jane, and I'll look for fresh meat," Crissy said.

They walked past each lane but didn't see many familiar faces. Finally on lane four, Kevin spotted a pink bowling bag. He wasn't positive at first, but then he noticed "CHAMP" on the cover. Immediately, he saw Jane returning from the lane, probably after another strike, and hugging another guy!

"Hey, isn't that her with that guy?" Crissy said, pointing toward them. "I can't believe she would be with him. Let's just say from personal experience that he doesn't have much."

"I can't believe she would be with anyone!" said Kevin, also realizing Jen was there with a date too. "We were the perfect team, like Abbott and Costello, Sonny and Cher, Big Mac and fries."

"Big Mac and fries aren't really a pair," Crissy said. "They go together but aren't equal parts. The fries are just a side portion."

"Whatever, let's not get overly technical," Kevin said. "I even proposed to her the other day."

"Well, she is pretty hot. What did she say?"

"Actually, she didn't say anything. I'm not sure she even heard me because it was over my cellphone."

"You tried to propose, over a cellphone? What a dumbass."

Jane noticed Kevin and Crissy standing a few lanes over, and she started walking toward them. Kevin turned and saw Jane heading their way.

"Let's leave," Kevin said to Crissy. "I don't even know why I'm here."

"Can I at least find a guy to take home?" Crissy said.

Crissy instead decided to stick with Kevin, but as soon as they walked out the door, they heard Jane running from behind, shouting to stop. Reluctantly, Kevin stopped, and so did Crissy.

"Kevin, what are you doing here?" Jane said. "I thought you were busy until the weekend!"

"Yeah, it was a mistake," Kevin said. "I wanted to explain that I'm not too busy for you. But I guess it doesn't matter anymore. I'm going back home."

"You can't go home in this weather!" Jane said. "We should talk."

"I'm not interested in talking right now," Kevin said. "I see what's going on with that other guy."

"That guy? He's just a friend. Jen started dating a guy, and she wanted me to go with them and his friend. I know him from calculus."

"Well that's great Jane, but I've gotta go. Maybe the roads will be cleared on the way home."

Kevin looked up at the clearing sky and started walking back to the dorms, with Crissy tagging along.

"Will you call me tomorrow?" Jane said.

But there was no answer. Jane wasn't sure what to think, so she went back into the bowling alley.

"So are you going to call her?" Crissy asked as they briskly made their way across campus.

"I don't know," Kevin said. "All of this seems useless now. I really love her, but it's not going to work, is it?"

"I guess you don't know until you go through with it," Crissy said. "So are you really leaving right now?"

"I might as well," Kevin said. "But maybe I'll call back to Malorett to see what the weather is like there. If it's bad, Jen would let me stay with her."

"Well you can always stay with me, baby." Crissy said.

They had already made it to the parking lot where Kevin's car sat.

"Thanks for going with me, Crissy," Kevin said. "We'll let you know something about .comU when we find out."

"Good luck!" Crissy said.

Kevin got into his car and dialed Sarina's number. He knew .comU would be shut down at midnight, and he knew Drew had bingo, so he was pretty sure Sarina would still be up at 1, possibly even at the office.

"I thought you stopped trying for booty calls a long time ago!" Sarina said.

"No, I'm over in Moxee, and I'm coming back tonight," Kevin said. "Are the roads clear there?"

"Not really," Sarina said. "Did something go wrong with Jane?"

"She was out with another guy!" Kevin said.

"Are you serious?" Sarina said. "Even though you guys were supposed to hang out tonight?"

"Well, no, actually she didn't know I was coming up here. And she was with my sister and some guy she started dating. And she said it wasn't a date. But they were bowling! That's OUR thing!"

"Kevin, how many times have you and Jane gone bowling?"

"Once, but that's not the point! She let me touch her resin bag after just three frames. Isn't that love?"

"For crying out loud, you are starting to sound like a teenage girl. Listen, it's after 1, and I need to check everything to make sure .comU is completely shut down."

"OK, OK ... maybe I'll call her tomorrow or something. So do you still think I shouldn't come back?"

"If you were going to be responsible, and not eat while you are driving, and drive really slowly, you might be OK."

"I can do that. Plus I'm not hungry at all."

"Did you just say you aren't hungry?"

"No because I keep thinking about Jane."

"Damn, maybe you are in love. All right Kevin, see you tomorrow."

"Bye, Sarina."

Still astounded that Kevin admitted to not being hungry, Sarina briefly checked to see if there were any comments about the site shutting down. There were zero. Considering how many people had been using the system, she was a little disappointed that no one had asked what was going on.

Sarina was ready for her trek home. With the fresh snow on the ground, and probably fewer than five cars out on the road, the run back would be peaceful.

For a moment, Sarina contemplated calling Rex, but surely he would be in bed. Rex rarely stayed up past 11, and even though he promised he would call, there was nothing she could do about it. She checked the email one more time, and there were still no inquiries. Sadly, she headed out the office door and started out the front door until Butch called from behind.

"I thought we had a meeting tonight!" said Butch, carrying possibly the largest tub of cheese puffs ever created. "Where was everyone?"

"No, there was no meeting," Sarina said.

"Then what are you doing here?" Butch said.

"I'm just shutting down .comU," Sarina said. "It's going to be down for the weekend, and we're having a press conference here tomorrow morning."

"A press conference? Tomorrow? I need to get this place cleaned up!"

"What are you going to do, wear a new smiley face T-shirt?"

"Why Sarina, that's a great idea. I'd better get to work. It's a good thing I have something to eat tonight. By the way, where's the rent check?"

Sarina scooted down the steps, avoiding the slippery parts.

"Talk to Matt about it when he shows up. He's giving his own press conference tomorrow."

"Two press conferences? This is big time. See you later!"

Butch waved to Sarina as she jogged away, and he almost dropped the cheese puffs due to the sheer girth of the container. Butch started back inside, but he noticed what appeared to be a drunk stumbling up the sidewalk. Butch peered out the door but did not recognize the man, which was strange because Butch knew just about everyone, especially someone in that sort of stupor who would be downtown at night. The man approached the steps, garnering Butch's full attention. Finally, Butch noticed the man was wearing sweat pants below a pair of nylon shorts.

"Rex old buddy," said Butch, trying to knock away some of the snow and ice from the door. "What in blazes are you doing out this late at night?"

"Butch is that you?" Rex said. "Butch Butch bo Butch, banana fana fo

Futch fe fi mo Mutch ... Bu-tch."

"Oh my goodness," Butch said. "What has happened to you?"

"Butchie-pooh, I had WAY too much apple cider," Rex said. He made it to the front door and practically fell into Butch's arms. "I came downtown earlier to see Sarina, but I was scared to come down here. But now I'm here. And you're here! But is she here?"

"I hate to break it to you Rex, but Sarina just left," Butch said. "I think maybe you should come in and rest though. Maybe you can call her in a few minutes when she gets home."

"What a splendid idea, Butchman," Rex said. "How about we run some laps around the building?"

Rex lifted his head off Butch's shoulder and started to run the other way, but he gradually leaned back on Butch. Rex wasn't too much of a burden, so Butch led him into the LAB.

"You are the bestest dude," Rex said, crawling on top of the LAB table and sprawling out on it. "You don't have a pillow, do you? At least a bedtime story?"

"How could apple cider make you this crazy?" said Butch, shaking his head. "Oh wait a minute, you are already pretty high on the crazy meter. I'll be right back."

"Wait, come back Butchie!" Rex screamed. Ten seconds later, Butch returned, with his cheese puffs in hand.

"I love those things!" Rex said. "Here, throw me some and let me catch them in my mouth."

Butch took off the tub top and threw a couple Rex's way. He missed all 12, although he was lying down, and Butch had problems throwing due to a torn rotator cuff.

"I guess I don't have anything better to do at 1:30 in the morning," Butch said.

"Well neither do I," Rex said. "Except sleeping. And calling Sarina. I almost forgot! Do you think it's too late?"

"No, she's probably just getting home right now," Butch said.

Rex found his phone in his left pants pocket, so he lifted it out through his shorts.

"But Butch, what do I say to her?" Rex said. "I like her, and I thought she liked me, but now she's not sure."

"From what I gather," said Butch, stuffing his face full of cheese puffs, "Sarina isn't really sure which side of the plate you're on."

"The side of the plate? Like baseball?" Rex said.

"No, you don't get it," Butch said. "She thinks you are gay. Look, we all think you're a cool dude, but I don't think Sarina wants to date a gay man."

"Gay?" Rex said. "Well I'm happy, but I like only girls. What would give her that idea?"

Butch started to explain, but realized it would be a losing battle.

"Maybe you should just tell her you're not gay," Butch said. "Even better, you could tell her you want to have sex with her."

"I don't think she would want to do that," Rex said. "I don't really think she's attracted to me. That's why I thought she didn't like me."

"I gotta tell you buckaroo, I think she would," Butch said. "Maybe you're just too nice to her or something. You seem like a nice fellow."

"All right, I'll call her," Rex said.

"Great," Butch said. "I'll give you some privacy."

Butch stepped out and walked into the small kitchen. He hoped Rex and Sarina could work things out because they seemed to be compatible. But what did he know? He was just the building owner, looking for a rent check.

Wondering how the conversation was going, Butch crept back down to the LAB. He put his ear to the door but heard nothing. He slowly opened the door and found Rex, spread eagle on the floor and sleeping. Butch still needed to finish tidying up the second floor, so he decided to leave Rex there for the time being.

Butch started up the steps until he thought he heard a noise at the front door. He went to the door and saw nothing. Damn squirrel, Butch thought. At least he won't get my cheese puffs tonight since they've been devoured. Unfortunately, Butch couldn't remember where he left the empty container, so he went upstairs to finish cleaning.

The noise wasn't Butch's imagination. Doug made his way through the snow to The Developers' office and started to knock on the door before he heard a loud thud inside. Upon hearing that, Doug darted back down the steps. He saw a man peep his head out but noticed that he went directly upstairs after closing the front door. Doug thought that was the building owner, and he thought it was odd the guy would still be there that late.

Doug walked back up the steps and tried to open the door. It appeared that the bottom part was locked, but the top part was left open. This would be daring, Doug thought, but he had to see the group's plans. He hoisted himself up to the door's top half, leaned through and did a flip inside. The short fall prevented injury, but he ripped the left side of his trousers. Since the door caught two belt loops, Doug decided to take off his belt and leave it at the door. Just in case, he might have to use it to climb out. Then again, his lei was still intact, and he realized that its orange color kind of matched his boxer shorts.

Doug tiptoed down the hallway. All the lights downstairs were off, and he was having trouble remembering which door was the room that had all the computers. There were three doors, and the first one he tried was locked. He thought the most sensible thing to do would be to test the doors, and if one was open, to check it out. If they were all locked, he would have to come up with a better alternative, possibly using a credit card to lift the lock. He hoped he didn't have to do that because Doug wasn't interested in being a burglar. He just wanted to get down to business.

Thankfully, the next door he tried was unlocked. Doug carefully turned the doorknob and opened the door slowly. He leaned over to feel for the light switch but suddenly, he heard steps coming from the staircase. Doug tried to close the door gently, but the steps got louder and louder. Fearful of being caught, Doug decided to hide inside the dark room. As he jumped forward, he stepped on something. Doug lost his balance, and his pants started to fall again as well. He reached down to grab his pants, but as he did, he slammed his head onto a table, which knocked him out cold. Doug fell to the ground.

Butch opened the LAB door but heard nothing. He noticed his cheese puffs tub sitting on its side with an indentation in the middle of it.

"So that's where I left the tub!" said Butch, closing the door. "I hope Rex wasn't anticipating a refill."

@8) & :)> = ROTFL

TWENTY-EIGHT

Gene Simons arrived early Friday for The Developers' press conferences. As he pulled into an empty parking lot next to the office building, he thought he may have arrived a bit too early.

It was 9 a.m., and he knew from previous trips that none of the group members kept firm schedules, yet there was always someone there by 8:30. The weather may have played a role in the absenteeism this morning, though, as many areas in the region reported up to 8 inches of snow. Downtown, though, the roads were completely clear, and the temperature was already above freezing, making Gene's trip from home fairly easy.

Gene noticed some movement through the window, so he assumed maybe whoever was in there had walked from home because of the snow. Gene climbed the steps and knocked on the door. No one answered, so he knocked again.

"Squirrel? Go away squirrel! No nuts or cheese puffs here!"

Gene didn't recognize the voice, but evidently, someone was there.

"Hello sir, I'm Gene Simons from the *Malorett Times*. I'm here for the press conference, a little early."

Gene heard footsteps heading toward the door.

"Sonny, you are a little early!" Butch said, waving Gene to come inside. "I'm not sure I remember meeting you, but your name sounds familiar. Were you ever in a rock band?"

"I played the clarinet in high school," Gene said, dusting snow off his jacket.

"Oh, never mind," Butch said. "Well I'm Butch the building owner. Say, that looks like a fancy camera you have there. Are you planning on taking pictures?"

"I figured I would bring this down in case something interesting happens," Gene said. "Then again, I guess nothing interesting can happen if no one is here!"

"I was here late last night trying to freshen the place up a bit," Butch said as they walked down the hallway. "I just live next door. Would you like a doughnut?"

Butch grabbed the box of doughnuts that was sitting on the kitchen counter.

"I ran down to the bakery just a few minutes ago," Butch said. "The gang really likes the chocolate alligator."

"The chocolate alligator?" Gene said.

"Yeah, it's a chocolate chip confection with chocolate icing on the top," Butch said. "What a delicacy. Even Leo likes it."

"Who's Leo?"

"He's my cousin. He comes down from Green Bay just to eat a couple of these. Of course, it's hard to get down here during curling season."

"When is curling season anyway?"

"You know, I've never quite put my finger on that. Maybe it's year round. You sure do ask a lot of questions, Gene!"

"I have to, I'm a newspaper reporter."

Gene made a mental note to exclude Butch from the .comU story, but that he would be a good person to interview if he needed ideas for something random to go into the newspaper. While they were enjoying their pastries, a noise came from down the hallway.

"Is someone else here?" Gene said, swallowing a bite of his alligator.

"Oh damn, there is someone here," Butch said. "A friend of Sarina's stumbled up here late last night, and I let him sleep in the LAB."

"Sarina? Is it her boyfriend?" Gene said. "I didn't know she even had a boyfriend."

"Well this is a funny one, but she doesn't know if she has a boyfriend or not either," Butch said. "And you would really think that a person should know that."

Butch and Gene approached the LAB doorway as the noise grew louder. Butch opened the door and flicked the light switch. They looked to the floor and saw Rex clutching a man, who had lost his pants, with his arms and legs.

"What in blazes?" Butch yelled. Gene grabbed his camera and took a few pictures. The flashing sound woke Rex.

"Where am I?" Rex said, dazed. "Who is this? Get him off of me! I think he's dead! Why am I wearing a lei? Wow, it's really pretty."

Butch stooped down to pick up the man on top of Rex. Butch immediately noticed a large bruise on his forehead.

"Gene, could you run into the kitchen and get some ice?" Butch said. "Hello, can you hear me!" Butch shook the man and he finally came to.

"I know that guy!" Rex said, holding his head, still thoroughly confused. "That's Matt's friend Douggie!"

"My name is not Douggie," Doug said, standing and wiping off his jacket. "My name is Doug Morris. You guys must have drugged me and left me with this man. You will hear from my lawyer!"

"I have one question for you, Doug," Gene said, returning with two pouches of ice. "Is there any particular reason you are not wearing pants?"

Doug looked down to realize his pants lay on the opposite side of the room.

"You took my pants?" Doug said. "How dare you! Give me my lei back too!"

Doug reached for the orange lei, but Rex turned away.

"No way, it's my lei now," Rex said. "You should be ashamed of your-self!"

"Who should be ashamed of what?" Matt said, entering the room upon hearing voices in the LAB. Katy followed.

"What the hell is going on here?" Katy said.

Matt and Katy were not sure about what to make of the pitter-patter be-tween Doug, Matt's liaison between the company and the United States government, and Rex, Sarina's estranged beau. Rex and Doug jostled back and forth, with Doug constantly grabbing the lei and Rex slapping his hands away. Gene returned with the ice, then stood in the far corner of the room, snapping pictures and occasionally laughing loudly. Butch tried to separate the bickerers but to no avail.

"Hold on a sec," said Butch, stepping from between Rex and Doug. "How did you two just happen to show up at the same time? In fact, I think I heard only one vehicle pull up!"

Butch ran out of the room, down the hallway and looked out the window. Before anyone had time to make a comment, Butch had already returned.

"Katy, your car isn't out there," Butch said, "so you two must have come together!"

"Well the roads were bad," said Matt, shrugging. "So I thought, um, I could just give her a ride."

"Yeah, what are you trying to say?" said Katy, taking a step away from Matt.

"Oh nothing," Butch said. "But aren't you two on opposite sides of this thing? And didn't you guys used to be a couple? Now I know how Lifetime gets its story ideas."

Gene set his camera down and pulled out his notepad.

"OK, I'm going to try to figure some of this out," Gene said to the crowd. "So we came in and this guy with the lei and this guy with no pants were sleeping together, is that correct?"

"No way, someone drugged me!" Doug said. "I came down here last night to find out the story behind .comU, but that's the last thing I remember."

"But how did you get to this room?" Gene said. "Did anyone see him come in here?"

"I was the only one here," Butch said, "and I didn't see him. Wait, Rex was already here, passed out."

"I was?" Rex said. "The only thing I remember is being down at Buckeye's, and drinking apple cider. Man, that stuff is good."

"Apple cider?" Matt and Katy said.

"That stuff gets me every time," Rex said.

"Yeah, big boy, you stumbled down from Buckeye's and ended up here," Butch said.

"OK, that's bizarre, but understandable, but how the hell did he get here?" said Gene, pointing at Doug.

"How many times do I have to tell you?" Doug said. "They captured me and put me in here with this, this ... monster."

"Well, we know that didn't happen," said Gene, scribbling on his pad. "First, how many monsters wear shorts over sweat pants?"

"Yeah, and how many have leis?" said Rex, taunting Doug.

"That's mine, you freak!" Doug said, trying to grab the lei again. "I mean look, they tore my pants too!"

Suddenly, Drew emerged from the hallway.

"Did anyone lose a belt?" Drew said. Then he looked up, surprised at the crowd. "Whoa, why are all these people already here. Am I late?"

Doug walked between Matt and Katy and grabbed the belt from Drew.

"Where did you find this?" Doug said.

"It was beside the front door," Drew said. "Along with this."

Drew held out a piece of cloth that clearly matched the tear in Doug's pants.

"This was attached to the door frame," said Drew, handing it to Doug. "Did you try to break in or something?"

"Now this is starting to make a little more sense," Gene said. "How did you get in here?"

"Well the door WAS open," Doug said. "At least the top part was. I didn't think that would be too bad just to climb through the door and see what was going on. I guess I had forgotten about that."

"Sure, you forgot," Gene said. "That still doesn't explain how you got into here."

"The last thing I remember is walking in one of the doors and trying to find the lights," Doug said.

"Wait a minute," Butch said. "I did come back in here to get my cheese balls container. Maybe he tripped over that!"

"That seems logical," Matt said. "What is your obsession with those things anyway?"

"They just taste great, but you need to make sure you drink something after you eat them and before you brush your teeth," Butch said "Because cheese balls and toothpaste are a terrible combination."

Drew glanced at his watch; it was 9:40 already.

"Guys, I think we'd better get ready for the conference," Drew said. "Come on Katy, let's head over to the WAB and get our stuff together."

"Wait, where's Sarina?" Katy said as they stood in the hallway. "She should be here by now."

"I'm here, I'm here," said Sarina, dusting off snow that had fallen on her as she entered the building. "My alarm clock was giving me problems. How did you get here, Katy? Your car isn't out there."

"Matt gave me a ride," Katy said. "Come on, we have to get our presentation together."

"Matt?" Sarina said. As she passed the LAB doorway, she noticed the cast of characters already assembled for The Developers' landmark event. She spotted Rex, who seemed to turn even more red in the face once he laid his eyes on his sweetheart.

"Rex, what are you doing here?" Sarina said, stopping for a moment at the LAB."

Rex started to say something but couldn't come up with anything.

"He stole my lei!" said Doug, as Matt tried to restrain him.

"Come on Sarina, we have work to do!" Drew shouted.

Sarina looked perplexed but continued down the hall.

"I ... I have to leave," said Rex, removing the lei and walking feverishly out of the LAB and out the front door.

"Yay, I got my lei back!" said Doug as he picked up the orange necklace and gently placed it over his head. "Well Matt, I guess you'd better get prepared for your gig too. But where is the boy wonder?"

"He got stuck over in Moxee last night, but surely he'll be back for the press conference," Matt said. "Too much is at stake."

"I assume the roads are cleared now, so that's no excuse," Doug said. "I'd better run home and get cleaned up. I wanted to be here for the .comU portion, but I'm not looking very professional. Sorry about the mess I caused here, Matt."

"Um, OK Doug," Matt said. "I'm still not sure what happened, but we can discuss it later. I've got my notes with me, so just meet me back here and we'll review if necessary."

Doug left, and Matt, Gene and Butch remained.

"Well, that leaves one question still unanswered," Butch said.

"What's that?" Matt said.

"Where's the rent check?" Butch said.

"If this morning's events are any indication," said Matt, already looking over his notes, "everything will be in shambles before you get another rent check."

***

"Good morning everyone, and thank you for coming. We are pleased you could make it, especially after yesterday's storm, so we could announce the new and exciting features of .comU."

As Katy began the press conference, she scanned the room to see who was in attendance. Coincidentally, the crowd was extremely similar to the last major meeting at the LAB. Phil Harris, obviously concerned with his advertising dollars for his hotels, was there, as was Susan Messer of the chamber and Lynn Harris of Malorett Public Schools. Of course Gene was still there, representing the *Malorett Times*, already taking notes. There were two other gentleman there who Katy did not recognize. Matt and Butch stood in the back of the LAB, while Sarina and Drew stood at Katy's right side.

Katy continued.

"So far, .comU has surpassed even the high expectations we originally had as a development firm. More than 75 percent of Malorett citizens have used the site, with 60 percent also becoming subscribers. Not only that, but there have been plenty of visits — and subscribers — from Moxee and surrounding areas as well. This shows that .comU has become a central depot for the Upper Peninsula, and it has also become a great place for companies to reach a wide variety of target audiences.

"Even though the system has been a great success, we feel there is more work to do, especially with the area children. So for the second phase of .comU, we are looking to the next generation of subscribers by placing a greater emphasis on things for the kids, many instructional, but also some fun and games.

"We have again teamed with Moxee Tech to provide tutors during the week to help middle school and high school students with their homework. We also hope to coordinate this effort with the public school system in order to raise the level of education.

"Our original mission with .comU was to provide a place where people could learn more about their neighbors via the Internet. Now, we just want to take it another step forward to build on that level of community through this powerful communication tool.

"In the upcoming days, as we launch new ideas, we'll have more information. But for now, does anyone have any questions?"

Katy gazed out to look for hands being raised. The first one she saw was from one of the men she did not recognize.

"Hello, Chuck Adams from the *Free Press*. I've perused your system, and it is definitely state of the art. Do you plan to market this system to other cities, and if so, what sort of time table do you foresee?"

Katy glanced over at Drew and Sarina, who both gave her blank stares.

"You're from the Free Press, like the *Detroit Free Press*?" Katy said.

"Yes, that's correct," Chuck said. "Currently I'm not aware of any other *Free Press* around here, are you?"

"Uh, no," Katy stammered. It wasn't clear whether she was finished, but Drew stepped forward to answer his question.

"Chuck, thanks for venturing all the way over to Malorett," Drew said. "It's an honor to think our little company could produce interest from the big city of Detroit. To answer your question, I have been in touch with the Green Bay Chamber of Commerce because an official there expressed interest in the system. As we continue to make improvements on the current one, we hope to make it portable to other cities as well. The estimates we have on hosting a solution for a bigger city are pretty rough, but we would definitely entertain the idea of moving forward."

"That's exactly what I needed to know," Chuck said. "With what I've seen so far, I wouldn't be surprised if more cities did want their own."

"Well thanks for your praise," said Katy, gathering herself following Drew. "Anyone else?"

Phil raised his hand and stood to speak.

"I'm somewhat confused about the recent talk of defection of The Developers group," Phil said. "So when you say that you are working on building these improvements, who do you mean?"

Katy again looked for help on the question.

"Phil, the 'we' Katy speaks of currently is myself, her and Sarina," Drew said. "Of course, we hope Matt and Kevin, two integral parts of the Developers, are in on this as well, but they have since decided to pursue other interests, at least for the interim."

"Other interests?" Phil said. "But isn't Matt the president of the group? How can the president not be involved in a major system upgrade?"

"We have been able to move ahead with the project, and we don't see any reason why we cannot handle it right now," Drew said.

"This just seems all a little shady to me," said Phil, increasingly becoming irritated. "I have a hard time believing a company could be OK when half of it is, as you said, 'pursing other interests.' Does anyone else think this is a little silly?"

Susan and Gene nodded, but the other unknown individual stood to speak.

"I'm Bob Clarkson, from the Green Bay Chamber of Commerce. Drew eluded to me earlier as I inquired about the system last week, and I thought I would come down and see what progress had been made. First Drew, thanks for sending me the proposal so quickly. I've looked over it, and I like what I see so far."

Drew acknowledged the thanks with a quick wave.

"At the same time, though, I am worried about the fallout of this development team. From what I've read on the website, and from what I'm seeing here, the company has split interests. I don't think our chamber is prepared to work with a company who has dissidence amongst itself, regardless of the type of work it can produce."

"Bob, I definitely understand where you are coming from," Drew said. "But I assure you, this is a temporary and minor thing. Could I speak to you briefly when the conference is completed?"

Bob nodded, then he sat back down.

Katy listened attentively at the exchange between Drew and Bob Clarkson, but she also attempted to gain eye contact with Matt. Unfortunately, Matt continued to re-read his notes and write more notes in the margins of his paper. Katy wondered how Matt could continue to prepare for a press conference that would go against what his company had already proclaimed.

"If there are no more questions," Katy said, "we will concede to the next press conference concerning the other half of The Developers' employees."

"And I must admit, the second half is the better half!" said Doug during his grand re-entrance into the LAB. Doug had cleaned up a great deal in just under an hour, and he left the lei at home.

While Doug immediately moved to the front of the room, Matt continued to read over his notes. When Matt looked up, Doug motioned for Matt to join him. Matt started to stand and noticed Katy looking his way, walking behind Drew and Sarina as they moved to the other side.

Matt made his way to the podium. Concern seemed to be expressed on just about everyone's face, with the exception of Doug, who seemed to be glowing even after his morning incident. Matt still wasn't sure whether or not he should start without Kevin. Matt thought about calling him, but he thought surely he wouldn't miss it.

But he wasn't there, and the audience, after intermittent instances of talking and silence, appeared to be settling in to listen to Matt's SIP speech. Now it was Matt's turn to display a look of concern.

"Thanks for hanging around. It's great to see familiar faces, and new ones of course. I also want to commend Katy, Drew and Sarina for the job they have done with .comU. They really have done a great job and have been great for The Developers. Thanks for all your hard work."

Matt paused and gave a small clap.

"There has been great work completed on .comU, and even greater things lay ahead for system development," Matt continued. "But what I am here to talk about is a system that will exponentially magnify the work we've completed on .comU and will bring The Developers to a new level of computer programming.

"The system is called SIP, for Super Information Portal, and even though it's in infancy stages, the system has already proved powerful and necessary to bring a central structure to the Internet. Unfortunately, I'm not allowed to get too detailed due to contract stipulations. But I can say for certainty that in the near future, everyone in the US will have to travel through the SIP during their Web experiences.

"Now here's the part I can tell you. As of now, myself and Kevin Gentry, who will be arriving shortly, will be working with Doug Morris of Foundation Technologies to develop this system for the government. We will be using many of the same technologies within .comU, only on a much larger scale. OK, I guess it's time for questions. Anyone?"

Matt realized his talk wasn't too informational, and didn't really apply too much to the people listening. Chuck Adams stood to address Matt.

"I guess I'm the new guy here, so I don't completely understand what's going on," Chuck said. "There's a single company, and you guys are going out on separate ventures? That seems a little weird."

"It's only for a limited time," Matt said, "until we can get back on track, with both projects."

"To me, it seems like both things will be ongoing," Chuck said.

"That's what I was thinking too," Phil said. "Are you planning to hire more people?"

"Not immediately," Matt said. "Until we can determine the workload, I don't see that as part of the plan, but it will probably happen some time down the road."

"So then who will be working on .comU?" Susan said.

Drew, sitting in the rear, leaned forward.

"We are not going to stop development on .comU," said Drew, staring down Matt. "I have a feeling it's much more likely that the SIP project will have an abrupt end before we'll have to worry about any conflicts."

Matt was shocked Drew would say something like that. While Matt thought about his response, Doug pushed Matt aside.

"If only you had a clue about the project," Doug said, "I don't think you would be making a farce out of this meeting. The SIP is going to revolutionize the way people and businesses send information. Having all the data bound tightly together will make everything more efficient across the country. If you think this is a fly-by-night project, well, you have something coming to you."

"What do I have coming to me?" Drew said.

"Well ... something!" Doug said. "And it's not nice!"

"Oh, maybe I'll wake up in an office, lying on top of another guy, with my pants down?" Drew said.

The crowd gasped, similar to when a murder mystery is solved, only lacking the organist. Of course at this point, Doug was livid.

"How dare you!" Doug said. "Why, I oughta ... " Doug started punching the air, while Drew motioned to Doug that if he wanted to fight, to come on down. Sarina, Katy and Matt all hid their faces, while Butch's eyes lit up. The outsiders appeared disinterested, and some even rose to leave. Kevin then walked into the LAB, looking pale and weak.

"Doug, come on, we have important things to discuss," said Matt, placing his hands on Doug's shoulders and nudging him to the side. "The other member of our team, Kevin Gentry, would like to have a brief word about the SIP."

Kevin stepped to the podium.

"I haven't eaten since yesterday!" said Kevin, beginning to sob.

Even though Doug was still bouncing around like Muhammad Ali, Matt left his side to console Kevin.

"There, there, I think there might be some leftovers in the fridge," Matt said. "You look terrible."

"I can't eat, I need to talk to Jane!" said Kevin, hugging Matt. The crowd let out a sigh this time.

"This is getting silly," said Phil, standing and stretching. "I've had enough. Katy, please give me a call this afternoon because I may be dropping all of my sponsorship responsibilities."

He exited, then Drew noticed Bob Clarkson also heading toward the door.

"Bob, hold on a sec," Drew said, catching up with Bob in the doorway. "I'm sorry this meeting wasn't what you had expected."

"You're right, this isn't what I had expected at all," Bob said. "From the proposal, and from talking to you on the phone, it seemed like this development company had it together, but now I'm not so sure. Drew, I like the stuff you guys have produced, but don't contact me until you are ready to make the step up to the big leagues."

With that, Bob left, and as Drew re-entered the conference room, it was hard to erase the pessimism that shone across his face. Susan Messer and Lynn Davis, whispering between each other, retreated outside as well. Gene and Chuck, the *Free Press* reporter, compared notes, and Katy and Sarina joined Matt in urging Kevin to go find something to eat. Kevin, though, continued to resist.

Meanwhile, Drew noticed Doug in the corner, apparently talking heatedly to himself. As Drew approached, he realized Doug was talking on his cellphone.

"No, I think we'll be all right," Doug said. "Wait, just let me ... yes, I know how important this is. We've already made progress and ... but we can't just stop now ... no, just give me a little more time and ... you can't do that! Just wait and it will work ... come on! OK, I'll let them know, but I can't believe you're doing this. All right, good bye."

Doug folded his cellphone and noticed Drew partially listening to his conversation. Doug then walked toward the others.

"I've got some bad news," Doug said. "I just got off the phone with Blake, and he's not too happy with what's going on here. I told him about the dual projects, and he's holding The Developers in breech of contract. He also said development has been suspended until it's firmly decided if you are to be the development team. But I can tell you, those guys are serious when it comes to breech of contract."

"How could we be in breech of contract?" said Matt, raising his voice. "We are still working on the project. Hell, I spent most of last evening building the administration pages."

"No, the contract stipulates all employees will work exclusively on this project, for a specific period of time," Doug said.

"That's ridiculous!" Matt said. This time, he threw his four-color pen near the back wall, narrowly missing Butch, who had fallen asleep. Butch awoke and noticed a piece of paper laying on the table near him.

"Whoa, this must be the rent check!" said Butch, who was severely disappointed after realizing it was just an old receipt from Dave's Burger Bonanza.

"Matt, I would suggest you get back with Blake today," Doug said. "I have to leave and get back to the office."

Doug exited, and Butch followed him out the door.

"Damn people, this is a mess!" Sarina said. "All clients, and even new ones, are dissatisfied now, so what the hell are we going to do?"

"Either way, it looks like we lose something," Katy said. "And that's why we have to keep the clients we have, instead of trying to create new projects."

"But the problem is a little bigger now," Drew said. "Like Doug said, if we don't build this other system, the company could be in deep trouble. This is tough, because we need a resolution immediately."

"Personally, I'm so furious right now that I can think of only one option," Matt said, retrieving his pen. "And that's to quit EVERYTHING."

Butch paced outside the doorway, up and down the hall. As he neared the front door, he noticed someone sitting on the small brick staircase in front of the building. Butch went outside and realized it was Rex.

"Rex, dumbass, it's too cold to be outside!" Butch said. "Let's go in!"

"No, I can't," Rex said. "I can't believe what happened earlier today. I screwed up everything, with Sarina, with the others."

"Actually man, they are in the middle of a problem that's far, far bigger," Butch said. "They probably forgot about this morning, and possibly have forgotten about you altogether!"

"I don't know if I like the sound of that!" Rex said. "It would be so much easier if I could just bake some cookies, and everyone would be happy again. Of course, they would be oatmeal raisin cookies, and some sort of fruit energy shake, because we need to be healthy."

Butch's eyes widened.

"Rex, that's a darn-tootin' great idea," Butch said. "I think we can solve the problem, and we might be able to do it without involving cousin Leo."

Butch extended his hand to Rex.

"Get up man, we have work to do," Butch said.

"Oh goodie goodie!" Rex said. "We are going to save the world!"

TWENTY-NINE

The Developers were stumped. Matt and Kevin sat on one side of the WAB, determining their next step with the SIP and trying to figure out how to keep the job. On the other side, Katy, Drew and Sarina reviewed client lists and attempted to figure out how they were going to keep their base from canceling all contracts.

Kevin appeared to be feeling a little better, at least after devouring a take-out sandwich from Buckeye's. He was still looking pretty scruffy, but considering he fell asleep in his car the night before, and woke up only because Tech students were pelting cars in the parking lot with eggs, it could have been worse.

"I know we're on deadline here, but couldn't we just hire a few more people to help complete the work?" Kevin said.

"If we had some people we knew who could do the work, that would be viable," Matt said. "But finding competent employees isn't something we can do overnight. I mean we haven't even received a decent resume since the developing 11-year-old."

"How long do we have?" said Kevin, looking through the infamous SIP binder.

"We have to show them something Monday!" Matt said. "We really can't be sitting here waiting for more workers to show up."

"What about Doug saying the project has been suspended?"

"We need to tell Blake we just need more time."

"More time? From Doug's reaction, that didn't look like an option."

"So what do you suggest we tell him?"

"Man, I don't know. Maybe we should just go get something else to eat instead."

Katy held the phone on her shoulder as she dialed Phil Harris' number. But before it rang twice, she quickly slammed the receiver down on the table.

"I don't even know what to say," Katy said. "Nothing has changed."

"Well, we need to tell him something," Drew said. "There's no way he's just going to back out of the project altogether. He has too much at stake."

"Precisely," Sarina said. "He's probably looking through the contracts right now to see if there's a way he can sue us."

The three Developers looked at each other with a sense of urgency.

"OK, we're not dead in the water yet because we still have some resources," Drew said. "Let's not forget about the Tech students. Crissy and the gang have done admirable work on .comU, monitoring and answering questions and stuff."

"Honestly, I don't think Phil is mad at the work we've done," Katy said. "It's the future that is bothersome. How can we continue to devote energy to a project if half of our full-time employees are sitting over in the corner, working on something else?"

Katy glanced over at Matt and Kevin, who tried not to notice. They continued their discussion though, and both sides huddled again. Without much to say, Sarina checked her inbox and noticed that a handful of clients had written. Each one of them contained concerns about the system and made mention of decreasing their contracts or dropping them altogether.

"Guys, it appears the word is out," Sarina said.

Drew and Katy scooted closer to Sarina's screen to see the sad state of the system.

"I guess we need to be calling more people than just Phil," said Drew, holding his head in his hands. "We just need to reassure them that we can handle whatever the future brings."

"But can we?" Katy said. "Plus, what about Green Bay?"

"I had totally forgotten about that," Drew said. "I guess that idea is history."

Butch and Rex entered the WAB. No one really seemed to notice, nor did they have time to care.

"You guys certainly look busy!" said Butch, circling the WAB slowly. "What are you up to, anyway?"

No one answered at first, but Matt finally muttered something, still looking at SIP papers.

"Butch, we are pretty busy here," Matt said. "There's a lot that needs to be decided today, or else we're not going to have a business anymore."

"What, no business?" Butch said. "What about that last rent check?"

"We don't owe you a damn rent check!" said Matt, standing to face Butch. "Could you please just leave us alone and ... why the hell are you wearing a miniskirt?"

The others turned to look as Butch was, indeed, wearing a black miniskirt to go with his new smiley face T-shirt. Near the doorway, Rex also happened to be wearing a similar skirt, although he wore nylon tights under his.

"I am?" said Butch, looking down to his waist. "Well duh, I just put it on. Thanks for reminding me, Matt."

Matt approached Butch.

"What kind of freak are you?" Matt said. "Here you are, coming in to bother WORKING people, dressing like ... that?"

"Actually, we have a meeting tonight, so we're just getting into character a bit early," Rex interrupted. "I had already taken the day off, so Butch and I were just going to catch up on old times beforehand. Oh, hi Sarina."

Sarina sat silently, nodding and turning away.

"A meeting?" Kevin said. "Are you guys in some sort of cross-dressing club? That's pretty exciting, but no, we're not interested in joining."

"That's funny, I don't remember inviting anyone to join," Rex said.

"You didn't Rex, it's OK," Butch said. "No Kevin, it's not a cross-dressing club. Actually you're not invited to join in the first place because you don't qualify for the standards."

"You have standards, and you're in a miniskirt?" Kevin said. "Please."

"Anyway, we are not here to talk about our club, but we are interested in helping you solve your problems," Butch said. "So tell me, what can we do to help?"

"Honestly there's not much that you can do to help us," Katy said. "Unless we could go back in time and plan for this, nothing much would change."

Rex walked closer to Katy.

"Let's see, I don't have my time machine working," Rex said. "One time I tried to fly around the world backward, like Superman, but I fell off the building. What if I sang that Cher song? IF I COULD TURN BACK TIME ... "

"Please, please no singing," Drew said. "Although I will say, you've got better legs than her."

"And I think you're out of luck on our end, too," said Matt, trying to hold back some of his current frustration. "Unless you'd like to explain to the United States government how we are going to be able to complete this project on time, and then explain it to us, I don't see any benefit to you being here."

"Then again, it's at least comic relief to see you in this fashion," Kevin said sarcastically. "Are you sure we can't join this little club of yours? If it came with a sandwich or two, I would be up for it."

"So I guess what you're saying is you wouldn't be interested in hearing this plan I have?" Butch said.

"Let me guess," said Katy, now circling Butch in the middle of the room. "You have come up with a plan that allows both sides here to work on their respective projects, keep all clients, continue future development, cure the sick and feed the poor?"

Butch thought for a moment.

"Hmm ... yeah, I think all of that is in my plan," said Butch, reaching for something in his pocket. "Then again, I just thought of the plan as you were spouting off those things, so it might not provide all of them. But I would wager everything in my pants pocket that it would be in the company's best interest to listen to this plan I have."

The others were interested and gathered beside Butch, Rex and Katy at the center of the WAB. Butch held something inside a tight fist and extended his hand outward. Everyone gazed closely at Butch's hand as he turned it over, opened his fist and revealed the contents of his pocket.

"You're betting a penny?" Matt said in disbelief.

Rex took it from Butch's hand for a closer look.

"No wait guys, look!" said Rex, jumping up and down. "It's a wheat penny! It's a wheat penny!"

"Ah yes, the magical wheat penny," Drew said. "Our company's fate now lies in a man with cheese puffs and a magical wheat penny."

"What do we have to lose at this point?" said Katy, pulling up a chair. "Let's hear your plan, Butch. And it better be good."

***

"Why on earth are we doing this?" said Kevin, carrying another set of chairs from Matt's 4x4 into the Malorett Community Center. "Have we been hypnotized? Have we been sabotaged? Are we crazy?"

"I've been hypnotized before," said Matt, closing his vehicle's back door. "And it seemed a little different than this. Of course, it was by aliens, and I don't remember a damn thing, so maybe they perform things like that differently."

It was 4:30, which left little time to complete the setup and transformation of the center. Luckily, Butch had stored away a bunch of folding tables and chairs inside the other building he owned, and the center was only three blocks away. Even still, trying to accommodate for an unknown amount of people for an event that was planned just hours earlier seemed a bit dubious to all of The Developers.

"There really is no way this is going to help us keep the SIP," said Kevin, rearranging the newest four chairs in the room. "Shouldn't we be back at the office, working on that system?"

"Yeah, probably, but honestly, I need some time to clear my head," said Matt, pulling out the legs of another table. "I've been staring at a damn computer for at least 332 days straight, and let's face it, we don't even know if we have the project anymore! I have a feeling that a couple hours out of the office will do us both good."

Kevin didn't agree, but he didn't completely disagree either. He knew the inevitable call to Blake had to come soon, and that could spell doom for the project. And at this point, the easiest way to avoid doom was to just simply avoid it.

Meanwhile, Drew and Sarina were on the other side of the community center, unfolding tables and chairs and organizing them accordingly.

"This might actually work," said Drew, handing Sarina another chair. "I don't know why we never thought about this before."

"I can tell you why we never thought about this before," Sarina said. "It is MADNESS! We are right in the middle of losing all of our customers, and now we're putting on some party that no one knows about, so no one is going to come to it, and it's going to ruin our chances to bring back .comU even more!"

"Wow, you really have your positive thinking cap on today, Sarina," Drew said. "You can be skeptical about all of this, but let's face it, your mind is elsewhere."

"What the hell do you mean?" Sarina said.

"I mean Rex. You guys have barely even talked since ... the incident."

"Oh yeah, Rex. I almost forgot about that guy."

Sarina and Drew walked back toward the entrance to grab more chairs from Drew's vehicle.

"Listen, he has had plenty of opportunities to talk to me," Sarina said.

"Yeah, but what if he doesn't know what to say?" Drew said. "You did break up with him, you know."

"I didn't break up with him!"

"You didn't?"

"No, not really. I didn't know we were dating!"

"Come on Sarina, that's a farce and you know it!"

The two procured another load and made their way back inside.

"You should address him," Drew said. "Maybe he's waiting for you to make a move."

"Or maybe he has just moved on," Sarina said.

"Moved on?" Drew said. "If that's the case, why was he sleeping in the office this morning with Doug? Better yet, why is he still here, walking around in that outfit like it's perfectly normal?"

Drew pointed to the back of the community center, where Butch and Rex were busy decorating.

"Do you think I should make more snowflakes?" Rex said to Butch, who was standing on a ladder, hanging red and blue streamers.

"I think we have plenty of snowflakes, actually," Butch said. "How did you make so many, so fast?"

"I just love arts and crafts," Rex said. "And do you want to know the best part? I used my three-hole puncher to make snow!"

Rex opened the hole puncher and waved it around like a lightsaber. Oodles of tiny circular specs of snow floated to the floor. Rex watched with delight, while Butch continued to adorn the room trestles in red and blue streamers.

Butch was more than satisfied with how easy it had been to talk everyone into the idea of hosting a gigantic party in downtown Malorett on short notice. As he prepared, though, he hoped his gut feelings about it were right.

"Look what else I have!" said Rex, dragging something from behind him. Butch gazed over to take a gander.

"What the hell, a Christmas tree?" said Butch. "Christmas has been over for months!"

"True, but everyone loves Christmas, so everyone MUST love Christmas trees!" Rex said. "They will be really pretty with some of this snow, too."

Rex shook his hole puncher over the 6-foot tree.

"Um, maybe it's time you go help the others," Butch said. "I'm sure Drew and Sarina could use a little assistance in positioning the tables."

"I would rather stay over here, Butch," Rex said. "I think Sarina is mad at me."

"Mad at you?" Butch said. "I told you, you just need to tell her that you love her, and everything will be OK."

"You make it sound so simple, but life doesn't work that way!" Rex said in a whiny voice.

Rex then bounced away. Butch hoped at the very least, he would go find more decorations.

Katy appeared in the doorway.

"Katy, baby!" said Matt, who started to make a motion to hug her, but instead, backed off. "What's the news?"

Finding a notebook and pen in her briefcase, Katy reviewed her list.

"First, I sent out the press release about the party, then I called the radio stations just to verify they received it," Katy said. "They seemed a little suspicious, but I assured them we were setting up and still had ample time to get everything going."

"Suspicious, that's the understatement of the century," Sarina said. "Who comes to a party when it was just announced hours earlier?"

"Shhhhhhhhh!" Butch said.

"Next," Katy continued, "I spoke with Gene at the newspaper. He jumped right on getting the word out, as he and some other people at the paper are calling a bunch of their contacts. They also posted the notice on the website."

"That's cool," Matt said. "But why was Gene so eager to help out?"

"Uh, I did promise him that Sarina would go on a date with him," Katy said.

"You what?" Sarina said.

"Come on, he's not that bad of a guy," Katy said.

"Yeah, but he grabbed my ass, without asking!" Sarina said.

"OK, we'll think of something," Katy said. "But I didn't get to the best news yet. I spoke with Phil Harris, and even though he was reluctant to participate, I managed to get him to come down for another contest. On top of that, Mayor Tillman will be coming down for the party."

"Holy shit, how did you round up all those people in such short notice?" Kevin said.

"I don't know ... but let's just hope they all really show," Katy said.

"I told you!" Butch said. "It was never in doubt. OK, maybe a little bit of doubt, but not too much doubt. The first-ever .comU Malorett Mayhem is only hours away!"

***

Matt, Kevin, Drew, Katy and Sarina all sat in a secondary room in the back of the community center. Kevin munched on a small bag of Fritos; Katy reviewed contacts in her PDA; Sarina stretched her arms and contemplated running in place in the corner; Drew stared at the ceiling and tapped his fingers on the table; and Matt spun his four-color pen in his hand. Everyone was silent, not necessarily because they were mad or frustrated with each other, but because there wasn't anything to say.

It was already 6:30, and the Mayhem, as it was being billed, was scheduled to begin at 7. The group members still weren't convinced of Butch's plan, but at this point, their only choice was to go ahead with it.

"Come on Matt, you said we were going to go back to the office after we helped set up, and clear our minds," said Kevin, pouring the remaining chip bits into his mouth. "We're wasting our time here."

"Maybe you're right," said Matt, standing. "Why are we all just sitting in here anyway?"

"I'm just resting," Drew said. "And waiting for this par-tay, if it's going to exist. And waiting for my wife, too, because I think she's coming down here. So at least there will be one person in the crowd!"

"Is she going to streak again?" Sarina said.

"Streak ... again?" Kevin said.

"Yeah, see you miss out on things when you're not in the Black Miniskirt Cult," Sarina said. "Which reminds me, Katy, we'd better get in costume."

Katy opened the door, and just after her and Sarina left, Butch entered, carrying a large cardboard box. The others weren't exactly sure if it was heavy, although Butch seemed to be wobbling a bit. He maneuvered forward and set the box on the table.

"Fellas, now we're in business," said Butch, gasping for air. "There's enough stuff in here for a load of people who come down to this great par-ty."

Drew stood, opened the top of the box and started sifting through the items. He pulled out a handful of toys that appeared to have come from kids' fast food meals.

"You're going to give this stuff away?" said Drew, still meandering through the box.

"Oh ... do you think I should sell it instead?" Butch said. "That's a good point, I wasn't really thinking."

"No, that's not what I meant!" Drew said. "You can't give away your old toys."

"They aren't mine," Butch said.

"They're stolen toys?" said Kevin, moving closer to gaze inside the box. "And they're from fast food places? This is great, I can still smell the grease!"

"Well, they are my toys now, but I found them," Butch said. "So they haven't been played with or anything. I've just been storing them in the other building for so long, and I thought it would be appropriate just to give them away."

"Oh," Drew said. "I guess you could give them away, if any kids show up."

"This isn't all of it; I have a couple more boxes out in the main room," Butch said.

The foursome scurried out of the room and back into the hall. There, Rex piddled through a few of the additional boxes Butch had mentioned.

"Hey guys, check this out!" Rex said. "There's a whole box of matching towels! Over there, I found a couple of brand new toasters and coffee grinders. But this, so far, is my favorite!"

Rex pulled out a bag full of little soaps from hotels.

"Isn't this exciting?" Rex said, acting like a kid who had just gotten patted on the head by his favorite professional wrestler. "Look at all this great stuff!"

No one was surprised at Rex's childlike characteristics, but some were astounded at the amount of random things that were in the boxes.

"I don't know how you accumulated all this crap," Matt said. "But I can see now why you recommended we say 'Free door prizes' on the press release."

"Yeah, I've been waiting to get rid of this stuff for awhile," Butch said. "I wanted to head over to the Moxee flea market, but every time I started to go, the squirrels got in an uproar, so I figured I should just stay here."

"Oh Matt, I meant to tell you," said Rex, wearing a colander on his head while playing with a can opener. "A group of guys wandered in, and they wanted to talk to you."

Matt whirled and noticed Doug, Blake and Rusty at the far left table in the hall. Confused, Matt briskly walked over toward them.

"Hey guys," Matt said. "What are you doing here?"

For some strange reason, Matt thought Doug resembled the Godfather, and Blake and Rusty two members of The Family. Matt also noticed Rusty punching his right fist in his left hand.

"First, Blake and Rusty decided to come back to town to set things straight," said Doug in a bad Italian voice. "Then we noticed on .comU that there was something going on down here. Since you weren't at the office, we thought maybe you were here. And check it out, you are here."

"Yep, I'm here," Matt said.

"Of course, you are here," Doug said. "Blake has some bad news for you."

"I have some bad news for you," Blake said to Matt.

"That's what I heard," Matt said.

"We've decided to cancel the contract for the SIP with The Developers," Blake said. "Frankly, we are tired of this lunacy of not knowing what's happening here. And it's readily apparent that you are not doing anything to work on the system."

Kevin and Drew inched toward the confrontation and overheard some of the conversation.

"Actually Blake, I was going to call you tonight," Matt said. "It has been a hectic day, but we are still in order to have something for you to test Monday and ... "

"I don't think you get it, Matt," Blake said. "We've modified the contract date, and it is set to terminate at midnight."

"If that's what you have to do, then fine," said Matt, shrugging. "Then I guess we're finished here."

"Not quite," Blake said as Matt started to walk away. "There are strict penalties for ending this contract."

"Penalties? What penalties?" Matt said.

"All the info is in the binder," Blake said. "And it said on the contract what would happen if you should bail."

"But we're not bailing, you are ending the contract," Matt said.

"That's not how we see it," Rusty interrupted. "We thought your entire staff would be working on the project, which obviously is not the case. Therefore, you will be subjected to the penalties."

Matt couldn't believe what he was hearing. Agitated, he contemplated what to say. He noticed Kevin and Drew standing a couple of steps behind, and he also noticed a few people entering through the front. Matt didn't recognize them, so he thought they must be early for Malorett Mayhem.

"So what's going to happen?" Matt said. "Do we owe you money or something?"

"Oh no, nothing like that," Blake said. "But you will never be considered for any sort of federal development contract again. And you won't be eligible for subsidies or any government-related funding. Don't be surprised if the government keeps a closer eye on you from now on."

Blake, Doug and Rusty reached for their coats. There appeared to be a larger influx of people entering the community center. Drew and Kevin looked at each other as Matt still tried to determine if he should say something.

"Good luck finding another development company like ours," Matt said sarcastically, "especially considering we've applied for patents on some of the stuff we've designed."

"Oh yes, I almost forgot about your patents," said Blake, stepping toward Matt. "Don't worry, those won't be accepted."

"Huh?" Matt said. "How do you plan to do that?"

"We're the government," Rusty said. "We can do whatever we want."

"And right now, I think we want to leave," Blake said. "What time is it?"

"It's 10 till 7," Doug said. "Can we really get out of here?"

The crowd grew rapidly, and people now surrounded the table at which the others were initially seated. There was no longer an easy way to leave, as all of the traffic flowed inside the building. Butch appeared at center stage.

"Ladies and gentleman, there are still plenty of seats available," said Butch over the loudspeaker. "Don't forget to hold on to your tickets for wonderful door prizes, which will be announced later in the program. GOOD LUCK!"

Kevin tapped Matt on the shoulder.

"Dude, we have to get going," Kevin said. "We have to get ready for our parts."

"Yeah, and getting through this mess, I don't know how we're going to get up there in time," Drew said, scanning the room. "This is madness."

Matt turned back to face Doug and the others.

"All I can say is, I'm sorry," Matt said.

Matt trailed Kevin and Drew as they crisscrossed the people now inside the community center. Matt turned to see if Doug, Blake and Rusty had figured a way out, but they appeared to be stranded right inside the hordes of partygoers. He finally lost track of them after he bumped into Kevin, who stopped at the base of the stage, and Sarina, who found the trio.

"Where have you guys been?" Sarina said. "You need to get back there and change. It's getting ready to start!"

Sarina led the guys to the dressing room, which was the same room the group occupied earlier in the evening. Katy was adjusting her black miniskirt when they opened the door.

"Come on, Butch is out there waiting for us," Sarina said. "Let's get the others."

"The others?" Kevin said. "We are the others, and we're here."

"No, the others in the club," Sarina said.

"There are others?" Kevin said. "And a better question, do they look good in a miniskirt, or do they look like Rex?"

"I guess you'll see for yourself in a little while," Katy said.

With that, Katy and Sarina went back out to the stage, and Matt, Drew and Kevin looked around the room to figure out just what they were going to wear.

"Surely we don't have skirts to wear, right?" Drew said.

They had a short laugh, which turned to dismay once they noticed three clear plastic bags, labeled with their names, filled with what appeared to be some sort of black material.

***

"Wow, I cannot believe there are so many people here!" said Butch, addressing the crowd. "Welcome to Malorett Mayhem!"

The people in the center let out a deafening cheer, especially considering the large amount of people who were crammed inside the building. Butch estimated at least 1,000 people were inside, with reports that there were even more people standing outside. Of course, this was totally unexpected, considering that they had set up only enough chairs and tables for about 400 people. Most of the people lined the sides of the hall and others sat on the floor near the stage. The community center resembled an '80s rock concert, minus guitars, torn jeans and big hair. Although Butch did notice a few women with big hair, and a teenage boy brought a guitar for no apparent reason.

"First, thanks for coming on such short notice," Butch continued. "We have tons of giveaways, so we're just going to try to move through them as fast as possible. Our .comU sponsors have supplied all sorts of gift certificates, so be sure to watch the various TV monitors to see if you have won. Let me assure you that many, many of you will be going home winners."

That incited another roar from the crowd.

"For those of you who don't know The Developers, the creators of .comU, I would like to introduce them to you," said Butch, turning around to realize that the guys just made it on stage, sans the black skirts.

"Matt Severson, Katy Terrill, Drew Davis, Sarina Metcalfe and Kevin Gentry are the full-time employees, and trust me, they are pretty much working the whole day. How do I know? Well I'm their building owner! I can tell, though, by this turnout, that they've really done something great for this community with the system. So here he is, the president of .comU, Matt Severson."

The crowd cheered, but as Matt stood, Katy stood and stormed toward the podium. Matt just stood and watched.

"Actually, I'm Katy Terrill, and I think it would be best if I addressed the crowd," Katy said.

Matt sat down amidst the catcalls in the audience. Yeah, she looks damn good in the miniskirt, Matt thought. Thank God it's her and not me.

"We'd also like to thank Butch Hodges, our emcee and the guy with the plan," Katy said. "As he said, thanks again for coming out. We have been on a roller coaster ride with the system, but thanks to you, we think we can continue to provide new exciting features in the near future.

"We want to host a Malorett Mayhem on a yearly basis, as a culmination of all we have done through .comU during the previous year. And tonight, we unveil a new rating process for all system users."

Drew stood and approached the podium. Sarina displayed a simple file on her laptop, which was shown throughout the hall on the monitors.

"Hi, I'm Drew Davis. Many of you are familiar with the ratings system used by eBay, so that users can tell which users are the best sellers, and which are a little shady. We've developed something similar, but it's not just for rating people auctioning products ... it's for rating anyone, for anything. It's called The Rater, and we should have it running within the next few weeks.

"Yes, you can rate people on anything ... looks, personality, online interaction, whatever. The higher rating you get, the higher you move on the .comU user level. More points mean more exclusive site info and better discounts from our sponsors. I guess that's it."

Drew moved back to his chair as the audience continued to clap. Butch again grabbed the microphone.

"Thank you, Katy and Drew," Butch said. "Now, we wouldn't be anything without this guy running the show, Mayor Tillman."

Mayor Tillman walked up to the stage from the front table and shook Butch's hand.

"This is unbelievable!" the mayor said. "When Katy told me there was going to be a party, I had no idea it would be like this. Let me just say that this system has been everything we expected, and more. I remember just a few weeks ago, when we were deciding when to launch the system, The Developers came up with a couple of slogan ideas. What's funny is the one I remember the best, and it still holds true, is this: 'There's an 'I' in community, but there's also a 'U.' And that 'U' really has become .comU. Thank you."

Mayor Tillman left the stage to a standing ovation. Katy and Matt looked at each other and smiled, remembering coming up with that slogan from the time they were an item, which seemed like eons ago.

Butch again went to the podium, but a policeman walked up the stage and said something before he could speak to the crowd.

"Mayor, thank you so much," Butch said. "I have some unfortunate news for the rest of us, though. Due to the sheer numbers of the people in the building, we are going to have to cut the party short. It wouldn't be fair to allow some to stay and some to go, so we all have to go."

The crowd booed.

"I'm sorry, I'm sorry, but there's nothing I can do," Butch said.

Some of the crowd started to disperse. Butch turned to the others, but Phil Harris jumped on stage instead.

"Wait, everyone, wait a second," Phil said. Everyone turned their attention back to the stage. "There is a way we can keep the party going ... we can do it through .comU! If The Developers will start up the system tonight, we can have our prize giveaways, chat, maybe test out this new rating system, even some bingo! What do you say!"

The crowd loved the idea, and even started chanting, ".comU! .comU!"

"Malorett has spoken," Phil said. "And they speak for me too. Looking at this crowd, looking at the excitement in the system ... watch out George Jefferson, because .comU is moving on up!"

Phil raised his fists, and again, the crowd reacted positively.

This time, Butch took his time to get back to the podium.

"OK, so maybe the party will continue," Butch said. "Some of The Developers will head back to the office and put the system back online, while the others will stay here. So if you can stay at the party from home, then go home! I hope that made sense. In the meantime, I'd also like to introduce the official .comU club. It's called the Black Miniskirt Cult, I mean, Club. Some of our initial members are walking around now, giving out BMC temporary tattoos. Take enough for the whole family!"

Drew knew he had to go to the office. He finally made eye contact with Jessica, who was handing out the tattoos.

"Hey, who's going with me?" Drew asked the others.

"I think I'll stay," Sarina said. "I have my computer here, and I can get on a wireless connection."

"It would probably be better if I stayed, to meet with the clients and such," Katy said. "So I guess you are on your own."

"Well I'll go," Matt said, surprising Drew. "Since the SIP stuff is history, I hope we can get back to working on this, right?"

"It's your project too, man," Drew said. "Let's get out of here."

Drew and Matt slowly made their way to the door, as many of the patrons were exiting as well.

Kevin waved to them leaving, but his attention quickly changed to a fine woman walking around in a miniskirt. He assumed she was one of the "other" members who Katy and Sarina mentioned, but he needed to get closer to get a better look. Then she came back toward the stage, and Kevin realized it was Jane! Kevin leapt off the stage and almost knocked over Jane in the process.

"Jane, I'm so glad you are here!" Kevin said.

"I heard about it, and when I got here, Katy and Sarina told me about this club," Jane said. "It seemed pretty cute, so now I'm a member!"

"You look great, babe," Kevin said. "Or, can I call you that?"

Jane gave Kevin a quick kiss.

"You can call me whatever you want," Jane said. "As long as you call me something."

Katy tried to track down other sponsors but seemed mostly unsuccessful. Instead, she ran into, of all people, Michael.

"Katy, I have something to tell you!" Michael said.

"Make it quick, I have tons of work," Katy said.

"I thought about what you said, and Martina is still coming here, but we are going to wait to get married," Michael said. "Maybe I should take it slow and see where it goes."

"That's great, Michael," Katy said. "That's the smartest thing I've heard you say in awhile."

"So does this mean I can join this club you all started? I have like eight of the tattoos now."

"We'll think about it. Send us an email or something."

While Sarina continued to test her Internet connection, Rex stood just behind the stage, mulling over what to do.

"It used to be so easy," Rex said to himself. "I could just run up and hug her or kiss her or whatever. But it's too weird now."

"Rex ... Rex! Go to Sarina." Rex heard the voice, resembling Darth Vader, but it also sounded somewhat familiar.

"Is that my imagination?" Rex said.

"No ... it is your conscience," the voice continued. "Tell her how you feel. Just doooooo it."

"OK, I will!" Rex said. He walked up to the stage and didn't notice Butch chuckling, standing behind a door with his mouth over an empty tub of cheese puffs.

Rex tapped Sarina on the shoulder.

"Sarina, I love you, and I want to have sex with you, tonight," Rex said.

The shuffling stopped in the hall, probably because the microphone was on, sitting in Sarina's lap for some reason. He realized what he had done, but the crowd just cheered. Sarina turned the microphone off.

"Why, Rex, would you want to do a thing like that?" Sarina said.

"Because ... I love you?" Rex said.

"Are you asking me?" Sarina said.

"Should I be asking you?" Rex was confused.

"No," Sarina said. "You should be telling me. And you can have me whenever, especially tonight."

"That's great!" Rex said. "Let's get some apple cider and party!"

Matt and Drew had just reached the door when they noticed Doug, Blake and Rusty, still sitting at their original table, being entertained by Ethel McMahan in her miniskirt.

"You guys are still here?" Matt said.

"We couldn't get out," Blake said. "And actually, I'm glad we couldn't. This has been an impressive display of community support for this system. Now I can tell why you guys were so torn about working on something else."

"Yeah, we spent a long, long time on it, that's for sure," Matt said.

"After listening to what the other people had to say, and seeing your dedication, I think we might still be interested in working something out with The Developers," Blake said.

"Seriously?" Matt said.

"Yeah, let's give it a week and get back with me then," Blake said. "We found out we have that much time to burn anyway. But we should really get out of here now. Hope to hear from you soon."

"No doubt, you will," Matt said.

Just before Matt and Drew walked out of the hall, Matt peered back in and noticed Katy looking his way. He gave her a thumbs up, and she blew him a kiss. Could the day get any better, Matt wondered. All of the sudden, his life — and his teammates' lives — seemed to be just right.

THIRTY

Matt lay in bed, still amazed at the turn of events that had just occurred in such a short time. Going from working like crazy to giving up to finding out he was in trouble with the government to having it all erased made it seem like Friday was more like a month, instead of just a day.

He didn't even know what time it was, but it had to have been well after midnight. Matt left Malorett Mayhem before it was officially over, but Drew and Sarina took care of things at the office and on the system. Kevin and Jane were busy making food runs for those users who stayed, while Rex and Butch just mingled with the crowd and handed out prizes.

Luckily, Matt brought home a prize as well.

"It's not that I mind wearing this damn skirt," said Katy, gently sliding her miniskirt over her thighs and down her legs to reveal Matt's favorite pair of white-laced underwear. "It just doesn't make sense."

"How so?" Matt said as Katy jumped into bed and in his arms.

"Well this is northern Michigan," Katy said. "The winter lasts like eleven months. It would make more sense to have something besides miniskirts as the garb of choice for a club."

"You should have thought about that when you guys started the club," Matt said. "It seems a little late now, especially considering you handed out those tattoos."

"I don't think people would mind if we changed the name. Then again, they did seem to like the style, even Ethel."

"Yeah, I think I saw Doug pull out money to pay for a table dance."

Matt and Katy were in great spirits despite being worn out. They were together, at least for the time being, and this time, it seemed right for both of them.

"So what do we do tomorrow?" Katy said, gazing into Matt's bright blue eyes.

"I think I heard we're supposed to get more snow," Matt said. "I know one thing: I'm going to stay out of the office. If I have to do stuff from here, I'll do it. Maybe we can run down and grab dinner at Dave's. I heard they have a swordfish special this week."

"Or we could go to Buckeye's, because they just got in some fresh perch."

"Those are two really great choices. We'll have to figure out some way to pick one or the other."

"That's easy," said Katy, snuggling close to Matt. "We'll just play Yahtzee until I win."

Matt didn't like to lose, but that seemed like the perfect option.

:-)